The Bitter Seeds of Hate
The Fourth and Final Novel in
The Spanish Saga

The Civil War is almost over. The last isolated bullets whine through the Spanish air. The final skirmishes. The pockets of resistance. The beginnings of an underground movement. More reprisals. A slow, uneasy return to normality.

The young men and women who lived through the war, still bearing their scars and their memories, themselves become the fathers and mothers of a new generation.

And then, a new explosion. A less violent one—yet challenging in a new way the piety, the austerity, the virginal morality imposed on the young. Tourism.

THE SPANISH SAGA comprises four novels:

The Bitter Seeds
of Hate

Stephen D. Frances

A Mayflower Paperback

THE BITTER SEEDS OF HATE
Stephen D. Frances

© Copyright Stephen D. Frances 1968

Published as an Original Mayflower
Paperback 1968

*This is a work of fiction and although almost all the
incidents described have happened, the characters I
have invented are imaginary and have no existence in
fact.*

MAYFLOWER Paperbacks are published by
Mayflower Books, 3 Upper James Street,
London, W.1
Made and printed in Great Britain by
Richard Clay (The Chaucer Press), Ltd.,
Bungay, Suffolk

To Remind The Reader

In CRIMINALS OF WANT, Book One, war breaks out between the elected Government and Rebel Army Officers led by General Franco, known as the Nationalists. Escoleras, happy and peaceful, is abruptly launched into horror by the arrival of a band of self-appointed terrorists who execute without justification a large number of villagers whom they suspect may be opposed to the Government.

In UNTIL THE GRAPES BLEED, Book Two, Escoleras is relieved by government troops who occupy the village. Teresa Barras has Captain Garon billeted in her cottage; she becomes his lover. Anselmo Ledesma deserts to France but is repatriated to Franco Spain where he is imprisoned as a suspected saboteur. Rafael Ledesma has won glory and rank, but his insane hatred of Communists drives him to the ruthless killing of prisoners. Miguel Barras, inwardly seeking to avenge the death of his young bride, has become an equally fanatical Communist and anti-Fascist. The Government launches a big, all-out attack but, with Franco receiving every help from Hitler and Mussolini, it seems doomed to failure.

In WHERE THE SUN DIES, Book Three, the Government forces fight their last great desperate battle. But defeat is inevitable. Retreat becomes a rout. The roads are blocked by fleeing civilians and government soldiers trying to reach France and safety from Nationalist vengeance. Teresa is violated by two escaping soldiers. Miguel Barras and Catalina cross to France where t' are interned with the remnants of the Spanis' Emil Serra, trying to reach Escoleras, i' executed on the road. Escoleras itself has been occupied by Nationalist troops. Anselmo, who has been allowed to join the Nationalist army, comes home on leave. He rejects Teresa when she confesses her affair with Captain Garon. Rosemarie Prada is turned out of her home because she is pregnant. Benito Vigon, who wants to marry her, is arrested and sent away as a suspected Socialist.

When Teresa learns that Anselmo is to marry someone else, she hastily marries the plain, faithful Narcisus Coruna . . .

The Bitter Seeds
of Hate

CHAPTER ONE

1

THE knock-up man limped along the darkened cobbled streets banging doors and waiting for sleepy answers growled from upstairs bedrooms, and as the first grey light of day peeked over the distant mountains the sleepy fishermen launched their dinghys and rowed out to the moored fishing boats.

The sea was still and the dripping oars spread silver ripples. Seagulls wheeled overhead and screeched mournfully as the engines started, their powerful piston thuds echoing across the water. Heavy anchor chains rattled across the wooden decks and out through hawser pipes.

The fishing fleet headed out to sea as the village came to life. Housewives and fish-buyers gathered on the dock to meet the small-boat fishermen who had spent the night with baited lines. Bidding for the catches was cautious; everybody needed food but few had money. The Civil War had ended, but not its hardships. Even fishing villagers were hungry. Fuel oil was rationed and fishing boats went out only one day a week. In the towns and cities the people were starving.

Isidro Barras shipped his oars and leaped nimbly on to the dock. His bare, brown foot warded the bows of his boat away before it rasped against the concrete. At once he was surrounded by villagers who shouldered each other to see his catch. It was small. For months the sea had denied its abundance, the breeding spoiled by those who'd fished with sticks of dynamite.

Isidro had two squids, an octopus, five scorpions and a sole, but the bargaining crowd fell silent as three Civil Guards approached. They had tommy-guns slung across their shoulders, their black, patent-leather hats were worn and their olive-green uniforms threadbare and yellowed. The villagers were sullen as they made way for them.

'Name?' demanded one guard crisply, eyes sizing up Isidro's catch.

'Barras.' Isidro scowled.

'You live here?'

'I was born here.'

'Papers!'

Isidro sighed and reached into his hip pocket.

'Nada. It doesn't matter. I've seen you around.' The guard pointed at the boat. 'Any contraband?'

Isidro smiled wryly. 'No contraband, Cabo.'

'Do we need to search? Shall we take up the floorboards?'

Isidro's face was stiff. 'I've nothing at all but ... fish.' He gulped. 'If you ...'

'Gracias,' said the Cabo instantly. 'Which do you want, Juan?' he asked his companion.

'I'd like the sole.'

'A couple of scorpions will do me,' said the third Civil Guard.

'I'll take a squid,' said the Cabo.

Amidst tense silence, Isidro stepped down into his boat and handed up the fish.

'Haven't you anything to wrap it?'

Isidro found a piece of rag and wrapped the fish.

'Gracias,' said the Cabo. He eased the strap of his tommy-gun, the crowd parted and the Civil Guards strode away.

Isidro scowled.

'You're lucky,' said a villager. 'Yesterday when they picked on Coll they took *all* his catch except an octopus.'

Isidro sighed. 'When there is no wine we must drink water.' He raised his voice. 'How much for these scorpion fish?'

Isidro sold his fish quickly, keeping his eye on Ines Brunet who was walking along the dock. He hurried to meet her and she reproved him. 'What will people think, the way you pay me attention!'

'Is it not polite to greet a neighbour and say good morning?'

'Very well, neighbour. Good morning.'

He walked beside her, one long stride to her two quick steps. The skirt of her work frock fell to her knees and although she was a brunette, the down upon her calves was silvery. 'See how everyone is watching us,' she protested.

'What of it? Can I not talk to you and walk with you at the same time?'

'Not without the gossips making scandal.'

'Why are you up so early?'

'Papa's fishing boat docked last night and all its catch was bought by a Barcelona merchant. Papa is packing the fish in ice and I'm taking him his breakfast.' She held up a rafia bag containing black bread, a slice of salami sausage and a bottle of wine.

'Why do you not wear shoes?' he criticised.

'Because I do not choose.'

'It is not seemly that a young lady should go barefooted.'

10

She giggled. 'A "Young Lady",' she mocked.

Isidro frowned. 'You do not make the best of yourself. Your father is a skilled carpenter who employs men. Also he owns a fishing boat. It is not necessary to demean yourself by going barefooted . . . like a peasant.'

Her black eyes danced. 'How many times have I seen your own sister, Teresa, barefooted and working like a man, drawing in the fishing nets and wading in the sea up to her waist?'

'Teresa is different. Everybody knows she is as strong-willed as a man. She will work with the men or sew with the women. She will dare argue her opinion against the schoolmaster and will even go into a bar unescorted. But you are different, Ines. You are *entirely* feminine. You should not ape man. You should be formal and more feminine. More . . . reserved.'

'What is it to you, the way I am?' she teased.

'I like to see you at your best.'

'He who bids the musicians play should make known his wishes.' She looked away shyly.

'Ines,' he said breathlessly. 'Will you go walking with me Sunday evening?'

'You are very forward, Isidro Barras.'

He said quietly: 'I ask. You have but to say yes . . . or no!'

She shrugged her shoulders. 'If you wish I will meet you in the Plaza next Sunday. We will walk there if you want it.'

'I *do* want it,' he said fervently.

'But there must be no nonsense about barefootedness!'

'I do not mind how you come . . . as long as you come, Ines.'

'I will wear shoes,' she said. Her eyes shone. 'Black shoes with high heels!'

'Walk with me a little now,' he urged.

She was scandalised. 'Impossible. My father awaits me.' She quickened her pace and he would have accompanied her had she not said sharply: 'It is better you leave me now. I will see you Sunday.'

He nodded obediently, watching her walk along the quayside to the fish market, then he sighed and went home.

Nobody was awake at this early hour and he crept up to his bedroom, stripped off his damp clothes and shivered as he snuggled between cold sheets. He quickly fell asleep and it was midday before he awoke and went downstairs to find Doctor Aldo attending his father.

A week earlier, Paco Barras had upset a pan of boiling water over himself and now he sat with his outstretched leg resting

11

on a chair while Doctor Aldo removed strips of dead, grey skin with tweezers. The leg was swollen, and as the skin came away the raw quick was exposed. Paco grinned wolfishly as the doctor worked and Elisa Barras hovered anxiously, giving her husband comfort. Pepita held an enamel kidney bowl into which the doctor dropped the slithers of skin. Despite her tender years she was becoming a woman.

Paco looked up. 'How was the fishing, Son?'

'It was not bad, Father. But the Civil Guard are hungry men.'

Doctor Aldo said angrily. 'Their appetites are more than fishermen can satisfy.'

'Did you protest, Son?'

'To protest is dangerous.'

'I am pleased you were wise, Son.'

'But I am also angry.'

'Do not worry, Son. Soon my leg will heal and we will fish together. We will have enough for all of us.'

Doctor Aldo removed a long slither of skin and, as Paco Barras clenched his teeth, Doctor Aldo asked : 'Have you no news of your son, Miguel?'

There were beads of perspiration on Paco's forehead. He said slowly : 'Miguel wrote that he has been released from the French concentration camp and is working for a farmer. Did I not tell you, Juan?'

'I remember you did,' said the doctor. He shook the tweezers and grey skin fell into the kidney bowl. It gave off a disagreeable odour and Pepita wrinkled her nostrils in disgust. The tweezers gripped another pucker of dead skin and peeled it away. 'Will Miguel not return to Spain?'

'I fear we have lost a son,' said Paco Barras sadly. 'The boy is obsessed by the murder of his bride. Those who have seen him tell me he is filled with hate. This is not good. Hate destroys. Already Miguel has grown apart from us. He is our flesh and blood but he is cold towards us and wishes to live apart.'

Isidro said quietly : 'I would have gone to see him, but to travel to Figueras requires a permit which is difficult to get. To obtain a passport and travel to France . . . was impossible!'

'And now France is at war with Germany we do not even receive letters from Miguel,' sighed Paco Barras. He shrugged his shoulders and smoothed his hair back behind his ears.

Pepita asked : 'If I volunteer as a nurse can I go to France and heal the wounded? Then I can find Miguel.'

'Have we not had enough of war that you must cross the border to find another?' growled Paco Barras.

'She's young,' her mother excused. 'She has a woman's urge to comfort the sick.'

'Then why doesn't she pour me brandy instead of toying with that enamel dish!' roared Paco, his eyes bright with pain.

'I will get it for you, Husband,' soothed Elisa. She took down the brandy bottle.

Doctor Aldo dropped the tweezers into the kidney bowl and took cotton wool and surgical alcohol from his doctor's bag. 'Drink up quickly, Paco. I'm going to clean up now and it will ... hurt!'

Paco Barras clenched his hands. 'Go ahead, Juan.'

As he cleaned the wound, Doctor Aldo tried to distract his patient's mind. 'What do you think of this war, Paco? Many say Britain and France declared war against Hitler only as a formality. The French are safe behind their Maginot Line and the Germans are safe behind their Siegfried Line. There will be no fighting. But the face of the Allies has been saved. They have fulfilled their treaty to declare war on Hitler if Poland is invaded.'

'What do I care for Britain's face and the honour of the French?' exploded Paco Barras. 'All I ask is that we are left in peace. To the devil with politicians and warmongers.'

Isidro said quietly: 'Many Spaniards now in France have new hope. They believe the Allies will fight Fascism; not only in Germany but also in Spain!'

'Listen to him,' choked Paco Barras. He was white with pain as Doctor Aldo sponged the exposed quick. 'Now he wants more war. Three years of misery and now he wants it to start all over again!'

'I do not want war, Father. I only repeat what everybody is saying.'

'What everybody says is nonsense!' roared Paco.

'Don't shout so,' soothed Elisa.

'I *will* shout!' he roared. Then he glared at Doctor Aldo. 'Why don't you cut my leg off and have done with it!'

The doctor chuckled and dropped a cotton wool swab into the kidney bowl. 'All finished, Paco. Now a soothing ointment and in a week or so it will be healed.'

'The entire Government army took refuge in France, Father,' said Isidro. 'They'll fight against Hitler.'

'Why talk about fighting,' roared Paco Barras. 'Nothing good is gained by war. It sows the seeds of hate. Do you want people to suffer? It is good to sit in the sun, to fish, to drink wine and help our neighbours. But not to fight wars! Look what war has done to us. I have lost a son and you have lost a

13

brother. But other families have suffered much more. So I shit upon your talk of war!'

'I do not want war,' said Isidro humbly. 'When it was useless to fight I surrendered and was taken prisoner. It was not pleasant to be a prisoner and now I am free again I want to live quietly. But I cannot pretend that there are not many Spaniards outside Spain who plan to return victoriously.'

Doctor Aldo bandaged deftly and said: 'France doesn't want to fight Hitler, only to pacify him. The French are afraid of Communism. They suppress left-wing hotheads more vigorously than the Fascists.'

Paco Barras's pain had been soothed by the ointment. 'We have no need of politics in Escoleras. Leave us in peace and we live contentedly.'

Doctor Aldo finished bandaging and rose to his feet. 'Unhappily, only you and I and a very few others know how to live well, Paco.'

'Let's hope things will soon get better,' said Elisa as saying 'Amen'.

Doctor Aldo picked up his battered bag, tugged out his watch and glanced at it. 'You have heard about our new neighbours?'

Paco Barras's eyebrows arched in curiosity. 'I know only that a family of gypsies with many children has occupied a bombed cottage.'

'They've come from Jaen, walking every step of the journey with all those children. It took them three years and two more children were born on the road. They've only got the clothes they stand up in. They've been begging. The Mayor offered them work, but they don't want it. They sit in the sun and sing and dance flamenco. Some of the children are very good and afterwards they go round with a hat. There've been a few fowls missing, also washing has mysteriously disappeared from the clothes lines.' Doctor Aldo chuckled.

'Where are they heading?'

'Maybe Escoleras will be honoured,' said Doctor Aldo with a twinkle in his eyes. 'They may stay. Nobody charges them rent. They're patching the hole in the roof with corrugated iron, begging bits and pieces of furniture and setting up a home.'

'Who owns the cottage?'

Doctor Aldo sighed. 'It belongs to the Plana family. But they were all killed and no relatives have claimed the property.'

'It's better the gypsies have it than the State should take it over,' said Paco Barras.

Doctor Aldo knuckled the door of Serra's cottage, opened it and stepped into the gloom of the stone-floored living room. The only furniture was a rickety table and two broken chairs. Maria Serra sat on the floor on a piece of sacking and used her bare toes to draw taut the fishing net she was repairing. She glanced up at the doctor and looked away quickly. 'Good morning, Doctor.' Her fingers flew as she patched. She was paid piece work and wouldn't waste a second.

Doctor Aldo drew back the sackcloth curtain at the window and crossed to the cot in the corner. It was made from two fish boxes and the child sleeping in it was pale and sickly.

'She's sleeping,' said Maria. 'Don't wake her.'

Doctor Aldo stared down at the child. 'She's not strong, Maria. How old is she now? Three years? She should be full of life and playing with other children.' His eyes glinted. 'You should be ashamed of yourself, woman. You neglect this child.'

She glared. 'What more can we do? We give her *every-thing*!'

'Feed the child,' he said flatly. 'Give her good food that makes bones and puts flesh on her.'

'We do what we can. But food's expensive. She eats more than we do.'

It was true. Maria's pinched cheeks, shrunken breasts and skinny arms showed she ate barely enough to keep herself alive. Vicente Serra was equally frugal. He worked every hour he could labour and never spent a peseta.

'If you and Vicente devote your lives to saving money it is your privilege,' said Doctor Aldo sternly. 'But you have a responsibility to your daughter. Her health is in danger.'

'She eats more than we eat. Last night we had boiled potatoes and half of them went on her plate.'

'Potatoes!' he stormed. 'She needs food ... *not* stuffing! Give her chicken, beefsteaks and lots of fish!'

Maria's eyes were black buttons gleaming in the dark hollows of her eye sockets. 'Such food is *impossible*, Doctor. It costs a fortune!'

'So what, woman! Spend a fortune. Make your child healthy!'

Her lips trembled and her eyes were shocked. 'We can't, Doctor. We *can't* spend the money.'

'You and Vicente have been saving for years. You've a small fortune stored away.'

'We can't touch our savings, Doctor. It's there ... in case we ever have need of it.'

'I shit upon your meanness,' stormed the doctor. 'What need is greater than the health of your child!'

'But, Doctor . . . she is not ill!'

Doctor Aldo lost his temper then. He swore and blasphemed, knowing strong language was more readily respected. 'Tell Vicente everything I have said,' he finished. He stumped to the door. 'Unless better care is taken of that child I'll report you both!'

But as he strode on to his next patient the doctor regretted his anger. Maria and Vincente were ill too. Their sickness was greed. They drove themselves relentlessly, aged themselves prematurely and denied themselves even the simple comforts of life.

His next call was upon Teresa Barras, now married to Narcisus Coruna. Manuel Coruna was weighing out dried beans for a customer and Narcisus was balanced on a high ladder, stacking rope-soled alpargatas on the top shelf. Teresa was setting out boxes of salted herrings on the display counter.

Doctor Aldo greeted them crisply, took out his watch and said: 'Let's see how it's going, shall we, Teresa?'

Emilia Coruna was preparing lunch in the tiny kitchen behind the shop when Teresa led the doctor through it and upstairs to the bedroom.

'How do you feel?' he asked, motioning her to lie down.

'I've never felt better.'

'Good.' He examined her, pleased that she did not embarrass him with mock modesty.

'Excellent,' he reported briskly. 'Excellent!' He washed his hands in the bowl of water on the washstand. Teresa stood up and shook down her skirts.

He turned to face her, drying his hands on a towel. 'Excellent,' he said again. 'You're as sound as a bell, Teresa. Everything is as it should be.'

'How about my need to keep running to the toilet?'

'That's quite natural. Your bladder's compressed. Everything has to give way a little. The baby makes everything move over to give it room. How's your appetite? Are you eating well? Any yearnings?'

'I'm always as hungry as a horse.'

He studied her, seeing her as a man and not as a doctor. She'd blossomed and was beautiful in a comfortable, matronly way. Her skin was clear and glowing and her eyes wise and peaceful. She was only nineteen, he recalled, but looked younger. The pronounced swell of her pregnancy above her coltish legs was incongruous.

16

'There's no way to tell if it will be a boy or a girl?'

He shook his head. 'What would you like?'

'A girl,' she said at once.

'Narcisus would like a boy?'

'A father always wants a son.'

'You're both young. You've plenty of time to have lots of both kinds.'

She nodded and he saw a hint of resignation in her eyes as though she could see the long years ahead unfolding monotonously, one pregnancy following another relentlessly, her youth swallowed up by wifely drudgery.

He thought of Anselmo's wife and said: 'It'll be a race between the Ledesmas and the Corunas.' He'd spoken thoughtlessly and he watched Teresa shyly, wishing he hadn't spoken, but was relieved when she looked at him with untroubled eyes.

'How is Silvana?' she asked.

'She is well. Quite well.' He frowned, thinking of women's different attitudes to childbirth. Teresa was active and helping her husband. Whereas Silvana, delicate and ethereal, made the household revolve around her while she lay in bed, imperiously demanding service and attention as though she was the only woman who had ever been with child.

'Is ... is Anselmo happy?' asked Teresa.

He looked at her steadily and because he knew how she had been devoted to Anselmo, he replied honestly, even though it hurt her. 'Yes, Teresa. Anselmo is very happy. He wanted a wife to bear him children and now a child is on the way.'

'I am pleased if Anselmo is happy,' she said quietly.

For a moment the bond of sympathy between them was so strong that he was tempted to ask: *'What went wrong with you and Anselmo? I was sure you two would marry.'* But instead he asked. 'Are you, Teresa? Are you happy?'

'Should I not be happy?' she asked with a sad smile. 'I'm married. I have a home, I am soon to become a mother and ... I have a good and kind husband.'

The doctor pulled out his watch and glanced at it. 'I must go.' Teresa and Anselmo would have been an excellent match, he reflected. Anselmo was a responsible young man, quite different from his brother, Rafael. He thought fleetingly then of Rafael and then of Rosemarie.

'Have you news of Rosemarie?' he asked.

'She hasn't written for a long time. She lost the baby. You knew about that, didn't you, Doctor?'

'Yes.' He sighed and took out his watch. 'I must get along.'

He had only one more patient to visit when he reached the outskirts of the village so he loitered to talk to Hernando.

3

Hernando had a cooking pot simmering on a bed of white-hot charcoal. He took off the lid, dropped in a handful of edible toadstools and a delightful odour wafted to the doctor's nostrils. 'It smells delicious!'

'A wild hare I shot this morning,' said Hernando proudly. 'One head of garlic, three bay leaves, one guindilla, half a litre of wine, some pepper and now the setas.'

'It makes my mouth water.'

'Come back in two hours and it will be ready,' said Hernando. He twirled his waxed moustache. 'Ilovet and Batana are coming with friends. Some are gathering mussels from the rocks and others are fishing. Coll will bring wine. We'll eat well, Doctor. You are very welcome.'

'No man can refuse an invitation to your cooking,' said the doctor. He tugged out his watch and thrust it away again. 'There is much hunger in the cities, Hernando.'

The old man nodded. 'So I have heard.' His face was serious. 'The soil of Spain is rich, but when men war instead of tilling the earth, they must starve.'

'I am told a donkey sells for a fortune in Barcelona.'

'Before the war,' ruminated Hernando, 'a donkey could be bought with a packet of cigarettes.'

'But now, Hernando, a donkey well salted will nourish a family for many months!'

'What other news have you got of the city?' asked Hernando.

Doctor Aldo shook his head. 'Things go from bad to worse. There is no confidence in the Government. Everywhere there is fear and suspicion. Industry is at a standstill and without capital. The factories stay closed and even if there was an abundance of food, few can earn money to buy it. All over Spain there is despair. There are few crops and only the Government has the money to buy them. It pays a pittance. Spain is dead, Hernando. Our roads were destroyed by trucks, tanks and bombs and all that is left are paths of hard-packed soil that turn into soft mud in the rains. They are not repaired because there are few trucks and buses to use them and no private cars. Only the secret police, the Civil Guard and the judges are active. The prisons are over-crowded with men who've been denounced. Those who are suspected of being Socialists get long terms of imprisonment. Those believed to be

Communists are executed. But what makes everything worse, Hernando, is the war between the Allies and Germany. If Europe was at peace Spain could ask for economic aid, but Europe is at war and all the frontiers are closed. Spain is isolated. Our problems are ignored by other countries which also have too many problems of their own.'

Hernando stirred the simmering pot with a wooden spoon. Steam wafted up with an appetising aroma. 'The Government that governs best is the one that governs least of all,' Hernando said philosophically. He looked up then as Father Delbos, the village priest, approached. His blue eyes gave no smile of welcome.

'Good morning, Doctor. Good morning, Hernando,' said the priest. He spoke in Spanish, but Hernando replied in Catalan.

'Bon dia,' said Hernándo.

'It is possible we shall have a shower towards evening,' said Doctor Aldo.

Father Delbos's nostrils quivered. 'Your stew smells delicious!' He still spoke in Spanish.

Hernando restrained an impulse to invite the priest to eat with him. Instead he said in Catalan. 'Send someone with a dish and it will be my pleasure to send you a sample of my cooking.'

Doctor Aldo relaxed. He had dreaded an open-hearted invitation to the priest.

'It is kind of you, Hernando. I will send my woman.' The priest frowned. 'You have noticed I always speak in Spanish. It is best we forget we are Catalans and weld ourselves into the Spanish nation and grow strong.'

Hernando hooked his thumbs into his black sash. 'I can't change what I am, Father Delbos. Catalan is my mother tongue and I always speak it, but I understand Spanish and will speak it to those who are not Catalan.'

'Hernando, by keeping the Catalan language alive you drive a wedge between the peoples of Spain.'

'I am driving no wedge,' said Hernando. 'There are some people who are very good and some who are very bad. But what they are does not depend upon the language they speak.'

'It is forbidden to speak Catalan,' said Father Delbos flatly. 'That is the law.'

Hernando stared at him unblinkingly. 'You are Catalan. Will you denounce me for speaking Catalan?'

Father Delbos flushed. 'Of course not.'

Doctor Aldo took out his watch and glanced at it. 'I must hurry.' He nodded briefly at the priest and spoke to Hernando in Catalan. 'I will see you soon.' He strode away.

Hernando took out a worn leather pouch and rolled a cigarette. 'Smoke?' he asked the priest.

The priest lit up and coughed at the acrid bite of the black tobacco. 'Where do you get your tobacco?' he asked curiously.

Hernando twirled his moustache and nodded towards the mountains. 'I grow it secretly.' He chuckled. 'It tastes better without government tax.'

The priest frowned. 'Tell me. Hernando. Why do you never come to church? Everyone says you are a good man. But you never worship God.'

Hernando laughed. 'What has the Church to do with God? In church you burn incense, chant in a strange tongue, sing sad songs and stand up and kneel down many, many times. I don't know God, but if all this pleases him, he must be a man of very simple tastes.'

The priest exhaled smoke through his nostrils. 'You are intelligent, Hernando. You can understand that the simple people have need of symbols to help them focus their faith.'

'The churches wanted war,' said Hernando slowly. 'They declared General Franco's rebellion a sacred crusade.'

'And so it was. Would you want the red scum of Moscow making us slaves?'

'I prefer that there is no slavery, either to Moscow or to the Church.'

Father Delbos's eyes narrowed. 'You presume to criticise, Hernando? Can you not see that mankind is on the threshold of greatness? Soon the one true faith will reign throughout the world. Hitler is gathering his strength and the Vatican and Mussolini are behind him. The red scourge will be stamped out. Britain and France will be destroyed and the forces of God's crusade will turn to the East and confront the twin evils of Judaism and Marxism.'

Hernando didn't have a watch to glance at. Instead he said briskly: 'Excuse me. I have an important job.' He disappeared inside his hut and pulled the sackcloth curtain across the doorway behind him.

Father Delbos stood frowning at the simmering pot for some minutes. Then he sighed and made his way along the beach to the quay. He stood watching the fish being unloaded and presently was given a rafia bag of fish. It was the custom.

Such men as Hernando and Doctor Aldo were dangerous, the priest reflected grimly as he paced homewards, his black skirts swishing. Clearly they were disbelievers. Such men had a disturbing influence upon simple-minded villagers.

CHAPTER TWO

1

MADRID was crowded with Nationalist soldiers. There were victory parades, the cinemas no longer feared bombing, the sidewalk bars were crowded and there was a surge of gaiety as though everyone was determined to forget the sad past and build a happy future.

Antonia Ledesma was on her way home from the University when she saw a group of officers standing under the gaily-striped awning of a hotel that had been commandeered by the Military. The familiar posture of one of the officers caught her attention and she ran across the road, her heart beating with excitement. It was her brother, Rafael.

He'd changed greatly during the last three years. He was taller, his pale forehead seemed higher because his black hair had receded and the skin of his face was drawn drum-tight over his facial bones. Antonia ran to him excitedly: 'Rafael. It's me, Antonia!'

He was surprised to hear his name called. He turned to her lazily, black eyes glittering and eyelids narrowing. She was shocked that he knew her and yet was so unmoved by their meeting. He said coldly: 'How are you, Antonia? I wondered if you were in Madrid.' His manner was so distant it killed her natural impulse to embrace him.

'We've been worried about you, Rafael. You haven't written.' Her voice tailed off because the other officers were eyeing her curiously.

'Señores,' said Rafael stiffly. 'I present my sister, Antonia!'

The officers gravely raised her hand to their lips. They were all very young and the smartness of ther uniforms with ribbons and medals made her aware that Rafael too had gained distinctions. He wore his medals with youthful arrogance.

'We must have a drink,' said Rafael.

The other officers tactfully excused themselves and Rafael urged Antonia into the hotel bar. They sat at an isolated table.

'It's been a long time, Rafael. Three years and not a word from you in all that time!'

He crossed his legs and his spurs jingled. He placed his riding crop upon the table and grinned sardonically. 'I no

21

longer belong to the family. I was turned out!'

'You ... you heard about father dying?'

He glowered. 'Murdered by the Reds!'

'I don't know what happened between you and Father, Rafael, but he loved you. He would want you to come back to the family.'

His face was a mask.

'I do not need the family. I prefer to make my own way.' He grinned mockingly. 'Anselmo can be a father to you all.'

She asked unhappily: 'What's happened to you, Rafael? You've changed. You're ... cold and heartless!'

'War makes a man hard.'

'You're breaking Mother's heart!'

His lips curled. 'She has two sons and daughters to fill the gap I leave.'

'You *will* come home, won't you, Rafael? Promise me.'

He shook his head arrogantly.

'You may have quarrelled with Father, Rafael. But a mother is always ready to forgive.'

He shook his head. 'The family and I are too far apart. Nothing can bridge the gap.'

'I do not know why you quarrelled with father but it is wrong to allow it to cut so deeply.'

He studied her thoughtfully. 'You know nothing of the quarrel?'

She shook her head.

'Father insisted I should marry Rosemarie Prada or leave home.' Rafael shrugged his shoulders. 'I was unwilling to tie myself to a cheap skivvy. So ... I left home.'

Her eyes were worried. 'Did Mother know of this?'

'Of course.'

'But there must have been some reason, Rafael. Father was a just man. Was there ... did you ... ?' She flushed.

He picked up his riding crop and toyed with it. His forehead gleamed like polished bone. 'I slapped her,' he said. 'She insulted my family so I hit her. She whined to Father that she was hurt and he gave me the ultimatum.'

Antonia was puzzled. 'That's not like Father.'

He shrugged his shoulders. 'Does it matter?' He slashed the table top lightly with his crop. 'We must be realists and accept things for what they are and *not* for what we want them to be.' He glanced at his wrist watch. 'I must leave in a few minutes. I've been summoned to Headquarters.'

'When will I see you again, Rafael?'

'That depends upon what I am doing.'

'How can I get in touch with you?'

He grinned mockingly. 'I move around a great deal.'

She wanted to reach across the table and hold his hand, but she knew he would resent it. She said in a low voice: 'Rafael. We are the same flesh and blood. We need each other and can help each other.'

'I need help from *nobody*,' he said flatly.

'Perhaps we may have need of you, Rafael,' she said gently.

He studied her coldly. 'You're twenty-eight, aren't you? You'd better watch it or you'll get left on the shelf and don't think I'll saddle myself with a spinster sister!'

She drew back as though he had smacked her face. 'That's a cruel thing to say, Rafael.'

'I'm a cruel person.'

She picked up her handbag and rose to her feet. He stood up at once, outwardly polite and gentlemanly. 'Allow me to call you a taxi.'

'I haven't taxi money. I walk.'

'It will be my privilege to pay.'

'Your privilege is to hurt those who love you.'

He saw she was close to tears and he turned away and called the waiter over to pay the bill. Then he escorted Antonia to the hotel foyer, his spurs jingling, his crop slashing his polished riding boots and the tunic of his uniform bright with medals.

'Must we part like this, Rafael?' she choked.

He glanced at his wrist watch. 'I have only a few minutes now.'

'I mean ... can we expect you to become one of the family?'

'It is better this way, Antonia. We've grown so far apart, we live in different worlds. I am content. I want no family ties.' He signalled to the door porter, who called up a taxi reserved for officers. Rafael spoke to the driver and gave him a currency note. The man saluted.

Rafael turned back to Antonia. 'He'll take you home.'

She looked at him steadily. 'When will we meet again, Rafael?'

He shrugged his shoulders. 'Is a brother and sister bond important? Would we bother about each other if we hadn't shared the same parentage?'

She stared at him for a long time. 'Something terrible has happened to you, Rafael. You're not ... not quite human.'

'That might be the best way to adapt to the world in which we live,' he said sardonically. He opened the taxi door, held her elbow as she climbed into the taxi and saluted her gravely. He bowed slightly from the waist as the taxi drew away from the curbside, then without another glance at her, signalled with his riding crop for the next taxi. 'General Headquarters,' he told the driver.

He arrived at Headquarters with time to spare and was shown into a large waiting room panelled with carved oak. The velvet window curtains were drawn and the cut-glass chandelier was the room's only source of light. Its glistening tear-drops turned the wine-coloured carpet warmly yellow and the gilt frames of the oil paintings that lined the walls into soft gold. Two colonels and a brigadier were also waiting. They glanced up at Rafael, nodded and looked away. Rafael seated himself, picked up a magazine from a small table and leafed through it.

The colonel was called away and then the brigadier. He marched up to the desk, stood stiffly at attention and saluted.

The general was a grey-haired man with tired brown eyes. He gestured wearily. 'Sit down, Ledesma. Forget the formalities.'

Rafael seated himself stiffly on the edge of his chair, almost as much at attention as when he was standing. He stared at the top of the general's head while he read through the dossier he had before him. He wet finger and thumb before he turned over each page and took an inordinate time to read each sheet. He closed the dossier, sat back in his chair, sighed and raised his eyes to Rafael. 'Your record is clean, Ledesma. You're very loyal to the regime.'

'It is my honour to be loyal to my country, mi General.'

'The loyalty of Spain's true sons is to be rewarded.'

Rafael lowered his eyes. 'I do not seek reward, only to do my duty.'

'These are critical times,' said the general. 'We have won the war. Now we must win the peace. Spain must be rebuilt, but we must guard against the red enemy still in our midst.'

'I am ever ready to be of service to my country, mi General.'

The general waved his hand. 'Relax, Ledesma. Let's dispense with the bloody military pomp.'

Rafael smiled restrainedly and relaxed slightly.

The general rummaged through his papers, picked up a folder, glanced through it, placed it under a paperweight and picked up another. 'All patriots who have shown their loyalty to their country will be rewarded. They will have preference for any job. Our Leader recognises Spain's indebtedness to them. But we still have a great deal of work ahead of us. Ah!' He'd found the paper he was looking for. He smoothed it flat and formed the words soundlessly with his lips as he read it. He looked up. 'Despite our victory, there are still many who oppose us.'

24

Rafael narrowed his eyes. 'The lower classes are traitors, ever ready to sell Spain to Moscow.'

'It is General Franco's wish that such traitors be combed out. All those who have been misled and influenced by red propaganda must undergo corrective training.'

Rafael leaned forward, eyes sharp with interest.

'There are many suspected left-wing sympathisers under arrest,' said the general. 'Such men cannot be given liberty to arouse discontent and preach dangerous philosophies. For their own good they must be re-educated before they can take their place in society again.'

Rafael nodded.

'You are young, Ledesma,' said the general. 'But you have initiative and determination. I believe I can trust you with the responsibility of setting up disciplinary camps to re-educate these social misfits.'

Rafael rose to his feet and clicked his heels. 'I assure you I will carry out this task to your complete satisfaction.'

2

All day Teresa had endured the warning pains in silence, but at seven in the evening a pain gripped her so fiercely that she knew her time had come.

She crouched over the counter, gripping her hands together until they were bloodless. Her eyes glazed and she said faintly: 'It is my time, Narcisus. Get Doctor Aldo and the taxi.'

Narcisus fled frantically as his mother took Teresa's arm and helped her to a chair. 'Is it a big pain?' she asked.

'The first big one.'

'Why did you not speak sooner, silly girl?'

Doctor Aldo hurried in with his worn leather bag. 'How long between pains?' He took out his watch to check for himself. 'You should have spoken sooner,' he scolded. 'It's a long way to Gerona and the roads are bad.'

The taxi was old, but was kept going by the mechanical genius of Juan Morales, who cared for it as though it was precious. The old car wheezed, rattled and bumped over the potholed road with Juan Morales torn between the necessity for speed and the comfort of his passenger.

Every time a pain came, Teresa braced back against the upholstery and gripped Narcisus's arm with such intensity that he turned pale.

Doctor Aldo timed the intervals. 'I think we'll be all right,' he said doubtfully.

Teresa summoned up a smile. 'Suppose our child is born in

the taxi, Narcisus.'

Juan Morales blushed and tramped down hard on the accelerator.

'You'll be all right,' said the doctor.

'And ... and Silvana, Doctor?' panted Teresa. 'What news of Silvana?'

Five days earlier Silvana Ledesma had felt her first pains. Doctor Aldo had been aroused in the middle of the night to accompany her to Gerona. But the pains had been imaginary and, after staying with her all night and most of the following day, he had finally left the clinic to care for his other patients.

'Anselmo telephoned,' he told Teresa. 'She's having more pains. This time it could be the real thing.'

'You said it would be a race between us!' Teresa broke off and braced her shoulders against the upholstery. Her body arched and the muscles of her face tautened and pulled down the corners of her mouth. Her nose was thin, prominent and wax-like.

'It's a big pain now,' the doctor told Narcisus.

It was dark when they reached the clinic. Two nuns took Teresa upstairs to a labour ward and helped her to undress. Doctor Aldo left Narcisus in a waiting room and went to see the hospital doctor.

'Another maternity, Pedro,' he greeted. 'This one held out as long as she could. I don't think she'll be more than an hour. How's the Ledesma woman?'

The doctor raised his eyes to heaven. 'More trouble than a dozen others. Screams every time she has a twinge. If she wasn't allergic to anaesthetics, I'd have quietened her long ago. She's just going to the theatre.'

Teresa was being helped into a hospital cot when she first heard Silvana who had a private ward alongside the ward. Its door was open and a trolley was wheeled in to take Silvana to the operating theatre. A pain started, screams rang out along the ward and echoed from the walls. The screaming dwindled to a whimpering and the hospital orderlies swiftly transferred Silvana to the trolley.

'She's been doing that all day,' said the woman in the cot next to Teresa.

'Some people are more sensitive to pain than others,' said Teresa.

'And some like to draw attention to themselves!' snapped the woman.

Teresa had to lay back then because another pain racked her. When it was over she propped herself up on her elbow. Silvana began screaming again. Teresa saw her trolley rolling along the corridor and a man who walked behind it. At first she didn't recognise the weary figure with bowed shoulders. Then she realised it was Anselmo, exhausted by remaining at his wife's side these last few days. Every scream she uttered punished him terribly. His guilt for her suffering had become an unbearable burden to him.

Narcisus came up to the ward and he and Doctor Aldo sat with Teresa for a time. Soon, Doctor Aldo was called away. Narcisus held her hand. Presently screens were placed round her and a nurse pulled long woollen stockings on her legs. There were only short intervals now between her pains and she sensed the urgency of the orderlies as they lifted her on to a trolley. Narcisus walked beside her, holding her hand until they reached the door of the operating theatre. He kissed her lightly on the lips and she was wheeled into the smell of ether and antiseptics. She was lifted off the trolley on to the operating table and a masked face loomed down upon her. She hadn't recognised Doctor Aldo behind his white gown and gauze mask but she knew his voice.

'You lost the race, Teresa. Silvana won.'

'What . . .?' asked Teresa faintly.

'A girl,' said Doctor Aldo. 'A beautiful little girl. On the small side, but healthy and screaming lustily.'

'Was . . . was Anselmo disappointed?' she whispered.

'All men want a son, but they become more attached to a daughter.'

There were metal stirrups to support the weight of Teresa's drawn-up legs. The hospital doctor made an examination. 'It won't be long,' he said. He looked hard at Teresa. 'It'll be a tight one.'

Teresa had another pain coming. Doctor Aldo went to the foot of the table and braced the soles of her feet against his shoulders. 'Bear down,' he said.

'Ahhh! That's good,' she said huskily. Her lips writhed back away from her teeth and her eyes bulged as the pain gripped her.

'Strain,' urged Doctor Aldo. 'Push down.'

It was a fine exhausting pain and her cheeks were wet with sweat when it eased. She glanced at the inspection window and smiled encouragingly at Narcisus who was watching her with worried eyes.

'Tell him to go away,' she told Doctor Aldo. 'It hurts him to see me.'

'He won't,' said Doctor Aldo. 'He insists on staying.'

Another long pain began, and when it was over the hospital doctor scolded angrily: 'Scream, woman. Don't bottle it up.

27

It's not natural!'

Teresa's eyes flicked to the window and she smiled weakly at Narcisus. 'I'm all right.'

'I can give you a whiff of something to make it easier. This is a tight one.'

'No,' she said quickly. 'I want my baby to be healthy.'

'It is better if you can do without it,' sighed the doctor.

'Will it . . . will it be long?' asked Teresa.

'Any time. But it won't be easy, young woman. The baby's gone full term and is big.'

The baby was born fifteen minutes later.

Narcisus saw the hospital doctor hunched down between Teresa's parted thighs. He straightened up and handed a lump of bloody pinkness to a nurse, who took it deftly and dangled it by its feet like a skinned rabbit. The nurse slapped, the wizened little face screwed up and the mouth opened enormously to cry. But no sound reached Narcisus on his side of the inspection window. The nurse swaddled the baby in a towel, placed it on one side and turned back to the operating table.

Narcisus's heart thumped painfully. An emergency? He stood on tiptoe to see over the white-overalled shoulders of the doctors but could see nothing. He studied Teresa's pale face. Her nose was pinched and waxen and her face bore the shadow of pain it had worn since her labour began. He clenched his hands tightly and there were tears upon his face. 'Please God, don't let her die,' he prayed aloud, but his lips trembled and he couldn't pronounce the words clearly.

He remained in tortured suspense until the gowned figures straightened up and pulled their masks off their mouths. With relief, Narcisus saw sheets being tucked around Teresa. A bell rang somewhere and hospital orderlies entered the theatre, lifted her on to a trolley and wheeled her away.

Narcisus looked at the baby. He saw the bloodstained towelling moving slightly, but no one took any notice of it. The doctors were talking, the nurses were dropping used instruments into trays and gathering up used swabs. He wanted to hammer on the glass and shout: '*The baby! What about the baby!*'

At that moment, Doctor Aldo turned and smiled at Narcisus. He nodded encouragingly and spoke to one of the nurses. She hurried across to the door of the operating theatre and called: 'You can come in.' There was a splash of blood on her white gown and the sharp tang of antiseptic stung his nostrils.

'Congratulations, Narcisus,' said Doctor Aldo. 'It's a boy.'

Narcisus stared at the moving bundle anxiously. 'Why don't

they do something for him?'

'Don't worry,' soothed Doctor Aldo. 'We give him a few minutes to adapt himself to his new environment. There. You see. Nurse is going to clean him up now.'

The nurse unwrapped the towel. The baby's wide-open eyes seemed to search for Narcisus and then stared straight at him. He thought: *'It's my son and he knows it. Look at the way the little devil's staring at me. He knows I'm his father.'*

The wizened features screwed themselves up, the eyes became slits and the mouth gaped. The baby cried lustily.

'Listen to those lungs,' said Doctor Aldo approvingly.

The nurse sponged the baby and as blood and mucus was sluiced away, Narcisus was horrified by the great mauve stains that covered its shoulders and buttocks.

'. . . is he all right, doctor?'

'Sound and healthy.'

'But, doctor. Will he always be like that, that mauve colour? Is it . . . is it a birth mark?'

Doctor Aldo chuckled. 'He'll lose that in no time. Imagine how you'd looked if you'd been cramped up for weeks like this little chap.'

'And . . . and Teresa?'

'She's fine, Narcisus. She's strong and healthy. She'll be sore for a time, but you can see for yourself what a big head your son's got.'

The nurse placed the baby on the scales and said contentedly: 'Four and a quarter kilos!'

'See what I mean,' said Doctor Aldo. 'Lots of stitches. But she'll soon be fit again.'

A week later Teresa was back in the shop and working as hard as ever, breaking off only to breast-feed her son.

Silvana stayed weeks more in hospital. She returned to Escoleras in an expensive limousine hired for the journey. She'd had new dresses made for herself while she was in hospital, clothes for the baby, crisp linen uniforms for the baby's nurse and costumes for the young woman who was to be her companion-help. For the christening, more than two hundred expensively printed luncheon invitations were sent out.

Narcisus and Teresa were invited, but shortly before they were due to set off for the Ledesma house Teresa had a headache. Although she insisted he should go without her, Narcisus stayed at home to keep her company.

3

The night was so silent that Miguel heard the men

approaching through the valley when they were more than a kilometre away. He waited patiently, as still as the mountains around him. When they were so close that he could hear their heavy breathing, the swish of the undergrowth, the scrape of iron-shod hooves on the pebbles and the metallic clink of weapons, one of them whistled a signal.

He whistled back and they grunted happily and hurried towards him, disturbing the night with their voices and heavy boots. Presently they reached him, a single file of armed men leading laden donkeys.

'It is you, Miguel?' the first asked softly into the darkness, speaking Spanish with an Andalucian accent.

'It is, Comrade Munez,' snapped Miguel. 'But I could easily have been a French gendarme or a German patrol. They'd have had plenty of time to prepare an ambush, warned by the noise you were making!'

'We did not use caution because we trust you, Comrade,' said Munez. 'You have the ears of a hound and I swear you see in the dark. You would have warned us if there had been danger.'

'That may be so,' grumbled Miguel.

'You will lead the way, Comrade?'

'Follow silently because in these mountains sounds carry swiftly from one hill crest to another.'

He led them for almost an hour, picking his way through the darkness with uncanny ease and walking with the sure-footedness of a goat. He halted at a belt of dwarf pines growing so closely together they seemed impenetrable.

'Keep close together,' he ordered.

He forced his way in among the trees, bending back branches to scrape past them. Soon he reached a cleared path where the pines had been uprooted to leave a passage a yard or more wide. This led on for a hundred yards to the rock face of a mountain. Miguel used a torch, knowing the thick canopy of pine needles above them effectively screened the light. At the rock face, Miguel pulled aside uprooted trees he'd placed across the entrance to a natural cave. He stepped inside and lit the oil lamp standing upon a ledge just inside the entrance. The guttering, yellow light revealed an enormous cavern with a roof so high that the light of the lamp did not reach it.

The donkeys were led into the cavern and their panniers unloaded. Boxes of ammunition were stacked high and covered with rubber ground-sheets. Tommy-guns were greased and swathed in oily rags, explosives and hand grenades were wrapped in waterproof papers.

Miguel surveyed the stock of ammunition with grim satisfaction. Week by week he'd watched it grow until there was enough to wage a minor battle.

The men sat down to eat and rest before their long journey back through the night. Some were Spanish refugees with bitter memories and others were French patriots awaiting the day they could strike at the Germans who occupied their country. There was one among them whom Miguel did not know. Munez introduced him. 'Comrade Miguel, this is Comrade Jean-Luis, second in command of our Resistance Corps. He has heard of you and wishes to meet you.'

Jean-Luis was a man of Miguel's age, dark, serious-eyed and with a high prominent forehead. His hand clasp was powerful and there were callouses on his fingers.

'Congratulations, Comrade,' he said. 'You've found us a perfect arms dump. When the time comes, we will have all the arms we need.'

'How long must we wait, Comrade?'

Jean-Luis shrugged his shoulders and his dark eyes studied Miguel's impassive face. Miguel's welted scar made him look cold and cruel. 'We must await the right moment. America will come into the war, Britain will launch an invasion and on that day all French patriots will arise and fight for freedom.'

'To fight blindly is not enough,' said Miguel. 'There must be organisation. We must hit the enemy where it hurts. We must harry him and destroy him with sabotage.'

Jean-Luis lowered his eyes. 'I'm told you are an indomitable fighter against fascism.'

'To destroy fascism is our only hope,' said Miguel. 'Britain and France betrayed us. They watched Italy and Germany turn Spain into a testing ground for war. But now *they* know the menace of fascist aggression. This is the life or death struggle of Europe and Spain's last chance to escape Franco's dictatorship.'

Jean-Luis said quietly: 'I need men like you. You're wasted in these mountains. You must work in the towns, in Perpignan or Narbonne, Dijon or Marseille.'

'There are difficulties, Comrade,' said Miguel. 'Who would lead your men to this cave?'

'I will leave a man to study the landmarks.' Jean-Luis scowled. 'There may not be many more trips. When France surrendered, many of us hid our arms and ammunition. Most of it is stored here. But we have no way to get more unless they are smuggled to us by the Allies.'

'There is a matter of documents, too,' said Miguel. 'I am a Spanish refugee and here in the mountains I am not suspect. But in the towns I will be quickly noticed.'

31

'The French officials will help us,' said Jean-Luis. 'You will have a French name and papers and a job like other Frenchmen. You will live with a family and keep contact with us for active work.'

Miguel's face was expressionless. 'I am not alone and I do not wish to leave my wife.'

Jean-Luis had been told of Miguel's brooding, silent wife who'd been made ugly by a facial disfigurement. 'It is better if your wife is at your side. It will help divert suspicion from you.'

'Arrange it then, if you will,' agreed Miguel.

'I will send someone for you when it is done.'

'What work will I do?'

'The factories work day and night. The demands of our German master are insatiable. You can learn quickly to be a machine minder or an assembler in an armaments factory.'

Miguel glowered. 'I will not labour to make armaments for the Germans.'

Jean-Luis eyed him steadily. 'There are many ways to work for the Germans,' he said softly. 'There are hand grenades that explode prematurely, shells that are duds, oversized cartridges that jam machine guns and range finders that fail when needed.'

Miguel looked down at his hands. 'I will do my best.'

After the men had rested they began their long trek back to their village. Jean-Luis shook Miguel's hand. 'I will arrange everything, Comrade,' he promised.

Three weeks later, a man brought Miguel and Catalina the documents they needed to start their new life in Perpignan.

4

Teresa heard the baby whimpering in the room behind the shop, quickly finished serving her customer and called to Narcisus: 'I must go now.'

'All right. Tell Father there's no need to come out unless I call him.'

In the back room Emilia Coruna was stooped over the kitchen range, fanning charcoal to a white-hot glow with a rafia fan. Beans were simmering in a blackened pot. Manuel Coruna was weighing out dried lentils into paper bags. He glanced up when Teresa entered. 'Good. You heard him. Until now he's been sleeping soundly.'

She crossed to the cot and stared down tenderly at her son, Leon. She stroked his cheek with her forefinger and felt such a sudden rush of love for him that she picked him up and hugged him. After a few moments he cried in protest.

'You're hungry, darling,' she soothed. 'Don't cry, little one. Mama will care for you. Mama will always care for you.'

She sat in the rocking-chair and unbuttoned her blouse. Her father-in-law turned his back towards her and she eased out her breast with gentle fingers. It was swollen with milk and she smiled, remembering how once she had feared that her breasts would never mature. She pressed the hardened nipple until the milk ran from it and lowered it to her son's greedy mouth. The touch of his lips made her gasp and she steeled herself to endure his rhythmic sucking. It was a sandpaper rasp across the quick. Her nipple was ulcerated and would not heal while she breast-fed.

'He can be weaned,' Doctor Aldo had told her. 'There are baby food preparations.'

'Will it be bad for him if I don't feed him, Doctor?'

He'd sighed. 'Spain is so poor that baby preparations are not what they should be.'

'Then I'll bear the pain, Doctor.'

He'd looked at her thoughtfully. 'You're a brave girl, Teresa.' He'd been thinking of Silvana who'd flatly refused to breast feed so she wouldn't ruin her figure. The baby food she ordered from Barcelona cost a small fortune in these hungry days when many starved.

Teresa endured the pain until it was time to change and then teased her son's greedily pouting lips with her other nipple, chuckling as his little face reddened wth anger before she lowered herself to him. Then she sat with closed eyes, rocking backwards and forwards and the soreness of the ulcer forgotten in the blissful pleasure of motherhood. When her son's hunger was satiated, he fell asleep at once and she tucked him up lovingly. Then she heated water in a pan and bathed her breasts. Her ulcerated nipple was split open and she covered it with a wad of gauze before she eased her breast back inside her blouse.

'Don't go back into the shop yet,' said her mother-in-law. 'Narcisus will manage. Sit quietly for a while. You tire yourself too much.'

'I don't get tired. I'm naturally active, Emilia.'

Nevertheless, Teresa sat and watched her father-in-law weigh lentils. The strain of child-bearing, caring for the baby, feeding him, washing napkins and working in the shop *was* tiring, she realised. She closed her eyes and dozed. Later, she drowsily acknowledged Anita Braguera, a friend of her mother-in-law who'd called, then almost fell asleep again. But abruptly she awakened, aroused by the name 'Ledesma' and sat listening with her eyes closed. Anita Braguera was the village gossip and a torrent of words poured from her.

'... absolute appalling extravagance, costing a fortune and how'll he keep pace with the taxes and everything and the farms not paying and a maid just for the baby and a companion too because she's so weak after it all and doesn't even know how to boil water. No matter how good the family, even if it's royal blood, a woman should know how to care for a man, and putting on airs as though she's a princess and giving orders to the servants as though they're slaves, but what can you expect from a chit of a girl who talks to my daughter, my own flesh and blood, as though she's dirt....'

Anita Braguera's daughter was employed by the Ledesmas and Teresa realised she was listening to gossip. Her impulse was to walk out and ignore it, but she yielded to the compulsion to hear more.

'... won't feed the baby, frightened to spoil her figure, spending all that money, criminal extravagance I call it. And what for, I ask you? Because, young as she is, she's already big and droopy and my Anna saw her in one of those French nightgowns you can see through and says they hang like a goat's udders. With all those fancy airs and young as she is, she's growing so fat I dare say without moving a finger to help in the house....'

Teresa was holding her breath. One part of her mind was vindictively triumphant. *'What did you expect, Anselmo, you fool? You found a well-bred, pretty face to flatter your pride but now it will cost you dearly.'* But another part of her mind was anguished. *'What have you done to us, Anselmo? We were right for each other. I would have cared for you, been an economical wife and helped you to succeed. How could you have been so ... so blind!'*

Anita Braguera's voice droned on: '... never seen anyone so lazy. Won't lift her finger to do anything, and all that paint and powder and never a drop of water to touch her skin and all those expensive see-through underclothes all smelly, and as soon as she leaves them off my poor Anna must wash them. She grumbles that the house is old and too cold and the bathroom's too draughty with never enough hot water, and in this weather she's so delicate she might easily catch cold if she doesn't take care. And my poor Anna with her hands swollen with chilblains washing in cold water and scrubbing away those smelly stains and the poor Señora Ledesma hardly daring to say a word because whenever there's a row she starts her shouting and screaming, and it's Anselmo who suffers most, poor boy, trying to keep the peace between mother and wife,

34

and she's got him right under her thumb because . . .'

Narcisus opened the door, smiled at Teresa and looked at the cot.

'He's had his feed and he's sleeping soundly,' said Teresa. She half-rose.

'No, no. No!' insisted Narcisus. 'Rest a little. We're not busy and I'll call you if it's necessary.' He frowned. 'Everybody's gone down to the beach. They say there's been an explosion.'

'Explosion?'

Narcisus shrugged his shoulders. 'I didn't hear anything myself.'

'Neither did I,' said Manuel Coruna.

Emilia Coruna said: 'I thought I heard a muffled bang a while ago.'

'Dynamiting fish,' said Manuel Coruna.

'It's not likely,' said Teresa. 'The penalties are too harsh now that it's illegal.'

Narcisus said: 'Somebody will come in later and tell us about it.' He went back to the shop.

Teresa closed her eyes and rocked herself gently.

Anita Braguera's butterfly mind gossip-flitted to the Pradas, her close neighbours. She droned on about the hours they worked, what they bought for the house, how Marcel Prada beat his wife and that Isabel Prada was a secret drinker, stealing money from the housekeeping, buying crude brandy and carrying it round in a bottle she kept in her apron.

The door burst open and a white-faced, wild-eyed Isidro choked: 'It's Pepita. It's Pepita!'

Teresa came up out of her chair, her heart hammering. 'What is it? What's happened?'

'It's Pepita. She's hurt badly.' Isidro was crying. 'Blood all over her,' he sobbed. 'Our little Pepita.'

Nervous tension made Teresa furious. She seized him by the arms and shook him. 'Don't stand there crying, you great fool. Tell me . . . what's happened?'

'They were playing on the beach and they found an old hand grenade buried in the sand. It . . . it went off!'

Teresa snatched down her shawl. 'Where is she?'

'She's . . . they've taken her to Gerona.'

'And Mama and Papa?'

'They've all gone in the taxi with Doctor Aldo.'

'Why didn't they come for me at once?' she choked. 'Mama and Papa will need me.'

'There . . . there wasn't room. The Farina boy was hurt and his parents went too.'

Teresa stared at Isidro. 'Sit down,' she said quietly. Isidro sank into a chair weeping.

Narcisus was hovering anxiously in the background. 'Pour him a drink,' she said, surprised at her calmness. She waited until Isidro had gulped down the brandy before she asked: 'How badly is Pepita hurt?'

'I ... I couldn't see. There were so many people and ... a lot of blood. Doctor Aldo ... he says ... says she's hurt badly.'

Teresa's jaw jutted. 'We're going to Gerona,' she told Narcisus.

'There's only the one taxi,' he said. 'It might not return until tomorrow.'

'We can't wait. Go to Girales and hire his truck.'

Narcisus hesitated. The extravagance of hiring a large truck as though it were a taxi shocked him.

'Hurry,' panted Teresa. She ran to the cot. 'We'll have to take Leon.'

Narcisus hurried away.

Teresa wrapped the baby in a shawl and turned to Isidro. His lower lip was trembling and his eyes were glazed with misery. 'You remain here, Isidro. Someone must look after the house.'

He nodded numbly and buried his face in his hands. She poured him more brandy.

The truck was seldom used and half an hour was lost finding fuel for it. It was a slow-moving monster with solid rubber tyres and jolted violently as it lurched over the potholed road. The bumping soon awoke Leon. Teresa crooned to him and cushioned him against the severest jolts, but the journey seemed interminable. Finally they reached the hospital. Teresa thrust Leon into Narcisus's arms, jumped down from the driver's cabin and ran up the steps and in through the swing doors.

Her parents were seated at the far end of the vestibule and she ran to them, a lump rising in her throat when she saw her mother's red-rimmed eyes. Her father rose to his feet and she saw he was old. She had never thought of him as old before. Yet now, startlingly, he had aged. His blue eyes were tragic and his face was drawn. He took her hand and held it tightly.

'How is she?' asked Teresa. 'Where is she?'

Her mother buried her face in her hands and rocked from side to side.

'Mama. Please, Mama,' comforted Teresa.

'She's ... in the operating theatre,' said Paco Barras.

Teresa knew overwhelming relief. 'She's going to be all right!'

Her father looked away. 'The Farina boy...' His voice was

36

husky. 'They did all they could but ... they couldn't save him.'

A black cloud of dread engulfed Teresa as she pictured Pepita, precocious and full of life. Suddenly she felt faint.

Narcisus came up behind her with Leon in his arms. She glanced at the baby to assure herself he was comfortable and turned back to her father. 'Papa. How bad is she?'

He stared at the floor and shook his head. 'The doctor didn't say.'

'How long ... how long has she been in there?'

'It seems hours.'

'Stay with Mama and Papa,' she told Narcisus. 'I'll find out something.'

A nurse took her up to the operating theatre. Doctor Aldo was standing outside in a white overall and talking with a surgeon. As soon as he saw Teresa he hurried to meet her, took her by the arm and led her along the corridor. His face was serious and his grip upon her arm was tight. 'It's a terrible thing,' he sighed. 'A terrible accident.'

'How ... how bad is she, Doctor Aldo?'

'The Farina boy ... all that was possible was done but ... he died on the table.'

'And ... Pepita?'

'She's being taken up to the ward now.'

Teresa's heart leaped. 'She's not going to die?'

'No. She's going to be all right.' His grip tightened upon her arm. 'But she's been badly hurt.'

'She'll get better, won't she, Doctor?'

He hesitated. 'Yes.' But there was such restraint in his voice that she eyed him sharply. 'What is it, Doctor Aldo? Tell me the truth.'

'Her face,' he said sadly. 'Her eyes.'

The world stood still.

Teresa held herself stiffly, and her voice was emotionally detached. 'Is she blind, Doctor?'

'No. But one eye was so badly injured it had to be removed.'

'She'll be scarred?'

'Scars are not important,' he said. 'They heal.' He frowned down at the floor. 'It's her hands too, Teresa. She ... she must have been holding the bomb when it exploded.'

'Poor Pepita,' choked Teresa. 'Poor little Pepita!'

'There was nothing we could do. There wasn't much left of her hands to save anyway.'

'Oh, my God!' Teresa closed her eyes and tears ran down her cheeks.

'She'll get better, Teresa,' said Doctor Aldo. 'Medicine and nature will heal her injuries. But we doctors can do nothing about the hurt to her mind. Only her family can help her recover from the shock of learning that she is no longer like other people.'

5

The prison in Gerona was so crowded that the cell doors were left open all night so that the prisoners could sleep in the compound.

Benito Vigon waited six weeks to be brought to trial. Every day batches of prisoners were taken away and new prisoners were crammed into the compound to take their places. The prisoners saw no visitors and received no letters. So it was with grim relief that Vigon found himself and others being taken to another part of the prison. They were locked in a stone chamber where they waited hours to go before the court.

Benito Vigon was the fourth to appear. Two armed soldiers marched him into the depressing gloom of the court room and at the far end, under a large photograph of General Franco, three army officers sat behind a trestle table draped with a bottle-green cloth. Before each officer was a blotting pad, paper for writing, a glass and a water jug. To the right of the judge's bench was a smaller table at which sat another officer and two civilians. This table was stacked high with folders, files and papers.

Vigon stood to the left of the judge's bench and his escort seated themselves on a wooden bench. The judges were discussing a dinner they'd attended the previous night and ignored the prisoner. One of them went out to relieve himself and almost a quarter of an hour elapsed before the president asked, without looking at Vigon: 'What about this one?'

The officer at the small table referred to a typewritten sheet. 'Benito Vigon,' he intoned. 'Age twenty-four, son of a peasant father, served with the Government forces and was captured wearing civilian clothes some months after the end of the war.'

The president glanced at Vigon momentarily. 'You are Benito Vigon?'

'Yes,' he said hoarsely.

One of the guards pounded Vigon in the small of the back with his rifle butt. 'Yes . . . SIR!' shouted the guard.

'Yes . . . SIR!' panted Vigon, arching his spine.

But the judges weren't listening to him.

'What else?' asked the president.

The seated officer reached for another typewritten sheet. 'He did not surrender and concealed his presence from the authorities. He had no documents and had destroyed his uniform. We have twelve depositions from citizens of Escoleras, where he was born. These state that he has socialist opinions, approves of the confiscation of private property and has many times declared himself in favour of trade unions. He has shown sympathy to the Federation of Anarchists.' One of the civilians handed the seated officer a sheaf of papers.

'These are the depositions,' said the officer.

The civilian gave him another typewritten sheet. 'The local Civil Guard report that his family are peasant farmers owning very little property and are without standing in the community. His mother attends church regularly but the father is indifferent and only goes to church when urged by the priest. The accused, Benito Vigon, did not attend church for many years prior to the outbreak of war and has often spoken disparagingly about religion. A number of witnesses affirm he has stated that he is an agnostic.'

'Anything else?'

'That's all,' said the officer. He placed all the documents into a manilla folder and handed it to the civilian.

The president took a packet of cigarettes from his pocket and offered them to his fellow judges. They all lit up.

'It seems clear enough,' said the president.

His companion judges nodded.

'A disciplinary correction camp is the obvious answer.'

Again his fellow judges nodded agreement.

'That's all,' said the president. 'Let's have the next one.'

Quite bewildered, Benito Vigon found himself being ushered from the chamber. 'Didn't ... I thought ... aren't I to have a trial?' he asked one of the guards.

The man chuckled. 'That was it.'

'But ... I didn't have a chance to defend myself.'

'You're guilty,' grinned the guard. 'You wouldn't be here if you weren't.'

'But ... what happens to me now?'

'You heard the judge. A disciplinary camp.'

'What's that?'

'You'll find out.'

Benito Vigon gulped. 'It was all over so quickly I didn't hear everything. How long must I stay in this camp?'

'He *didn't* say,' said the guard. 'You just stay until they decide to let you out.'

For a week Vigon was locked in an underground cell with other men and when there were so many that no more could

39

be packed in, they were marched out under armed escort to the railway station, herded into a cattle truck and padlocked in.

They remained seven days in the cattle truck while the train rolled slowly across Spain, lingered in sidings and shunted back and forth in marshalling yards. During the long stops their guards unlocked the doors to let in fresh air, passed round canteens of water and gave them a few stale loaves of black bread. They were not allowed outside to relieve themselves. The heat generated by their close packed bodies, the jolting in the trucks and the stench of excretion and urine caused nausea and added the smell of vomit to their discomforts. When the train stopped for the last time and they were ordered out of the truck at bayonet point, many men were too weak to stand.

New guards took over. They were tall, strong men who showed no pity for their hungry, filth-soiled prisoners. They were men from Navarra and Andalucia who nourished a hatred for Catalans. They goaded their prisoners with insults about Catalonia, its people and its traditions, and whenever a prisoner was stung to retort they beat him.

The prisoners were herded along a highway, along a track and then up a steep path that led to a hillcrest overlooking the Mediterranean. The view was magnificent but the prisoners were given no time to enjoy it. They were hurried on another three kilometres to an enormous open compound surrounded by a perimeter of stakes and coiled barbed wire. The double gates of the compound entrance flew the Nationalist flag and had the words '*Todo por la Patria*' emblazoned above them. Outside the gates was a row of barracks huts where off-duty guards were sunbathing, reading or dozing. They were well fed, sun-bronzed men who ignored the prisoners herded up to the double gates. The compound doors swung open and the prisoners were driven inside with blows from rifle butts.

Benito Vigon looked round with bitter eyes. He was caged by a high wall of coiled barbed wire which could blind and shred flesh. The inmates of the compound were scarecrow figures in fluttering rags, their skin burned black by the sun and their limbs so thin and dry they looked as if they could easily snap and dissolve into dust. He saw gaunt faces, wild eyes set deep in black hollows, ulcerated sores, blood and pus-stained bandages made from ripped up underclothing. They were too weary to rush to greet the newcomers and watched them with flat, dead eyes.

A bearded man with long, corn-coloured hair rose to his feet unsteadily and staggered across to the new batch of prisoners. His eyes were blue and his mouth lopsided as though his jaw had been broken and reset badly.

'Welcome to the camp of no hope,' he said in Catalan.

They gathered round him, bombarding him with questions until he raised his hands in a plea for restraint.

'Please. Please! I cannot answer a thousand questions.'

The questions died into expectant silence.

'Understand this, friends,' he said bitterly. 'We are Catalan swine who must suffer because we perpetuated the war. You are prisoners and must do the best you can for yourselves. There is all the water you need in the communal tap. Food, a little every day. Sometimes a little soup which is no more than hot water. On these rations you must work eight, sometimes ten, hours a day. Your clothing is what you stand up in. When it rains you must still sleep on the ground ... if you can. If you are strong you will live. If you are not ... you die quickly.'

Vigon asked quietly. 'How long have you been here, friend?'

The blond Catalan stared at him steadily. 'Five months.' He raised his hand to his jaw and stroked it tenderly. 'My first day here I talked back at a guard. His rifle butt smashed my jaw. I was strong when I arrived. Now look at me.'

He held out arms like sticks from which tattered clothing fluttered. His chest was sunken and his ribs stood out starkly.

'This is ... inhuman!' choked Vigon.

'Our bodies must suffer for our thoughts,' said the blond man bitterly.

It was Sunday, a day of rest. But at six o'clock the next morning a factory siren awakened them. Vigon climbed stiffly to his feet with every joint aching from the chill of the morning and the hardness of the ground. The prisoners shuffled into a long queue at the entrance gates. When they were opened the men filed out past a water tap from which each man drank. A prisoner, supervised by a guard, presided over a wooden crate filled with hunks of black maize bread. He gave each man a ration as they filed past.

The guards shouted orders, the prisoners shuffled into ragged formation and they were marched away from the compound, up over a hill and set to work cutting a road through a mountain.

Vigon thought it looked like a scene out of hell. Starved skeletons wielding picks and shovels with feeble strength hacked a wide road through solid rock. The work could have gone ahead much more quickly if dynamite had been used. But the road had to be made with men's suffering. So the picks swung, shovels filled, wooden wheelbarrows and scarecrow figures swayed as they laboured and often fell.

Benito Vigon wielded a pick axe. Again and again he smashed at a boulder, splintering it and reducing it to a heap of large rocks. Whenever he rested to get his breath or wipe his forearm across his sweat-dewed forehead a guard snarled: 'Keep at it. No slacking!'

Benito Vigon glowered and swung the pick, but without muscle behind it.

The watchful guard snarled: 'That's not the way. Put your back into it. *Cojones* is what you want, man. You Catalans all lack *cojones*. You're a bunch of *maricones*!'

Benito Vigon fought off his rage and swung the pick until sweat blinded him. The boulder became the face of the guard and he smashed at it, battering it with a terrible fury.

At lunch time there was a break of half an hour. The wise prisoners had saved their ration of bread and now they gnawed it slowly, savouring every crumb. Benito had gulped his down hungrily while marching to work and now he could only watch them enviously with hunger gnawing at him.

All through the long afternoon they laboured on while the sun beat down. At six in the evening, when the whistle blew, Vigon ached in every limb. One man who fainted and couldn't get to his feet was beaten until blood ran from his lips. Benito Vigon and another were ordered to carry him back to camp.

Back at the compound Benito and the other men let their burden fall and sank down exhaustedly on to the hard earth. The bearded, blond man settled down beside them. 'What do you think of the Catalan's private hell?'

Vigon said faintly: 'When do we eat?'

'Tomorrow morning we get another crust of bread.'

Vigon stared disbelievingly. 'That's all the food we get?'

'You can live on it. Look at me. I've lived on it for five months.'

Benito Vigon gulped. 'Is there no way out? No way of escape?'

The blond man nodded. 'There is a way,' he said. 'The way of the *Piojo Verde*.'

Vigon frowned. 'What is this of the Green Lice?'

'It is an illusion,' said the blond man. 'Often prisoners suffer from it.'

'How does one use it to escape?'

The blond man's deformed mouth tried to smile. 'He who catches it is taken away ... to die!'

6

Before he had been a prisoner a week, Benito Vigon resolved

to escape before the appalling conditions robbed him of his will and strength.

He planned the escape with a prisoner named Ignacio and for several days they collected every scrap of discarded cloth or rag they could find. One night they bound their hands and wrists and limbs with these rags, crept through the darkness to the barbed wire perimeter and stealthily wormed their way into it. The long coils of wire were springy and the barbs were long and vicious. They knew the metal thorns would tear their flesh but they'd brace themselves to suffer pain if it meant escape from hell. They believed they could burrow through the barbed wire to freedom.

A trip wire embedded in the heart of the barbed wire sounded the alarm. A siren wailed mournfully, lights sprang on everywhere, whistles blew, guards shouted and powerful spotlights swept out over the startled, sleepy eyed prisoners.

The guards turned out, a sergeant shouted orders and bayonets were fixed. With jabs and blows the guards herded the prisoners into one corner of the compound where they were stood at attention. A patrol headed by a sergeant set off at a trot round the barbed wire perimeter until they found the two escaping prisoners.

Ignacio had made more progress into the barbed wire forest than Vigon and only his feet protruded from it. The guards seized his ankles and heaved mightily. Ignacio's tortured scream was a warning to Vigon who had time to clamp his hands over his face before he too was dragged out. They were beaten and herded to the punishment huts which stood just inside the compound entrance. Both of them were streaming with blood and Ignacio had his hands clasped over his eyes. They were thrown inside separate huts and the guards went to work on them with boots and rifle butts, leaving them insensible before they slammed the iron doors and shot home the bolts.

For three days and nights they remained in the darkness with neither food nor water. Ignacio went out of his mind with pain and raved deliriously.

On Sunday they were dragged out into the blinding sunlight. Ignacio babbled incoherently. His face was a mask of congealed blood and a black scab oozed pus where his right eye should have been. His good eye rolled wildly.

The prisoners had been on parade at attention for three hours, waiting to see the punishment meted out to the would-be escapers, and they stared at Ignacio and Vigon with lacklustre eyes devoid of sympathy. The night of the attempted escape they had been forced to remain standing until dawn and they blamed the escapers for their increased misery.

Vigon's mouth was as dry as sandpaper and his tongue so swollen that it impeded his breathing, but he tried to stand upright and glare defiantly at the guards.

'We've our own methods of punishing escapers,' said Sergeant Ares. He gestured to the guards. One of them unrolled a canvas flour sack. Baling wire was threaded through its bottom corners and loops of the wire were attached to its mouth. The guards held the sack flat against Vigon's back and passed the wire round his waist and over his shoulders. Pliers twisted the ends of the baling wire together until it cut into his waist, shoulders and armpits.

'Fourteen days,' the sergeant told Vigon. 'Day and night, asleep and awake, that sack lives with you. Try taking it off for just one minute and it won't be fourteen days. You'll wear it then for the rest of your life!'

Another sack was fastened to Ignacio's shoulders. Then six prisoners were ordered out to bring small rocks and to fill the flour sacks.

The sacks were large and as they were filled up, Benito's eyes smouldered. When the sack was full and its neck closed with a twist of wire, fifty pounds of rock was bowing him down. The baling wire cut into his shoulders like a knife.

Ignacio was too weak to support the weight. His knees bowed and he sank to the ground. He was booted and rifle butts swung, but not even the steady pressure of a bayonet point could goad him to his feet.

Vigon shouted: 'Can't you see you've driven him out of his mind? What do you want to do? Kill him?'

Sergeant Ares was a powerful man. He swung his fist like a professional boxer and Vigon's upraised arm was smashed aside by a blow that hurtled him backwards and stretched him flat on the ground. Vigon stared up at Sergeant Ares with his mouth full of blood. He tried to scramble to his feet, but the weighty sack pinned him down. Pointed rocks gouged into his spine and he felt ludicrously like an overturned tortoise.

'Talk back at me and I'll kill you,' raged Sergeant Ares.

Ignacio was thrown back into the punishment hut. Vigon rolled over on to his hands and knees, gathered his strength and rose to his feet. He waited with downcast eyes until the prisoners were dismissed and then stumbled across to the water tap, turned it on with shaking fingers and slaked his terrible thirst.

At first it was the weight of the sack that punished him. He had to work as hard as the other prisoners, swinging a pick or wielding a shovel. If he slacked, he was beaten. At night he

44

could not rest properly, lying on his back with no support for his head or lying face down with the weighty sack compressing his lungs. By the third day the baling wire had cut through his clothes and his raw flesh weeped blood. During the night scabs formed round the wire which tore away with his first movements the following morning.

Ignacio must have been taken away while the prisoners were out working on the road. They never saw him again.

Vigon had caused the other prisoners a miserable sleepless night and they showed him no sympathy. But what happened next to Ramon Puig welded all the prisoners together in hatred for their oppressors.

Ramon Puig was a stocky, slow-thinking youth who'd been a butcher's assistant in Barcelona. During the week a guard overheard him speaking Catalan. Sergeant Ares announced that Ramon Puig would be punished on Sunday. The unhappy youth spent long, tormented days of suspense wondering what would happen to him.

On Sunday the prisoners were lined up. Sergeant Ares warned them solemnly not to disobey camp laws and two prisoners were ordered to dig a deep hole. Other prisoners were sent to cut down two slender birch trees, trim them and joint them together in the form of a cross.

The cross was laid upon the ground, Ramon Puig was ordered to strip to his drawers, was placed upon the cross and lashed to it with baling wire. A cardboard placard was hung round his neck reading: 'I must not speak Catalan!' Then the cross was stood upright in the hole and the earth filled in round it.

All through that long Sunday the crucified Puig hung by his lacerated wrists, moaning piteously. The prisoners were forbidden to approach him or speak to him. The sun blazed down upon his tortured body, his thirst increased and he pleaded ceaselessly for water to moisten his lips.

The prisoners tried to put him out of their thoughts, but wherever they went within the confines of the compound the crucifix dominated them. The tortured figure on the cross couldn't be escaped.

At first one prisoner, then a second, a third and then many went to the compound entrance and stood with their backs to the crucifix as they stared at the guards. It became a spontaneous demonstration. All the gaunt and weary prisoners stood shoulder to shoulder in close ranks, their eyes a sullen and disturbing challenge.

The guards became uneasy. They swore at the prisoners and made threatening motions.

The prisoners stood firm.

Three of the guards picked up their rifles, fixed bayonets and lounged across to open the compound gate. Their threatening manner showed that they intended to walk in among the prisoners, clubbing with rifle butts and jabbing with bayonets.

But the prisoners stood waiting unflinchingly, watching the guards with sullen, hate-filled eyes. There was an ominous, breathless tension. One guard was about to open the door but another stopped him. They glared in at the prisoners.

The prisoners stared back with hate-filled eyes and the guards walked away, strangely afraid.

Hour after hour the prisoners stood silent and unmoving with their united hatred flowing out through the barbed wire.

All the guards were turned out and posted round the compound entrance with fixed bayonets. Sergeant Ares was in the town and a messenger was sent to find him. At dusk the searchlights were switched on and in their merciless blaze the shadows were deep and the prisoners' staring eyes became black holes in white skulls. And behind their close-packed ranks the crucifix stood out starkly, towering over them all. Ramon Puig's rasping breathing could be clearly heard as he hung insensible with black trickles crawling down his arms and his under-drawers stained by his tortured bowels.

Sergeant Ares had intended Puig to be crucified for forty-eight hours. He returned to the compound in a tearing rage, furious that his guards had not used their initiative. But when he saw the silent, close-ranked prisoners and felt their united hatred lick out at him, he too was afraid. The seething bitterness of the prisoners was powerful enough to burst apart the entire camp.

Sergeant Ares suppressed his fear, walked up to the compound and stood with feet astride facing the prisoners. They stared back grimly. Their eyes were a hostile barrage and their united hatred beat at him with a physical force. He was handling human dynamite, capable of tearing apart barbed wire walls and destroying its captors with bare hands.

Sergeant Ares ordered loudly: 'Listen to me, swine. No more breaking regulations and no talking Catalan. Now take that man down. Save the cross. We'll need it another day.'

The hostile eyes beat at him savagely. Then the prisoners slowly turned and flooded to the crucifix, swamping round it as it bobbed in the air and then sank down out of sight.

Sergeant Ares ordered crisply: 'Double the guard for the rest of the night and keep the searchlights turned on. If anything happens send for me at once. I'll be in my quarters.' He frowned as he strode away, knowing the fear he had sensed had been germinated by his own men. Fear is contagious.

The prisoners destroyed the crucifix, but nobody was punished. And afterwards the guards drove the prisoners less fiercely and punishments were milder.

7

It was Sunday in the disciplinary camp and the prisoners sat in the sun trying to draw comfort from its warmth. Vigon took off the filthy rag that was his jacket, picked live lice from the seams, squashed them between his thumbnails and listened for the pop as their blood-gorged bodies burst. His chest was shrunken, his ribs stood out and his abdomen was hard and distended. All the prisoners were so weak that they could not work as hard as previously and progress on the road they were making grew less and less.

Vigon had a headache, his limbs throbbed, he felt light-headed and was disinclined to move. He didn't even want to cross to the water tap to slake his thirst. It was the weakness of starvation he realised and wondered how long it would last. The previous week, despite the bootings of the guard, some men were too weak to go to work. They'd been left lying in the compound in a fevered stupor and had died. Vigon wondered if their illness was contagious and the following morning knew it was. He tried to climb to his feet but could not because of the peculiar muscular rigidity of his limbs. The guards booted him disinterestedly, as though knowing it was useless, and left him. Presently the pain of his head and the ache in his bones sent him into a pain-misted stupor where his thoughts wandered hotly. There were fleecy cool clouds against a pale blue sky and the cool tang of the sea. Cooked meat sizzled succulently, there was the crisp rustle of white linen, lacy edging to dainty underwear and the lavender smell of clean laundry. A great knot was tied in a ship's cable so big that it filled his head. It kept tightening, groaning and expanding. Thirst raged and burned his bowels and his mouth. He had lucid moments when he was aware of the cold hardness of the earth and the blue of the sky. Then came the nightmares of leering faces and fevered distortions. At some time he became aware of the blond bearded prisoner with the broken jaw hovering over him.

'What's . . . what's the matter with me?' choked Vigon.

'It's the Piojo Verde,' said the man. 'Look at yourself.'

With an effort Vigon sat up and looked at the mulberry-coloured blotches mottling his chest, arms and stomach. They were great mauve blisters and when he pressed them they ached in his joints and his head.

'Will I die?' he whispered. He was mildly curious.

'Almost certainly,' said the bearded prisoner. 'But not here. They will take you and the others away. They do not care if prisoners die but they must stamp out the epidemic before it spreads.'

He was only vaguely aware of the truck that drove into the compound. Its brakes squealed when it stopped beside him. Strong hands grasped his ankles and shoulders and he was swung up into it. He landed on something soft that moved and whimpered. The truck jolted on, stopped again and a smothering weight falling upon him jolted the breath out of him and rushed him down into the cool, green sea while silver tinsel flowed along his limbs until he flashed like a mackerel. There were black voids of pain and the huge knot groaned greasily in his head, never disentangling.

Slowly he became hazily aware of white walls, a white ceiling and white-coated orderlies. There was a drain tube drawing off pus from his infested arm. The wounds caused by baling wire hadn't healed and during his illness infection had run riot.

He'd had typhus, they told him. The doctors were proud of him. All their other typhus cases had died, but miraculously Vigon had survived.

They'd operated on his arm.

'What do you work at?' asked the surgeon some time later when the arm was healing.

'I help my father. We have a vineyard and an olive grove.'

'You are lucky it is your left arm. You'll never use it properly again. The muscles are shrivelled.'

Vigon's face showed his bitterness. The surgeon said sternly: 'You're lucky to have an arm at all. Most doctors would have amputated and saved themselves a lot of headaches.'

Vigon's arm healed and he regained strength as the hospital food, although monotonous and inadequate, put flesh on his bones.

There came the day when a doctor told Vigon: 'There's nothing more we can do for you. Keep exercising your arm and when you get out of here, feed yourself well.'

Vigon asked tonelessly: 'Will they send an escort for me?'

The doctor knew he had come from a disciplinary camp. He said quietly: 'You won't be going back.'

Vigon stared at him hopefully.

'I have your identity card and papers,' said the doctor.

'But . . . have I been released?'

The doctor said quietly: 'Eleven men were brought here.

48

Typhus is contagious and we put you all in isolation. It was thought you would all die. To avoid complications all you eleven men had your release papers signed and dated the day you entered hospital.' He smiled encouragingly. 'You're free to go home, Vigon.'

CHAPTER THREE

1

MANY years had elapsed since Escoleras had been
bombed, but the rubble of destroyed cottages had not been
cleared away. Yellow grass, weeds and nettles grew on the
mounds of broken stones and the villagers used the bomb sites
as rubbish tips.

Vicente Serra regularly combed through the rubbish tips
searching for anything which might have value, and today he
was especially lucky. Someone had thrown out a rusted pram.
With a hammer he'd reduced it to old iron and firewood. The
tyreless wheels, axles and springs he carried in a sack slung
over his shoulder. The firewood was in another sack carried by
his daughter, Asuncion. She was now eight years of age, a
pale, skinny little girl who was surprisingly pretty despite her
pinched features. Serra was teaching her how to scavenge
rubbish tips and was confident she would soon be able to do it
alone.

Father and daughter walked to the next bomb site. The little
girl's shoulders bowed under the weight of her sack and her
bright, black-button eyes watched the heels of her father's
alpagartas as she followed him.

The bomb site was surrounded by a dozen or more young,
conscript soldiers who were stationed in the military camp on
the hill just outside Escoleras. They shouted excitedly to each
other as they cordoned off the rubbish-strewn area. Some
flourished wooden stakes and others had gathered rocks to
throw.

'It disappeared in there,' pointed one soldier excitedly. 'It's
got a hideaway.'

Serra swung the heavy sack down off his shoulder and rested
it on the ground. He found a piece of wood to use as a club
and picked up a large rock. Asuncion rested her sack on the
ground and eased her aching shoulders. She rubbed her bare
foot against her other calf and watched the soldiers with dull
interest.

They half crouched as they closed in slowly over the rubble.
Their shabby uniforms were ill-fitting, most of them wore
alpagartas without socks and their shirts were patched. Their
meagre ration of beans kept them ever hungry, and added to

the thrill of the hunt was their genuine need to eat.

They closed in steadily, reducing the size of the cordon until one soldier was close enough to jab a long stick into a hole in the rubble. He kept jabbing. 'There's something here ... I think,' he said.

'Don't jab,' advised a companion. 'Apply steady pressure.'

The soldier probed. 'I think I've got it.' His eyes gleamed as he increased pressure on the stick, thrusting strongly.

A split second later there was an abrupt animal-squealing explosion which made the soldier jump back in shock. A furry, raging tornado shot out from the hole, spitting and clawing and darting first one way and then another, desperately trying to break through the cordon of excited soldiers who shouted, whooped, threw stones and slashed wildly with their clubs.

It would have escaped through the cordon, but Serra was suddenly there, driving it back with a shrewd blow from his club which made it squeal. The half-starved, half-wild cat drew back, snarling at the circle of men, one claw upraised threateningly and showing long, yellow teeth as it hissed. The animal was fighting for its life and was so fierce that the soldiers were a little afraid and unsure how to tackle it.

Serra called loudly: 'You, soldier. You with the curly hair. Keep feinting with your stick so it watches you all the time.'

The soldier made tentative jabs at the cat. It arched its back and spat. Serra hefted a heavy rock calculatingly, aimed carefully and tossed it so it dropped cleanly on the cat's back. It landed solidly and the cat howled in fury and spun round. But the way its haunches twitched showed it had received a crippling injury. Emboldened, the soldiers pounced and grasped it despite the flashing claws that raked their hands. One of them drove his thumb into its scrawny throat and squeezed tightly until the convulsive struggles diminished and ceased. He held up the cat by its tail, a hunter proudly displaying his prey. Others sucked bites and licked deep scratches. One took out a penknife, cut the fur at the cat's throat, edged the knife point under the skin and slit it open down to the groin.

Serra claimed: 'It's mine.'

The soldiers instantly united against him. 'We saw it, we hunted it and caught it. We killed it too!'

'It would have escaped if I hadn't prevented it. You didn't know how to kill it until I told you what to do.'

They stripped the skin off the dead cat as though it had been a rabbit. 'There's not much to eat anyway,' said one of the soldiers.

'If we share it out what we get won't be worth cooking,' said another.

Serra's eyes glinted slyly. 'Cook it here, now. Then we can all have some.'

Doctor Aldo was passing and walked over to see what had happened. He heard Serra's offer and took an onion and three potatoes from his pocket, a present from a grateful patient that morning. He said: 'I'll contribute these.'

The soldiers stared suspiciously. 'What do you want in return?' asked one.

Doctor Aldo pointed to Asuncion who was waiting patiently, shyly rubbing the sole of her foot against her other shin. 'See that she gets a share too. She's hungrier than any of you.'

The soldiers agreed at once.

Serra was delighted. 'Some of you boys get a fire going.' He glowered at Asuncion. 'Run to Maria Joncols and ask the loan of a cooking pot.'

While the soldiers blew the kindling to make the fire flame high, one soldier tugged at Serra's sleeve. 'D'you buy pen-knives?'

'I buy anything if it's cheap enough.'

'What will you give me for this knife?'

Serra glanced at it and laughed. 'Throw it away!'

'Give me *something* for it,' urged the soldier.

Serra shook his head.

The soldier sighed. Then he took from his pocket an oddly designed hexagonal watch charm with the letters SRR embossed upon it, curiously entwined. 'What about this?'

Serra was fascinated by the object. He turned it over in his leathery fingers, testing its hardness with his thumbnail. He was struck by the coincidence that SRR spelled his name. It was very old, he realised. Perhaps three or four hundred years. But it was a common metal and had no value. To his surprise he heard himself saying: 'I'll give you a duro for this and the knife.'

'A deal,' said the soldier delightedly.

'Where did you get it?' asked Serra, frowning down at the watch charm.

'When I first came here a soldier who'd served his time gave it to me in exchange for a book. He said it was lucky.'

'And was it lucky?'

The soldier wrinkled his nose as though there was a bad smell. 'Not so you'd notice.'

Asuncion came running up with a cooking pot.

'Fill it with water,' ordered Serra gruffly.

2

When Doctor Aldo left the soldiers he walked on through the village, pleased he'd been able to help Asuncion yet unhappily aware of his strange lassitude. His legs were leaden and it tired him to walk. *'I'm a young man,'* he reflected, *'I shouldn't be feeling old yet. At forty-five I'm a boy compared with Hernando.'* Yet the years were passing quickly. Children he'd brought into the world were springing up into adolescence. He passed Marcel Prada who nodded to him. 'Good morning, Doctor.'

'Bon dia, Marcel.'

'Perhaps I need a rest,' Doctor Aldo thought. A new thought came to him and he knew instantly he was right. *'I must eat more,'* he told himself with surprise. *'I'm probably more undernourished than most of my patients.'*

The doctor went to the quay. A fishing boat had recently docked and crates of fish were stacked on the quayside. Doctor Aldo shouted to a fisherman sluicing down the deck with pails of water: 'What fish have you got for me, Jaime?'

'It's all sold.' Jaime nodded along the quay towards Paco Barras who was standing on the quay looking out to sea with a black cheroot jutting from his mouth. 'Barras bought the entire catch.'

Doctor Aldo strolled over to him. 'What fish have you for me, Paco?'

'It is mostly *merluza*, Doctor. Let's see what takes your fancy.' There were half-a-dozen stacked fish boxes and he took them down one by one. The Doctor selected two large codfish. 'How much do I owe you?'

'Nada, Juan. All you have done for me and you want to pay me?'

Isidro drove up on a motor tricycle which had been converted into a small van. The engine was twenty years old but overhauled so thoroughly that it would still give many years of service. Isidro unloaded a box of broken ice and helped his father to cover the fish with it.

'Have you got your travel permit?' Paco asked.

Isidro patted his pocket. 'Here, Father.'

'You'd better get going. Talk to Apierra in Barcelona. He may have goods to deliver to Figueras that'll help pay for the return journey.'

'Will do, Father,' said Isidro. He and Paco loaded the crates and Isidro winked at Doctor Aldo as he climbed on to the saddle of the motor-truck. 'Plug your ears,' he warned and started up the engine. It throbbed deafeningly and the doctor was relieved when the engine phut-phutted away into the distance.

Paco Barras grinned contentedly. 'Another consignment on its way to Barcelona.'

'You're an astonishing man, Paco,' said Doctor Aldo. 'Apart from Serra, you are the only man in Escoleras earning money. These are hungry, workless days.'

Barras nodded soberly. 'I am lucky,' he agreed. 'Most of my life I've been a fisherman, but I have learned to buy fish and know the business by instinct. I look at a case of fish, estimate its weight and bid for it. I rarely make a mistake and succeed because others bid too high and lose money or do not bid high enough and lose the opportunity to buy.'

'You will become a rich man, Paco. It pleases me.'

Barras's face was moody. 'I have no need for money. I am happier fishing. But I have responsibilities, Doctor. I will not live for ever and provision must be made for Pepita.'

'It is a responsibility,' agreed Doctor Aldo. He pulled out his watch and glanced at it. 'I must go, Paco.' He hurried away with the two codfish dangling from his forefinger and his pace increasing as he drew closer to his home. Thinking of eating had stimulated his salivary glands and he was suddenly ravenously hungry.

Paco Barras picked up a handful of fish he had placed on one side, took off his clogs and trudged back along the beach to his cottage. Pepita was seated outside in the shade of a cane canopy Isidro had built. The scars on her face were hair-thin white lines and not very noticeable. But the closed lid of her blind eye was curiously distorted.

'Do look at this, Father,' she thrilled. 'It's a new one!'

'I'll be with you in a moment, Daughter.' He went inside the cottage and into the kitchen. He kissed Elisa's cheek dutifully and placed the fish on the table in two heaps. 'These are for us,' he said. 'And these are for Teresa.'

'Did you have a good buy?'

'Reasonably good. Isidro is on his way to Barcelona now.'

She smiled at him affectionately. 'I know you are unhappy with the work, Paco, but it is necessary.'

'I do not complain, woman,' he said sternly and went outside.

Pepita sat at a flat-topped table upon which were scattered multi-coloured mosaic stones. On the stumps of her arms were fastened tightly laced leather sleeves which ended in hardened points. Between them she could pick up the small stones and arrange them in gaily-coloured designs of her own invention. She was engaged now upon a view of Escoleras. It showed the

54

beach, the sea, the high mountain behind the village and a sailing boat. It was a neatly executed work of patience and as Paco Barras watched his daughter he marvelled at the facility with which she picked up the tiny stones and manoeuvred them into position. Later on, when she'd changed the design until she was satisfied with it, he'd prepare the cement into which she set the stones.

'You like the scene?' she asked happily.

'It's . . . excellent.'

'Better than the others?'

'Much better.'

'Will they pay more, do you think, Father?'

All her work was bought by a customer in Barcelona who was a figment of Paco's imagination. 'They're sure to,' he said. 'I'll certainly ask for more.'

'If we can get a lot of orders, Father, and employ other people to work at it too, we might make a big business.'

'I certainly hope we can, Pepita.'

Since her accident she had avoided meeting people and although she was now twenty-two she was strangely out of touch with the world around her. She got up from the table, walked across to the cottage and glanced inside. 'Has mother gone out?'

'Isn't she in the kitchen?'

'I can't see her.'

'She's taken the fish along to Teresa then.'

Pepita said: 'Oh!'

'Did you want something, Daughter?'

She hesitated. 'It's . . . I need mother. I want to go.'

'She won't be long.'

'I don't think I can wait.'

'That's all right, Daughter. I'll go with you.'

'I'm sorry to worry you, Papa.'

'Nada, Daughter. We'll all do anything for you, you know that!'

'Thank you, Papa,' she said as he helped her.

'What is it?' he asked.

'Big jobs.'

'Call when you want me. I'll be outside.'

Presently she called.

'I feel awful about this, Father. So . . . helpless. This is when I notice it most . . . when even the simplest, natural things I can't do for myself.'

'Don't worry, Daughter. It gets done, anyway, doesn't it?'

'It's awful . . . for you too!'

'Nonsense. When you were a tiny girl sitting on a potty I

looked after you. It's the same now. You're a little older, that's the only difference.'

'I don't know what I'd do without you and Mama.'

'You still wouldn't need to worry. The world's full of good and kind people.'

'Most of the time I don't worry, Papa. I do my mosaic and I help Mama a little. But there are moments ... there are things a girl has to do ... things that make me *so* dependent.'

'You can only feel like that for a few moments,' he consoled. 'But there are twenty-four hours in every day.'

'You always comfort me, Papa.'

In Coruna's grocery store along the street, Elisa Barras watched her grandson, Leon, march up and down behind the shop counter shouldering a roughly fashioned wooden rifle. He was a well-built child with very fair, curly hair, blue eyes and apple-red cheeks. He bore no resemblance to his father, but at times his face held an expression of blue-eyed wonder that was startlingly like his grandfather's.

Teresa gutted the fish while her mother watched. Her father-in-law was bowed over a worn accounts book. These were hard days and those who did buy always asked for credit. The Coruna family, like most others, lived frugally while absorbing their meagre savings. Few people could afford clothes and meat and fish were luxuries. There was so little work in the shop that Narcisus had gone out with an old shot-gun and faint hopes. So many hunted the valleys and mountains that they were almost denuded of game.

'Are you going to be a soldier when you're a big boy, Leon?' asked his grandmother.

He shook his head. 'I want to be a fisherman. I want to go out in Grandpa's fishing boat and catch the *biggest* fish ever caught.'

Elisa Barras nodded wryly. 'Grandpa will take you fishing,' she promised. 'When you're older he'll teach you to be the best fisherman in the village.' There were tears in her eyes. 'Grandpa taught your uncle Miguel to fish and he was an expert.'

But Leon had already lost interest in fishing and was using his rifle as a bayonet, attacking an imaginary army and lunging lustily with gleeful shouts.

Elisa Barras sighed. 'The war is almost over in Europe, they say. Perhaps Miguel will come home soon.'

'If he wants to come home, Miguel will find a way,' said Teresa.

'The terrible wars,' choked Elisa Barras. 'We mothers suffer most. All the pain of birth, the sacrifices to bring them to maturity ... only to lose them.'

'I'm Manolete,' Leon announced shrilly. His wooden rifle was now a matador's sword as he thrust and parried.

'Ole!' he shouted.

3

It was a moonless night but the men worked swiftly. Long practice had accustomed them to the darkness of the marshalling yards. They taped plastic explosives to switch points and on the axles of the locomotives waiting in sidings. They had little fear of being caught. They'd dropped hints in the right quarters and the French night-workers had invented good excuses to be elsewhere.

The saboteurs completed their work and retreated, reeling out the firing cable until they reached cover behind a brick wall some hundred yards away.

'All set?' asked Miguel.

His men nodded.

'Blow it, Comrade,' ordered Miguel.

The men crouched low, the firing plunger was thrust down and immediately the night was split apart with an earth-shuddering explosion. Dust and small stones hailed down like rain and a jangling grind of metal proclaimed that at least one locomotive had crashed over on its side.

'Let's go,' said Miguel.

He led the way through the darkness and after a few moment's fast walking he hissed in warning and stopped dead. His men held their breath and listened. Presently they heard what Miguel's sharp ears had already noticed, the thudding of heavy boots and guttural voices.

There was a soft rustle and a clink of metal against metal as Miguel unslung his tommy-gun. His men fanned out beside him, holding their weapons waist high. There was no need for others. They would slip away into the night if they could. But if they had to fight, they had the advantage of surprise.

The Germans approached rapidly, shouting to each other. One of them was lighting the way with the feeble, yellow rays of an exhausted battery torch.

The saboteurs tensed in the darkness. The Germans came straight at them.

When they were close enough Miguel shouted: 'Action!'

A saboteur blazed a powerful torch into the Germans' faces, blinding them. In the same instant, Miguel and the men pressed the triggers of their weapons, firing short, devastating bursts. It was a German patrol of eight and none had a chance to fire back. Lead cut them down and those who did not die instantly were given the coup-de-grace by saboteurs with bitter memories.

The Germans' weapons were gathered up and twenty minutes later the saboteurs were safely hidden in the basement cellar of a farmyard barn with concealing bales of hay stacked upon the trap-door.

There were ten saboteurs, all Spanish except Rene Dalfois, a French Resistance liaison man who spoke Spanish fluently. His mother was Spanish. He was intelligent and fearless, hated fascism and was a member of the Communist Party.

'We can be pleased with tonight's work, Comrades,' he said with satisfaction. 'Germany is being hit hard everywhere, on the fighting fronts, at sea, in the air and in the occupied countries too!' His eyes gleamed. 'Hitler is doomed!'

Miguel scowled. 'So much talk of destroying Hitler. But what of fascist Spain? *Now* is the time for the free world to strike. Now Hitler is beaten, the Allies must attack Franco.'

Rene Dalfois's eyes narrowed. 'Franco is a minor issue, Comrade. First the Allies must destroy *completely* our major menace. Then, at leisure, the fascist lick-spittles will be mopped up.'

'Patience!' sneered Miguel. 'Always patience. Meanwhile our people live under a reign of terror.'

'It will not be for long,' said Rene Dalfois. His eyes glowed. 'When France is free from the German hell, every true Frenchman will fight for the freedom of his comrades on the other side of the Pyrenees.'

4

One day when Felipe and his three sons rode back to the farmhouse, he was suddenly struck by his daughter's appearance. Violante stopped to lift a carafe of wine and he saw the thickness of her hips and the swell of her belly. Too startled to believe his eyes and shocked by the enormity of his suspicion, he strode across the stone kitchen floor and placed a calloused, exploratory hand upon her.

She twisted away, her flat, brown eyes glaring and her thin lips drawn back in a snarl, as defensive as a mountain wild-cat.

'Come here, girl,' ordered Felipe.

'No,' she panted. 'No!'

She had never before dared to defy him and he felled her with a backhanded blow.

Her flat brown eyes were glazed as she pushed herself up into a sitting position. Then she sprang to her feet, snatched up a pick-axe handle and swung it at her father with all her strength. His upraised forearm broke the force of the blow, but there was enough power behind it to beat him to his knees with blood streaming from his head.

Violante was so angry that she would have struck him again and again, but her brothers sprang at her and held her while she writhed furiously. Felipe climbed to his feet with blood pouring down his face and staining his shirt. 'Hold the bitch still,' he ordered thickly. 'Hold her!'

Violante's eyes smouldered and her chest heaved as she strove to break free. But her brothers were strong. Her skirt was lifted and her father's coarse fingers explored her knowledgeably, probing deep into her soft flesh as though she were a farm animal.

'The bitch is with child,' he said disbelievingly.

Violante broke away from her astonished brothers, shook down her skirts and glared at her father.

He wiped his hand across his forehead and flicked it, spraying red droplets around him. 'Who's its father, you bitch?' He demanded, towering over her, his face dark with rage.

Violante retreated into a world of her own. Her flat eyes became dead to emotion, her lips clamped shut and her face became impassive.

'You whore!' roared her father. 'Who's was it? He'll marry you! There'll be no sin in *my* family!'

She held her head high, bracing herself against his anger.

'Tell me!' he roared. 'Who is it?'

She faced him, unafraid and defiant.

'You won't deny me, you bitch.' He seized her, threw her to the ground, pinned her down with his foot upon her back and unbuckled his belt. 'You won't defy me!'

She lay quite still, her eyes closed and her hands clenched tightly to help her to bear what must come. He flipped up her skirt and slashed. The weal was edged with pin-points of blood. Violante bit her forearm.

'You'll tell me, my girl,' thundered her father. 'You'll tell me!'

His sons watched with troubled eyes as he slashed again and again. But although Violante's teeth drove into her arm until it bled, she made no sound.

At last he stopped. He wiped his belt and said gruffly: 'That's to think about. The next time I ask who's the father you'd better be ready to tell me.'

Violante climbed to her feet and stumbled away. Her flesh burned as though seared by a branding iron and blood ran down her legs like molten lead. She was alone, so dreadfully alone in a man's world and tears trickled down her cheeks. She made her way to the hayloft and lay there enduring her pain.

During the following weeks she was often severely beaten, but steadfastly maintained an obstinate silence. But there came a time when her swollen belly proclaimed her motherhood so abundantly that the beatings had to cease.

'You whore!' Felipe raged, his face dark with anger. 'No daughter of mine will sin! No daughter of mine will bear a child out of wedlock.'

Violante retreated into her own maternal world. She moved among her menfolk but was apart from them. Her face was serene, she smiled secretly and held herself with care as though her heavy hips and swollen belly housed a precious jewel.

Felipe and his sons spent hours pondering over who might be the father of Violante's child. The farm was isolated and visitors were so rare that they could easily be remembered. A long time ago Benito Vigon had stayed with them for some months but since then no man had visited the farm.

'Is it a married man?' Felipe raged at his daughter.

She seemed not to hear him and smiled secretly, detached from their maleness, impervious to their blows and insults.

They thought of a shepherd whose goats grazed the valley on the other side of the mountains and father and sons rode away for three days to visit him. He was a stupid man with a foolish smile and slack lips and although they turned his fool's face into a bruised pulp, he said nothing to reveal his guilt.

They remembered a band of gypsies who had camped for one night a mile away from their farm and racked their memories for dates and made calculations, all of which proved that the gypsies could have had no part in the affair.

'Tell me, you bitch of a whore,' raved Felipe. 'Who is the father of the bastard?'

But Violante seemed not to hear him. She smiled contentedly and moved around carefully, protecting the new life which would burst triumphantly from her loins.

'Don't mock me, you bitch,' raved Felipe. 'No daughter of mine will sinfully give birth to a child. It is against the wishes of God, your own mother and Jesus Christ!'

Violante serenely went about her work.

Father and brothers watched her preparations for the baby with scowling resentment. She cut down a thin, birch sapling and trimmed it with an axe. She cut the thin trunk into equal lengths and notched the ends. With cords made from esparto grass she made a cot. The slender birchwood branches were its ribs and old sacking stuffed with a straw was its mattress.

'No daughter of mine will sin and give birth to a child out of wedlock,' stormed Felipe.

But Violante ignored him and busied herself round the house in which everyone had become a stranger. She was healthy and as strong as a bull. Her appetite was voracious. She was not an attractive girl, her Mongolian features, slack lips and receding chin made her ugly. But her face was suffused with a glow of maternal happiness which made her radiant. The happiness shining in her eyes turned her father frantic. 'You bitch of a whore!' he raved. He knocked her down and had to be restrained by his sons from kicking her. 'No daughter of mine will give sinful birth to a child out of wedlock!'

They remembered that three herdsmen had driven two hundred goats through the mountain valley and father and sons spent a week searching them out. But the herdsmen were so transparently innocent that Felipe and his sons had to ride away disgruntled.

It was Virgil, the most thoughtful son, who advanced a new theory. It was a startling one, but since they could find no other explanation, they finally challenged Violante about her relationship with the stud stallion.

At first Violante seemed not to hear them. Then her lips twitched. Then she laughed and her laughter peeled away their self-confidence, exposed the quivering quick of their obtuse minds and humiliated them with her contempt.

'You can laugh, whore,' snarled Felipe, shaking his fist. 'But I am a man of God. I vow you will not bear a child out of wedlock and sin in God's eyes.'

She locked the men out of the secret and mysterious woman-world in which she moved alone. Surreptitiously they watched her peaked but contented face and the steady swelling of her belly, amazed that she felt no shame and could stand so proudly, with feet astride, shoulders braced back and the great swollen bulge of her shame thrusting at them flauntingly. They saw how it grew difficult for her to move around, how stooping made her grunt and presently, how even simple movements cost her an effort. And they marvelled that she was so radiant with happiness. It was a happiness that was infectious and despite themselves they did things to make her life easier. They ran to pick up things to save her stooping and did work which only a woman would normally do.

'Who is the father?' panted Felipe.

Violante looked at him steadily. 'If I tell you, you will not believe me.'

'Who is he?'

She shrugged her shoulders. 'I do not know. He was a man I

met in the valley. We talked and he touched me and then ...
this happened.' She rested her hand upon her belly.

'You are lying!'

She shrugged her shoulders. 'You see, Father. You do not
believe me!'

'Who is the man?' he stormed. 'We must know who he is.
Even if he is married, it matters not. The child must have a
father.'

'When I tell the truth you do not believe me.'

'You are shit upon the name of your mother,' he stormed.
'You are shit in the eyes of God. You are a whore. You have
sinned, but I promise God the religion of your mother will be
respected. I vow you will not give birth to a child out of
wedlock.'

She turned away from him sadly, hands clasped around her
swollen belly. 'The will of God and the seed of life is stronger
than you, Father,' she dared to say.

He towered over her, his face crimson and his clenched fist
upraised. 'Jezebel!' he roared. 'You are damned. You are
sinful and corrupt. You have eternally disgraced the mother
who gave you birth.'

She hurried away, undisturbed by his words. She was thrilled
by the stirring of the child within her womb.

'Jezebel!' he roared after her. 'Jezebel! No daughter of
mine shall give birth to a child out of wedlock.'

Three weeks later the severe pains struck her. All day she
had borne the minor pains that scourged her, but when the big
pain hit her she dropped her pitchfork, clasped the underside
of her swollen belly and moaned aloud.

Zacarias was working with her. 'What is it? What has
happened?'

'It is my time,' she choked. Then as the pain tore her apart,
she went down on her knees in the hay, biting the stalks until
crimson flecked the yellow straw.

Zacarias shouted for the others. 'It is Violante. It is her
time!'

Felipe came running with Tomas and Virgil on his heels.
They stood over Violante and watched her roll over upon her
back.

'Yes,' said Felipe sadly. 'It is her time. Now we must obey
the will of God!'

5

Felipe and his three sons rode into Escoleras just before
dusk. Those who saw them were surprised because on the rare

occasions they came to the village they usually led a caravan of mules and donkeys laden with crops. Now they came empty-handed.

They dismounted in the Plaza and tethered their mounts to a plane tree. The three brothers squatted on their haunches in the shade with their wide-brimmed, straw hats pulled down over their eyes and Felipe stumped off along the cobbled street to the church. He pushed open the door and plunged inside. A few minutes later he came out and strode back to the Plaza. He nodded to his sons, confirming an unspoken question and sat down with them. They smoked, talked a little and waited for time to pass.

The villagers wondered about the four men as they went about their business. Night came and father and sons remained in the Plaza smoking, chewing raw vegetables which they took from their panniers and sleeping.

By mid-morning the following day wild rumours were sweeping through the village. Everyone who saw the four men sensed the strangeness of their relentless patience.

Jose Corbera, the mayor, spoke to them, passing the time of day and then casually enquiring the reason for their visit. They at once became evasive. 'We shall be leaving soon,' said Felipe uncomfortably.

'You have a great deal to do in the village?' asked Mayor Corbera politely.

Felipe avoided his sharp eyes. 'Presently we shall go,' he said uncomfortably. 'When it is time.'

'Then you are waiting for something?'

Felipe felt trapped. 'Yes,' he said. 'When it is time. . . .' He broke off and looked away quickly, betrayed by his own tongue. Nothing more could be got out of him.

The mayor told Doctor Aldo of the strange behaviour of the mountain men. Other villagers mentioned that Felipe's first act when he arrived at the village was to visit the church.

The mayor and Doctor Aldo called upon Father Delbos who received them coldly. 'Yes,' the priest snapped. 'There was a man who stormed in as though he owned the church. He smelt abominably. People should have respect for the Church and wash before they come here.'

'Did you talk to the man, Father Delbos?' asked Mayor Corbera.

Felipe had offended the priest. Father Delbos said tartly: 'It was not a conversation.'

The doctor took out his watch and glanced at it. There was a sheen of perspiration on his forehead and without knowing why, he was gripped by a sense of urgency. 'Please, Father

63

Delbos. Tell us why he visited the church?'

The priest shrugged his shoulders. 'Merely to show his contempt for the Church, I imagine.'

The mayor sensed the doctor's self-control was escaping him and said tactfully: 'Will you tell us exactly what happened, Father?'

Again the priest shrugged. 'The man's little more than an animal. He strode in here, stinking like a pigsty, gave me no sign of respect and shouted questions at me.'

The mayor asked quickly: 'What questions, Father?'

'A ridiculously naïve question. He asked: "Is it a sin in the eyes of God for a woman to have a child out of wedlock?"'

There was a long silence.

'And you replied . . .?' asked Doctor Aldo.

'There is only one true reply,' said Father Delbos stiffly. 'The Lord does not condone immorality. Clearly it is a sin.'

'Thank you,' said the mayor. He hastened after Doctor Aldo who was already hurrying away.

When Felipe saw them approaching he rose to his feet unhappily.

'Felipe,' said Doctor Aldo. 'Where is your daughter, Violante?'

'She is at home, Doctor.'

'Why did she not come with you?'

There was a long pause. 'Someone must take care of the farm,' said Felipe.

'Why do you come here with your three sons, empty-handed?'

Felipe stared over his head and said tonelessly: 'When it is the time, I will tell you.'

They could get nothing more from him.

Somebody remembered that Benito Vigon had once spent some months with Felipe in the mountains and he was brought from his labour in the vineyard. He wore a sweaty handkerchief tucked under his straw hat to protect his neck from the sun, his sun-bleached shirt was sweat-rotted at the armpits and the black hairs on his arms glistened moistly. He listened to the mayor and Doctor Aldo and nodded understandingly. He had a tick which made his cheek twitch, a result of his detention in a disciplinary camp. Doctor Aldo hoped he would lose it in time, but nothing could be done about his left arm. Its shrivelled muscles drew up the limb as though it was held in a sling and his fingers drooped like the weeping branches of a willow tree.

Felipe and his sons greeted Vigon without enthusiasm. He sat with them, pulled out his worn pouch of tobacco makings and while they smoked, talked of the days he had spent with them. But they wouldn't talk. They stared down at the hard-baked earth, sun-dappled through the leaves of the plane trees and remained silent.

Presently Vigon ventured: 'And Violante. How is she?'

Felipe spat to one side disgustedly.

His three sons stared stolidly at the ground.

'Violante is well?' persisted Benito Vigon.

Felipe said explosively: 'I shit upon my whore of a daughter.'

'You are angry with Violante, Felipe?'

Felipe's tongue had betrayed him again and he relapsed into determined silence.

'What is this about Violante?' persisted Vigon.

Virgil eyed him steadily. 'Do I enquire for your sisters? Do I ask about your mother? Go away. Leave us in peace. We have no wish to question you . . . nor that you question us!'

It was the final word. Nothing more would be said. Sadly Benito rose to his feet, bid them good day and returned to Mayor Corbera and Doctor Aldo. 'They will not talk,' he sighed.

'And what of Violante?'

'Felipe is angry with her. He shits upon his whore of a daughter.'

The doctor's vague suspicions fused into conviction. 'Remember Felipe's question to the priest? If Violante is pregnant it would explain everything.'

'But who . . .?' doubted the mayor. 'What man would want . . .?'

'Whoever the woman, when she has the need she can always find a man to serve her,' said the doctor.

'But why. . . .?' began the mayor.

'I'll talk to Felipe,' said Doctor Aldo grimly and hurried over to him. He confronted Felipe challengingly. 'What is this of your daughter, man. Is she pregnant?'

Felipe stared impassively. 'She is *my* daughter!'

'She is your daughter. But she is also a human being. Answer me, man. Is she pregnant?'

Felipe hesitated a moment. 'Yes,' he admitted.

'Tell me why you have come to the village.'

Felipe stared into the far distance. 'She betrayed the law of God. She sinned.'

'This may be so, Felipe. But why have you come to the village?'

Felipe rose to his feet, stepped out from under the shade of the trees and looked up into the blue sky. He squinted his eyes against the sun, gauging the time. 'It is a sin for a woman to give birth unless she is wed,' he said.

'It may be a sin in the eyes of the Church,' said Doctor Aldo. 'But it is an oft-repeated sin which should make God happy since we are all God's children.'

'The mother of my children had a deep reverence for God,' said Felipe. His weathered face shone with an uplifting inner conviction. 'Her whore of a daughter shall not disgrace her.'

Doctor Aldo said in a low voice: 'You are the father of Violante and responsible for her. Whatever happens ... *you* are responsible!'

Felipe nodded his head with grave dignity. 'I accept that,' he agreed. 'I am responsible.'

'Then tell me why you are here, man!' thundered Doctor Aldo.

Felipe gently shouldered him to one side and again stared up at the sun. At least thirty hours had passed since they had left Violante and he judged it was sufficient.

'You can go to her, Doctor,' he said quietly. 'It is her time.'

Doctor Aldo paled. 'You mean ... she is in labour?'

'Yes,' said Felipe. He stared up at the sun while his sons looked mutely at the hard-packed earth.

Doctor Aldo wiped the back of his hand across his forehead. 'You must be mad!' he choked and turned towards home and his medical bag. 'How could you leave her at such a time?'

Felipe's voice was remote. 'You will go tend upon her, Doctor?'

'As soon as I can get there.'

'Take the Civil Guard with you,' said Felipe. 'It will be right and proper.'

A Civil Guard sergeant and two men accompanied Doctor Aldo. Teresa Barras volunteered to act as midwife.

It was twenty-four hours before they returned.

Felipe and his three sons were arrested. They meekly accepted handcuffs and climbed into the truck which took them to the jail in Gerona.

Violante's body was wrapped in a Civil Guard's grey cloak, brought down on the back of a mule and taken to the mortuary.

Doctor Aldo hurried home, poured himself a stiff brandy and relaxed in his armchair. He drank slowly, glared at a crucifix on the wall and swore softly under his breath.

Teresa kept herself under control until she reached the sanctuary of her kitchen. Then she broke down. Narcisus comforted her. 'What is it, my love?'

'They're beasts,' she choked. 'They're ... animals!' She

looked down at Leon playing happily and her voice trembled. 'How could they do such a thing?'

'What did they do, my love?'

'They're not men. They're ... monsters. Felipe vowed that Violante would not bear a child in sin. So when her labour began, they shackled her ankles together and rode away.'

6

Doctor Aldo dropped a hint to Teresa that Señora Ledesma would like to see her and Leon. It was only then that Teresa realised she hadn't seen Anselmo's mother for almost two years! With a husband and son to care for, serving in the shop and helping Pepita, the days and weeks passed quickly.

She brushed her long hair, tied it in a pony tail with a strip of black velvet and put on a short-sleeved blouse and a pleated skirt. She'd had the skirt since before Leon's birth but it still fitted neatly round her slender waist.

She dressed Leon in white shorts and shirt, combed his hair and put on his best shoes. He strutted proudly beside her as they walked to the Ledesma residence. 'Where are we going, Mummy?'

'To visit a lady.'

'I don't want to visit ladies, Mummy. I want to play at soldiers.'

'No nonsense now,' she said firmly. 'You'll play when it's time to play. Now you'll do what I tell you!'

He pouted but accepted her decision. 'What kind of a lady, Mummy?'

'She's a very gentle, elderly lady.'

'More than a hundred years old, Mummy?'

Teresa chuckled. 'Only in wisdom.'

'Why do snails have horns?' Leon asked abruptly.

Teresa seldom visited this side of the village and she was shocked at the way the Ledesma residence had been neglected. From gossip she knew the Ledesma family were having hard times, the farms lost money, Anselmo's debts were increasing, he'd got rid of the servants and at a time when nobody wanted to buy, he'd sold some of the farms for a song to meet his need for ready cash.

Even so, Teresa was astonished when she saw the state of the grounds. Weeds choked the once carefully tended herbaceous borders, nettles stood waist high, the gates hung awry and weeds sprouted in the wide cracks and potholes of the drive. When she climbed the steps to the terrace, she couldn't recognise it. Tiles were missing, broken flower-pots and withered plants were scattered around, dirt lay thickly as if it was never swept away and baby excretion hadn't been cleaned up.

The door stood wide open. Teresa pushed aside the mosquito netting and called. 'May I come in?'

From within a voice called: 'Who is it?'

'It's Teresa Coruna.'

'Come straight through,' shouted Silvana.

Teresa took a firmer grip on Leon's hand as they crossed the threshold. He wrinkled his nose in disgust. 'Mummy. What a smell of caca!'

'Now don't start,' she warned him angrily. 'Don't speak until you're spoken to!'

Silvana was in the dining room. It had been an impressive room with a great chandelier hanging from the ceiling, a long polished dining table which seated twenty guests, high-backed chairs with wine-coloured upholstery and a long sideboard loaded with delicate china.

Now the dining table was pushed away into a corner of the room, the chairs were stacked against the wall and the middle of the room as a playground for Silvana's three children. They were naked and playing happily amidst their own baby-messes. The smell of stale urine and excretion was sickening.

'Nice to see you, Teresa,' greeted Silvana cosily. 'Get a chair and make yourself comfortable.' She was sprawled out in a sun-bleached deck chair and made no attempt to get to her feet. She'd been steadily gaining weight and now her arms and thighs were fleshily over-plump. Her cheeks were moist and beads of perspiration made a glistening moustache across her upper lip. She wore a sleeveless cotton dress which stuck to her damply and at her armpits, black hair curled out over the edge of a soiled under-garment.

Teresa said: 'I called to see how you all are.'

Silvana gestured with a plump arm and wheezed with the effort. 'It's as you see, Teresa. A woman's work is never done.' She'd become cheerfully placid as she'd put on weight, but there was a note of discontent in her voice. 'If you're like me, Teresa, you're wondering why we ever got married. Why did we? We were young and enjoying life and then...!' She pointed at her three children. 'I'm saddled with *that* lot! I don't mind because I love them. But they're a terrible responsibility and they rob you of your youth.'

'But they become part of your life too!'

'Don't misunderstand me, Teresa. I wouldn't part with them for anything now I've got them. But being stuck with them makes a girl think. Especially with a man like Anselmo. I think all he married me for was to have a son ... and here we are with three girls! But I've put my foot down. I'm not a machine. I won't go on and on like this just because he wants a son. Perhaps in a few years' time when I've got these off my hands we can think about it again. But I can tell you now, I won't do *much* thinking!'

'I can understand Anselmo,' said Teresa quietly. 'He wants to carry on the family name, to preserve the traditions and the way of life of a cultured family.'

Silvana nodded and the flesh under her chin wobbled like jelly. 'I know all that, Teresa. But it cuts both ways, doesn't it? Anselmo wasn't honest with me. I know he had lots of property. But what does it add up to now? He's broke, Teresa. The farm brings in barely enough to eat and we haven't a peseta to spend. I haven't had a new dress for over a year and I have to do everything myself ... not one servant! It's my own fault. I was silly. I should have got it written down in black and white. I thought I'd have everything, dresses, parties, nurses to take care of the children and a loving husband. But you'd hardly recognise Anselmo these days. He's so gloomy and grumpy that it's better to keep out of his way.'

'And how is Señora Ledesma?'

Silvana raised her eyes to heaven, lifted her plump arms in despair and let them flop back on her fat thighs. 'She's the end! I do what I can but you know what a mother-in-law is like. Nothing's good enough for her son. Without saying a word she faults everything I do. So I let her get on with it. If she wants to live like a hermit, that's her affair.'

'It's been a long time...' began Teresa. 'Do you think I might...?'

'Of course.' With a grunt and a wheeze Silvana heaved herself out of the deck chair. She crossed to the sideboard where dirty crockery was stacked high and reached for a pot of honey. 'You like honey?' she asked.

'We have it from time to time.'

'You want some?' She thrust the pot at Teresa.

'No thank you. Not now. I ... I don't often eat between meals.'

'It's good honey,' said Silvana. She ran her forefinger round the pot, scooping up a yellow ball of thick, waxy honey, popped it into her mouth and licked her forefinger clean. 'How about you, Leon?' she asked.

Leon stood stiffly, very conscious of his clean shirt and shorts. He shook his head solemnly. 'No thank you, Madam.'

'What a polite little boy he is. Just look at my lot over there. Look at Silvana. You'd never think they were the same age!'

Silvana was playing with her sisters and her hair was encrusted with the excretion of the youngest child.

Teresa looked away quickly. 'It's a long time since I saw Señora Ledesma,' she said.

'She shuts herself up in her own room. I'll take you to her.' Silvana beckoned Teresa to follow and shuffled along a corridor to the back of the house. She pounded on the panels of Señora Ledesma's bedroom.

'What is it?'

'A visitor to see you,' shouted Silvana. 'Teresa Coruna.'

There was a pause.

'Thank you,' said Señora Ledesma.

Silvana smiled. 'I'll see you before you leave.' She shuffled back to the dining room, her hips wobbling fleshily under her tight dress.

Teresa gently knuckled the door panels. 'It's me, Señora.'

The key turned in the lock, the door opened and Señora Ledesma said in a frail voice: 'This is a pleasant surprise, Teresa. Do come in!'

The room was the elderly woman's sanctuary and would have been musty had not the french windows been open. Teresa saw a four-poster bed with fresh, white pillow-cases, comfortable chairs, a lace-making pillow and a table with washed-up crockery.

Señora Ledesma stared down at Leon and her eyes glowed. 'What a beautiful child, Teresa. He's *so* handsome!'

'Be careful what you say, Señora Ledesma. He's a big head.'

'What have you got to say to me, Leon?'

He stared at her solemnly. 'I'm very pleased to meet you, Señora.' He held out his hand.

She shook hands solemnly. 'I'm enchanted to meet a young gentleman with such charming manners.'

Teresa had a lump in her throat. 'Do you think he's like his grandfather?'

'Very much,' said Señora Ledesma, staring at Leon intently. 'Very much like the grandson I would have liked to have had.'

Teresa looked straight at Anselmo's mother and there was an immediate understanding between them.

'Leon,' said the older woman. 'You'll like this book. See ... here are all the animals of the jungle. You can look at it while I talk to your mother.'

'I'm always intending to call and see you,' apologised Teresa. 'But time flies and ...'

The older woman nodded understandingly and placed her

hands together. Teresa noticed how frail and bloodless they'd become. 'What went wrong between you and Anselmo, Teresa?'

'There was another man. He meant nothing to me. It was a purely physical thing. I wanted to be honest with Anselmo and I told him about it.' Teresa spread her hands ruefully.

Señora Ledesma sighed. 'It was a pity. You were right for Anselmo. This other one, she's a child. I do not criticise her. I simply cannot live her way. I cook my own meals and try to close my eyes to the travesty she is making of my son's life.'

'It is difficult for her too,' said Teresa.

'I am old enough to see both sides, Teresa. Silvana was a butterfly in fairyland who wanted to marry a prince and live happily ever after. The pain of childbearing and financial setbacks ask more of her than she is capable of giving.'

'It is sad to see her,' said Teresa. 'She's let herself go.'

'*You* would have been right for Anselmo,' said Señora Ledesma. 'You would have strengthened him, economised and encouraged him when he was despondent.'

Teresa nodded sadly. 'I loved Anselmo.' She took a deep breath. 'I *still* love him!'

The older woman propped her lace-making pillow against the back of a chair and flipped bobbins through her frail fingers. 'Anselmo's handicap is that he is a gentleman. He has made his bed and he will lie upon it. He will suffer and grieve but he will be loyal to Silvana. She's his wife and he will bear everything, her laziness, her dirtiness, her neglect of the children and her tantrums.'

'Tantrums?' asked Teresa.

'You've no idea, my child. She's fat and placid and looks good-natured. But when Anselmo comes home she's transformed. You can't imagine it. She screams, shouts insults and uses appalling language. If I had dared once to talk to Baudillo in that way he would have beaten me. But you young people live in a new era, Teresa. She talks to Anselmo as though he is dirt and he only lowers his eyes and allows her words to beat upon him. I'm too old, Teresa. I come from a world so different from all this that there can be no understanding between Silvana and I. I loved my husband but I revered him too. He was the master and withal I was content that it should be so. But this is a new generation. Now the woman is the master and although my son accepts this, I cannot believe he is happy.'

'Silvana is still very beautiful,' said Teresa.

'Her *face* is beautiful. But should my son live in deference to a beautiful face? I am worldly, Teresa. If you say my son is

71

enchanted by her physical charms, I can understand it. But when it is only a face without physical attraction, I am unconvinced.'

'I cannot comment upon these things of which you speak,' said Teresa.

'I am sorry, my dear. We are talking of something that is too close to the hearts of both of us.'

'Anselmo made his decision,' said Teresa quietly. 'But I do not complain. Narcisus is a good husband.'

'I'm sure he is.'

'Also I have Leon. He is a good boy.'

'I see that,' said Señora Ledesma. She smiled at Leon. 'He is strong and well built.'

'Why is that lady outside so fat?' asked Leon.

Señora Ledesma smiled gently. 'Because she is.'

'And why does she smell so nasty?'

'She does not always smell nasty,' said the older woman gently.

'And why don't those children do it in the lavatory?'

Anselmo arrived home as Teresa was leaving. He'd bought an old motor-cycle to do the rounds of his properties and was dismounting when Teresa, holding Leon by the hand, came down the steps from the terrace.

It was a long time since he'd seen her and he was impressed by the crispness of her white blouse and the slenderness of her waist. Her pleated skirt swayed across her knees and emphasised her shapely calves and she smelled of lavender. He found himself strangely breathless. 'Hello, Teresa.'

'Hello, Anselmo.' She stared at him steadily for some moments and then urged her son: 'Say good afternoon, Leon.'

'Good afternoon, Señor Ledesma,' said Leon solemnly.

'*A son*,' Anselmo thought. '*Ah. If I too could have a son!*' He said: 'Good afternoon, Leon.'

'I have visited your mother,' said Teresa.

He knew instantly she must be aware of the conflict within his home. 'Mother is not quite herself,' he said awkwardly. 'She hasn't been well for some time.'

'She seems very frail, Anselmo.'

He looked away from her, determined not to remember the past, but acutely conscious of her closeness. 'She lets trivial things worry her.'

'I will visit her again soon.'

'I hope you will. She's always pleased to see you.'

There was an awkward silence.

'Your children look very healthy and happy, Anselmo.'

'Yes,' he said. He was compelled to look at her and saw her

flush. 'Have you seen Silvana?'

'Of course, Anselmo.'

He was ashamed of his wife and hurt that others should see her laziness. 'Silvana has ... not been well for some time.'

'It's a great strain to have so many children so quickly,' said Teresa gently.

He was grateful for her understanding. 'It *is* a lot for Silvana to manage, isn't it?'

'I've only Leon and he's more than a handful!'

He looked down at Leon and thought of a son of his own who would hand down the family wine and traditions. 'I'm sorry I wasn't at home when you called, Teresa. Will you take a glass with me?'

'Thank you. I've already stayed too long. Narcisus needs me in the shop.'

His clothes were old, she noticed. The jacket elbows darned crudely. Silvana's darning!

'Say goodbye,' she encouraged Leon.

'Goodbye, Leon. Goodbye, Teresa.'

'Come again soon,' he called after her when she reached the entrance to the drive.

'Mummy,' panted Leon, trotting to keep up with her. 'Why are you crying?'

She wiped her hand across her cheek. 'What are you saying, silly boy? I'm not crying!'

CHAPTER FOUR

1

JULIO GARCIA was miserable as he sat at the wheel of his taxi. He had a good wife and two pretty daughters, but he couldn't earn enough to feed them properly. His taxi was pre-war and battered, its upholstery sagged, its rusted mudguards were paper thin and the worn engine needed careful nursing. But it was reliable enough to take a passenger from one side of Barcelona to the other through the almost trafficless streets. But few people could afford his modest taxi fares. The end of the war in Europe had made little difference to Spain. There was acute depression. Business had never been so bad. There were no exports, people had no money to buy, many factories were closed down and others simply ticked over, hoping for better times. Even lucky men with jobs couldn't live on their wages. Beans, rice and potatoes were the staple diet and a family was well-off if it could taste fish or meat on one day of the week.

So Julio Garcia, who was a much thinner man than he had been, sighed sadly as he took a pouch of black tobacco making from his pocket. Ten years ago, he reflected wryly, the Ramblas had been crowded with well-dressed men smoking expensive cigars and flaunting comfortable paunches. Now he couldn't remember the last time he'd seen a fat man.

Three men sauntered towards him and Julio Garcia sat up straight, scenting clients. They wore thin, blue and white striped linen suits and two carried worn, leather bags. Nobody had the money to buy smart clothes and a man's social position couldn't be judged by his clothes. One man opened the door, the others climbed inside and Julio Garcia threw away his loosely-made cigarette. It was dangerous to smoke while driving because it let drop glowing particles of tobacco.

One of the men told him where to go in Catalan and when Julio Garcia repeated the address, the man knew by his accent that he was not from Catalonia and switched to Spanish. 'There's no hurry,' he said. 'We're early for our appointment so take your time.'

The three passengers were strangely silent and when Julio Garcia slyly looked into his driving mirror, he found himself staring into cool, grey eyes. He looked away and pretended he was checking if he was being overtaken.

The silence of the three men was strangely ominous. They shared an inner tension which they communicated to the driver and although it was a cool September day, he began to sweat. He cruised along the Diagonal with its wide, tree-lined rambles deserted of traffic and overtook one of the city's few trams. It was overflowing with passengers massed on the steps and hanging on to the hand rails like clusters of grapes.

'You were here during the war, driver?' asked the man with the grey eyes.

Julio Garcia nodded sadly. 'We were bombed. We lost all our windows three times.'

'It was better before the war, wasn't it, driver? Then Spain was building a new world, but now there's only ... despair.'

Julio Garcia hunched his neck down into his shoulders, clamped his lips and stared doggedly at the road ahead of him.

'Don't you agree, driver?' asked the man softly.

Julio Garcia didn't answer.

'Are you deaf, driver? Or are you one of *them*?'

Garcia gulped. He said hoarsely: 'Why lose your head for just talking?'

They liked his reply. They chuckled and quite suddenly the atmosphere had changed. They were all friends and the tension had vanished.

'We're a little ahead of time,' said the man with the grey eyes as the driver pulled up outside a marble-fronted bank.

Julio Garcia stretched his hand towards the meter.

'Keep the engine running, driver. We've got other calls to make.'

They waited. The city looked dead. Only a few people were on the streets. A Civil Guard paced towards them, his tommy-gun slung across his back and his patent leather black tricornio gleaming dully in the sun. He glanced at the men waiting in the taxi without curiosity and strolled on.

'Wait for us, driver. We won't be long,' said the man with the grey eyes. He and one companion picked up their brief-cases, unhurriedly crossed the pavement and entered the bank.

The third man sat on the edge of his seat breathing down the driver's neck.

'How long will they be?' asked Julio Garcia.

'Only a few minutes.'

'I don't like to waste petrol. It's rationed.' Julio Garcia reached for the ignition key.

'Leave it. Don't turn the engine off.' The man's voice was so sharp that Julio Garcia turned round slowly and stared at him.

'Leave the engine running,' said the man. His face was pale and beads of perspiration had gathered round the wings of his nostrils.

Julio Garcia sensed his fear. 'Don't tell me what to do,' he said.

'Don't get rattled, driver. Just leave the engine running.'

'It's my cab. I'll do what I want!'

The man's eyes glowed. 'I hired this cab and you'll do what I say.'

'We'll see about that,' said Julio Garcia grimly and reached for the ignition key.

The pistol the man was holding out of sight slid over the driver's shoulder. Its sight cut the driver's cheek. 'It's the last goddam thing you'll do, driver!'

Julio Garcia's hand fell back. He was breathless with shock. Nothing like this had ever happened in all his years as a cab driver. He held his breath until the pistol slipped out of sight again. His mouth was dry and tasted of copper.

'Just sit quietly.'

Julio Garcia sat as still as a statue.

Only minutes had elapsed since the men had entered the bank and the Civil Guard who'd passed a few minutes earlier was returning. His pace was steady, unhurried and assured. Julio Garcia felt momentary relief. Then he pictured himself in a gun battle and tommy-gun bullets drilling through his innocent chest. He gulped as he pictured himself crumpled and dying.

The Civil Guard drew level and Julio Garcia stared at him glassy-eyed.

The man behind warned: 'Just sit quietly.'

The Civil Guard passed and looked straight at the driver. Then his eyes went to the passenger.

Julio Garcia sweated.

The Civil Guard glanced both ways along the pavement, took a deep breath and with unhurried stride, paced into the bank.

When the two men had entered the bank they'd gone to separate desks, seated themselves and written out paying-in slips. There were only a few clients in the bank and the shirt-sleeved clerks were getting out the day's balances.

The two men glanced up when the Civil Guard entered and watched him intently. The aged, uniformed porter seated at the entrance door hastily got to his feet. 'Can I help you, Guardia?'

'Tell your chief I want to see him. It's urgent.'

The old man limped away and the two men with briefcases

watched him raise the counter-flap and pass through.

The Civil Guard took a small wedge of wood from his pocket and thrust it under the door. He straightened up, unslung his tommy-gun, held it waist high and said in a voice that resounded through the bank: 'Attention everybody. This is an emergency. Everyone listen!'

A sea of startled faces stared towards him.

'This is an emergency. All of you stand against that wall over there.'

After a moment's startled hesitation there was a wild shuffling and pushing as clients and bank employees moved over to the wall.

The two men with briefcases ignored the order.

The aged porter had found the manager who came hurrying, his face worried. 'What's wrong, Guardia?'

'Stand on one side. The rest of you back right up against the wall.'

The bank manager fluttered his hands nervously. 'I'll help in any way I can and ...'

The Civil Guard had raven-black hair with cotton wool sideboards. A ridged welt like a sabre scar ran from the corner of his eyes to the point of his jaw. He nodded. 'Attend to those gentlemen quickly.'

The bank manager looked at the two men. 'What can I ...?'

'Take us to the vaults. Quickly!'

The bank manager's eyes narrowed. 'I don't think ...'

They pulled out revolvers.

'No,' said the bank manager flatly. 'Don't think I'll ...!'

The man with the grey eyes pistol-whipped him. The manager clutched at his face and blood spurted through his fingers. The second man tripped him up and he whimpered as he lay on the cool tiles.

The man with the grey eyes stooped and prodded his chest with the pistol. 'Don't waste more time or I'll kill you.'

The bank manager had a son he wanted to support through medical college. He got to his feet and mopped his cheek as he led the two men to the vault.

The men cleared the shelves of stacks of one thousand peseta notes. It was many years since new currency had been printed. All the notes were old and untraceable. There were not enough to fill the two briefcases so they topped them up with one hundred peseta notes. The rest of the currency notes, stacks of bonds, stocks and shares they swept on to the vault's stone floor. They applied a lighted match to the paper mountain and when it was well ablaze they ushered the manager outside and shut the steel door.

77

The man with the grey eyes left the bank first. He took a firm grip on his bulging briefcase, walked out unhurriedly, crossed the pavement and climbed into the taxi.

The second man followed him a few minutes later.

The Civil Guard waited until they were in the taxi. Then he drew his pistol and held it menacingly while he slung the tommy-gun over his shoulder. 'The first to follow me outside gets shot in the belly.'

He walked swiftly across the pavement and slid into the seat alongside the driver. 'Get going, driver. As fast as you can.'

They sped up the Paseo de Gracia, turned left at the Diagonal and drove hard until they reached the outskirts of the city. Julio Garcia trembled when they ordered him to pull over to the side of the road.

'All right, driver. Get out.'

Julio Garcia knew he was going to die and a lump in his throat choked him as he thought of his wife and daughters and the futility of his dying.

The man with the grey eyes snapped: 'Didn't you hear me, driver? Go behind that hedge.' His hand was in his pocket holding his gun.

'I won't talk,' panted Julio Garcia. 'I *swear* I won't talk. I won't say a word to anyone.'

The cool, grey eyes were impatient. 'Hurry, man. Hurry!'

Julio Garcia stumbled round to the other side of the hedge. 'Kneel down.'

Julio Garcia knew men were killed this way during the war. Taken for a ride, told to kneel and then shot in the back of the head. 'Please don't!' choked Julio Garcia. 'Please don't!' But he sank on to his knees, resigned to what must come.

The man with the grey eyes placed his foot against Julio Garcia's shoulders and thrust hard. The driver fell forward on his face and lay still, wondering if he'd been shot in the back. The man snapped a handcuff on his left wrist, doubled up his right leg and snapped the other handcuff round his ankle.

'This is for your trouble, Comrade.' The man thrust some thousand peseta notes into the driver's pocket.

Julio Garcia was too astonished by his reprieve from death to understand anything clearly.

'Be a good comrade. We'll borrow your taxi. Give us a fair chance to get away before you cry for help.'

Much later, Julio Garcia's taxi was discovered only a quarter of a mile along the road where the change-over car had been waiting.

The four men were playing a card game called Manilla. The cards were Spanish, forty-eight to a pack and the suit designs were gold coins, drinking cups, green cudgels and blue swords. It would have been difficult for a foreigner to understand the game by watching it because the nine of each suit was the strongest card.

Catalina busied herself at a mahogany-stained buffet, cutting black maize bread into slices on which she spread mashed potatoes and beans flavoured with garlic. As she prepared each slice she placed it at the elbows of the players. There had not been an acute shortage of food in southern France during the war and although she was slim, she was strong and wiry. If her scarred cheek and drooping eyelid had not made her look sinister, she would have been attractive.

The hand of cards ended and Miguel Barras pushed back his chair and got to his feet. He stretched himself and yawned. 'I've no interest in cards!' He crossed to a window, edged the curtains to one side and stared down into Barcelona's busy Mayor de Gracia. Up and down the street he saw the grey uniforms and flat caps of Barcelona's special police. 'The sons of whores! The city's crawling with them!'

'But they've bolted the stable door after the horse has run,' said Adolfo and chuckled nervously, remembering the long, anxious minutes he'd waited outside in the taxi. He shivered.

'The horse *didn't* escape,' said the man with the grey eyes. His name was Marin and the flat was rented by his mother and his sister, Helena.

The fourth man, Jaime, complained petulantly: 'They're too well organised!'

'What do you expect of a police state?' said Miguel.

'It was madness to show yourself with your scar, Miguel. You're a marked man now.' Adolfo glowered.

'So I made a mistake!' snarled Miguel. 'But *I'm* the one who'll pay. They're looking for me . . . not you!'

'But we're together and it . . .!'

'One minute, Comrades,' Martin held up his hand soothingly. 'The plan was good. Slip across the border, rob a bank, hide out a while and then home again. But we couldn't anticipate a police cordon would be maintained round the city.'

'Only one thing matters,' said Miguel. 'The money's got to get back to France to work for the Party.'

'Patience,' advised Marin. 'Even if we have to wait a month. Patience!'

They tensed at the click of a key in the lock, but relaxed

when Helena shut the flat door behind her. She came into the room and glared at the men resentfully. 'Did mother call?'

Marin's mother was in her eighties, bedridden, deaf and partially blind.

'She's sleeping,' said Marin.

She scowled at the invaders of her home, hating them and her brother. 'How much longer are you going to stay?'

Marin's grey eyes were as hard as steel. 'Who wants to know?'

'I want you all out of here,' she said. 'Didn't you hear it on the radio? In some districts they've started house to house searches.'

'That doesn't mean a thing, Helena.'

'Why did you come back, bringing us all this trouble? Mother and I were all right until you returned.'

'What's happened to you, Helena? You're a Party member. Are you turning traitor?'

She glared. 'What's bank robbing got to do with Communism?'

'The Party needs money,' he explained patiently. 'We've got to buy arms and equipment.'

Helena pleaded with her brother. 'Can't you see it's hopeless? What can a handful of you achieve by making raids across the border? When the Allies didn't turn against Spain after Germany was conquered, our last hope was destroyed. You're crying for the moon, Marin!'

He flushed angrily. 'What can you know of these things. You're a woman!'

'Any fool knows a handful of armed men can't overthrow a dictator and his army.'

'The masses are suffering,' said Marin. 'They've not enough to eat and are ripe for revolt. They're living in a police state where freedom is suppressed. All we need is a revolutionary situation and they'll rise!'

She said sadly: 'Are you so blind you can't see reality, Marin? The people suffer. But anything is preferable to another civil war. Nobody wants all that again, the bombing, the killing and the atrocities.'

'Don't argue, Marin,' said Miguel quietly. 'She's a victim of propaganda. She listens to *their* radio and reads *their* newspapers.'

Helena glared. 'It's not *your* mother you're putting in danger.'

'The cause is important, not individuals.'

'I want *that* out of here at once!' She pointed to a brown paper bundle. 'If they search here that's a giveaway.'

80

Marin said quietly: 'Get rid of it, Adolfo. Leave it some-where, in a park or in a cafe.'

'Me!' exploded Adolfo. His eyes widened in alarm.

'That uniform doesn't leave,' said Miguel firmly. 'We got it the hard way and we'll need it again.'

'Helena's right. If they come here it will betray us at once,' Marin said quietly.

'So would my scarred face,' said Miguel. 'And so would the money.' His black eyes glittered. 'Or are you suggesting Adolfo dumps the money too?'

Marin dropped his eyes. 'I'm thinking . . . of my mother. . . .'

Helena glared at Miguel. 'He's my brother, otherwise I'd turn you all out. But once you leave here don't ever come back. If you do, I'll call the police at once.' She stormed out of the room.

Marin shrugged his shoulders apologetically. 'Women!' he said, and smiled wryly. Then his eyes met Catalina's and he added: '*You* are different, Comrade.'

that I can't sympathise with Helena,' she be *sure* of our contacts. It's a mistake to get where we can't depend absolutely on everyone.'

I was sure I could rely on Helena,' protested Marin. 'We were both Party members. Her fiancée was killed leading the attack on the Arcazana's barracks.'

'That was ten years ago!' snapped Catalina. 'People change!'

There was a ring at the doorbell and everyone listened while Helena answered it. But it was an expected comrade and they pulled up chairs and sat round the table with him. Nolano was a dark man, thirty-five years of age and worked in the docks as a ships' carpenter. Most days he spent in the slipway and was ideally placed to make contact with the crews of foreign boats.

'I've fixed it so two of you can sail tonight for Marseilles.' Nolana took a manilla envelope from his pocket and drew out two Spanish seamen's identity cards. 'These will get you into the docks. A banana boat's leaving for the Canary Islands and you're the new crew.'

Miguel examined the documents. They were genuine but the original photographs had been changed for those of Miguel and Marin. 'My scar doesn't show in the photograph,' said Miguel.

'It would be fatal if it did!'

'How do I get round it?' asked Miguel.

'Take a calculated risk,' said Nolana. 'I've left a suitcase

81

outside in the hall with sailor's clothes and two kitbags. Fill the kitbags with the money, put dirty underclothes on top and walk through the dock gates showing the passes.'

'And the scar?'

Nolana smiled slowly. 'Carry the kitbag over your shoulder as all sailors do,' he said. 'Pull it hard up against your cheek.'

Miguel grinned. 'A nice touch, Comrade. Walking straight out under the noses of the bastards with the money in a kitbag!'

'How about the rest of us?' asked Adolfo anxiously.

'You'll have to be patient. They're checking everyone, everywhere, at the railways and the port. They're even stopping cars leaving the city and making spot searches of cafes. You'll have to wait until they relax their vigilance.'

Miguel asked: 'Did you learn anything about Gomez, Comrade?'

Nolana nodded. 'He was arrested three months ago on suspicion. They interrogated him and he _____ another man did. Gomez has been ident_____ ber and sentenced to death. No date's bee_____

Miguel's eyes smouldered. 'There'll be _____ workers take power.'

Nolana scowled. 'For the present we must _____ struggle with limited means. We must make it clea_ workers that the American imperialists are building up _____ at reserves of arms to strike at the Soviet Union. Already in Korea a revolutionary situation is developing. We must prevent the American warmongers from intervening.'

Nolana talked on and on.

'That summarises the Party line, Comrades,' he concluded. He thumped his fist on the table. 'These are the facts we must get over to our Spanish comrades.' He looked round at his small audience. 'Any comments?'

Miguel Barras nodded broodingly, his features markedly peasant as he stored away in his mind all that Nolana had said.

Marin commented: 'Although Stalin united with the Allies against Hitler, it was evident that Soviet Russia was using the imperialists.'

Nolana looked at Adolfo who nodded quick agreement and smiled nervously.

Jaime frowned. 'I wanted a better world for Spaniards. When the revolution started I fought for it.' He held up his hands and looked at them. 'I've killed men and wept afterwards. I'm not a killer, but if it's necessary to kill to free my people, then I will do it. But all this talk of the Soviet Union and American imperialists bewilders me, Comrades. I am only a simple man.'

Nolana nodded understandingly. 'We cannot all have the wisdom of Comrade Stalin. We can only be true to our cause by giving tactical help to our Russian comrades. *La Pasionaria* says we must disrupt the goodwill between the Allies. They must *not* unite against the Soviet Union. And when the times comes, Comrade Stalin will strike hard at the roots of *every* fascist dictatorship.'

'Including Spain?' asked Miguel quickly.

'As soon as tactics permit,' said Nolana. His voice rang with conviction.

3

A new but dusty coupe lurched along the mud-packed road from Figueras. Long ago its macadam surface had been eroded away by wind, rain and sun. Now, the high-wheeled peasants' carts had torn deep furrows along its centre. It was difficult for the driver to avoid dropping his wheel into these deep ruts, and when it happened the exhaust pipe or sump scraped the ground.

The car entered Escoleras at a snail's pace and came to a standstill in the Plaza under the shade of the plane trees. At once the villagers came hurrying to see the strange, modern car and news of its arrival spread like wildfire as children ran to tell their parents.

The car bore British number plates and was startlingly modern, with headlights set into streamlined wings and its radiator honeycombed with chromium plate like an enormous mouth organ.

The driver climbed out of the car. He was a man of thirty-five with cropped, fair hair. He wore a white, twill shirt with rolled-up sleeves and khaki shorts. His face was burned red by the sun, but his bowed legs were thin and very white. The villagers stared at him with hungry curiosity as though he was a visitor from an alien planet.

The Englishman was embarrassed by the silently watching crowd and the dark, staring eyes which watched his every movement. They were very poor, he saw, their drab clothes patched and patched again. All the women wore shapeless black dresses with black scarves over their heads. Their faces were grey with sadness and pinched with hunger. He wondered if he had broken a village tabu. He couldn't understand why they hurried to watch him and why the crowd was swiftly growing bigger. Their faces were sullen and their manner ominous and he wondered for a moment if they might fling themselves upon him. But he shrugged the thought away. Spain was a civilised country even if it was a dictatorship. So he gave them a sickly smile and said: 'Buenas dias.'

It was like pressing a light switch in the darkness. The eyes and faces lit up, delighted smiles greeted him, heads nodded and a dozen villagers tried to talk to him at once, their expressive eyes and actions telling more eloquently than words that they were thrilled to meet a foreigner and awed by the magnificence of his car.

He spoke a strongly-accented pidgin-Spanish. He told them he had come from England across the sea and had driven through France. He said it was very hot and that the view of the sea was wonderful He stooped and spoke to his wife through the car window. 'You can get out. I don't think they'll eat us.'

Mary Tweed was fair-skinned like her husband, but had sunbathed at home in the back garden. She was beautifully tanned and proud of it as she stepped out of the car. A cigarette dangled from her crimson lips and her yellow linen dress with slender straps completely exposed her arms and shoulders. Her short skirt showed bare brown knees as she balanced on high-heeled white sandals.

There were gasps from the older women of the village. Some covered their eyes, others crossed themselves, many hurried away and some muttered under their breaths. The men and youths stared blankly, unable to believe their eyes.

But the British couple were unaware of the consternation. Mary took a beach bag from the back of the car while her husband happily interrogated the villagers.

'Swim?' he asked, making swimming motions and looking the question.

A dozen hands were at once pointing, heads nodding, eyes smiling. 'That is the beach, Señor. There are many kilometres of beach.'

'Deep?' he asked, hands demonstrating shallowness and then deepness.

'Good for swimming,' they encouraged. 'Very good.'

He nodded his thanks. 'My car. It is good? Parked here?'

They were perplexed. Parking was a problem they didn't know about. They stared blankly.

He tried again. 'The car? Here? It is good?'

They nodded reassuringly. Yes. The car was good where it was. But their assurances were dubious and their eyes unhappy. They felt they had failed him.

The Englishman nodded and took his wife by the arm.
'Adios.'

'Adios,' chorused the villagers, and stood staring after the couple as they made their way to the beach. After a few minutes most of the younger men set off after them.

Robert and Mary walked some distance along the sand before they sat down.

The village youths sat at a distance and watched the foreign couple do something unheard of. They held towels for each other and changed into swimming costumes *on the beach.* The youths watched breathlessly and then stared incredulously when Mary dropped her towel to reveal a crimson, skin-tight swimming costume. She was quite shameless and stood at the water's edge flaunting herself. The youths watched the couple swim, rub oil on themselves, doze in the sun and then swim again. When the couple returned to the village the youths followed them persistently.

'The way they act you'd think they'd never seen a woman swimming,' commented Mary.

'Perhaps they haven't,' said Robert.

They wanted to buy food to make sandwiches and Teresa was behind the counter when they entered her store. They shut the door behind them and stepped into the cool interior, but the villagers who'd clustered round the door opened it again so that they could listen.

'Food,' said Robert Tweed in his primitive Spanish.

'We have dried sardines and salted cod,' said Teresa. 'There is also sausage meat and tinned tunny fish.'

He did not understand her so she showed him the goods and then, because she had studied French which is similar to Catalan, Teresa spoke to him in that language. He answered delightedly, his accent strong and his grammar atrocious, but his vocabulary was extensive enough for them to converse.

'My wife and I love this village,' he said sincerely. 'It is like ... something you read about in a book ... like a paradise. The blue sea, the deserted white-sand beaches and ... everything.'

'I like it too,' smiled Teresa. 'We live simply but we are happy.'

'Is there an hotel?'

'There's the Hotel Catalana in Figueras.'

'I mean ... *here!*'

She chuckled at his foolishness. 'Nobody ever stays here.'

'We want to.'

'But ... you're different.'

'You *must* have some people who visit here.'

'Not often.'

'Where do they stay?'

'They can always find a room in the village.'

'Will someone in the village give us a room?'

Teresa smiled wryly. Such wealthy foreigners couldn't live in a village cottage. 'People here live very simply,' she explained. 'There are few conveniences.'

'We don't mind the simple life.' He chuckled. 'We've just lived through a war. That wasn't luxury living either.'

'But ... there's no running water, the lavatories are in the back yard ... it's not what you're used to.'

'We won't mind,' he assured her. 'Who will rent us a double room?'

Teresa took a deep breath as she swiftly rearranged the household mentally with herself and Narcisus sleeping at the Barras cottage. 'I have a double room. Would you like to see it?'

She led them up the steep, narrow stairs and hesitantly showed them her bedroom. They looked round without dismay. 'This will do,' Mary told her husband. 'It's spotlessly clean.'

'We'd like to stay,' he told Teresa. 'How much is it?'

She told him.

She noticed his slight hesitancy and feared she'd asked too much, but then he astonished her by asking: 'Is that each day or for the week?'

'For the week,' she said, and was surprised when he laughed.

'You're making a mistake,' he said.

'Am I?' She checked mentally, adding a little to the normal price charged for a double room overnight. 'No,' she confirmed. 'I haven't made a mistake.'

'We won't argue,' he chuckled. 'We'll square up when we leave. Now what about eating? Is there a restaurant here?'

'A bar or a cafe will prepare a snack. But if you want regular meals ...' Teresa took a deep breath and plunged 'You can eat here if you don't mind eating in the kitchen behind the shop.'

'I'd love it!' Mary said delightedly. 'We'd *much* prefer to live with a family!'

They stayed three weeks. They sunbathed on the beach all day, returning only for lunch. In the cool of the evening they took long walks along the rocky coast, exploring little bays and coves and looking down from the high cliff tops into water so clear and transparent that the sea bed could be seen clearly.

Robert Tweed studied Spanish grammar books, showed a remarkable aptitude for the language and practised upon

Teresa and the family. Mary was enchanted with Leon, played with him endlessly and bought him sweets. He was seven years old and Mary couldn't get over his blond, nordic appearance.

'Our family has always been blond,' said Teresa proudly. 'My father is known as "El Rubio".'

Everyone was delighted by the friendliness of the English couple. Teresa tactfully explained that the older women of the village were narrow-minded and without demur Mary wore a coatee, stubbed out cigarettes before she left the house and used less lipstick. The couple drank a lot of wine, visited all the village cafes, stayed until the early hours of the morning and invited fishermen and everybody else to drink with them. They ate all that was set before them, even snails. Robert Tweed told Teresa that eating snails was as nauseating to the average Englishman as eating rats or mice.

Teresa startled him by saying: 'What's wrong with eating rats or mice?'

He stared. 'Have you eaten rat?'

'I haven't. But many people have. You would too if you were starving.'

Robert Tweed bought one of Pepita's mosaic pictures and he asked: 'How many pictures can Pepita make a year?'

'It's hard to say,' said Teresa. 'It's ... tiring for her.' She thought of the leather-tipped stumps of arms painstakingly searching among the stones for one of the right colour and delicately edging it into position in the picture.

'There'd be a good sale for them back home.'

'Pepita does it to pass the time.'

'They're not works of art,' agreed Robert Tweed. 'But the colours are gay and the scenes have charm. They're a novelty. If you like, I'll show them round and try to get some orders.'

'It would make Pepita happy,' said Teresa.

On their last night in Escoleras they bought champagne to drink with the family.

Robert Tweed said: 'We're coming back. This is one of the most beautiful places I've seen.' He eyed Teresa thoughtfully. 'Why don't you open a boarding house or a small hotel?'

She smiled tolerantly at his grand ideas. 'But nobody ever comes here.'

He leaned forward and spoke intently. 'They will. I'm employed by a big firm that's started a travel agency. I'm its manager and I know what I'm talking about. People have suffered years of war and want to escape. This place has got everything. It's cheap, the climate's wonderful, the surroundings are beautiful and the beach is perfect. Believe me, Teresa. This is a tourists' paradise.'

She was amused by his enthusiasm and touched by his dream. 'Provide me with clients and I'll find the accommodation,' she chuckled.

'I'll take you up on it,' he said seriously. 'I'll keep you busy all summer and into autumn.'

'But ... nobody has ever heard of Escoleras. Why should anyone come here?'

His eyes gleamed. 'I did, didn't I? Despite bad roads, language difficulties and frontier guards who kept me an hour, checking my papers and turning out everything in the car.'

'You're different,' said Teresa slowly. 'But most people going on holiday don't want problems.'

'The problems will ease,' prophesied Robert Tweed. 'Spain can become Europe's most popular tourist resort. And as soon as your government realises it, the frontiers will be thrown open, money will be found to build new roads, transport services will improve and everyone will grow prosperous. The birth of a tourist trade is a wonderful thing, Teresa. I've seen it happen in other countries and in England. I've seen a seaside village with a handful of houses turned into a thriving town in a few years.'

Teresa said thoughtfully: 'Supposing I could find some good, clean double rooms ... would that do?'

'They must be clean. And you'll have to arrange for food.'

'I could rent a big room with a kitchen.'

'Why not get a loan from a bank and build a small boarding house?'

Teresa was horrified. 'We couldn't afford *that*!'

'Then find out how many villagers have got rooms to let.'

When the Tweeds left the following day, Robert Tweed paid exactly twice what he'd been asked.

'It's too much,' Teresa said.

'For us, it's not enough,' he insisted. 'We've had much more than value for money.' He chuckled. 'We've been looked after too cheaply and you think you've been overpaid so ... we're both happy!'

After they had gone, Teresa sat in deep thought. Presently she took a pencil and paper from the sideboard and made calculations.

'What are you up to?' Narcisus asked.

She smiled softly. 'Making our fortune.'

CHAPTER FIVE

1

GREY-UNIFORMED guards with tommy-guns stood at the foot of the flight of marble steps leading to the cool vestibule of the building. It was hot in Madrid at this time of the year and the guards were grateful for the shade thrown by the tall building.

Renato Maroto approached briskly, flashed his police badge and glared when a guard stolidly barred his way. 'I've shown you my badge,' he snapped. Spots of red burned high up on his cheeks.

'Orders,' said the corporal tersely. 'Papers, please.'

Maroto scowled while his credentials were scrutinised. The guard waved. 'You may proceed.'

Maroto hurried inside, angered that he had been harassed by a low-ranking guard.

A sergeant sat at a desk in the vestibule. 'You have an appointment?'

'At eleven-thirty,' said Maroto.

The sergeant opened a ledger and ran his finger down a column of names. 'Correct,' he confirmed. 'Take a seat over there, please.' He nodded.

Maroto sat on a wooden bench and scowled at the tiled floor. He was a government official and resented being treated like the public.

The sergeant spoke softly into the telephone then busied himself folding printed sheets.

Time passed.

The telephone rang a number of times but the sergeant answered it without once glancing towards Maroto who presently got up and paced the vestibule.

The sergeant eyed him disapprovingly.

Another guard entered, glanced enquiringly at the sergeant and then beckoned to Maroto. 'This way, please.'

Maroto was shown into a well-furnished office with deep chairs, leather upholstery and oil paintings in gilt frames. An enormous desk was weighed down by files and behind it sat a silver-haired man with a lined face as brown as a chestnut. He was known by his staff as the Old Man.

'Sit down, Maroto.'

'Thank you, Señor.' Maroto seated himself.

The Old Man referred to typewritten notes, then looked across the desk at Maroto. He saw a man about forty years, tall and thin with a dark face and piercing eyes. His neck was too long and, as though conscious of it, he hunched his shoulders which made him look strangely like a hungry vulture.

'You've a good record, Maroto,' said the Old Man. His sharp eyes collected the basic data from the typewritten sheet. 'You served as lieutenant in North Africa when our leader launched our sacred crusade, commanded Moorish troops with distinction, served in the Vizcaya campaign and were at the Ebro. Twice wounded and decorated and ... where were you wounded, Maroto?'

'Once in the chest and once in the thigh.'

'Badly?'

'The chest wound smashed a rib and collapsed a lung. I was in hospital three months. The thigh wound was shrapnel. The bone wasn't touched.'

'When you left the army you were recommended for secret police work.'

'That's right, Señor.'

'You have excellent recommendations, I see. You have influential friends, Maroto?'

'My family has always been traditionalist in politics, Señor.'

The Old Man pushed himself back in his chair and looked keenly at Maroto. His eyes were so sharp and his face so alive that if it had not been for his silvery hair he would have seemed a young man. 'I've picked you for a tough job, Maroto.'

Maroto smiled. 'I am honoured, Señor.'

'These damned counter revolutionaries.'

'Yes, Señor?'

'They want to fight the revolution all over again. It's time we put men with military experience up against them.'

'You mean ... Scarface and his gang, Señor?'

'Catalan bandits,' growled the Old Man.

'Yes, Señor.'

'They've got to be stopped,' thundered the Old Man. His eyes glowed. 'They're bank robbers and murderers, criminals of the worst type. But they're more dangerous than ordinary criminals. They're masquerading as a People's Army. The only way to stop their activities is to deal with them in a military fashion.'

'You mean ... impose martial law?'

The Old Man scowled. 'A declaration of martial law won't help. It wouldn't look good in the foreign press either. These guerillas are a cancer, Maroto. They've got to be cut out. But the less fuss while doing it the better. No publicity. They mustn't be called revolutionaries. They're bank robbers and that's a job for the Secret Police.'

'What are your wishes, Señor?'

'Take over, Maroto. Choose the men you need. The Civil Guard will give you any assistance you require. Your primary objective is to stop these guerillas quickly and quietly. If you have to step outside the law, that's at your discretion. I don't want you to be hampered by red tape. Make them talk!'

'I'll need an authority signed by you, Señor.'

The Old Man picked up an envelope and flipped it across the desk. 'Here's everything you need, signed and sealed.' He stood up and stretched his hand across the desk. 'Good luck, Maroto. Good hunting.'

'Thank you, Señor,' said Renato Maroto. He looked very tall and very thin now that he was standing. He held his head slightly to one side with his long neck still hunched into his shoulders.

2

The garage was on the outskirts of the town near the main highway to Toulouse. It was a long, two-storey building with accommodation for two hundred cars and bays for oiling, greasing and car washing. The name painted above the entrance was: GARAGE BACHET and in the office of the Town Hall the proprietors were listed as Miguel and Catalina Bachet.

It was dark when Jean-Luis arrived. He knocked on the glass window of the garage office and Miguel took off his warehouseman's coat with the name 'Bachet' blazoned across its front and hung it on a peg. 'Take over, Charles,' he said in bad French to the short, balding little man at the enquiries window. 'I won't be back tonight.'

Miguel and Jean-Luis walked down the path which ran alongside the garage to the rear of the building where a steep flight of steps led up to the first floor. The door was bolted on the inside and didn't open until Miguel had been studied through a spyhole.

This first-floor room was wide and spacious and ran almost half the length of the garage. There were racks of rifles and hand grenades, bren guns and boxes of ammunition stacked neatly round the walls. There were mines, walkie-talkies and sticks of explosives. Most of the material was United States

91

issue, stolen by G.I.s and sold cheaply. Pinned round the walls were detail maps of the mountainous frontier between France and Spain and picture diagrams showing the component parts of weapons so that they could be taken apart and reassembled. A large framed picture of Lenin was draped with red bunting and along one whitewashed wall was the slogan: 'They Shall Not Pass' printed in blood-red letters. In one corner stood a pirate radio station.

Eight men and two women were awaiting them. One of the women was Catalina, wearing a black jersey and black ski-pants. She smiled at Miguel when he entered and the stern lines of his face softened momentarily. He'd visited a plastic surgeon in Switzerland and the ridged, red welt which had scarred his cheek was now only a hair-fine, white line.

Jean-Luis said crisply: 'I've had a word from Pivot and clinched the final arrangements, comrades. We'll check through once more to make sure everyone understands his part.' Jean-Luis crossed to a wall map and the others gathered round him.

'We hit next Thursday afternoon, comrades,' he said crisply. 'We set off tomorrow night, cross the border and hide out during the day on Comrade Pivot's farm. Then we disperse, each group making its own way to Barcelona. It's to be at one forty-five, so everyone please synchronise their watches with the radio. They're making it difficult for us, comrades. An armed guard sits inside all the banks and one stands outside. No car is allowed to park within fifty yards of any bank entrance.' Jean-Luis's eyes flicked to Clara and Catalina. 'It's up to you two to persuade the Civil Guard who's outside to step inside. When he does, you all go into action. Now ... we can't expect to make a big haul. The banks now keep their money permanently in a central safety vault. All we'll get will be the day's takings. But our objective is to show the masses that we mean business. They'll know we're using the money to buy arms to fight for freedom.'

The others listened intently.

'Any questions?' asked Jean-Luis.

'If things go wrong, Comrade?'

'Use your own initiative. Avoid capture at all costs! If they take you alive they'll make you talk!'

'We'll be armed,' said Miguel succinctly.

3

It was nearing the bank's closing time and the grey-uni-formed guard outside the entrance noticed how last-minute clients hurried to get in before the doors closed. There was a rush of businessmen with briefcases, two uniformed messengers and two nuns. Nuns visited business houses pleading for charity for orphans and their unselfish requests were seldom refused. The guard eased the strap of his tommy-gun, squared his shoulders and glanced casually along the pavement. The sun was overhead and it was hot, but it would soon be time to break for lunch. He looked at his watch. Not long now and the bank porter would close the doors. The guard stifled a yawn, glanced down at his heavy boots and shiny leggings and spat thoughtfully at a winged ant scurrying across the pavement.

Then he became aware of the nun, eyes wide and worried and hands fluttering nervously. Her face was very white and pure against the blackness of her veil. 'Please come at once, guard. Your companion is ill. He's asking for you.' She gulped. 'He is dying, I fear . . . a stroke!'

He couldn't believe that big and powerful Pedro could be tak⸻ ⸻ssible. Pedro with his flushed face . . . ⸻ . . . a blood clot lodging in the ⸻ pushed in through the swing ⸻ wooden bench. He hurried

⸻and

from his shoulder and spun round threatening everyone within range. 'I don't want to hurt anybody. Just back up against the wall quickly.'

With her nun's robes rustling loudly, Catalina was pushing small wedges of wood under the door. Clara was lowering the blinds as though the bank was shut.

Miguel snatched up the other tommy-gun when the second Civil Guard went down. The guard's head had hit the marble floor solidly and at once blood ran from his ears.

The onlookers were terrified. They pressed back against the walls, eyes fearful and their trembling hands raised high above their heads.

Miguel and Marin covered the bank clerks and clients while their companions vaulted the bank counter and scooped currency and coins from the tellers' tills. Clara and Catalina helped, their nuns' habits swishing loudly.

'Don't worry, Comrades,' Miguel reassured everyone. 'We won't hurt you. We fight only the people's oppressors.' He nodded down at the dead guards.

Worried eyes stared at him, fac... ...re dry. Nobody was reassured.

'We fight for liberty,' Mi... 'We rob your fascis... freedom.'

clients hurried to get in before the doors closed. There was a rush of businessmen with briefcases, two uniformed messengers and two nuns. Nuns visited business houses pleading for charity for orphans and their unselfish requests were seldom refused. The guard eased the strap of his tommy-gun, squared his shoulders and glanced casually along the pavement. The sun was overhead and it was hot, but it would soon be time to break for lunch. He looked at his watch. Not long now and the bank porter would close the doors. The guard stifled a yawn, glanced down at his heavy boots and shiny leggings and spat thoughtfully at a winged ant scurrying across the pavement.

Then he became aware of the nun, eyes wide and worried and hands fluttering nervously. Her face was very white and pure against the blackness of her veil. 'Please come at once, guard. Your companion is ill. He's asking for you.' She gulped. 'He is dying, I fear . . . a stroke!'

He couldn't believe that big and powerful Pedro could be taken. But it *was* possible. Pedro with his flushed face . . . perhaps high blood pressure . . . a blood clot lodging in the brain. . . . He ran up the steps, pushed in through the swing doors and saw Pedro lounging on a wooden bench. He hurried over to him.

'Are you all right, Pedro?'

Pedro looked up in surprise. He drank heavily off duty and his fleshy features were flushed. He said irritably: 'Of course I'm all right. Why shouldn't I be?'

'There was a nun who . . .' The guard glanced round and was reassured to see the nun standing behind him. 'Didn't you say Pedro was ill?'

The nun frowned. 'There must be a misunderstanding.'

'I was outside and you came up to me and said Pedro was ill!'

A small crowd was gathering round them.

'I asked if you and your companion would donate to the orphans' fund,' said the nun.

The guard stared at her incredulously. Either she was mad or he was. Then he became aware of the men who hemmed him in and the sharp pressure against his back. The shot was muffled by clothing and his shocked brain wondered that he felt no pain until he heard Pedro's choking grunt. It was instantly drowned by another shot which he heard this time with his body instead of his ears. The pins and needles in his spine detached his limbs from the swift darkening of his vision.

Marin, dressed as a messenger, eased Pedro's tommy-gun

from his shoulder and spun round threatening everyone within range. 'I don't want to hurt anybody. Just back up against the wall quickly.'

With her nun's robes rustling loudly, Catalina was pushing small wedges of wood under the door. Clara was lowering the blinds as though the bank was shut.

Miguel snatched up the other tommy-gun when the second Civil Guard went down. The guard's head had hit the marble floor solidly and at once blood ran from his ears.

The onlookers were terrified. They pressed back against the walls, eyes fearful and their trembling hands raised high above their heads.

Miguel and Marin covered the bank clerks and clients while their companions vaulted the bank counter and scooped currency and coins from the tellers' tills. Clara and Catalina helped, their nuns' habits swishing loudly.

'Don't worry, Comrades,' Miguel reassured everyone. 'We won't hurt you. We fight only the people's oppressors.' He nodded down at the dead guards.

Worried eyes stared at him, faces were pale and lips were dry. Nobody was reassured.

'We fight for liberty,' Miguel said fiercely. His eyes blazed, 'We rob your fascist oppressors to buy arms to fight for freedom.'

Frightened eyes stared at him from shocked faces.

They left the bank as it had all been planned. Miguel first, followed by two business men and then a uniformed messenger, all carrying briefcases. The two nuns stood outside the almost closed door of the bank to lull suspicion while Marin and others inside kept the bank clerks covered.

Miguel strode along the road, turned sharply to the left and crossed to a parked car with false number plates. The driver started up the engine as Miguel and his companions climbed inside. 'Don't drive like a madman,' warned Miguel.

The driver pulled away from the curb and Miguel gave the car parked behind it a signal. The two cars slowly rounded the corner and speeded up. Miguel's car drove on straight past the bank but the second car slowed to a standstill. The bank door opened and other men carrying briefcases hurried down to the waiting car.

Marin was the last to leave. 'I don't want to kill anybody,' he warned. 'But if anyone puts his head outside this door within the next ten minutes, I'll blow it off.' He unloaded the tommy-gun, placed it on the floor and slipped outside. The two nuns followed him across the pavement, their presence reassuring to anyone suspicious of seeing a car parked before a bank.

Marin climbed into the car and beckoned urgently to Clara and Catalina. They crossed the pavement solemnly, serene and pure in their white headdresses, black veils and flowing robes.

One of the bank's clients who'd found himself lined up against the wall was a Falangist and an ex-Nationalist soldier. He had a gun permit and carried a small automatic. It nestled neatly in his jacket pocket and he burned with frustration as the robbers left the bank one by one. But as soon as the door had shut behind the last of them he raced to the nearest window. It was too high to see out of so he ran for a teller's stool, carried it to the window, climbed up on it and looked out through the thick glass. A car was drawn up at the curb, one nun was climbing into it and the other was behind her, pushing her gently.

The Falangist smashed the window with his pistol butt, swore when a slither of glass lanced his hand and aimed carefully. He squeezed the trigger only once. He'd cut a tendon and the gun fell from his nerveless hand as it poured blood.

Clara was almost into the car when the shot rang out.

Catalina was just behind her, stooped over. The bullet hit her between the shoulders, ripped through her neck, severed an artery and tore out through the hollow of her throat. She went down on her knees, blood spraying from her in a miniature fountain.

Her companions didn't realise what had happened. 'Hurry,' they urged. 'Hurry!'

She was numbed and frightened by the sound of her blood pattering on the pavement.

'She's been hit,' choked Clara.

'Pull her inside,' ordered Marin.

'We'd better get out of here quick,' said Adolfo, the driver. His white face was wet with sweat.

'Grab her,' ordered Marin, who was farthest from the door.

Hands reached out to seize Catalina but from down the street came the staccato rattle of a tommy-gun as an alert Civil Guard fired into the air to raise the alarm.

Adolfo acted without thinking. He slammed in the gear, let up the clutch and the car shot away with the open door swinging wildly.

'Are you crazy?' roared Marin. 'You've left her behind!'

'Do you want us all killed?' Adolfo hunched over the steering wheel, driving desperately.

They looked behind at the swiftly receding black-robed figure kneeling on the pavement. The tommy-gun burst had spread the alarm and people were running to her. As the first man reached her, she slowly slid forward on her face into a pool of blood.

The cars raced out of Barcelona and on to Badalona where they garaged them in a warehouse belonging to a comrade and spent the hours until it was dark. The radio made only a brief mention of the raid. A gang of criminals had murdered two guards while robbing a bank. A woman accomplice had been shot dead.

They waited until the early hours of the morning before they set off again. Miguel hardly spoke. He radiated the bitter hatred that burned within him.

'You left her,' he told the others tonelessly.

'There was nothing else we could do, Comrade. If we had carried her into the car we would all have been killed!'

They drove on through the night, their headlights boring a tunnel through the tree-lined roads. Presently, ahead of them, a red light was waved from side to side.

Two Civil Guards with bicycles had stopped them, their patent leather tricornios shining in the car headlights as it braked to a standstill in the centre of the road. The guards stood one each side of the car. 'Your papers, please,' asked one, stooping to look inside.

'They're here,' said Miguel. He brought up the Sten gun from between his knees and fired a burst which all but cut the man's head from his shoulders. Nolana fired his pistol at point blank range into the other guard's chest.

They drove on.

Twice more they came upon patrolling Civil Guards. Each time they stopped and when the Civil Guards came over to them they gunned them down.

'Take it easy, Comrade,' urged Marin. 'I know you're upset about Catalina, but it won't help our cause to become a bunch of murderers.'

'There's only one way to deal with fascist swine,' said Miguel tonelessly. 'Kill them!'

Later that night they hid their cars in a barn belonging to a sympathiser, changed their clothes and tramped off into the mountains. Twelve hours later they were back in France.

4

'This way, Señor,' said the grey-uniformed attendant and Renato Maroto followed him down the stone steps to the basement and along a wide corridor to the iron door at the far end. The attendant swung the door back slowly until it clanged against the brick wall and switched on the lights.

The walls were whitewashed, the floor was concrete and the air was dank. Maroto felt the cold strike through his thin, summer suit and the sweat at his armpits turned icy.

There were three marble slabs but only one was occupied. Respectfully, the attendant pulled back the sheet to show the corpse's face.

'Strip her, man,' snapped Maroto. 'We don't use delicacy with scum!'

The attendant pulled the sheet right down.

Renato Maroto stood staring, his long dark face brooding and his shoulders hunched. His thin nostrils quivered, stung by the smell of formalin and antiseptic, and deep down in his mind a chord of memory was lightly touched.

She was about thirty, a strong, wiry girl with firm flesh. A peasant type who'd worked hard and grown tough. Her body was wax-like and the wound in her throat a small black plug of congealed blood. But even in the coldness of death her breasts were flabby pouches, pocked and pitted with the scars of surgeon's knives. Her abdomen bore the ridged scars of many major operations. Her long, black hair was drawn back tightly into a bun and her cold face was serene. She would have been attractive but for the scar on her cheek which pulled down her eyelid until it drooped, giving her a sinister appearance. He looked at her fingers. The nails were short, but he saw no work callouses. He looked at her face and again memory stirred as he tasted the hot dust of Andalucia, saw the shiny faces of grinning Moroccan soldiers, felt the bitter hatred for the Reds who'd killed his brother and smelled iodine.

He knew then why his memory had been stirred. This one lying here naked recalled those other red bitches who had also been starkly exposed. This one was dead, but those others had been alive ... for a time.

'Spawn of a whore,' he growled at the corpse. He stooped over her, shoulders hunched like a vulture about to peck at its prey and spat upon the cold flesh.

The attendant's face was impassive, but his eyes were shocked.

'Red scum,' Maroto snarled.

'Si, Señor,' agreed the attendant bleakly.

'Cover her up,' said Maroto. 'I've seen all I want of the Red whore.'

All the witnesses of the bank raid had been detained and statements taken. Maroto studied them and personally interviewed some of the witnesses.

'I'll see Señorita Bolero next,' he told the guard. 'Don't bring

97

her here. I'll see her in ... private!'

He kept her waiting an hour before he strolled along the corridor to the interrogating room. The suspense of waiting always made people jittery even though they were innocent.

At a gesture from Maroto, the guard unbolted the door and held it open. Maroto stepped into a bare, windowless room with a solitary chair bolted to the floor below the arc lamp. The door shut behind him and he studied the seated girl speculatively. She was mousy, wore thick-lensed glasses and had a large mole on her cheek. She was scared and her stubby fingers nervously twisted a moist strip of handkerchief. She wore a plain grey dress over her dumpy figure and her legs were thick and unshapely.

He said curtly: 'I've read your statement and there are some questions I must ask you.'

She pleaded, 'Will it take long? My parents expected me home long ago. They'll be worried.'

'You'll leave when I've finished with you,' he said flatly.

'It's almost midnight and mother will be terribly worried. If I can send a message...?'

'Hold your tongue,' he snapped so fiercely that she at once lapsed into silence.

'You say you recognised one of the men who entered the bank? You say his name is Marin?'

She nodded unhappily, regretting she had remembered anything.

'Tell me about Marin.'

'It's all in my statement,' she sighed. 'He used to live across the road from me just before the war. But we moved away and I haven't seen him since.'

'Tell me about him. What does he look like? What did he do? Who are his friends?'

'It's so long ago,' she wailed. 'It's hard to remember, and I'm tired. I haven't had a thing to eat. They wouldn't even give me a drink of water.'

He stood beside her and his long fingers gathered up the hair at the nape of her neck and held it tightly.

She sat petrified.

'You'll answer my questions, do you understand?'

'Yes,' she whispered.

'Murderers won't run around loose because you're too tired to talk. Understand?'

'Yes.' Her eyes watered as he increased the pressure on her hair, pulling her head back. His long, dark face was poised like the rending beak of a vulture.

'Tell me about him. What did he look like?'

98

She talked, telling all she could remember, even trivial and unimportant details. Two hours elapsed before he was satisfied.

'That's all,' he told her. He yawned and stretched himself then walked to the door and knuckled it.

The girl asked with relief. 'May I go now?'

He watched her with dark, sombre eyes while the guard unbolted the door. 'You'll have to stay,' he said.

Her eyes widened. 'What more can I do? I've told you everything I know. The only reason I was in the bank is because I work there!' Hysteria edged into her voice. 'I've done nothing! I want to go home. I want to see mother!'

'You'll go home,' he promised. 'We'll release you in a few days when we capture Marin.'

Her eyes rolled. 'A few days!' A frantic note rang in her voice. 'I've done nothing. Please don't keep me here. I want to go home!'

He nodded to the guard. 'Keep her on ice.' He walked away quickly leaving the guard to take whatever steps he thought necessary to quieten the girl.

During the following days records were painstakingly checked, the secret police interviewed dozens of people and asked subtle questions and a thick dossier was built up about Marin. He'd been a left-wing university student, president of the debating society and author of fiery articles in a splinter-group political magazine. Official records were searched and photographs of him as a young man were found. These were reproduced and nearly all the witnesses of the bank raid recognised Marin's photograph.

Maroto gave precise orders to the captain of the Civil Guard. 'This is the first time we've had a clue to the identity of any of these criminals. If I get my hands on one, he'll lead me to the others, If that Red whore hadn't died she'd have talked by now.'

The captain looked doubtful. 'They're the martyr type. They'd rather die than betray their comrades.'

'Let me get my hands on Marin,' said Maroto grimly. 'He'll talk!'

The captain looked sceptical.

Maroto took a pair of pliers from his pocket. His long, dark face was satanic. 'I'm not squeamish, Captain. When these tighten on a man's *cojones*, he'll talk. He'll sacrifice his mother!'

The captain looked away quickly. 'What are your orders?' he asked tonelessly.

'A dog always returns to its vomit. In a few days, in a few weeks or even a few months, Marin will visit his mother and sister. Their flat must be watched day and night. Study its location carefully and take over three or four flats with a dominating view of the one we're interested in. Set up a secret day and night watch. When Marin shows up I want him taken alive.'

The captain said doubtfully: 'It's a thickly populated area. Innocent people will get hurt if a gun fight starts.'

'As soon as Marin shows up, call me and I'll take over,' said Maroto.

5

Teresa had listed fifteen neighbours with double rooms to let. But Robert Tweed had written that he could send her ten times as many guests. She had a feeding problem too. There was no room big enough in the village for more than twenty people to dine at table. And even if such a room had been available it would still need a large kitchen.

Teresa spent hours figuring with a pencil and paper. One day she left the shop, walked to the far end of the village and along the beach. She called a cheerful 'Bon dia' to Hernando who sat outside his stone-built hut repairing a fishing net and walked on until she reached the sand dunes. She stood on them and sent a long, searching glance round her. The white beach of silvery sand stretched along the bay as far as she could see. In the other direction, only two hundred yards away, was the village. In the winter when the great gales blew, the sea swamped over the beach and flooded the low land between the village and where she stood. The high ground upon which she stood became then an island, a long wide bar of sandy soil stretching for more than a kilometre, tufted with coarse, yellow grass and yellow weeds.

The owner of the land was a widow who lived in Figueras. Teresa went to see her.

'But why do you want to buy worthless land, my child?' asked the widow. 'Nothing can grow there. Even the weeds are poor, starved things.'

'I am thinking of building a house,' said Teresa carefully.

'A house! Are you mad, child? Surely you know that with the winter storms the land becomes an island.'

'That happens for only a few days each winter. And it is not difficult to wade across to the village.'

'If you have thought about it carefully then I will sell.' The widow's eyes were sharp. 'How much do you offer?'

'As you have pointed out,' said Teresa. 'The land is use-less . . .'

'You don't expect me to give it away!'

'I have thought about it in this way,' said Teresa. 'I will pay a good price for the land, but I will not pay all the money at once. I will need eleven years to pay you. Each year I will pay a tenth of the purchase price. Any year I fail to pay, the land will revert to you and I will forfeit what I have paid.'

'The conditions are fair if we agree upon the price,' said the widow. 'But have you talked this over with your husband, child?'

'I will do so when I know I can reach agreement with you,' said Teresa, and smiled.

The widow chuckled. 'Since you are set on this madness, go and talk to him because we will not quarrel over the price.'

But Teresa did not at once speak to Narcisus. Instead she went to her father.

'Do you know Widow Bruton's land just along the beach, Father?'

He was painting his boat. He was shirtless and the muscles of his brown arms rippled as he stooped to load the brush and then drew it smoothly along the scraped, bare wood until it glistened green. 'I know it.'

'I can buy it cheaply, paying only ten per cent every year.'

He glanced up quickly and then deliberately turned back to his work. He made no comment.

'If the land is mine I can build on it,' she said.

He made long, skilful strokes with the brush. The new paint gleamed brightly. 'Have you not a house big enough to live in?'

'I want to build a big house, Father. Twenty bedrooms overlooking the sea with a terrace and a large dining room and a big kitchen.'

'What nonsense are you talking now?'

She forced herself to speak calmly. 'Big changes are coming, Father. We can be among the first to reap the benefits and earn money.'

'Have you not learned that the only happy man is one without a shirt to his back?'

'I am not thinking of myself, Father. I have Leon and perhaps ... there may be other children. There is also Pepita.'

'I have two strong hands. Neither Pepita, your mother nor any of your children will go hungry while I can work.'

She said quietly: 'You will not live for ever, Father. What will happen to Pepita then?'

His paintbrush faltered as he drew it along the curve of the bow. 'So what do you want of me?'

'Money.'

'Money!' he snorted. 'What money have I?'

'I am not deceived, Father. You work hard buying fish and live simply, saving every peseta. You have money in the bank.'

'If I have money in the bank it's no business of yours, girl!' he said gruffly. 'It is for Pepita and you others if the need should arise. It is only a little and not to build great hotels or even think of it!'

'You have more than the money you've saved, Father. There is the cottage, the vineyards and the olive grove. I have talked to the manager of the Savings Bank and he will lend money against these properties. You take out a mortgage and it is twenty years before you must repay.'

Paco Barras exploded. 'What is this talk of borrowing money! I owe no man. I'm not a slave or a pauper. I look every man in the eye. I have no debts. Nor will I yield to . . .' Paco Barras broke off. Teresa had braced herself to receive this expected tirade and was staring stonily at the sand while his words washed over her.

'Don't wear that face!' he snapped.

'I'm sorry, Father. I'm your daughter. Don't you think I know how you feel about owing money?'

'Well then?'

He resumed painting. Minutes passed and he still could not trust himself to speak.

'I have talked to Juan the Builder,' she said simply. 'He says that labour is very cheap. Everyone wants work. Materials are not expensive either. There's a quarry on the other side of the village and dynamite will break out the rock needed for construction. He too will mortgage his house and his vineyard to get the capital. Then when the house is built it can be mortgaged and the builder paid!'

Paco Barras's paintbrush slapped furiously, expressing his suppressed anger. Yet he was strangely willing to be convinced.

'I don't deny it's a risk,' said Teresa. 'But all of life is a risk. We'll get co-operation from everyone. I can build this hotel if you'll mortgage your property and lend me some money. Juan the Builder will give me credit and Narcisus can get loans against the shop and the olive groves. I've calculated it a hundred times, Father. If we get tourists, Father, we'll soon pay back every penny.'

'And if it is a failure, Daughter?' He thrust his brush into the paint pot and recklessly spattered the sand as he slapped the brush furiously up and down the woodwork.

'Then we will be unhappy, Father,' she admitted. After a

102

pause she added. 'But we will not have been too cowardly to have taken the risk.'

Paco Barras scuffed the sand with his bare foot, covering up the fallen paint. Then with great care he trimmed the brush on the edge of the paint pot and drew the bristles along the side of the boat in a swift, sure stroke which left no brush marks.

'Well, Father?'

'I've never owed anyone a penny!'

'I'm not asking about the past, Father. I'm talking about the future.'

'Don't come here arguing with me, Daughter,' he stormed. 'You know you can wheedle anything you want out of me.'

Teresa gave a secret smile. 'Then I can go ahead, Papa?' Calling him Papa was like a hug of gratefulness.

'You're a mad one, Daughter,' he said, shaking his head in despair. 'A mad one!'

Paco Barras had enough money to pay the first instalment on the land. The mortgages on his house and vineyards plus the property of Narcisus's family got the building started.

Juan, the builder, had a friend in Barcelona who was an architect. He was young and bursting with modern ideas. He visualised for Teresa an hotel with streamlined curves and walls of glass.

'It will cost you more,' he warned. 'Also you must look ahead. You must prepare for success. Dig your foundations deep and make them wide and solid. Cement beams are not good enough. Use iron girders. If you build only one storey it is expensive. But if you build six, seven or eight storeys, as they build on the French Riviera, you will have your solid foundations already laid.'

'Iron girders then,' said Teresa recklessly. 'Deep foundations.'

Mortgages were arranged and contracts signed. The land flanking the beach became Teresa's in name and the foundations were dug. Workmen grew suntanned as they laboured in the hot sun and expensive iron girders were brought down from Barcelona.

Every day Teresa walked along the beach and watched her dream take shape. Sometimes she had qualms and was afraid her optimism had inspired unjustified recklessness in her father and others. Every day too, Paco Barras came to see the building and walked away shaking his head sadly.

But Teresa's correspondence with Robert Tweed was reassuring. The hotel must be ready for June, he insisted. He guaranteed every room would be occupied until the end of September. She must not fail him, he urged. The hotel must have all conveniences and showers in every double bedroom.

Juan, the builder, worked his men sixteen hours a day. All through the autumn and winter the work went on ceaselessly and in spring the painters, decorators and electricians were encouraged by an untiring Teresa.

On the first of June the first group of English tourists arrived in Escoleras escorted by a Spanish-speaking English guide. They were welcomed by a smiling Teresa and Narcisus. The kitchen was beautifully equipped and a dozen village girls were dressed in white and blue striped dresses with big red bows in their hair and lacy white aprons tied round their waists. They lacked experience, but made up for it with enthusiasm. They talked to the tourists in Catalan and with smiling gestures. And the tourists, enchanted by the sun, the blue Mediterranean and the simple friendliness of the Catalans, delighted in trying to understand them.

'How goes the business?' Paco Barras asked Teresa one day.

'I've been wanting to talk to you seriously, Father. We've twenty double bedrooms. That means forty guests. They pay us double what it costs to have them. It's good business and if it continues we shall grow rich.'

'I do not wish to be rich, Daughter. I want only that my children are happy.'

'We *are* happy, Father. So I beg of you, leave the business side to me and I will deal with it.'

'We must not forget Pepita.'

'Father! I've more than a hundred orders for her mosaics.'

'Then I am happy too, Teresa. Talk to your mother and tell her how good things are.'

'And how are things with you, Father? Are you still fishing?'

He looked at her laughingly. 'I have no need of an hotel to bring a happy flush to my cheeks!'

'You do not yet need the money I borrowed?'

'Have you not said things are going well? So why can you not repay me?'

'Business prospers or it withers and dies,' she said. 'Business cannot stand still.'

He eyed her warily. 'What now then?'

'Another twenty bedrooms. A playground and a paddling pool for children at the back of the hotel. A long bar and an open air dance floor for dancing in the evening under the trees.'

'Trees!' he scoffed. 'Where are the trees?'

'I'll bring palm trees from Andalucia where they have so

104

many they give them away. I'll sink their roots deep and pack good fertile soil from the valley round them.'

'Forty bedrooms,' he snorted. 'Trees. A garden and a dance floor! What do *you* know about the hotel business and its problems?' He spoke gruffly, but she sensed his pride in her.

'This is only the beginning, Father. Our guests are delighted, the weather is perfect and they love our food. Meat is still rationed in England, Father. They're delighted that they can eat here as much as they want.'

'Only because it's too expensive for most of us to buy,' said Paco Barras quickly.

'But to the English it's cheap, Father.'

'Do what you will then,' he sighed. 'Use my money if you must. I urge only that you do not ruin me.'

'Do not worry, Father. Your money is safe.'

'When you have lived as many years as I have, you will know nothing is safe.'

'Then I will tell you this in confidence, Papa, so that you will not worry. Businessmen from Gerona have visited me. All the Costa Brava is being opened up for tourists. The land I bought upon the beach, which I will pay for during ten years, is ideal for building flats. They can be let to foreigners for the summer.'

'Flats!' scoffed Paco. 'A handful of tourists in the village and suddenly it's a European invasion.'

'Time will show, Father,' said Teresa placidly. 'The men from Gerona will pay me double what it cost for the land.'

'Then sell it and make a good profit.'

She shook her head, smiling secretly. 'I refused to sell. I have only a little capital invested in it and ten years to pay. Next year I will sell it perhaps, when the price has increased three or four times. Or perhaps even five times!'

Paco Barras threw up his hands. 'How can I understand such madness when worthless land is sold to crazy people for a fortune!'

Leon came running up, his fair hair gleaming in the sun. He was a beautiful child and Teresa watched him fondly as he piped excitedly: 'Take me fishing, Grandpa. *Please* take me fishing.'

The boy spoke in English and ruffling his hair, Paco Barras asked gruffly: 'What's all this gibberish you're telling?'

'It's English, Grandpa. I can speak English now.'

'He spends all day with the English,' said Teresa. 'They make a great fuss of him. He shows them the best places to swim, how to find cockles in the shallow water and takes them for walks along the cliffs to see the caves. I encourage him. I do believe he's becoming bi-lingual.'

'Can you count to ten in English?' asked Paco Barras.

Leon made a disparaging gesture. 'I can count to a thousand!'

'You'll need to and many times over if your mother has her way,' said Paco Barras. His blue eyes twinkled as he held out his hand. 'Come, Leon. You can row while I bait the hooks.'

CHAPTER SIX

1

Two men waited in the stuffy room with the curtains drawn to keep out the sun. Although they were stripped to their underpants sweat gleamed moistly on their bodies. One was stretched full length on an iron cot, the other sprawled in an armchair. A cheap clock on the sideboard ticked loudly. Two tommy-guns were propped against the wall.

Both men were drowsy and negligent of their duty. In the beginning, tension had kept them alert. But as the months passed, the monotonous, uneventful days bored them until they fretted with impatience. They became irritable and relaxed only when the oppressive midday heat made them sleepy.

They were drowsy now after a lunch washed down with wine and when the knock came upon the door, rapping out the signal, neither of them stirred.

The knuckles rapped again, urgently.

'All right, Alfonso,' said the man sprawled in the chair. 'I'll get it.' He padded barefoot to the door of the flat and opened it cautiously.

The caller slipped inside quickly, his black eyes bright with excitement. 'He's here!' he choked. 'He's *here*!'

'Who's here?'

'Who do you think, Pedro. It's Marin. He's here!'

Pedro stared at him. He wiped the palm of his hand up his hairy torso and stared stupidly at his sweat-beaded fingers. 'Marin's here?' he said dully. Then he spun round, raced to the living room, crouched down at the window and stared out through a peephole cut in the curtains.

The window of the flat opposite was curtained as it usually was.

He straightened up. 'You startled me, Juan.'

Juan said grimly: 'We haven't all been taking a siesta. Marin's in there, I tell you. Marin ... or some other man. I saw him myself!'

The man on the bed swung his legs round off it and rested the balls of his feet on the floor. 'Are you sure, Juan?'

'I can't swear it's Marin. But I saw a man.'

Pedro groaned. 'The entire gang might be in there!'

The man on the bed wiped his arm across his sweat-dewed

forehead. He said quietly: 'This could be the end of all of us. You,' he pointed at Pedro. 'And me.' He tapped his chest with his forefinger.

'Don't be so damned ghoulish,' snarled Pedro.

'Face facts,' said Alfonso. 'This is just a job. We've all got families. We don't want to kill anybody or be killed. But these men are mad. They're not afraid of dying and want everyone to die with them! There's something ... uncanny about them. They never get hurt although dozens have shot at them.'

'You took the job,' growled Pedro.

Alfonso got up and padded across the room to his tommy-gun. He carried it to the table and put it down ready to hand. His face was pale. 'I'll do my job,' he said. 'But I wonder how many of us will get out of this alive.'

His grim acceptance of death was unnerving.

'There's enough of us,' argued Juan. 'Alberto's in our flat keeping the windows covered. Then there's the upstairs flat too. That makes six of us!'

'It's one thing waiting for Marin when he's a sitting duck,' said Alfonso darkly. 'But it's a different thing taking him alive! Do you know how many Civil Guards have been murdered these last few weeks? Do you know how many have been shot in the back at night, up in the mountains? I'm not a coward, but I don't shut my eyes. If Marin's in there he won't be taken without a fight. But if I were Marin I'd rather go down fighting ... than be taken alive!'

Pedro was staring through the peephole. 'No sign of him.'

'What do you expect?' growled Alfonso. 'A red flag waving from the balcony!'

'You've alerted the flat upstairs?' asked Pedro.

'I warned them first.'

'You'd better phone Headquarters.'

Juan frowned. 'I only got a quick glimpse of him.' He smiled wryly. 'You know how it is if you alert Headquarters for nothing. They shout as though you don't know your job.'

'Is his sister in there?' asked Alfonso.

'She hasn't moved out of the flat all day.'

'Nobody else saw Marin?'

'Rudi was downstairs in the cafe. But you know how careless he is. He could have been reading while Marin slipped past.'

Alfonso sighed. 'We'll keep watching until we're sure. Alert Rudi. Perhaps you made a mistake. But if it is Marin, as soon as we're *sure*, we'll ring Headquarters.'

'That makes sense,' said Pedro. He padded through to the bathroom and returned with two towels. He tossed one to

Alfonso and used the other to wipe his sweat-moist chest and armpits.

'Identifying Marin won't be difficult,' mused Alfonso. 'Taking him alive will be tough.'

The others knew what he was thinking. They pictured the door of the flat as they approached it and the blast of sten-gun bullets cutting through the wooden panels.

'Keep watching,' said Juan. There was a film of sweat on his forehead. 'I'll tell them in the apartment upstairs to do the same. Then as soon as we're sure . . .!'

'Perhaps it was a tradesman,' said Alfonso hopefully.

Pedro and Alfonso took fifteen minute spells watching the curtained windows opposite as the heat of the afternoon diminished into the hot humidity of early evening. It was tiring crouched at the window and the temptation to doze was strong. But as it became twilight, Pedro saw the curtain opposite twitch.

He called in a low voice: 'Alfonso. Watch this.' At the same time he raised his tommy-gun.

With one pace Alfonso whipped up his tommy-gun from the table and kneeled beside Pedro. Both Civil Guards watched from either side of their window as the curtains opposite twitched and then parted.

They could see the man only indistinctly in the twilight, shirtless and with his arms spread, holding apart the curtains as though he was drinking in the cool evening air.

'Is it Marin?' whispered Pedro shakily.

'I can't see him clearly,' said Alfonso.

'Step forward, you bastard,' whispered Pedro fiercely as though the man opposite might hear and obey him. 'Let's look at you!'

'It *could* be Marin,' whispered Alfonso. 'Would a tradesman take off his shirt?'

'Don't forget his sister,' said Pedro. 'You know how these Reds are. They're all whores!'

'I want just one glimpse!' breathed Alfonso. 'Just one look at his face.' He sounded as though he was praying. Pedro pictured them advancing up the staircase while Marin fired a burst from his sten-gun through the door and scythed them down.

'You bastard son of a bastard whore,' growled Pedro. 'Let's see your face!'

As though he'd heard him, the man opposite stepped forward until the failing daylight dispersed the shadows that concealed his features. They saw the face they'd seen so many times in blown-up photographs.

'Holy Jesus Christ! It *is* Marin!' choked Pedro and levelled his tommy-gun, his mind hearing the sten-gun bullets splitting through the door panels and tearing him apart.

'Look at him,' choked Alfonso. '*Look* at him!'

The man opposite leaned forward slightly, drawing in the cool air and relishing it. Then he glanced up and his eyes stared straight at Pedro, riveted upon the curtain peephole as though he could see the two men crouched behind it.

Without moving his gaze, Marin's hand went to his trouser pocket.

In that instant of panic, convinced Marin had seen them, the guards lost their heads and triggered their tommy-guns. They nourished a superstitious fear that Scarface's men could not be killed and when the man opposite was blasted back away from the window, they continued firing. Now, from the flat to the inside and from the other guards, all were firing furiously.

In the street below, women screamed and men threw themselves flat. White splinters flew from the shutters opposite, dust and stone chips spurted from the brick surround and ricocheting bullets screamed. The torrent of lead pouring into the room tore plaster from the walls until white dust billowed from the window like smoke. The guards' fingers vibrated on the triggers until the last weapon emptied.

Alfonso's gun was hot in his hands. A spiral of smoke curled upwards from its muzzle and great drops of sweat ran down his cheeks. His black eyes were glazed as he stared at the room opposite. 'Holy Jesus Christ,' he whispered. 'It's Marin. *It's Marin!*'

'Do you think he's had it?' asked Pedro anxiously.

Alfonso crossed himself. 'Please God he's dead!'

Juan burst in on them wildly. 'There'll be trouble about this,' he choked.

Pedro said quickly: 'We've got to stand together. It was self-defence.'

Juan picked up the telephone. 'Holy Jesus Christ!' he said as he dialled.

A contingent of Civil Guards sealed off the surrounding streets. Since the shooting, there'd been no signs of life within the apartment. But they all knew that cornered animals are the most dangerous.

Renato Maroto was icily furious. 'My instructions were precise. I was to be called as soon as Marin showed up.'

The Civil Guard captain was torn between anger with his men and a duty to defend them. 'They explained that . . .' he began.

'We'll deal with the explanations later,' said Maroto grimly.

'Your men started this. They can finish it. Send them upstairs to take a look round.'

The six Civil Guards unhappily reloaded their tommy-guns.

Maroto glared at them. 'Open up that apartment and arrest everybody.'

Apprehensively they climbed the stairs and stood outside the apartment door. They were so cramped in the narrow corridor that their tommy-guns were as much a menace to themselves as to others.

They flattened themselves against the walls on either side of the apartment door and Alfonso pressed the bellpush.

It rang out loudly.

There was no sound from within the apartment.

Alfonso ran his fingers across his forehead and flicked away the sweat drops. He rang the doorbell again.

The stillness of death answered him.

From below Maroto called up through the stairwell: 'What's happening up there?'

'Sweet Mother of God,' prayed Alfonso. He stood at the crossroads of life and death. Inside the flat, crouched down behind a barricade of furniture and mattresses, were desperate men who were waiting to rip him apart with American-made, steel-jacketed bullets.

'Holy Virgin Mary have mercy upon a sinner,' prayed Alfonso devoutly. He nodded at his companions, placed the muzzle of his tommy-gun against the door lock and fired a burst.

The door vibrated beneath the hammering and swung inwards.

The Civil Guards flattened themselves against the walls on either side of the door. They waited, tense, sweating and very much afraid.

'What's going on up there?' roared Maroto.

Alfonso drew a deep breath and made a suicidal leap through the doorway, tommy-gun levelled and eyes searching desperately for the target which he must fire at before he himself was killed.

'What's going on?' yelled Maroto.

Pedro came to the head of the stairs. There was a bleak note in his voice. 'You can come up.'

Maroto and the Civil Guard captain entered the flat, walked along the corridor to the living room and stood staring into it.

Marin lay on the tiled floor in a pool of blood, his chest and head dissolved into a raw, bloody mess. Still seated upright in a chair was Marin's sister. She'd received the brunt of the bullets

111

which had blasted through the window. Blood ran from her as though from a sieve and snaked towards the door.

'Marin's sister!' said the Civil Guard captain. He felt sick.

'She's Red scum like the rest of them,' said Maroto. 'There's no need for tears.'

Juan called from the next room. 'There's an old woman here. She's dead too.'

The old, bedridden woman had died because a ricocheting bullet had freakishly spun into her bedroom and smashed through her ribs above the hip.

'We've got one of the gang at any rate,' said the Civil Guard captain.

'Precisely,' said Renato Maroto icily. 'We've got one!' His hand was in his pocket and his fingers tightened round his pliers. 'And if he'd been taken alive we'd have had the rest of them!'

The men who took away the bodies were inured to unpleasant tasks. They wrapped a cloth round Marin's head, lifted him on to a stretcher and covered him with a sheet. But they were upset by handling Marin's sister. So many bullets had ploughed into her that she was a soggy mass that came apart in their hands.

Nothing was published in the newspapers about the incident and it some days before Miguel Barras learned from underground contacts how Marin had died.

'The Spanish Civil Guards are murderers,' he told his comrades fiercely. 'Marin and his sister will be avenged. We will never cease to fight for liberty.'

2

Señora Cornelia Ledesma was dying.

There was no medical cause. Cornelia Ledesma had lost the will to live and was fading swiftly. She remained in her room shut away from the rest of the household, pale, remote and listless. Anselmo tried to comfort her and interest her in everyday events. But she listened to him detachedly, nodded disinterestedly and quietly faded.

Silvana accepted death as placidly as she accepted everything. She shrugged her shoulders, slumped in her deck chair with her plump legs outstretched and sighed helplessly: 'What can I do?'

Anselmo was ageing rapidly, worried by financial problems, selling off properties to pay debts and irked by Silvana's laziness. She would have lived cheerfully in a pigsty. Although only in his thirties, Anselmo's face was lined, his hair was thinning and his hands trembled nervously.

Señora Cornelia Ledesma became so weak that she couldn't lift her head from her pillow to take nourishment. Pilar and Antonia came from Madrid and spent their days at her side. Manolo, the youngest son, now a student in Barcelona, came home.

Rafael also came.

He swaggered home in his officer's uniform, his riding boots gleaming and his uniform ablaze with medals. His face was brooding and he erected a hostile barrier between himself and his brothers and sisters. He came as a duty, to attend the funeral of his mother and to claim his share of the dwindling estate.

With her family at her side, Cornelia Ledesma died quietly during the night, fading away as gently as a light breeze.

Teresa called to pay her respects and saw the calm, serene features that now knew peace. Death had released her from sorrow. Teresa looked down upon the face of Anselmo's mother, who had wanted what Teresa too had wanted, and cried unashamedly.

Anselmo stood stiffly erect, dressed in black and sadly receiving friends and relatives who gave him their sympathy.

'I'm sorry, Anselmo,' Teresa choked, her hand in his. It was their first contact for months.

'Thank you, Teresa.' His eyes were moist.

Teresa joined the other women. Many were crying. The older women recalled when Ledesma was lighthearted and gay, remembered their garden parties and their barbecues with Cornelia presiding, gracefully circulating among her guests, skilfully using her black lace fan and imparting an air of culture and wisdom to everything she did.

The house filled up as more and more sympathisers called. Silvana wore a black dress and a suitably sad expression, but she had been too lazy to put on black stockings. Her plump white calves and bedroom slippers aroused the silent resentment of many.

Pilar and Antonia were red-eyed and deeply moved, but Rafael stood apart, smiling sardonically and watching Anselmo with sharp eyes that proclaimed that he wanted a swift settlement of the estate.

Father Delbos and choir boys formed up outside the house and pall bearers carried the coffin down to the hearse. The funeral procession set off and all the men of the village walked bareheaded behind the coffin, following it to the church and then to the cemetery.

The women remained in the house to cry, to comfort each

113

other, to talk reverently about Cornelia Ledesma and to prepare the food and wine for the returning men.

Silvana was happy to leave Pilar and Antonia to cut the
meat and chickens which had been cooked the night before.
Teresa helped, making sandwiches and setting out glasses.

Teresa was alone in the kitchen when Anselmo entered. He
crossed to the kitchen range, where so often as a boy his
mother had cooked before the blazing fire, rested his arm and
his forehead upon the chimney and cried uncontrollably.

Teresa went to him. He held her tightly, his head on her
shoulder. 'My God, Teresa,' he choked. 'My mother. My
mother!'

She comforted him, knowing his misery and crying with
him.

'My mother,' he choked brokenly. 'My mother!'

She pressed him to her.

'I loved her,' he whispered brokenly. 'I loved her.'

'I loved her too, Anselmo,' she whispered. She wanted to
beat her fists against his chest and shout *'How could you have
been so blind?'* Instead she choked, 'I loved her too!'

'Yes,' he whispered. 'We both loved her.'

3

Rosemarie had no appointment that evening so she
showered leisurely and dressed slowly, admiring herself in her
mirror and delighting in the gossamer delicacy of her lingerie.
She took a long time making up her face and varnishing her
nails.

Outside her apartment block she called a taxi and directed it
to one of the most fashionable restaurants in Barcelona. She
caused a minor sensation sweeping into the restaurant, with
her platinum hair tumbling down over her shoulders.

But Rosemarie was accustomed to being stared at. She
walked to a table with queenly aloofness, allowed the head
waiter to take her coat and seated herself with confident grace.
She seemed quite oblivious to the stir she created. She held the
menu with crimson-tipped fingers, studied it with her pencil-
line eyebrows arched critically, and when the waiter hurried
away with her order she glanced round the restaurant, seeing
everyone without seeing them. She took a cigarette holder
from her bag and lit up, coldly indifferent to the eyes which
watched every movement of the exercise. Men watched admiringly. Women eyed her furiously.

Although Rosemarie was modishly dressed, she shouted
'*sex*'. She'd arrived at night and unescorted. Her peroxided

hair and lacquered nails were a feminine lure and although her tightly-fitting black dress was neat and modest with its long sleeves, the cut-away holes under her armpits that revealed the softness of her skin were as shocking as exposed nipples.

After she'd eaten, Rosemarie rose and walked the length of the restaurant to the lounge. She wore very high heels, her skirt was short and her stockings were sheer nylon. She was aware her sinewy movements were watched admiringly and accepted the admiration as her due, as do all beautiful women. She settled in a low armchair, gathered her skirt around her and ordered coffee and brandy from a hovering waiter. There was severe unemployment in Barcelona, shortage of food and little money circulating. But there were still some people who could afford to frequent high-class restaurants. Rosemarie gave a sweeping glance round her as she reached into her bag for her cigarette holder, reassured to know that all the men present were watching her covertly.

She held her cigarette holder gracefully, sipped her coffee and moistened her lips with brandy. Then after a time she became aware of the Man.

There was always a Man.

She noticed this one because he stared more intently than the others. Once, when she glanced towards him casually, his face lighted up eagerly. But her glance swept on, failing to observe him. He would probably be the one, she decided as she took the cigarette holder from her red-painted lips and blew a thin plume of smoke towards the ceiling.

She had only a vague idea what the Man looked like. But then, she never really saw any of them: They'd become faceless, animated objects. This one would be faceless like all the others, neither young nor old, ugly or handsome, stupid or wise!

The waiter brought her a note. The Man invited her to drink with him. Such an invitation sent to a respectable woman would have been an insult. But her manner of dressing and smoking in public proclaimed her profession.

She glanced towards him and smiled. When the waiter set the drink before her she gestured that he should join her.

The Man sat opposite her and said the usual things, that she was attractive, looked intelligent and that her dress was charming. She said the usual things too, smiled at his comments, occasionally gave a low chuckle and preened herself so that he could study the firm thrust of her breasts.

The Man was shy about the basic subject so she raised it herself when he casually mentioned that everything was so expensive these days.

115

'Especially me,' she smiled.

'How expensive?' he asked, emboldened by her bluntness. She told him, and although the corners of his mouth turned down she knew she had him.

'It's too much,' he protested.

She shrugged her shoulders and looked through him, suddenly remote and disinterested.

'Why so much?' he asked.

'I give *complete* satisfaction.'

'You'll make a fuss of me?' he surrendered.

'Of course, darling. You'll have to pay for the room too.'

'Can't we go to your place?'

Her face hardened. 'I *never* take anybody home.'

Having clinched the deal, he became eager: 'Another drink before we go?' he invited, but was pleased when she shook her head.

As soon as they were in the taxi he forced her knees apart and slid his hand up between her thighs.

She concealed her annoyance. 'Don't rush it, darling. We've got all night!' She hated him for handling her as though she were something he'd bought on a market stall.

They went to the 'Green Sanctuary', an expensive 'meuble'. The rooming hotel for lovers took great care that their clients could enjoy their amorous adventures in secret. Wealthy business men brought their secretaries to these love nests, a man could bring his best friend's wife or the wife her best friend's husband. Only high-class whores had clients who could afford to spend the night here.

Not far from the centre of Barcelona the taxi swung in between gate posts and swept up a shrub-lined tarmac drive to a long row of garages. Some of the garage doors were open and above them a green light glowed. The taxi eased into one garage and stopped. The garage doors slid shut and roof lights came on. While they waited, the Man paid the driver. Presently a narrow door opened and a white jacketed steward said impassively: 'Follow me, please.'

They passed through the door into a warmly lit passage with a thickly carpeted floor and followed the steward to the reception desk. They were allocated a room and the steward escorted them up a wide carpeted staircase. There was no chance of meeting other clients on the stairs. Nobody left his room until the steward had made sure that nobody else was around.

The steward opened a door, ushered them inside and checked that all was in order, clean bedsheets turned back, newly laundered towels and hand napkins. He pocketed his tip

116

with suave satisfaction. 'Will you be staying the night, sir?'

'We will. Bring up a bottle of champagne and some glasses.'

'Very good, sir.' The steward smiled. 'May I remind you, sir? We ask all our guests *not* to leave their rooms. If you wish to leave, telephone for a steward who will escort you down to your car or call a taxi for you.'

'I understand, steward. You'd better bring up some sandwiches with the champagne.'

'How's that, darling?'

She smiled automatically. 'Lovely, darling. Lovely.'

The bed was low and large enough for two couples. The crisp, white linen sheets were monogrammed. The walls and the ceiling were lined with mirrors and a panel of switches at the head of the bed controlled the room lighting. It could be blended down from a merciless white blaze to a cosy glow. The background radio music was romantically soothing.

Rosemarie was no stranger to the 'Green Sanctuary'. She put her bag on the bedside table, placed her cigarettes and lighter beside the ashtray, checked that the drawer contained napkins and used one of them at once. She wrapped it round her forefinger and wiped her lips clean of the crimson lipstick. It was a symbolic action, showing her submission to the Man yet forfeiting rights over him. The betraying blonde hairs on his jacket or a smear of lipstick on his shirt collar which could arouse the suspicions of a jealous wife she avoided as assiduously as the Man himself.

She threw the stained napkin into a basket and reached for another. She peered into a mirror, arching her eyebrows as she scrubbed them clean, coaxed mascara from her eyelashes and rubbed the colouring from her cheeks.

The Man was fascinated, flattered that she was stripping her face naked for his protection. 'You *are* ... beautiful, darling,' he breathed.

Her face was strangely pale now and the dark shadows round her eyes made her wan and interesting. 'Do you still want me without my war paint?'

'More than ever.'

'Make yourself comfortable while I undress, darling.'

She posed, stretching her arms above her head and circling her hands gracefully, clicking her fingers like a flamenco dancer. Her black dress exposed the softness of her armpits and she saw the hot gleam in his eyes with unemotional satisfaction. It was a way of life, to enter a bedroom with a stranger and submit her body to his wishes. The pay was excellent and if she paid attention to apparently unimportant details, the Man was greatly satisfied and sought her again.

She unzipped her dress and moved provocatively as she peeled it down over her arms and hips. She was emotionally unmoved, but her acting was flawless. Her eyes, smile and mock-modesty implied a sensuality he believed she shared with him. Her black lingerie was sexy and she teased him skilfully, unclipping stocking lingeringly, peeling nylon slowly down her shapely thighs. She was unhooking her stocking girdle when the steward knocked. She called to him to enter and waited while he placed the champagne and sandwiches on the table. When he left the room she giggled saucily at the Man, unhooked the girdle and gave it to him.

Inevitably he tugged the stocking tabs, let them slap back against his hands and chuckled. She wondered why all men were so childishly alike. She eased her slender petticoat straps off her shoulders and the garment whispered down round her slim calves like a cloud. She took off her brassiere quickly, knowing that complete exposure brought an end to the teasing that pleased men and thrust her breasts at him, laughing joyously as though kneading her nipples into hard prominence gave her exquisite pleasure.

He was deeply aroused. She knew this by instinct without looking at him, knowing too that if she were to meet him in the street the next minute she would not recognise him. She shock-exposed herself, flipping her filmy pants into his face and giggling girlishly as she posed with legs brazenly astride, busy fingers displaying her body's secrets. He blundered to his feet, his cheeks moist and his eyes gleaming.

'Don't rush, darling. I'll go and wash while you get ready.'

She took a ribbon from her bag and ran into the bathroom. She gathered up her hair and tied it in a pony-tail and adjusted the bidet taps to a steady flow of warm water.

He padded into the bathroom and she sensed his moment of surprise when he saw her scarred back. But he made no mention of it as he took the soap from her. 'I'll do this, my love.'

'Aaayeee!' she whimpered in mechanical ecstasy as he washed her. 'Aaaaeeeh!' She leaned back against him, eyes closed, arms hanging limply and his aroused manhood burning against her cool shoulders.

And because she knew his pride would be flattered, she presently whispered: 'No more, my love. No more! You'll tire me out!'

She washed him with a matter-of-factness which cooled his passion, but as soon as they returned to the bedroom he seized her fiercely. She teasingly twisted away, but his hands were strong and his lips whispered down her cheek to her throat. He slobbered when he reached her breast and she arched away from the inner moistness of his mouth, vaguely hoping that *this* Man might have the patience to arouse her. But she was disappointed. All too soon he became compelling and although she used all her skill to prolong his pleasure he was quickly satiated.

Languidly she reached for her cigarette holder and lit up. She blew a thin plume of smoke up at the mirrored ceiling and studied her reflection. She seemed to be looking down on herself with the naked Man doubled up at her side lying in the foetal position.

'How are you, my love?' she asked after a while.

'Wonderful,' he murmured. 'And you?'

'It's never been so good,' she said, and watched the secret smile of pleasure which touched his lips.

Presently she tapped the stub of her cigarette out from the holder, crossed to the table, poured champagne and carried glasses and sandwiches back to the bed.

She ate and drank with relish but he merely nibbled a sandwich and refused more than one glass of the sparkling wine. She replaced the remains of the sandwiches on the table and sat beside him. 'How do you feel now, darling?'

'Very happy, satisfied.'

She giggled. 'You don't look satisfied to me.'

'But I am.'

'I don't believe it.' She touched him. 'There. You see?'

'Don't.'

She pouted. 'I want you.'

'I'm longing to awake and find you in my arms!' he said.

'Tonight too!' she urged.

'Darling. I have my limits.'

'Not with me.' She caressed him.

He became alarmed. 'NO!'

'Don't you like it?'

'You're ... you're wasting your time!'

'Want to bet?' she mocked. 'I'm expensive, darling, but I'm worth it.'

A little later he was astonished that she had aroused him again and as her gasps of ecstasy synchronised with his own he swelled with masculine pride. After the hammering of his heart had ceased he rolled over on his side and almost instantly fell asleep.

Rosemarie sat up, reaching for the glass of champagne, sipped, ran the sparkling wine round her mouth and then swallowed it. She fitted another cigarette in her holder and as she lit it she looked down contemptuously at the Man.

119

She would finish the cigarette, she planned, douche, drink a little more champagne and then sleep. She'd disposed of the Man satisfactorily. Too often in the past she'd had her sleep disturbed by the Man reaching out for her in the middle of the night. She'd learned. Now the Man slept deeply and exhaustedly, his passions so skilfully aroused and dispersed that even in the morning he would not be passionate again.

4

The Cafe Azul was at the not-so-fashionable end of the Ramblas, close to the port and the Christopher Columbus monument. But because its snacks were hot and tasty and its wine good, its customers kept it busy until the early hours of the morning.

This night among its customers were three strangely assorted couples. One pair were clearly professional entertainers. The man wore long, black sideboards and carried a worn, leather guitar case.

The second couple talked intently as though discussing a serious family problem. The man's briefcase looked as though it might contain family wills and legal documents.

The third man had a suitcase. He was about thirty-five years of age, dark-faced and scowling. The woman with him looked sulky and a casual observer would not have been surprised if the man had snatched up his suitcase and walked off. But presently he glanced at his watch, got to his feet and nodded at the woman. She picked up her large handbag and hurried after him. Outside he hailed a taxi.

Five minutes later the musician picked up his guitar and held the door open for his partner. She wore a large handbag slung from her shoulder. They crossed the road to a taxi with a large iron cylinder welded to its side. Petrol was rationed and many taxis had adapted their engines to sawdust combustion. The girl climbed into the taxi, the musician handed her his guitar as though it was precious and climbed in after her. The taxi rumbled up the Ramblas in a thick cloud of blue smoke.

The third couple followed them out, the girl holding the man's arm and looking up earnestly into his face. They walked the full length of the Ramblas to the Plaza de Catalonia before a taxi overtook them and was flagged down.

In a Plaza just off the Mayor de Gracia a dark-eyed man with silvery streaks in his raven black hair sat outside a cafe and moodily sipped brandy. He was at least ten years older than the girl at his side. She had a white, pinched face, strangely burning eyes and thin, colourless lips. They spoke little and presently when he glanced at his watch and nodded, she got to her feet at once.

She held his arm as they walked along the street and when he saw the distant green light of a cruising taxi, he stepped out into the road and held his hand high.

The taxi took them to the 'Green Sanctuary'.

The man paid off the taxi and as they followed the white-coated steward, the girl looked with shy interest at the gilt-framed pictures on the passage walls, the wine-coloured carpeting and the glass tear-drop chandeliers which hung from the corridor ceiling.

When they reached the booking desk, the receptionist gave a searching glance at the pale-faced girl who was so obviously embarrassed. He said gently, 'We cannot accept guests who are under age. By law a girl must be twenty-five. . . .'

'She's twenty-six,' said the man gruffly.

The steward sighed. 'I do not doubt your word, señor. But the law requires me to ask for proof. . . .'

The girl fumbled in her handbag and pulled out her identity card. The steward was surprised. Her age was twenty-six. She didn't look twenty.

'Thank you, señorita.' He returned the card to the girl and reached for an invoice pad. 'Do you require the room for a period or for all night?'

The man glanced at the clock on the wall behind the reception desk. It was two thirty-five a.m. 'We'll take it for the night.'

The steward totalled the invoices. Cost of room, napkins, soap, gratuity for staff and government tax. 'Do you require a condom?'

The man hesitated. 'Yes.'

The cost was added to the bill which was receipted.

The man paid, left the change as a tip and sheepishly thrust the contraceptive into his pocket. As they followed the steward upstairs, the receptionist frowned after them. He was practised at calculating ages and was surprised he could have been so wrong about this girl.

The steward showed them into the bedroom, pocketed their tip and went away. The man slid home the door bolt and relaxed. The bolt gave privacy although, in an emergency, the stewards had a special key to open bolted doors from the outside.

The girl put her handbag on the bedside table, took off her coatee and smiled wryly. 'I felt *terrible*!' she confessed. 'I wanted the earth to swallow me up. I know it's *bourgeois* but I can't help my background, can I? Without reason, I felt . . .

ashamed of myself!'

He took off his jacket and threw it over a chair. He crossed to the bed, sat on it and bounced up and down, testing its springs. 'Shame is a conditioned bourgeois reflex, Comrade,' he said. 'It takes time to escape from conditioning. Lenin said, *"Religion is the opium of the masses."* Guilt feelings about sex result from generations of religious teaching.' His voice was patient as though he was bored with giving the same lesson. He kicked off his shoes, lay back, clasped his hands behind his head and stared up at the ceiling. The bright light showed up the wrinkles round his eyes and the hair-line scar which stretched from his cheekbone to the point of the jaw.

'What time is it, Comrade?' she asked.

He glanced at his watch. 'We've more than an hour. Sleep if you feel tired.'

She kicked off her shoes, sat on the bed, drew up her nyloned legs and tucked them under her. 'I *couldn't* sleep,' she said.

'Too nervous?'

'Too excited ... too tense.'

'Breathe deeply,' he said. 'Learn to relax.'

'When he asked for my identity card I was scared, Comrade.'

'Don't ever worry about identity cards,' he reassured her. 'Only an expert can detect that ours are forgeries.'

She looked round at the mirrored walls, the chromium-plated bathroom fittings and the erotic symbolism of the furniture. 'Have you been here before, Miguel?'

'Twice. I had to study the layout.'

'I mean ... have you ever brought a girl here?'

He hesitated a moment. 'Once.'

After a while she said softly: 'What we're doing is very dangerous, isn't it?'

'I've never pretended otherwise.'

'If everything goes wrong we might ... we might not live through it?'

His dark eyes turned to her.

She looked back calmly.

'Are you afraid?' he asked.

She shook her head. 'No, Miguel. I know the risks and I am ready to die for our cause. It's just that ... in case anything goes wrong ... I want you to know I've always admired you, Miguel. So much so that ... that if you want to make love, I will be happy too.'

His black eyes stared at her and into her.

She flushed. 'Have I said something ... bourgeois?'

122

'No, Maria-Luise. But you've said something very ... disturbing.'

'We're fighting for a new way of life, aren't we, Comrade?' she said fiercely. 'A new economic system, a new philosophy ... free love ... and all that!'

'You're very sweet,' he said softly. But when she moved closer to him, he lay quite still.

'Your father is a much older man than me,' Miguel said. 'He was a sound Party member whom I looked up to and admired. We fought at the Ebro and I was with him at the end when the Civil Guard ambushed us in the mountains.'

Her eyes burned. 'I hate fascism.'

He talked on as though she had not interrupted. 'Your mother escaped to France with a group of refugees, tugging you along by the hand. That is how I always see you, Comrade. As a child who is the daughter of a comrade.'

Her cheeks burned. 'So that's it! You regard me as a child!'

'Don't be angry,' he soothed. 'I'm explaining myself. I have always seen you as a child. But tonight you are a woman and I need time to adjust myself to this new idea.'

'You don't want me?'

'On the contrary,' he said quickly. 'I am deeply honoured. But I am not a good partner. I am old and scarred in mind and body. Often I feel I am not quite ... wholesome.' He held out his hand with his fingers hooked into claws. 'There is a hate inside me that destroys the good. I cannot help it. The ugliness is uncontrollable. I hate bitterly because life has taught me to hate. But this hate is destructive. Yet all I have is hate and I've nothing else to give anyone.'

'You are lonely, Miguel,' she soothed. 'Since you lost Catalina you've become a brooding shadow. You need a woman at your side, Miguel. You need understanding, sympathy and ... love!'

He stared at her intently.

She said softly: 'Miguel, I will try to give you what you need.'

He sighed. 'This is not the time.' His hands clenched into hard fists. 'This is the time for hate!'

She watched his face intently. 'Yes, Miguel?'

'Afterwards, Maria-Luise. ...' His hand fell back on the bed. 'When we have done what must be done ... later!'

'Yes, Miguel,' she said contentedly. She settled herself more comfortably and smiled quietly.

At five minutes to four he put on his shoes and jacket and opened his suitcase. He took from it a long-barrelled pistol, loaded it and dropped it into his pocket.

The girl put on her shoes and looked at him with burning eyes.

'Relax,' he said. 'I'll send for you.'

He stepped out into the corridor and made his way past all the other bolted doors to the head of the stairs. When he reached the floor below he met Adolfo. 'Nice timing,' he said and they went down the next flight to the ground floor.

In the reception office two stewards were playing cards with the receptionist. When they saw the two men they scrambled to their feet and the receptionist said reprovingly: 'We ask guests not to leave their rooms unescorted, gentlemen. It can be embarrassing for other guests. There is a telephone and ...'

Miguel took out his gun and levelled it. The receptionist's eyes widened, and the tip of his tongue moistened his dry lips. The two stewards gaped.

Miguel said softly: 'We won't harm you. Co-operate and you'll have no trouble.'

Adolfo ran his hands over the stewards. None of them was armed. But three long night sticks hung from leather thongs on the back of the door and Adolfo tucked them under his arm. 'These will be useful,' he grinned.

Miguel scowled at the receptionist. 'A lie will cost your life. How many more of you in the building?'

The receptionist gulped. 'Only the relief. He's asleep in the back office.'

'Take us there.'

The back office was a windowless room with a cot. Miguel ordered the stewards to remove their white jackets and he and Adolfo put them on.

Miguel asked one steward, 'What's your name?'

The man swallowed nervously. 'Burgas.'

'All right, Burgas. You come with us.' He jabbed his gun at the others. 'Stay here, keep quiet and you'll stay healthy.'

Miguel locked them in the back office and tapped on the door with the barrel of his gun. 'Can you hear me?'

'Yes,' quavered the receptionist.

'We're going to be around a long time,' warned Miguel. 'One squeak out of any of you and you get lead!'

Miguel and Adolfo, wearing stewards' jackets, returned with Burgas to the reception office.

'How many rooms are occupied?' demanded Miguel.

Burgas studied the key rack. 'Fifteen on the first floor, fourteen on the second and ten on the third.'

'Will you get any more callers tonight?'

'It's not probable, but possible,' said Burgas. 'Perhaps a drunk with a pick-up.'

'When you're full up, how do you indicate it?'

'We turn off the entrance lights over the garages. Then taxis know we've a full house.'

'How do you turn the lights off?'

Burgas pointed to the control panel. 'That's the switch.'

Miguel turned it off and looked up as Greco padded along the carpet towards the office, closely followed by Nolana. Both men carried sten-guns.

'We'll lock the entrance doors, too, Burgas,' said Miguel.

The steward's hands shook slightly as he bolted the doors.

'What's the biggest empty room on the second floor?' demanded Miguel.

'They're all the same size.'

'Is there one without a window?'

'Room two-two-two,' said Burgas.

The five men went up to the second floor, the thick carpeting muffling their footsteps to a whisper. Burgas opened the door and switched on the lights. Miguel glanced round and nodded. 'This will do. Now remember. Work quickly but don't run risks by being negligent.'

They went down to the ground floor and stopped outside the first occupied rooms. Obeying Miguel's orders, Burgas quietly inserted his master-key in the lock and opened the door bolt. He looked at Miguel and nodded.

Miguel turned the handle, stepped into the room, switched on the lights and levelled his pistol. Adolfo closed the door behind them.

The man stirred, grunted and went on snoring. The girl's eyelids fluttered as she screwed up her eyes against the light.

Adolfo went to the foot of the bed, gripped the sheet that covered them and ripped it down.

The girl sat up, startled into wakefulness. The man groped for the sheet which wasn't there, blinked his eyes, became aware that his privacy was invaded and sat up slowly. His face mottled with anger and he tried to cover himself with his hands as though ashamed of his nakedness.

Adolfo grinned savagely and flourished his night stick. 'On your feet, quick,' he ordered. 'And not a sound!'

The girl's eyes were terrified, her gaze hypnotised by Miguel's pistol. The man said with a show of bravado: 'Now what do you think...!'

Adolfo swung the night stick. It cracked loudly against the man's elbow, paralysing it with pain. 'Make a sound and you'll get another like it,' warned Adolfo.

The man hugged his elbow in silent agony.

'Hurry. Or do you want another one,' Adolfo leered at the girl. 'You too, big tits. Get moving.'

The night stick was an ideal weapon. It cracked against the man's shin when he was slow moving and raised a red welt on the girl's shoulder. Miguel opened the door so that Adolfo could herd them outside. The girl hung back. 'Can't I put something on?'

'Why worry?' grinned Adolfo. 'It's not cold.' He flourished the night stick and drove them out into the corridor. Nolana was waiting with his sten-gun. His black eyes were so merciless that the naked couple scampered hastily along the corridor in front of him when he gestured. They climbed the stairs to the second floor and into room two-two-two where Greco was waiting.

'Stand over there,' ordered Greco, pointing with his sten-gun.

The man and the girl crossed the room and stood in a corner. The man rubbed his bruised elbow and the girl gulped as though about to burst into tears.

'Don't make a noise,' warned Greco. 'Otherwise . . .' He grinned viciously and swung his sten-gun, spraying the room with invisible bullets.

'Those rings,' said Greco, slitting his eyes. 'Put them on that table.'

Tears filled her eyes. 'It's . . . my wedding ring.'

'Put it on the table.'

'But . . . please. Have pity. What shall I tell my husband?'

'Tell him the truth.'

She was furious then. She stalked to the table, spent some seconds pulling the rings off her finger and flung them down. One bounced on to the carpet.

'Pick it up,' said Greco ominously.

His tone frightened her and she stooped for it quickly. Her buttocks were too much of a temptation for Greco. He booted her, sending her sprawling on her face. She scrambled up and flashed him a glance which should have killed him.

'Now the earrings,' said Greco.

She took them off and banged them down.

'Back in the corner,' ordered Greco. He leered at the man. 'Your ring now.'

The man rubbed his elbow and glowered sullenly as he pulled off his ring.

Nolana rejoined Miguel and Adolfo. They'd entered a second room and aroused its occupants. Adolfo's swinging night stick drove them out into the corridor and Nolana herded the naked pair upstairs.

Steward Burgas was co-operative. He'd received one clout on the kneecap from Adolfo's night stick and wanted no more. He unbolted the doors with his master key, turned the door handle, switched on the lights and stepped to one side so that Miguel and Adolfo could do their work. Couple after couple were herded upstairs by Nolana.

Maria-Luise and the other girls now played their parts. They ransacked the vacated bedrooms, searched clothing, wallets and handbags and packed money and jewellery into their large handbags.

When Rosemarie was awakened, she was so sleep-drugged that she was only vaguely aware of two threatening figures. She thought it was a police raid, checking for girls under age. The Man was sleepily befuddled. He whimpered when the night stick cracked against his shin. When it dawned upon Rosemarie that the intruders were thieves she was relieved. The contents of her handbag was all they could steal. She'd left her expensive jewellery at home and her savings under the mattress. It wasn't until she was being herded through the door that she saw the man with the pistol clearly. Her memory peeled the years away from his lined face, recognised the weak mouth, long jaw and flashing eyes. She gasped. 'Miguel. You're Miguel!'

His black eyes glittered and the gun jabbed. 'Shut your mouth and keep moving!'

Adolfo swung the night stick and she hurried out. But she dared to glance back and Miguel was scowling after her. His stance was so familiar that she could picture him standing on the beach outside his father's cottage, trousers rolled up to show his bare, brown legs. It *was* Miguel Barras, she realised with amazement as she was herded along the corridor.

Miguel and Adolfo steadily worked their way up to the second floor. Only one man showed any resistance. He leaped for his jacket where he kept a revolver. Adolfo brought him down in mid-leap with a cracked skull and he was led, semi-conscious, to join the others menaced by Greco's sten-gun.

One couple they surprised bathing and laughingly they herded them along the corridor coated with lather.

Miguel found the man he was looking for on the third floor.

He was fifty-five, bald, athletically slim and with clean-cut aristocratic features. His eyes blazed as he sat up in bed and glared at the intruders.

The girl was about twenty-five. She had a voluptuous figure and a simple peasant face. On the bedside table there was a little mound of bracelets, rings and other ornaments.

Miguel told Adolfo: 'Get Nolana.'

Nolana came in and covered the pair in bed with his sten-gun. Adolfo took out a camera.

'Move over,' Miguel told the man. 'I want the two of you side by side.'

The girl grinned foolishly. Her sleep-drugged mind didn't yet feel fear. She moved over and embraced the man. He shrugged her away. 'This is an outrage!' he stormed. 'I'll have you pay ...'

The night stick bounced off his elbow and his face turned pale.

'Snuggle up,' said Adolfo through his teeth.

The man glared.

The night stick swung and the man cried out. 'Snuggle up,' said Adolfo.

The man leaned against the girl.

'Put your arm round her. Good. Now hold her breast.'

The man hesitated.

Adolfo gently swung the night stick and the man obeyed.

'You, girl,' ordered Adolfo. 'Get hold of him. You know how.'

The girl's sleepy eyes showed only mild surprise and her audience did not deter her.

'That's fine,' said Adolfo. 'Hold it.'

He took three flashlight photographs before he put away the camera.

The man glared. 'Why do you want those photographs?'

'Blackmail,' said Adolfo and grinned.

'You'll be sorry. You won't get away with it.'

'Cry for me when I start to be sorry,' grinned Adolfo.

'I'll stay here,' said Miguel. 'You and Nolana finish up quickly and come back.'

Miguel held the night stick in one hand and his pistol in the other. He flourished the night stick threateningly every time they moved.

'I'll remember you,' said the man. 'I could pick your face out from a million.'

'Shut up,' said Miguel wearily.

The girl asked: 'Are you going to steal my jewellery?'

'Yes.'

'I've a diamond brooch of sentimental value. It belonged to my mother. I'll willingly pay ten times its value not to lose it.'

'We'll come to an arrangement,' said Miguel bleakly.

'Thank you,' she breathed gratefully. Compared with the older man's leathery, wrinkled skin, her soft voluptuousness was very womanly.

'Why do you want a man old enough to be your father?' asked Miguel curiously.

She giggled. 'He's ... sweet.'

'But he's ... old!' said Miguel. He was thinking of himself and Maria-Luise.

'That's why he makes love so nicely. He's experienced!' She giggled again and her breasts quivered.

Presently Adolfo returned. 'All finished,' he reported.

Miguel said: 'Tie them up.' He gestured to the man. 'You first. Stand over there facing the wall.'

The man hesitated until the night stick swung. He hastily walked to the wall and faced it.

'Kneel down.'

He kneeled awkwardly because of a war-wounded hip.

'Hands behind your back.' Adolfo tied them swiftly with one of the girl's stockings.

'Now you,' Miguel ordered the girl.

Placidly she rolled off the bed and joined the man. Her ample breasts quivered and she smiled, pleased that men were watching her nakedness.

'Kneel down and hands behind you.'

She knelt and Adolfo tied the stocking with a big bow.

'Foreheads against the wall,' ordered Miguel.

They obeyed him and Miguel took a quick step forward and locked his fingers in the man's hair. In the last split second the man knew what was going to happen. He'd seen it done before. He tried to rise to his feet but the barrel of Miguel's pistol pressed against the bone behind his ear and as the man strained his head away, Miguel pulled the trigger. He saw the girl's astonished eyes staring at him, released the man and locked his fingers in her hair. The upturned eyes and their surprise made him turn away her head before he pulled the trigger.

The man died instantly but the girl still breathed. Miguel fired again and this time she died.

The girl's handbag was turned out on to the bed. Her identity card was placed prominently upon her pillow with her jewellery. The man's identity card was placed upon his pillow and to show that robbery was not the motive for the crime, nothing belonging to the couple was taken.

Miguel and Adolfo returned to the second floor where the other guests were prisoners. They were tired of standing and cold. They were afraid too because they'd heard the muffled shots. They eyed Miguel apprehensively.

He said quietly: 'We had to shoot a couple who made trouble. They're in room three-four-four. Be warned. We're not leaving yet!' He nodded at Greco. 'I need you now.'

Adolfo swept up the jewellery on the table and stuffed it in to his pockets. He winked at the prisoners and sauntered out after Miguel and Greco. They locked steward Burgas in with his clients.

Their four women companions were waiting in the reception office with their handbags bulging.

'Ready to go?' asked Adolfo.

Miguel nodded. Adolfo picked up the telephone. When a voice answered he glanced at his wrist watch. 'Ready in ten minutes.' He replaced the receiver.

They waited. The minutes ticked past slowly. Miguel's face was set like stone and Adolfo watched him slyly, sensing he was suffering an inner tension.

Adolfo glanced at his watch. 'We can go now.'

They unbolted a door, passed through into a garage and out into the grey dawn. Just inside the entrance gates two cars were waiting. Four hours later they were all sound asleep in a barn only two hours climb from a mountain pass leading to France.

5

Renato Maroto instantly understood the motive of the double murder and took steps to counteract it.

The murdered man was an influential politician. His reputation was spotless. He was a pillar of the church, a leading light in the new Spain and his wife was related to one of Spain's aristocratic families.

The public would have been shocked to learn that he slipped away from Madrid to spend a night in a Barcelona meuble. It would prove depravity and corruption in high places and give anti-Franco agitators a powerful propaganda weapon.

But much more dangerous to the regime was the identity of the girl. She was the daughter of a wealthy family at the forefront of Spanish society. She was related to royalty and the niece of an ambassador. Many town and village streets bore her grandfather's name and she was married to a young member of the Government. It would rock Spanish society to its foundations to learn that she had an elderly lover.

But another factor turned the incident into dynamite. The girl was the wife of the older man's son!

Renato Maroto destroyed all evidence of the girl's identity and ordered her body to be removed to the mortuary. It was recorded that she was found in the park behind a clump of bushes with a suicide gun in her hand. She was entombed namelessly. Her husband and relatives would be anxious and search for her unsuccessfully. In time she would become one of those rare cases of people who are inexplicably missing.

The man's body was sent to an undertaker and prepared for a journey to Madrid with all pomp and splendour. According to Renato Maroto's fiction, he died a hero. Single-handed he fought murderous criminals who he came upon engaged in a robbery and died bravely . . . as he had lived.

A carefully worded news report of the fictional robbery was issued, Civil Guards who may have seen too much were promoted and transferred to other districts far away and a campaign against Soviet Russia and its unscrupulous criminal agents was launched.

Renato Maroto should have been congratulated, but there was a brittleness in the Old Man's voice when he spoke to him from Madrid.

'You have shown great initiative, Maroto. *Great* initiative! But initiative in preventing scandal is not your basic task.'

'I understand that,' agreed Maroto faintly. He wanted to hurl the telephone across the room.

'Get those men, Maroto. Shoot them down like dogs. Have no mercy. I don't care *how* you do it . . . get them!'

Maroto was inwardly writing from the memory of that conversation when the guard unlocked the door of the interrogation room. Maroto stepped across the threshold and the guard shut the door behind him.

The girl slumped on the chair looked up at him with weary, dark-ringed eyes.

He hunched over her, holding his head on one side.

'Your name?'

There was infinite weariness in her voice. 'Again! Can't I go home and answer more questions tomorrow. I'm exhausted.'

'You'll answer *now*,' he said.

She sighed. 'Rosemarie Prada.'

'What do you do?'

She hesitated. 'I'm . . . I have independent means.'

His long neck craned over her and his long, thin face posed to rend like a vulture's beak, but his voice was silkily soft. 'I asked what you do.'

She said wearily: 'I have men friends who give me presents.'

'Why do they give you presents?'

She showed a flash of anger. 'Lots of men give presents to girls.'

'You're a whore,' he said flatly.

'All right.'

'Now tell me what you are.'

131

'What is this?' she flared. 'Music hall comedy? You know what I am!'

'I want to hear *you* tell me,' he said softly. 'Or are you too ashamed?'

'I'm ashamed of nothing,' she flared. 'All right. You want to hear it? I'm a whore. A *whore*! Do you hear that? I'm a *whore*!'

He sighed. 'It needed an effort, but I finally got you to make a truthful statement. I hope I won't have as much trouble with the rest of your answers.'

She glowered.

'You don't realise the seriousness of your position....' He glanced at the card in his hand, '... Rosemarie?' He put one hand in his pocket and toyed with something. 'You are a whore,' he said flatly. 'You should know that girls in moral danger are sent to a correction centre for moral re-education.'

Rosemarie's face became an expressionless mask. She'd heard tales of correction centres and had been careful to keep out of trouble with the authorities.

'We rounded up a batch of girls last week and sent them away,' he said casually. He cocked his head on one side. 'Do you know about correction centres, Rosemarie? They shave your head. No pretty underclothing. Just a rough, canvas smock that rubs your skin raw. And all day long you scrub floors. Your knees grow calloused, your nails break and your hands swell. The food's adequate, but the girls burn up so much energy that they lose their curves. No man will look at them when they come out.'

Rosemarie stared up at him.

'You don't want to go to a correction centre, do you, Rosemarie?'

She slowly shook her head.

'I didn't hear you.'

'No,' she said loudly.

'All right. Now let's get ahead more quickly. You have scars on your back?'

'Yes.'

'Let me see them.'

She unhooked her dress, eased it off her shoulders and rounded her back.

'I want to see the scars,' he said tonelessly.

'You can see them. They're the fine, white lines.'

'I can't see them properly.'

She gave him a hard stare. 'You want me to take my dress off?'

'Yes.'

She pushed her dress down over her hips and stepped out of it. She pulled the hem of her petticoat up under her armpits and showed him her back.

His voice was toneless. 'I can't see them clearly.'

She turned to face him, her eyes bitter. 'You want me to strip. Is that it?'

'I want to see the scars.'

Nudity meant nothing to her. She quickly removed her clothing and stood with her back to him, wearing only shoes and stockings. She grew impatient of waiting while he studied her and said in exasperation: 'What are you doing? Counting the stripes?'

'Who did it?' he asked.

'A lover I had when I was young.'

'Why did he do it?'

'He found me with ... another.'

'And then what happened?'

She answered glibly because it was the story she had told many times: 'He ran away and joined the army. He was killed.'

'You may sit down.'

She reached for her clothing.

'You can dress later.'

She sat down, watching him curiously, already resigned to accepting him as a lover and wondering how she could turn it to her advantage.

He asked quietly: 'Who is Miguel?'

She froze. Panic leaped inside her. She'd answered all her interrogator's questions but had made no voluntary statement. She realised the Man had not only told about her scarred back but also how Miguel's name had escaped her when she recognised him. She said in disgust: 'That big mouth!'

'Is that how you insult a patriot?' he said softly.

'I made a mistake,' she said. 'I thought I recognised one of the men. But it wasn't him.'

'A mistake?' he said gently.

'Yes.'

He reached out and she tensed, expecting to be hurt, but instead his finger and thumb gently rolled her nipple between them until the stimulation made it stand out starkly. 'Who is this man?'

'I ... er ... I can't remember where I last saw him.'

'You can't?' he said gently. He brought his other hand out from his pocket and she saw the pliers. She watched the open jaws draw closer and shuddered.

'You're not afraid, are you, Rosemarie? Only traitors to the

133

State and those who obstruct authority need have fear.'

The pliers gently held her nipple, their coldness an icy fear deep down in her bowels.

'What shall I do, Rosemarie? Apply pressure and squash flat? Or twist and tug like pulling a tooth?'

She was petrified and didn't dare move a muscle. She sensed that he was capable of putting his threat into effect.

'Tell me about Miguel,' he said gently.

Her voice was husky. 'His name is Miguel Barras. He lived near me in Escoleras.' Words poured out in a torrent.

He interrupted. 'That will do.' He squeezed gently with the pliers and she arched forward grasping his wrist.

'All right.' He dropped the pliers into his pocket. 'Let me see it.'

She whimpered and showed him her bruised flesh.

'Stop fussing. I didn't even draw blood. Get dressed.'

When she was ready he took her out of the building and flagged down a taxi. He handed her into it and climbed in after her.

'Tell the driver,' he said.

'Where . . . where are we going?'

'Your apartment.'

She shrank into her corner, unutterably weary and with her breast aching. Her usual carefree self-confidence was scared out of her. She was submissive and willing to do whatever he wanted.

They reached her apartment block and waited while she paid the driver. There were power cuts every day in Barcelona, but they were lucky and the lift took them up to the fourth floor. She opened the door of her apartment and he followed her inside, looked round and nodded approvingly.

Her flat was her castle, her refuge from her public way of life. She'd furnished it expensively. Here was home, where she could be completely herself. Apart from workmen, Maroto was the first man to enter the flat.

He scowled as he browsed round. He opened drawers and rummaged through them, upended their contents on the floor and stirred them with the toe of his shoe while Rosemarie watched with dismay.

He turned out the living room and kitchen and in the bedroom found the wooden box hidden in the wardrobe under her shoes with unerring instinct.

'The key,' he demanded.

She took the key from her purse.

He opened the box and examined the necklaces and brooches, bangles and earrings. 'It's profitable being a whore,' he said coldly. He locked the box and tossed it back into the wardrobe.

'What ... what are you looking for?' she ventured timidly.

'Anything that's interesting.'

He found her savings, notes of large denomination, wrapped in brown paper and thrust away under the mattress. He rifled through the wad, grunted and replaced it in its hiding place. 'How long did it take to earn?'

'Since I came to Barcelona. I was nineteen then.'

He nodded, took off his jacket, slung it across a chair and flopped down on her bed. He cushioned his hands under his head and the heels of his shoes soiled the delicate hand-made lace covering on the bed. 'This room's seen action!' he said and chuckled.

She stared down at him expressionlessly. 'This is my private apartment. I never bring anyone here.'

'I'm here,' he said.

'Please be careful with your shoes. You're tearing the cover.'

'You mean ... like this?' He snagged his heel in the open lacework, ripped and laughed at her pained expression. 'Take my shoes off.'

She sat on the foot of the bed and drew off his shoes.

'A nice flat,' he said approvingly.

She said nothing. She was completely in his power.

'I'm tired of living in a boarding house. This will suit me fine.'

She was numb with dismay.

'How are you at cooking?'

'Very bad.'

'You'll learn.'

Her shoulders drooped.

'Don't just sit there,' he said. 'You know why I'm here.'

Tiredly she reached behind her and unhooked her dress.

'What's the matter?' he asked after a while.

'I'm tired. No sleep last night and I've been interrogated all day.'

'You can do better than this!'

'I'm doing my best.'

'It's a lousy best for an expensive whore. Show some feeling.'

'I ... I can't switch on emotions like turning on a tap.'

'You're not responding.'

'It doesn't mean anything to me. If the man gets pleasure that's all that matters.'

'You've never been deeply stirred?'

'I must have been with all my experience.'

He said softly: 'Relax and leave everything to me.'

She was tired and it was easy to close her eyes while his hands ran over her. She feared she might fall asleep while he amused himself with her. His hands were a soothing rhythm and sleepiness became dreaminess, his knowing touch invading until abruptly she was sharply aware of her alerted pleasure. She had never known anything like it. Every pleasure nerve responded as the explorative rhythm of his hands aroused tender and exquisite sensations. She floated on a cloud of dreamy rhythmic pressure, breathlessly understanding that she had not known this before because she'd never had a lover patient enough. His knowing arousal of her desires presently brought her to the brink of frenzy and she cried out, drove her nails into his shoulders and jerked convulsively until the tempest of ecstasy slowly died and became peace.

'Happy?' he asked.

'I . . . I've never known anything like it.'

'Do you love me?' There was a mocking note in his voice that rang alarm bells. His brooding black eyes were calculating.

'I like you much better when you're making love.'

He chuckled. 'Don't be so sure. I've studied women anatomically and know their pleasure points like a Judo expert knows pressure points.'

'Don't be so cold-blooded.'

He narrowed his eyes. 'I'll pleasure you until you're in heaven at first. Then I'll ration you until you'll do anything I want.'

'You conceited bastard.'

She felt his hands upon her and stiffened. But she was already tired and she thought she could ignore his caresses until she became aware that she was aroused again, eager for the sweet pleasure, trying to exert its power, but her loins dominating her hands so that she clung to him fiercely while urgency dissolved into a great spasm of shooting stars, spurting high and slowly drifting her back to reality.

A little later he took her bruised nipple between finger and thumb and twisted until she moaned.

'Tell me more about Miguel Barras,' he urged.

6

The Civil Guards came for Teresa just after lunch. A loud clatter of crockery came from the kitchen, waitresses wearing pretty print dresses were setting tables for dinner and the dining-room blinds were drawn against the afternoon sun. Most of the guests were sunbathing on the beach in front of

136

the hotel. Sunbathing, reading in the shade of gaily-coloured parasols while they sipped iced drinks, or swimming and sporting in the sea with paddle boats which Teresa hired out.

The Civil Guards were young men. 'The Captain would like to see you at Headquarters.'

Only a few guests were seated on the high stools at the hotel bar and Teresa was using this slack moment to check stock. 'I'm busy now,' she explained. 'I'll come down within an hour or so.'

The young guards were embarrassed. 'The Captain wants to see you *at once*, Señora.'

Then she understood. One Civil Guard could bring her a message, but two were an escort! 'What wicked thing have I done? Am I arrested?' She chuckled.

They were shocked. 'You're not arrested, Señora.'

'Wait a minute while I comb my hair.'

They allowed her to walk ahead of them to the Civil Guard Headquarters but as soon as she entered the vestibule she sensed trouble.

Captain Romero was worried. He bowed formally. 'Thank you for coming, Señora.'

Teresa knew the sergeant and most of the Civil Guards quite well. During their long, weary hours of patrolling they often dropped in at her hotel and could count upon a sandwich and a drink. Now they eyed her anxiously as though they knew something she didn't.

'What's the trouble, Captain?' she asked.

'There's ... there's somebody from Barcelona to see you. Come this way please.'

She followed him along a corridor. He knocked on a door and ushered her inside to meet a tall, thin man with a long, dark face. 'Señora Teresa Coruna?' he asked.

'That's right.'

'All right, Captain.' He dismissed the captain like a menial. When the captain closed the door behind him, Maroto locked it and dropped the key in his pocket. He turned to face Teresa and stood with his head cocked on one side, scrutinising her intently 'Police,' he said and turned back the lapel of his jacket to show a small badge. He pointed to a solitary wooden chair. 'Sit down, please.'

Teresa perched on the edge of the chair and looked up at him curiously. 'Is there trouble?'

'No,' he said gently. 'Just a few questions. You have a brother ... Miguel Barras?'

Her eyes lit up. 'You have news of him?'

Maroto took a blown-up photograph of Miguel from his

137

pocket. He'd found its original in the Admiralty files with Miguel's application for a fishing licence. Teresa said at once. 'Yes. That's Miguel.'

More than thirty witnesses had identified the photo despite its being twenty years old.

Maroto returned the photo to his pocket. 'Where is your brother now?'

Teresa was dismayed. 'Don't you know? I thought you had news of him.'

'How did he get the scar on his face?' he countered.

'He was wounded...' Teresa broke off. 'None of us have seen Miguel for many years.'

'You know about the scar?'

She was puzzled by his manner. 'I was told by friends who met him.'

'You've heard of Scarface?'

'You mean ... the bank robber ... the murderer?'

'I mean ... Miguel Barras ... your brother!'

She was incredulous. The assertion was so ridiculous that she wanted to laugh. Gentle Miguel, so slow-thinking and placid ... a bank robber! It was impossible.

But her mind worked fast. There'd been a startling change in Miguel after the death of his wife. He'd brooded and developed a fanatical hatred for those who'd started the war and she'd heard stories from men who'd seen him at the front. He'd turned Communist, he was in the Steel Corps, he'd retreated to France to carry on the war!

'Miguel,' she whispered. 'My brother...! You can't mean it!'

'When did you last see him?'

She smiled wryly. 'Before the war. He enlisted and we haven't heard from him since.'

'How about your Catalan friends who bring you his messages?'

'Tell me who they are,' she asked quietly. 'I'd like to meet them.'

'They are scum who hide him when he crosses the border, traitors who conspire with him to destroy their country.'

'I know nothing of Miguel. Tell me where he is and I will talk to him and learn the truth.'

'The truth!' he sneered. 'The truth from a ruthless murderer who kills, tortures, steals and rapes.' Maroto lashed himself into a fury. 'Scarface and his followers are monsters. They destroy and defile everything that's good and decent.' His lips sprayed spittle. 'These monsters must be destroyed. Only when they are buried can Spain know peace.'

She turned pale, shocked by the accusations.

'And you will help me to trap him,' he said.

'Are you sure ... it is hard to believe that my own brother...'

'You will answer my questions?'

She nodded bleakly.

'Tell me who brought you his messages.'

'We've had no messages from Miguel.'

The blow was totally unexpected. His knuckles smashed against her cheek and hurled her to the floor. Half dazed, she got to her knees and stared stupidly at the red drops falling on the mosaic tiles.

He gathered up her long hair, wound it round his hand and strained her head back until her eyes looked into his.

'Listen, you Red whore. I'll get the truth if I have to tear you apart.' Spittle spattered her face. 'I've got ways of dealing with Red whores!'

She couldn't believe this was happening. 'I can only tell you what I know,' she whispered.

'You'll tell me ... everything!' he said grimly.

Juan Prenga was the only Catalan Civil Guard in Escoleras. He hovered in the corridor and heard Teresa's cry of pain. He hurried to the vestibule where Captain Romero was talking to the sergeant and reported breathlessly: 'She cried out, mi Capitan.'

Captain Romero scowled. 'This is not our affair,' he said bleakly. 'It's out of our hands.' Then he stared thoughtfully at Juan Prenga and said deliberately. 'Take a couple of hours off duty, Prenga. You may have friends you want to talk to.'

'Thank you, mi Capitan,' said Juan Prenga and hurried away.

He went to his good friend, Enrique Godes, and talked to him earnestly. Fat Godes got out his cycle and sweated profusely as he pedalled along the dusty road to the Marrista Hotel. Narcisus was entering accounts in the ledgers and was astonished to learn that Teresa was at Civil Guard Headquarters. 'What's it about?' he asked.

Godes hurried him to the door. 'Nobody knows,' he said. 'But it's the secret police from Barcelona!'

'I'll go and ...'

'No,' said Godes. He tightened his grip on Narcisus's arm. 'First get the priest. You've got to have somebody with some standing to back you.'

Father Delbos was sleepily relaxed after a well-cooked lunch and good wine. He was irritated by the visit of Narcisus and Godes. 'What is it?' he snapped.

Narcisus said: 'If you please, Father . . .'

Enrique Godes broke in: 'It's about the wife of friend Narcisus. The police from Barcelona are interviewing her. Narcisus wishes to be present and asks you to intervene, Father, so his request may be granted.'

Father Delbos eyed them slyly while his thoughts raced. He burned for an appointment in Barcelona. He wasn't interested in the good opinion of the peasants among whom he was forced to live but, on the other hand, if he interfered with the Barcelona police, word of it might spread and prejudice his hopes of a transfer. He scowled at Narcisus. 'When did you last come to church?'

Narcisus gulped. 'Since the tourist season began, Father, we've been very busy and . . .'

'I'm sure the police have good reasons for what they do,' snapped Father Delbos. 'Also it is quite improper to disturb me during my meditation period.' He wiped the back of his hand across his moist forehead. 'Don't ever worry me again at this hour.' He shut the door in their faces.

Narcisus was furious, but Enrique Godes was tugging his arm. 'Doctor Aldo,' he urged. 'We've got to find Doctor Aldo.'

'But it's the duty of a priest . . .' argued Narcisus.

'We can do without him,' panted Godes. 'Hurry!'

Doctor Aldo was lancing a fisherman's finger which had been infected by a rusty fishing hook. While he bandaged, Godes talked, and while the doctor washed his hands Godes had a chance to whisper: 'They're beating her up!'

Doctor Aldo's face was set as he hurried along the street with Narcisus and Godes. They went to the town hall where Poca, the new mayor, and Conill, the Justice of the Peace, were brooding over a disputed land title. Doctor Aldo spoke to them without Narcisus hearing and with grave faces they set off to Civil Guard Headquarters.

Already the news had spread magically and a large, sullen crowd had gathered outside the Headquarters while Civil Guards stood at the entrance doors trying to look unconcerned.

The deputation headed by the mayor, Doctor Aldo, Conill, Narcisus and Godes strode purposefully up to the Civil Guards who saluted and parted to allow them through. In the vestibule, Captain Romero hurried to meet them with relief.

'What's the trouble, Captain?' asked the mayor.

The Captain spread his hands. 'It's the Secret Police from Barcelona.'

'They've got her in there?' The Mayor nodded along the

140

corridor.

'Yes. There's only one man.'

'We want to see him, Captain.'

The Captain scowled. 'My orders are not to disturb him in any circumstances.'

'I'll accept all responsibility, Captain.'

'I've been given my orders. You can't relieve me of that responsibility, Señor Roca.'

Doctor Aldo pushed forward. 'Teresa Coruna is my patient. Excessive nervous strain can make her seriously ill. I insist that this officer from Barcelona is warned of it.'

'As Justice of the Peace I must be informed about every infringement of the law in the area under my jurisdiction,' said Conill grimly. 'I must remind you, Captain, that I am appointed by the Governor of the Province.'

Captain Romero smiled with relief. 'In these circumstances, gentlemen, I must comply with your wishes.' He led them along the corridor and knuckled the door loudly. Maroto called sharply: 'What is it?'

'A deputation wishes to see you and Señora Coruna. It's the mayor, the Justice of the Peace and the doctor. Señora Coruna's health may be endangered.'

There was a pause. 'Tell them to come back later,' said Maroto.

'They insist that they see Señora Coruna at once.' The Captain moistened his lips. 'A large crowd has gathered outside ... we want to avoid public unrest.'

There was a long silence. Then Maroto said quietly: 'Very well, Captain.' The key turned in the lock and Maroto stood on the threshold, his dark face sullen and his black eyes smouldering. 'I'm to be snarled up in red tape, am I, gentlemen?' he said bitterly. 'Murderers escape so that you can uphold the letter of the law!'

Narcisus choked: 'Teresa!'

She appeared behind Maroto, staring glassily and swaying. Her hair was dishevelled, the bruise on her cheek had half-closed her eye and blood trickled from the corner of her mouth. Her blouse was torn and a shoulder strap was snapped.

They stared at her in shocked silence. Then Narcisus sprang at Maroto. They went down together, Narcisus raging and hitting out wildly. Captain Romero and Enrique Godes fought to pull the enraged Narcisus away and Civil Guards came running to hold him.

Maroto got to his feet, scowling.

'I'll kill you,' panted Narcisus, struggling furiously. 'I'll kill you!'

Captain Romero took Maroto by the arm and urged him along the corridor towards the rear of the building. 'Let's talk this over and see if we can handle it differently,' he soothed.

Teresa's dazed eyes stared at Narcisus happily. 'You really care!' she said delightedly.

'Are you all right, Teresa?' Doctor Aldo asked anxiously.

She held her breast. 'He hurt me a little.'

'If you wish, Teresa,' said Conill. 'We'll prepare an official complaint and take statements from witnesses.'

The doctor and the mayor frowned and shook their heads quickly, advising against it. Everyone knew it was unwise to complain against those in authority.

'It's up to you, Teresa,' said Doctor Aldo.

She tried to smile. 'Let sleeping dogs lie.' Only a few years earlier, any criticism of authority had implied opposition to the regime.

'What was it all about, Teresa?' asked Mayor Roca.

'My brother, Miguel,' she said slowly. 'They say he's ... Scarface!'

CHAPTER SEVEN

1

THE Civil Guards patrolling the foothills of the Pyrenees were doubled, strict discipline was enforced and day and night vigil was kept.

Two Civil Guards saw the man through their binoculars. He trudged over the loose, dry soil of the vineyards and they studied the direction in which he was heading and circled round in front to wait for him. One guard concealed himself behind a clump of bushes and his companion stood out in the open. 'I can see him clearly now,' he said. 'I don't recognise him as from round these parts.'

'I'll keep him covered.'

The man trudged on and when he saw the Civil Guard his stride didn't falter. He wore a faded blue shirt, black corduroy trousers and rope-soled alpagartas. He greeted the Civil Guard in Catalan.

'Bon dia.'

'Can't you speak Spanish?'

'Esclar que si. Buenas dias. Can you understand me now?'

'Papers,' demanded the Civil Guard.

The man raised his eyes to heaven in mute disgust and drew out his identity papers from his breast pocket. The sun beat down. It was tiring tramping across loose soil. Sweat stained his armpits and had moistened the papers. The Civil Guard scrutinised them. They were quite in order. The man lived in a small village some five miles away and had received permission to travel to Figueras. The guard returned his papers. 'Where are you going?'

'To Figueras.'

'For what purpose?'

'To buy seed.'

'You intend walking?'

'I missed the bus. But if I walk to a highway I may get a lift.'

The guard gestured. 'All right. Carry on.'

The man grinned slyly. 'Bon dia,' he said in Catalan.

The guard scowled after him. He called sharply: 'Just a minute.'

The man stopped and half turned. He still grinned.

'What's that in your back trousers pocket?'

143

'Food. A hunk of bread and a piece of sausage meat.'

'Let me see it,' said the guard.

'You won't make me go hungry, will you, Guardia?'

'Let me see it.'

The man shrugged his shoulders and thrust his hand into his pocket. He pulled out a black object, levelled it and fired so casually that the guard knew no danger until lead smashed into his chest.

With one burst of his tommy-gun the guard concealed in the bushes brought down the killer. He ran to him and stood over him trembling with anger. Only obedience to orders, hammered into him again and again that such men must be taken alive, stayed his finger on the trigger.

The Civil Guard died before he reached hospital. His killer was badly wounded, his legs smashed and the muscles severed. He was taken to Barcelona, his wounds were treated and a blood transfusion given. While he was recovering from the anaesthetic witnesses filed past him, studied his pale features and unhesitatingly identified him as a Scarface accomplice. He was removed to a private room and two plain clothes policemen guarded him day and night. A news flash was released that an unidentified man had fought a gun duel with a Civil Guard and both had died after admission to hospital.

Some days later when the man was stronger, Renato Maroto visited him. He visited him every day, steadily extracting more and more information. And each day when Maroto left, Greco wept, not only for his own suffering but for his comrades whom he had betrayed.

2

Renato had telephoned that he would arrive early for dinner and while Rosemarie basted the roasting chicken a thoughtful pucker wrinkled her forehead. She closed the oven door, went through to her bedroom and took out her savings. The postman had just delivered a bill for the quarter's rent and she was shocked to find that she had only just enough to pay it.

It was amazing how swiftly her savings had dwindled away. Renato liked to eat well and food was expensive. He also liked whisky which was a prohibitive price. Money had melted away and she had no income now. When Renato had first moved in with her she'd tried to keep going, but he so often made her stay home and let down regulars that she'd lost them all. She didn't regret it. Her way of life had changed and the thought of other men now filled her with revulsion. But she felt insecure. Renato was so unpredictable. He always expected her

144

to be on hand when he needed her, but once she had waited in for him three days and nights without a word from him. Then he'd calmly come home as though he'd stepped out for a packet of cigarettes. The previous week he'd brought back a frightened slip of a girl with terrified eyes and had insisted that Rosemarie watch him make love to the girl. She'd been sickened and angry as he gave freely to a stranger the pleasure he deliberately denied her.

Rosemarie took out her jewels, calculated what she'd paid for them and was reassured that she had reserves to depend on until she summoned up the courage to ask Renato to contribute to the household expenses.

Renato was in a vile mood when he arrived home. She scurried round anxiously, serving the dinner efficiently and trying to appease his bad temper. She opened a bottle of excellent wine and this mellowed him. He wasn't so grumpy when she'd got him seated in his comfortable armchair with black coffee, an over-generous tot of whisky in a tall glass and a Havana cigar.

She washed up quickly, took off her apron, prettied herself and went to him. 'More whisky, darling?'

'All right.'

She poured.

'More coffee?'

'No.'

'Do you want more ice?'

'No.'

'Why are you bad-tempered, darling?'

He scowled. 'Inefficiency makes me angry.' He shrugged. 'It doesn't matter. I couldn't have got much more out of him.'

Her face became impassive. She deliberately tried not to see Renato's faults.

'He managed to steal a small plate off his dinner tray,' said Maroto disgustedly. 'He broke it under the bedclothes and cut his wrists. With two trained policemen in the room with him all the time, mark you. Yet they noticed *nothing* until the blood soaked through the mattress and dripped on the floor. By then it was too late!'

'He must have had a great wish to die,' she said quietly.

'Naturally. That was why he was being watched.'

She sighed. 'You frighten me, Renato.'

He chuckled. 'Why don't you sit down?'

She placed a cushion at his feet and half sat, half knelt on it, resting her arm on his thighs and her chin on her clasped hands.

He tapped an inch of white ash from his cigar. 'I didn't tell you what I did to him yesterday.'

Her face was pale. 'Don't tell me, Renato. *Please* don't tell me.'

'You're too squeamish.'

'I worry about *you*,' she said seriously. 'You're ... sadistic!'

He drew on his cigar and considered what she'd said. He exhaled blue smoke thoughtfully. 'I wonder if I am? I don't derive sexual satisfaction from inflicting pain. But later, I discover my lovemaking ardour has been stimulated.'

'Must you be cruel, darling? Aren't I stimulating enough?'

'A man likes variety.' He rolled his cigar from one corner of his mouth to the other.

She pleaded. 'Please, darling. Be nice tonight. I've waited so long.'

He reach for his whisky and sipped it. 'It won't be long before we have your friend Scarface.'

'He means nothing to me,' she said. *'Nothing!'*

'Stimulate me,' he suggested. 'Stimulate me until I want to give you what *you* want.'

3

Six came through the mountain pass, all Spaniards. Miguel carried the rucksack of explosives to destroy a many-spanned train viaduct built high across a gorge. In winter it bridged a foaming torrent which swept all before it down to the sea. Its destruction would sever rail services between France and the Costa Brava and deal a crippling blow to Spain's booming tourist industry.

Adolfo and Nolana carried walkie-talkies and the other three men had sten-guns. Their hideout was a farmhouse belonging to a secret member of their band and they arrived in the early hours of the morning and at once rolled themselves up in blankets in their host's hay loft. They were tired by their long trek over the mountains and slept soundly, unaware that their arrival had been observed through powerful telescopes.

Telephone calls were made, ammunition was issued, jeep tanks were topped up and pale-faced Civil Guards shivered in the night air, with fear like a leaden stone in their bellies.

Just after dawn Miguel's host shook his shoulder vigourously. The man's face was grey with strain. 'The Civil Guard,' he choked.

Miguel threw off his blankets, snatched up a sten-gun, leaped the stairs and ran to the nearest window. He saw at once glance the hopelessness of their position. The farmhouse was surrounded. Civil Guard's patent-leather tricornios could

146

be glimpsed behind mounds of earth thrown up during the night in hedgerows, ditches, behind trees and within the shelter of farm outbuildings.

The men looked to Miguel, acknowledging his leadership.

Miguel picked up a shepherd's staff, placed a hat on it and showed it at a window. Glass splintered, lead hummed and plaster flicked from the walls.

Miguel's face was grim. They could be starved out or, if artillery was brought out, the farmhouse could be reduced to rubble.

Miguel said without hesitation: 'We've only one chance, Comrades. To attack and break through their lines.'

Adolfo was pale. 'They'll cut us down before we get half way.'

'It's the *only* chance,' said Miguel.

'He's right,' agreed Nolana. 'The longer we wait the more men they can bring up!'

'It's suicide,' protested Adolfo.

Miguel stared at him steadily. 'Are you afraid to die?'

Adolfo gave a sad smile. 'Yes, Comrade. Nevertheless...'

They armed themselves from their store, each man taking a pistol, a sten-gun, two hand grenades and ammunition.

Miguel placed six hand grenades on the floor. 'If we're fearless we've a good chance to get through,' he said. 'I'm going to open the door. From time to time I'll lob out a hand grenade. They're too far away to be hit but the explosions will worry them.' Miguel looked round to ensure that the men were listening intently.

'The shortest distance between us and *them* is to our right. They're sheltering in a shallow ditch and that's the side we'll attack. I'll lob out three hand grenades with a five minute interval between each. Let them get used to it. Then I'll lob out three more, one on top of the other. While they're still exploding we get out through the door ... fast! Turn right round the house and run for the ditches. Fire short bursts to make them keep their heads down. Once you're over the ditch keep running on into the trees. There's a steep slope down into the valley. Go down it on the seat of your pants. Losing skin off your ass can save your lives. There are pine trees at the bottom of the slope and they'll give shelter along the valley. Make for the railway, cross the tracks and we'll meet in the sidings. Any questions?'

'It's all too clear, Comrade.'

The man who owned the farmhouse went to the fireplace, took down a crucifix and put it in his pocket. 'It's all I've got left of my wife's,' he said apologetically. He cast a sad glance

147

round him. 'I knew this would happen some time but it's still sad, leaving your home.'

'Don't worry, Comrade,' Miguel assured him. 'Party funds will recompense you.'

'How about French papers? Will I get French citizenship?'

'Don't worry, Comrade. We'll fix it.' Miguel looked around. 'Are you ready?'

The men nodded grimly.

'Stand back while I open the door.'

After a time the Civil Guards tired of firing into the empty doorway.

The first hand grenade was lobbed out and exploded close enough to spatter some of the Civil Guards with earth. They poured lead into the open doorway until their gun barrels were hot.

A second hand grenade was lobbed outside and trigger-happy Civil Guards whose nerves were sorely strained fired at windows and doors until their magazines were empty. A haze of smoke hung on the air like a blue mist.

The third hand grenade exploded.

Only a few Civil Guards reacted, firing unenthusiastically through the whirling dust, vaguely wondering why hand grenades were being thrown which could injure nobody.

Miguel nodded grimly at his men and they tensed. The next three hand grenades exploded quickly, one after the other. Earth geysered and smoke swirled thickly.

Miguel went through the door in a fierce leap with the others following. They were deafened, smoke was in their eyes and soil pattered down like rain. They ran round the farmhouse and fanned out, firing as they attacked.

The Civil Guards sheltering in the ditch were taken by surprise. A few fired over-excitedly and then the sten-guns hammered viciously. A raw guard lost his head and fled, spreading panic among his comrades, some of whom followed him and became clear targets for desperate men who scythed them down.

Miguel and his men ran fast. Already they were more than half way to the ditch. But the smoke was clearing and now the guards on their flanks could see them. Rifles cracked and tommy-guns chattered.

The owner of the farmhouse was the first to go down. He fell like a stone, his sten-gun flying from his hands. The man behind tripped over him and was riddled with lead as he tried to scramble to his feet.

The firing was deafening as Miguel reached the ditch and leaped it. He plunged into the undergrowth beyond and hurled

148

himself down the steep slope, rolling and sliding. He pounded against rocks, tore through trailing vines and thorn bushes, ripped his flesh and his clothes and brought up in the protective screen of the dwarf pine trees. He'd kept his grip on his sten-gun and he lay panting, gritting his teeth against the pain of the bullet which had torn through his shoulder. His shirt was blood-soaked, the wound was serious and he needed swift medical attention.

There was a crashing through the shrubbery close to him and he raised his sten-gun and aimed it. But it was Adolfo and Nolana. Nolana grinned wolfishly and managed to stand up. Blood soaked his trousers from a flesh wound in the thigh. Adolfo had fallen more than thrown himself down a slope. He stared at them unseeingly, the dark blood that ran from his mouth and the gaping wound in his chest showing that he was beyond human aid.

'Let's get out of here,' said Miguel. He offered Nolana his good shoulder and they stumbled along the floor of the valley.

They heard orders being shouted across the valley and jeep engines revving up. Police cordons were being thrown up all round them.

Nolana came to a standstill.

'Keep going,' growled Miguel.

'Leave me, Comrade,' said Nolana quietly.

'Don't be a fool. We can make it.'

'Look at my leg.'

Nolana's boot was full of blood and left a red trail which was easy to follow.

'Sit down, you fool,' growled Miguel.

Although he scowled with the pain of his wound, he ripped open Nolana's trousers, tore off a strip to make a pad and used a stout twig to apply a tourniquet above a severed artery. 'That's the best I can do,' panted Miguel.

'Go,' said Nolana. His face was pale with pain. 'This is the end for me, Miguel. If I move I'll lose more blood. Go, Comrade. There's a chance you can make it . . . alone!'

'Don't be a fool. I'll help you up.'

Nolana was determined. 'I'm done. But *you* can make it. You must. You're more important to the cause than any of us.'

Miguel glanced all round him and far behind them, the undergrowth crackled as men forced through it.

Nolana patted his sten-gun. 'I'll wait and take some of the bastards with me.' He raised his clenched fist. 'They shall not pass, Comrade. They shall not pass!'

Miguel stared at him unhappily.

149

'I shit upon your stupidity, Comrade,' said Nolana. 'Go!'

Miguel clenched his fist and choked: 'They shall not pass!'

He stumbled away without looking back, heading along the valley towards the railway track. When he reached it he limped along beside it until he came to a siding and a gravel quarry. An old steam engine huffed black smoke. There was no sign of the driver and stoker but Miguel found them on the other side of the train, seated on a stack of old sleepers with napkins spread over their knees as they ate. They stared as though he was an apparition. He gestured threateningly with his sten-gun and, as though in a trance, the two men stood up and raised their hands above their heads. Their food cascaded to the ground.

'Is this your train?' demanded Miguel.

The driver nodded stupidly.

Miguel backed to the iron steps and climbed up into the cabin, keeping the men covered.

'Come on up.'

They climbed up reluctantly.

'Start her up,' ordered Miguel. 'Take her out on the track.'

'I can't do that,' protested the engine driver. 'It's a single line. I haven't got a clear way until two o'clock.'

Miguel turned his face slightly so they could see the hairline scar. 'I'm Scarface. Now ... get this train moving!'

The driver flung a startled glance at the stoker, pulled levers and spun handles. Slowly the train pulled out of the siding. 'Give me more steam, Pedro,' said the driver.

The stoker opened the furnace door, threw in a shovelful of coal, expertly blocked the flame backlash with the flat of the spade and drove it deep into the coal again.

'Open her out!' ordered Miguel. Sweat ran down his face and he could have swallowed a litre of water. Pain made his heart hammer and his thoughts were hazy, as though he were drunk.

'We have to build up steam,' said the driver. 'It takes time.'

The stoker's strong arms rippled powerfully as he shovelled.

The driver eased the train out on to the main track. He warned unhappily: 'We might meet a passenger train!'

'That's a chance we'll have to take,' said Miguel grimly.

Above the loud huffing of the engine they couldn't hear the sound of firing but bullets spanged loudly on the metal roof.

'They're shooting at us,' choked the driver.

'The sooner you get beyond range the better for all of us,' said Miguel.

The stoker redoubled his energies and the driver crouched low. The train rocked on and presently there were no more

150

bullets.

Miguel was trying to concentrate, but thoughts eluded him. They knew he was on a train and he wondered if they would be waiting at the next station or if they could shunt him off into a siding. He swayed as a black wave washed over him and closed his eyes, fearing he would faint. He exerted will-power, opened his eyes and saw the driver staring at him hopefully. The man's eyes slipped away guiltily.

Miguel looked down at the embankment sliding away past the train. 'Tell me how you stop this train?'

'You spin this wheel and then pull this lever.'

'How do you reduce steam pressure?'

'It's this lever here.'

'All right,' said Miguel. 'Jump.'

The driver gaped. 'What?'

'Jump!'

'You mean . . . leave the train running by itself?'

'That's right.'

The driver shook his head. 'I won't leave a runaway train on the line.'

Miguel raised his sten-gun. 'Have it your way,' he gritted.

The driver looked at the gun, crossed to the steps of the cab, descended them and stood on the bottom step. He looked up at Miguel, wanting to say something but not daring. When Miguel pointed the sten-gun at him he shrugged his shoulders and jumped.

He jumped badly, with both feet together and forgetting to throw himself backwards. He was hurled forward on his face and lay making feeble movements as the train rumbled on.

A few minutes later Miguel told the stoker: 'You jump now.'

Without a word the man crossed the cab and went down the steps. He jumped, rolled over and over, climbed to his feet and stood watching the train disappear.

Miguel watched the countryside sliding past. Pain surged up in another wave of dizziness and he knew he must act soon. He sat on the floor of the cabin with his feet on the iron steps. The swaying jolted his smashed shoulder agonisingly, but he peered ahead until he saw the landmark he was awaiting.

He watched it approach and prepared to jump. He was vaguely aware that the train was going much faster and remembered he'd anticipated this and asked how to reduce speed. But it didn't seem important now. He watched the landmark coming towards him and then tearing at him.

He jumped without thinking, feeling himself flying and then swashing against the gravel in black, splintering agony, rolling down the embankment with a thousand knives tearing at his shoulder until he screamed aloud. There was a long drop, a hovering in space and another smashing impact which numbed all awareness.

He recovered consciousness lying on his back in tall grass. The late afternoon sun beat down on his exposed face and the world swam sickeningly. He wanted to lie quite still, but the instinct to escape goaded him to his feet and the crawling black mass on his shoulder and chest buzzed angrily. He smeared away the great clot of ants and blow-flies, reeled in the wrong direction for many paces before he realised it and painfully retraced his steps. He saw his sten-gun lying on the ground, stooped to pick it up, his head swam and he almost fell. The gun was so heavy that he could only carry it slung over his good shoulder.

He stumbled on, his sun-blistered eyes painful and his vision blurred. Vaguely he wondered where he was going. Then a little later, or was it a long time later? he suddenly knew where he was going.

He was going home!

His legs were leaden and every thump of his heart made his head swim. Something deep down inside him was badly hurt and sometimes the agony of his shoulder made him cry aloud. But he stumbled on determinedly, eager to reach the beach and show his mother the fish he had caught. A great fish, all silver and alive and leaping in the bottom of his boat while his strong brown calves were cool in the sea and the boat's painter cut painfully into his shoulder as he hauled the boat up the gently sloping beach.

The sand was hot and heavy and clung to his feet so it needed a great effort to lift them. He plodded along the beach interminably, the hot sun burning his shoulder and the sea a black, buzzing cloud. He saw a figure ahead of him and it was his father. He stumbled on more quickly then, wanting to shout: 'Father. I'm coming.' But his mouth was so dry he could only croak the words. Then when he got closer, he saw it wasn't his father but in a moment of lucidity he recognised the face.

4

Benito Vigon's back ached as he stooped and swung his sickle, trimming the grass lining the shallow ditch. He could have set fire to the grass, but there had been no rain for many months and a spark could start a fire which would consume crops and olive groves.

His sickle flashed and the curling black hairs on his arms glistened with sweat. With every stroke the long grass fell and the cropped stubble was as yellow as straw. Vigon had been married nearly two years and as he laboured he thought of his baby daughter and pictured her in her cot, cooing with pleasure, drawing up her chubby legs and kicking. He had wanted a son, but was more than delighted with a daughter.

Vigon straightened up, eased his aching back and reached for the sharpening stone. He passed the sickle to his bad hand. Shrivelled muscles drew his arm up against his chest, but the fingers that hung from his curved wrist like the drooping branches of a willow tree could hold the sickle firmly while he honed its gleaming edge.

The stone rang against the metal like a high-pitched bell. The hot air was loaded with the hum of insects and the smell of pine trees. He tested the blade, tucked the honing stone into his sash and took the sickle in his right hand.

It was then he saw the man. He was the width of a field away and stumbled drunkenly. His head was lowered and he peered through half-closed eyes as though his vision was blurred.

Vigon watched the man approach, wondering who he was and then knew who he was when he saw the sten-gun slung over the man's shoulder and the blood-encrusted shirt. He dropped his sickle and waited for the man wth a breathless constriction in his chest. He'd heard on the radio at lunch time of the battle between the Cvil Guards and a gang of criminals.

When the man drew close he unslung his sten-gun but was so weak that he held it with the barrel pointing at the ground. He swayed to a standstill, peered hard and croaked. 'Benito!'

Vigon recognised the care-worn face, the swarthy skin, the raven-black hair and the long Barras jaw. 'Miguel!' he said quietly.

'Thirsty,' croaked Miguel. 'Mouth . . . parched.'

Vigon stooped for his wineskin lying in the shade of a bush and gave it to Miguel. He rested the barrel of his sten-gun on the ground and used his teeth to unscrew the stopper. He raised the bottle to his lips and gulped greedily. Wine ran from the corners of his mouth and dripped into his bloodstained shirt. He sighed and wiped the back of his hand across his mouth. He could think more clearly now although the high fever in his blood was nibbling at the outer fringes of his consciousness. He said hoarsely: 'They're after me, Benito. They . . . got all the others.'

'I heard it on the radio.'

'Help me, Comrade. Hide me. Take me home with you.'

Vigon stared at him steadily. 'I'm married, Miguel. I've got a baby and there's another on the way.'

'Help me home, Comrade. Mother will hide me and care for me until I'm well.'

'Why don't you give yourself up, Miguel?'

Miguel said incredulously: 'They'd shoot me on sight!'

'What would happen to my family if I hid you? What would happen to your family if they sheltered you? Go away, Miguel. You'll bring bad trouble to everyone.'

'I don't understand you,' Miguel panted. 'We're friends, Benito. We played as kids, went to school, teased the girls together. We're comrades of war. I'm hurt. I need a doctor. You can't deny me.'

'We were friends a long time ago, Miguel. You're not the same man. You've done ... terrible things!'

Miguel's eyes were feverish. 'I've carried on the fight for freedom. What's happened to you, Comrade? Have you been corrupted?'

'Come with me, Miguel,' persuaded Vigon. 'I will take you to a doctor.'

'No! My mother will care for me.'

Vigon shook his head. 'Your family are my friends. I won't bring your troubles on them. They are good people.'

Miguel swayed. He couldn't understand. 'What do you hold against me? That I killed? We all killed, didn't we? Can you refuse help to a comrade?'

'We've stopped speaking the same language, Miguel. You can't see yourself as others do. You've stopped being a fighter for freedom, Miguel. You're a fanatical murderer!'

Miguel's face set hard. 'Is that what you think?'

'It's what you've proved yourself to be, Miguel.'

'If I'm a murderer I'll kill you ... now!'

Vigon drew himself up proudly.

'Leave me,' choked Miguel. His thoughts and vision were blurred and he was unutterably weary. 'Go away,' he croaked.

Vigon stared at him steadily for some seconds then turned deliberately and walked away. He walked fifty paces before he looked back. He'd half expected to be shot down but Miguel was slumped on a flat rock with the sten-gun across his knees and his chin on his chest.

Vigon reached the highway and followed it towards the village. Presently a jeep packed with Civil Guards lurched towards him over the potholed road and without hesitation Vigon stepped into its path and spread his arms.

The jeep squealed to a standstill and white dust swirled round him like a mist. A sergeant demanded: 'What's the trouble, man?'

'I've seen Scarface.' There was instant tension.

'Where?' panted the sergeant.

Vigon pointed. 'Take the path a hundred yards along on the right which leads to the Vila farm. The second path on the left leads through an olive grove to a meadow. He's badly wounded. He's sitting there on a rock armed with a sten-gun.'

'Show me your papers,' demanded the sergeant.

A corporal said: 'I'll vouch for him. He lives in Escoleras.'

The sergeant slapped the jeep driver on the shoulder. 'Let's go.'

The jeep roared off and Vigon watched it come to a stand-still farther along the road. Civil Guards leaped from it and ran along the path he had indicated. When they were out of sight he turned and walked on towards the village.

He walked slowly and presently he heard the distant rattle of small arms fire. The firing didn't last long.

Benito Vigon kept walking and wiped his calloused hand across the corner of his eye.

5

Rosemarie loved pretty things and sold her jewellery reluctantly. But money vanished swiftly and all too soon she had to break her resolution not to sell her pearl necklace. She returned to her apartment with the money and knew at once that Maroto had been home and gone out again. He'd left the telephone standing dangerously close to the edge of the table.

She showered leisurely, painted her toenails and fingernails, scented herself and put on freshly laundered underwear. She loved the gossamer touch of dainty garments on her skin.

There was a worry nagging at her, but it was some time before she realised what it was. Maroto's slippers were not under the bed and his dressing gown was missing. She opened the door of the wardrobe and stared in astonishment at bare shelves. His two suitcases had gone too. He'd taken everything that was his.

She searched the apartment for a note but all that remained was his hair oil stain on the pillowcase and the stale scent of cigar smoke.

She sat down calmly and reasoned it out. He'd been elated since he'd destroyed Scarface's band. Without doubt he'd been promoted and switched to other work. He'd probably had to pack and leave at a moment's notice. Rosemarie resigned herself to patience, anxiously awaited the postman and spent long, lonely nights watching the telephone.

There was not a word from Maroto.

The electricity bill was heavy and the telephone account with Maroto's many long-distance calls aroused new money worries. It was ironic that when she had resolved to discuss money with him he should have left so unexpectedly.

She knew he would resent her intrusion into his professional life, but after two weeks she went to the Commissary. The officials were polite to an attractive young woman but not helpful. She showed her papers to a succession of different officials, answered many questions, but could only learn that Maroto had been recalled to Madrid. Nobody knew his address.

Bills came for wine, whisky and cigars, an invoice for new curtains she'd fitted the previous week and a reminder from her landlord that the next quarter's rent was due. Rosemarie made calculations and learned that she was in pressing need of money. If she worked again it would take time to build up a clientele and she would have to borrow money until she was earning again. But the very thought of 'working' filled her with revulsion. What she wanted more than anything was to have Maroto to look after and care for. To have him dominate and bully her, yet sometimes be as loving as only he knew how.

Rosemarie decided to join Maroto in Madrid. She sold her furniture and adornments for almost nothing. Shopkeepers shook their heads sadly. Times were bad, nobody had any money and stock stayed in the shops gathering dust. It was the same with her expensive dresses. They brought her very little. She used up most of the money paying outstanding debts and travelled to Madrid by train with only two crammed suitcases and a slender purse. She told a taxi driver she wanted cheap accommodation for a few days and he took her to a modest boarding house.

It was difficult to trace Maroto. Government offices only opened in the mornings and there were always long queues. Often she waited an hour or more only to be told to try another office where another queue was waiting and where the doors closed before it was her turn.

Finally she located him. The uniformed receptionist said: 'He's very busy now. You must telephone later.'

She walked the streets waiting for time to pass and phoned him from a cafe. But he'd left the building and wouldn't be back until tomorrow. She telephoned many times the next day but he was never there. Finally she called again at the office.

'He can't see you now,' said the receptionist. 'Will you call back?'

'It's very important that I see him. I'll wait.'

'You may have to wait a long time.'

'I don't mind.' She crossed to a bench and sat down, wondering which of her dresses she should sell next. After two hours she persuaded the receptionist to ring through again.

'The young lady is still waiting,' he reported. 'She says it's very important. She doesn't mind how long she waits.' The receptionist listened. 'All right.' He nodded at Rosemarie encouragingly and beckoned a uniformed guard. 'Take the Señorita to room fourteen.'

Room fourteen was a windowless interrogation room. She sat on a chair under an arclight and remembered that it was just in such a room she had first met Renato.

He kept her waiting an hour and when he stepped into the room he was a stranger, emotionally cold and detached. She wanted to embrace him but his icy coldness rebuffed her. She stared up at him with pained eyes.

'What do you want?' he demanded tonelessly.

'I ... didn't know what had happened to you. You left without a word!'

'Was there anything to say?'

'Don't be this way, darling.' Her eyes swam wth tears. 'I want you, Renato. I *need* you. I'll cook for you, clean for you, care for you. I'll do *everything*!'

He stared bleakly over her head. 'That's all over now. This is Madrid.'

'Please, Renato. Let me be with you. I'll do anything you say.'

'Go back to Barcelona.'

She choked. 'That's all I mean to you?'

'Is there anything else you want?'

'I've given you everything,' she choked. 'My love, my money, my jewellery and my clothes. You can't cut me off this way, Renato. I've got nothing ... *nothing*!'

He frowned, pulled out his wallet and took out two currency notes. 'Here. Is that enough?'

She threw the notes at him. 'Don't treat me this way. I'm human!'

He carefully picked up the money. 'Why refuse payment? You're a whore, aren't you?'

'Let me stay with you, Renato.' Tears trembled on her eyelashes. 'Weren't you happy with me?'

'I need a change,' he said brutally.

Her pride was broken. If it would have helped she would have fallen to her knees and begged him to take her back.

'It was an episode, Rosemarie,' he said quietly. 'Ships that pass in the night. It's all over now. I've got other interests.' He nodded casually and strolled out of the room.

She dried her eyes, composed herself and left the building with her head high. But as soon as she was outside a black loneliness swamped her and her misery was so great that she almost ran back into the building. Instead she waited patiently on the other side of the road until he ran down the steps and strode away. She ran after him, caught his arm and hurried to keep pace with him.

'I've got to talk to you, Renato. There's something I must explain.'

He was embarrassed, tugging his arm free and glancing round anxiously, worried that anyone should see them. He flagged down a taxi.

'It's important, Renato,' she said. 'Terribly important.'

He jerked open the taxi door, but she stood in his way.

'Rosemarie,' he said urgently, 'I've got important business. I'll see you later at the Black Sheep Tavern. Be there at ten tonight.'

She knew he was lying but let him go so that his lie would be proved and waited at the Black Sheep for more than an hour before she went back to her lonely room and cried herself to sleep.

The next morning when Maroto arrived at the Commissary she was waiting for him. 'You didn't come,' she accused.

His eyes avoided hers. 'I couldn't get away.'

'I must see you alone, Renato.'

'It's all been said, Rosemarie. There's nothing more to talk about.'

'There's *much* more!'

'If it's money . . .?'

'It's not money, Renato. It's *you* I want. We've got to talk about it.'

He sighed and glanced at his watch. His dark face poised over her like a vulture's beak. 'Do you know the Nouvelle Bar near the Plaza del Sol? Wait outside at ten tonight and I'll pick you up.'

'You promise, Renato?'

'Yes.'

'Last night you broke your promise.'

'Tonight it will be different.'

She arrived at the Nouvelle with ten minutes in hand and walked up and down slowly, ignoring men who ogled her, while anxiety grew inside her. At a quarter past ten there was still no sign of Maroto.

Two tall men stopped on either side of her. One pulled back his coat lapel to show his police badge and she sighed with relief. 'Come with us,' he said. He had a broken nose which had been set crookedly.

'Did Maroto send you?' she asked.

He looked at her curiously. 'That's right.'

'Is it far?'

'Only a few steps.'

One walked ahead of her and the other followed, along the main street, up a side street and up the steps of a Commissary.

'Identity card,' said the man with the twisted nose.

She gave it to him.

'This way.' He led her down a long corridor. At the end was an iron door. A guard drew back bolts and opened it. It was a large cell crowded with women of all types and ages. They stared out sullenly.

'Inside,' said Crook nose.

Rosemarie stared in astonishment. 'What?'

'Don't get awkward *now*,' he pleaded.

'I don't understand . . .' she began.

'Will you step inside like a lady or . . .'

'You *can't* do this,' she choked. 'I demand that Señor Maroto knows about this!'

He eyed her curiously. 'He does!' He eased her over the threshold and the cell door slammed.

Something happened to her mind during the long night which anaesthetised her suffering. Some of the women were drunk and sang unmusically until guards came and laid night sticks across their shoulders. There was only a small hole in the stone floor to serve their physical needs and the air was thick with the stench of vomit, excretion and stale urine. Some of the women had sores and those who weren't lousy soon began to scratch. Rosemarie's mind retreated to an inner remoteness and although horror touched her, she retained her sanity.

The next morning she was taken to the railway station with five other girls and locked in a compartment. The glass windows were painted so that nobody could see in, the seats were wooden and it had been left in a filthy condition by previous occupants who'd made this same, sad journey. But nothing could reach Rosemarie through the numbed hurt that gripped her.

At the correction centre her long hair was sheared off and her head razor-shaved. They held up a mirror and she stared at the gleaming baldness of her head, unmoved by the horror she saw in the eyes of her companions who wept as they awaited their turn. They gave her a coarse canvas smock to wear that chafed her skin where it touched her.

159

Stern women warders kept them working. Nuns led prayers for sinners a dozen times a day and there were punishment cells for girls who did not conform, where they spent days in darkness with a ration of cold water and stale bread.

Rosemarie scrubbed floors. She was on her knees from early morning until bed time. She scrubbed courtyard flagstones and stone steps with cold water and caustic soda. Her nails split to the quick, her hands swelled and became so tender that it was painful to hold the scrubbing brush. She scrubbed every flagstone three times over, rinsed it clean and scrubbed it yet again. When all the flagstones in the courtyard were spotless, sheep from the farmyard were herded across it and scrubbing began again. Her knees were swollen and the skin calloused. The food was insufficient, her feminine curves withered and as she scrubbed, her shrivelled breasts swung and chafed against her smock.

Each day was an eternity of numbed misery.

CHAPTER EIGHT

1

THERE was one part of the beach where the younger villagers gathered and swam during the summer months. Silvana Ledesma spent all day there, wheezing as she eased herself on to her towel, mechanically scolding the children and then relaxing to read a paper novelette. Her plump shoulders gleamed with oil and her generous breasts swelled out over the neckline of her swimsuit. She remained on the beach until dusk, wading into the sea when the sun was too hot and sitting down with the surf swirling round her until she was cool enough to lie in the sun again.

Her eldest daughter, Silvana, was fifteen. At lunch time she was sent home to cut bread, smear it with tomato pulp, add olive oil and bring it back in a rafia basket. Spending her days on the sand saved Silvana work. Her older children looked after themselves and the younger ones played naked, not soiling clothing if they messed themselves. Her daughter Silvana was always on hand to stop them drowning themselves and to wash them in the sea when they were dirty.

Other villagers had caught the sunbathing craze of the tourists. Benito Vigon's wife came to the beach every day with her two children. So did Anita Morales, Camila Vigon, who'd married a building contractor from Figueras and had three children, Helena Guitart and her two young sons and a dozen others.

There was a natural pigmentation in the villagers' skins and they tanned easily. They swam like fish, and when they waded out of the sea with gleaming droplets clinging to them and threw themselves down on the hot sand, they fitted into their background.

But the tourists, a hundred yards along the beach, lived in a different world and stood out starkly from their surroundings. The Marvista Hotel was six storeys high now and workmen were extending its foundations to double the length of its façade. A wide, tiled terrace ran the full length of the hotel and swim-suited tourists sat under gaily coloured awnings and sunshades or relaxed in deck chairs while pretty waitresses in crisp, linen dresses brought them drinks. Rich, black soil had been brought down from the mountains in trucks, trees and seeds had been planted and now cool shade was spread by the foliage and a lawn of lush green grass stretched from the terrace to the sea's high water mark.

The Marvista accommodated two hundred and fifty guests, but there seemed to be many more as they stretched out on the lawn with dark glasses turned to the sun and their white-skinned bodies turning pink. The beach was littered with deck chairs and the white flutter of newspapers flown into Barcelona the previous day. The tourists romped in the sea like lobster-coloured seals, paddling and splashing, learning to swim and floating on inflated air cushions. They rented pedal boats or languidly drifted in glass-bottomed canoes and studied the floor of the sea with breathless wonder. From breakfast until one o'clock this stretch of beach was like photographs the Spaniards had seen of Coney Island, Brighton or Nice. Then magically, long before the Spaniards thought of lunch, the tourists simultaneously disappeared, leaving only empty deck chairs and slanting sunshades to show where they had been.

Leon Coruna lived in the hotel during his summer break from school, but he always joined his Catalan friends in the mornings. He was tall for his age. His silver hair and laughing eyes were inherited from Teresa and his grandfather, El Rubio. He was slim but well-muscled, he swam effortlessly and when he waded out of the sea, tossing his head and spraying droplets widely, the young Silvana watched him secretly.

Leon came across to their group. 'Bon dia, Señora Ledesma.'

Silvana was reading and glanced up absently. 'Bon dia, Leon.'

Leon smiled round at all the elders. 'Bon dia.'

The younger ones were sitting in a large circle. Leon sat down between Asuncion Serra and Diego Munez, a gipsy boy who was strumming a guitar and singing softly.

'Have you heard about the new promenade, Leon?' asked one boy.

'I heard mother talk about it,' he said knowledgeably. 'But it's still under discussion. They want to build a wide promenade along the front of the village and a road for cars with street lamps and laid-out gardens.'

'It'll cost millions,' said Jaime Guitart, his eyes wide with awe.

'It's for the tourists and they bring millions into the country,' said Leon.

They looked at him respectfully. Although he was one of them he had a foot well placed in the other impressive world of wealth and foreigners.

162

'My father says it's a boom period,' said Asuncion Serra. They listened to her too with respect. Everyone knew her father had made a fortune buying and selling old iron. Now he owned a factory in Barcelona which manufactured chicken wire for all Spain. And on the slopes beyond Escoleras he'd bought a vineyard for a song and an army of workmen were pegging out plots for the bungalow village he was building. With typical frugality Serra had hired a truck, driven to Andalucia where there was acute poverty, signed up labourers for a minimum wage and brought them back to Escoleras.

'Mother says Spain's passed its crisis and is on the up-grade,' said Leon. 'She says prosperity's like a snowball rolling down a hill, growing bigger and bigger and bigger.' He glanced towards the Hotel Marvista and thought he could see the hotel's façade spreading relentlessly along the bay for many miles.

'Are there *so* many tourists?' asked one girl. 'Not everyone in the world will come here.'

'This is only the beginning,' said Leon. He spoke with conviction because his mother's enthusiasm was contagious. 'The Government will soon have to open more frontiers otherwise there won't be enough to let them all in.'

'I don't mind as long as the tourists leave us a little sea to swim in,' said Silvana, and they all laughed.

Some of the boys did headstands. The girls tried it too and there was laughing and horseplay as they rolled in the sand. Then they played handball.

Every morning they met on the beach and it was fun because they were young. But the older boys and girls were beginning to show shy interest in one another. Leon often swam a long way out to sea and one day when he came back he found a folded note lying on his towel. While he wiped himself dry he glanced at it, folded it quickly and thrust it away into the band of his bathing trunks. The wording was written in tiny crosses representing kisses and read simply: 'S loves L'.

Leon glanced around furtively. Maria was being buried in the sand by the others and nobody was watching him. But Silvana was nearest and he felt a thrill of excitement, knowing instinctively that she had written the note.

A little later he invited: 'Walk with me along the beach, Silvana?'

She got to her feet at once.

'Don't go far,' snapped her mother. 'I can't keep getting up to stop Freda falling in the water.'

'You'll look after Freda, won't you, Asuncion?' pleaded Silvana.

'All right,' agreed her friend amiably.

They walked along the beach side by side, past the tourist zone and on beyond. 'Did you write the note?' he asked.

She didn't ask what note. She said: 'No!' and flushed.

'You can admit it,' he said.

'It's not up to the girl.'

'I . . . like you too, Silvana.' He had to say 'like' because the word 'love' stuck in his throat.

'Do you want to be my boy?'

'All right,' he agreed, and instantly the decision frightened him because it seemed binding.

That summer passed happily for them. They swam together and sat next to each other on the beach and took long walks, far enough away from the others to share their secret thoughts.

It was an eventful year. There was an abundance of fish, of ambition, of planning and of social activity. It was a year of great events and of sad happenings. It was a year of farewell to old traditions and of welcome to the new way of life.

It was the last year of Hernando and Father Delbos.

2

Although they were now wealthy, Vicente Serra and his wife, Maria, still lived in their old house and never spent a peseta if it could be avoided. They drove themselves from morning to night and although Serra's bungalow project was sweeping, neither he nor his wife were above prowling round the piles of broken and discarded bricks for those they thought could still be used.

They put Asuncion to work in a grocer's store where she started at eight in the morning and remained until it closed at ten at night. The only concession that Serra made to his affluence was an arrangement with the grocer during the summer months that Asuncion needn't start work until after lunch and could spend the mornings on the beach.

When she was young, Asuncion had been taunted by other children about her parents' meanness. The wounds of the jibes never quite healed and she was always ill at ease with others of her own age. She felt she was looked down upon and was always shy and uncertain. She was astonishingly beautiful. Despite childhood illnesses and chronic lack of nourishment, she'd grown fit and strong and although somewhat thin, she had rich blue-black hair and symmetrical facial bones which made her features delicately lovely.

Father Delbos noticed her. One day after confession he said before she left the box: 'Meet me in the vestry, Asuncion.'

It was dark in the vestry and it smelled of the bleaching chemical used to clean the choir boys' surplices.

'Come, Asuncion,' said Father Delbos in his fatherly way. 'Sit by me.' He patted the wooden bench beside him. 'You're growing quickly. You'll be a woman soon.' She wore a sleeveless cotton dress and his fingers teased her armpit, gently tugging a moist black tendril of underarm hair. 'This shows you're growing into a woman, Asuncion.'

'Yes, Father,' she said with a note of doubt in her voice.

'It's also elsewhere too, isn't it?' he asked, and the question was so natural that she answered unhesitatingly and thought he must have some special all-knowing power if he could know about *that*.

'Now, Asuncion,' he said seriously. 'I want you to grow into a *sensible* young woman. I'll help you as I've helped hundreds of girls. It's my duty.'

'Yes, Father.'

'Nevertheless, it must be a secret between us, because I haven't time to spare for everyone. Do you understand, child?'

'Yes, Father.' She was curious to know what she could learn.

'You promise?'

'I promise.'

'On the book,' he said, and held it so that she could place her hand on it when she vowed.

'You understand this is a secret between we two. You must never tell anyone, not even your mother and father. If you do, you will go to hellfire.'

'I won't tell anyone, Father.'

'Very well. I want you to read the Bible to me while I teach you new mysteries.'

'Yes, Father.'

'Come here, child.' He pulled her in between his parted legs and sat her upon his thigh. She wasn't afraid because he was a priest and must be good. But she felt strange.

'Can I not sit on the bench, Father?'

'Are you not comfortable, child?'

'Yes ... but ...'

'Read to me,' he said, handing her the open Bible.

She read slowly and timidly and her voice didn't falter when his hand rested on her knee. But when it slid higher between her thighs she stopped abruptly.

'What is it, child?'

'Please, Father. I feel strange. It is not right you should touch me thus.'

He chuckled. 'But I am different, child. I am a man of God.

165

What I teach is with the wisdom of the Holy Spirit.'

'Yes, Father.' But she clamped his hand tightly between her thighs.

'Don't resist me, child.'

She gulped. 'I am afraid, Father.'

'You must not be afraid, child. You are safe and I will guide you as I have many others.'

She yielded to his insistence and he touched her in a disturbing way. She made a sighing sound and he said: 'You now feel the secret of becoming a woman.'

'Yes, Father. But ... please stop!'

'Are you afraid?'

'No, Father.'

'Is it not pleasant?'

'Yes, Father. But ... it is a pleasure I should not have with you because it is not right.'

'You are impatient, child. Wait a little and you will learn of the deeper pleasure which will make you happy to be a woman.'

And it was so.

Two nights later in the vestry he taught her more. It was difficult to concentrate on reading while he taught her the pleasure of becoming a woman and she was relieved when he took the Bible away and placed it on the bench. 'Do you know what is Adam's rib, my child?'

The delight of his touch was marred by his smelly breath. She closed her eyes and thought of Diego Munez whose olive skin and handsome gipsy features made her heart leap whenever she saw him.

'The rib of creation,' said Father Delbos. 'Adam's rib.'

Intuitively she knew what he meant, having sensed it while she sat on his lap. But learning about it was prolonged for many sessions in the vestry while her timidity and shyness were lulled and slowly lured to the intimacy of mutual caressing.

'You have learned well, child,' Father Delbos told her.

Her knees were trembling, she was sticky and wanted to wash her hands. He opened a wardrobe, unlocked a drawer and took out a slab of chocolate. 'A present, child,' he said.

All her inner guilt feelings dissolved then as she recalled how other girls giggled secretly as though at a great joke while they ate sweets that Father Delbos had given them. She went away reassured. Other girls did it too.

Three weeks later at a critical moment with Father Delbos, the vestry door, which he had forgotten to lock, burst open and they were caught by the woman who came to clean. She was deeply religious and gave her services freely to the church. After Father Delbos had spoken to her long and seriously she was almost persuaded to believe his explanations. She spent days in an agony of irresolution and finally turned to the only other man in whom she had confidence.

Doctor Aldo listened quietly and assured her she could leave everything in his hands.

He called upon the Serras and asked to see Asuncion in private. He talked to her alone, gently breaking down her reticence and worming out the story. She gave him the names of other girls whom she thought had lessons with Father Delbos.

Doctor Aldo talked to all of them. Silvana Ledesma admitted that Father Delbos had once embraced her and touched her, but she had pulled free and run away. Other girls had had similar experiences. Two girls were at the same stage of intimacy as Asuncion.

Doctor Aldo and the parents called upon the mayor and the judge and later a small deputation called upon Father Delbos.

Like wildfire the news ran round the village. Father Delbos had left suddenly. Nobody knew where or why.

Three days later another priest arrived. He was a middle-aged Catalan, fat and jovial. He smoked cigars in the street, laughed heartily at doubtful jokes, slapped people boisterously in greeting and wasn't above swearing. He quickly learned everybody's Christian names, joined the chess club, paddled in the sea with his cassock rolled up over his knees and organised picnics for the children every Sunday. Outside the church he never reproached villagers who did not attend Misa, but his church filled up and within a month he was holding services for larger congregations than had ever been known.

3

That year the town hall was enlarged. The house next door was taken over, the intervening walls knocked down and the offices expanded. The council's secretary, a permanent official, engaged an assistant. Business men from all over Europe bombarded the town hall with letters asking where they could buy land, the conditions of building permits and the facilities available for water and lighting.

Escoleras was becoming a popular tourist resort and the price of land beside the sea soared. Allotments, disused vineyards and neglected olive groves, once thought worthless, were eagerly sought after, while astute Catalan peasants forced up

167

the price. Twice a week a lawyer from Figueras came to Escoleras to untangle land deed problems. When land had been worthless the boundaries were not maintained. Fierce disagreements now waged between owners and many disputes were scheduled for legal proceedings. There was even one involved case of four different Catalans indignantly claiming ownership of land which had already been sold to a Swiss by a fifth Catalan.

Foreign capital flooded into the new, unexploited tourist market and the Spanish Government encouraged it by giving Spain a face lift.

The Governor of the Province appointed twelve new councillors for Escoleras, a plan of development was drawn up and money was made available for the scheme to start at once. A promenade was to be built along the front of the village between the harbour and the beach. Flowering palm trees would be planted, there would be gardens with flowers, public benches and neon lamp posts. The beach would disappear and the fishermen would have to draw their boats up out of the water elsewhere, but even although the promenade existed only on the drawing board, a business man in Barcelona applied for a deck chair concession.

The work went forward quickly. A long line of stakes was placed from the harbour along to the beach. They stood far out in six feet of water. A long armed crane was brought down from Barcelona and the great concrete blocks an army of workmen made with wooden moulds were lifted into position. These concrete blocks made a long wall outside the stakes. Then six tipping trucks arrived. They loaded up with earth and stones in a quarry at the back of the village and tipped it into the sea inside the stone wall, steadily filling in what would become the promenade.

Hernando's stone hut on the beach came within the marine zone. He did not own the ground and town development couldn't be held up for one man. Hernando would have to go. Everyone regretted it, but it couldn't be helped.

Hernando listened with dignity, stroked his neatly trimmed beard and nodded sadly while it was explained to him by the secretary, the architect and the mayor.

But he didn't leave his stone hut.

Paco Barras, Doctor Aldo and many others offered him the hospitality of their homes.

Hernando thanked them gravely, smiled sadly and rolled the waxed ends of his moustache until they bristled like needles.

But he did not leave his hut.

The mayor and the councillors convened a special meeting.

They voted Hernando the use of a piece of land the Council owned behind the village for his lifetime. A councillor started a subscription list to build Hernando a small villa. Then the mayor and the councillors visited Hernando and told him what was arranged. He thanked them gravely and offered them his wineskin.

But he did not leave his hut.

The tipping trucks had started work at the harbour and steadily filled in the space behind the wall, replacing sea with gravel and building a promenade of earth which marched inexorably towards Hernando's hut.

Hernando sat on the beach, baiting his fish hooks, weaving his lobster pots and showing no sign that he would leave.

The mayor and others called to reason with him. But Hernando did not argue. He listened, nodded solemnly and offered them his wineskin. And always when they left they felt ashamed and a little ridiculous. Hernando was solemn and dignified, but there was a hint of pity in his blue eyes which made them feel like thoughtless children.

The tipping trucks worked on. They reached Hernando's hut, skipped it and filled in on the other side. Finally, Hernando's hut and its strip of beach was surrounded by a high dyke. The tipping was concluded but for Hernando's hut.

The villagers gathered early the next morning to see what would happen. But there was an anti-climax. During the night Hernando had disappeared, taking his bedding and cooking pans, his fishing line and his shotgun. All had been loaded into his little fishing boat and he had sailed away. He was never seen again.

The tipping began. The gap was filled in, pickaxes demolished the part of Hernando's stone hut which was higher than the earth around it and steam rollers flattened, levelled and prepared the ground for the New Spain.

4

This same year Pepita became engaged.

Teresa had built her a small factory at the end of the hotel garden where Pepita worked with six girls making mosaic pictures. They were a colourful novelty and Teresa never ceased to be surprised at how well they sold. Despite their weight, tourists paid handsomely, packed them in their suitcases and took them home, a thousand miles away. Pepita earned money and felt useful and independent. She had learned to overcome almost all her disabilities. She had attachments made for the leather sleeves laced to the stumps of her

169

arms. She could cut up her own food and even write in a large scrawl. But she never overcame her self-consciousness about her scarred face and always turned her good profile to people.

Luis Jova was twenty-six, good-looking, alert and eager to make his way in life. His parents were elderly and owned only their cottage and a small allotment. Luis knew that in this new and quickly changing world the only way to keep pace with it was to work hard. Luis worked hard!

He gave satisfaction to Teresa who made him her under-manager. At lunch time he wore a white suit with a black tie, supervised the waiters, helped at the bar when it was over-busy, handled kitchen problems and answered guests' questions. After seven in the evening he changed into a black dinner jacket and carried on doing the same job.

One day at the end of the season when business was slack. Teresa asked him up to her rest room-cum-office on the top floor. The room had a terrace and an excellent view of the sea and bay and was tastefully furnished with comfortable arm-chairs, a lounging couch, a writing desk and a portable bar.

'Pour yourself a drink, Luis,' said Teresa.

'How about you, Señora?'

Teresa smiled wryly. He always addressed her as Señora and she never quite got used to it because it made her feel old.

'Just a little one, Luis,' she said, and realised with a shock that she would soon be forty. The years had flown. She'd been so busy with her son and business that time had concertinaed. It seemed only yesterday that Leon had been born.

'What will you drink, Señora?'

On the spur of the moment Teresa said: 'Pour me whisky. It must have something if so many clients like it.'

He sat on the edge of his chair, toying nervously with his glass while she sat back comfortably.

'Relax, Luis,' she urged. 'Don't be so edgy. You'll wear yourself out.'

He sat back in his chair, still uncomfortably tensed.

Teresa asked bluntly: 'What do you think of my sister, Pepita?'

'She's . . . very pleasant, Señora.'

'You see a good deal of her, don't you, Luis? You handle the orders for mosaics.'

'Yes,' he agreed. 'This year we sold more than last year and I suggested to Pepita . . .'

'You think Pepita's a nice natured girl?'

He was startled. It was the word 'girl' that bothered him. 'Pepita's more than thirty, isn't she?'

'Only a little,' said Teresa quickly. 'I call her a girl because

170

she's unmarried.'

'She's pleasant,' he agreed carefully. 'Much more even-tempered than you'd expect...!'

'She was very pretty before the accident.'

'You can see that even now, Señora.'

Teresa looked down into her glass and swirled the whisky round. 'What plans have you for your future, Luis?'

He smiled. 'Work hard, earn money, save and get out of the rut.'

'You haven't got a girl?'

'I haven't time, Señora. I've got to take a position for myself and ...'

'Why don't you marry Pepita?'

'I beg your pardon, Señora?'

Teresa repeated. 'Why don't you marry Pepita?'

A flush spread up from his neck and turned his cheeks crimson. He looked away in embarrassment. 'I ... I hadn't thought about it.'

'She's not an attractive proposition, is she,' said Teresa bluntly. 'She's maimed, she's older than you, she's unsightly and she often snaps bad-temperedly.'

He took out his handkerchief and wiped the sweat from his forehead. 'I didn't say those things, Señora.'

'I said them for you,' said Teresa. 'They're all valid reasons for not wanting to marry her. But in Pepita's favour we can say she is a very sweet girl who needs a husband's love and children. Not having them is embittering her.'

He listened miserably.

'I'm a down to earth woman, Luis. I like everything clean cut. I'll tell you something else about Pepita. The day she's engaged I'll start building a new hotel as a wedding gift to her and her husband. The day she's married it will be ready and furnished and handed over, lock, stock and barrel. With good management their future and the future of their children will be assured. What do you think, Luis?'

He stared at her with wide eyes.

'There are drawbacks in being married to a handless woman older than yourself,' she said. 'There are times when Pepita is totally dependent upon others. But in marriage you expect to take the ups and downs. There can be plenty of ups too.'

Teresa finished her drink. 'This conversation is private, Luis. I don't want to persuade you. Think about it and decide. If you don't refer to it again before the beginning of next month, I'll know you're not interested. And whatever you decide won't affect your future with me.'

A month later Luis and Pepita became engaged. Teresa gave

171

a dinner party for friends and relatives. Pepita sat at the head of the table and was so radiant that her guests quite failed to see the disfiguring scars on her face.

5

When she left the correction centre, Rosemarie was given a train ticket to Barcelona, a little money and a letter of introduction to the Mother Superior of a convent who might give her shelter. The train was a slow one and was often shunted into sidings while expresses raced past and it was early evening before she reached Barcelona.

Rosemarie gave up her ticket, stepped out into the station hall and looked round slowly as though coming back to life after a long, long death. The familiar smell of scorched iron, burnt coffee and stale tobacco rushed in on her. Scurrying crowds, the anxious voices of passengers hurrying for trains and the static loudness of the station loudspeaker were familiar.

Rosemarie went to the station cafe and recklessly squandered some of her money on coffee and a roll, standing at the counter while she sipped the rich, milky liquid laced with sugar and relishing the soft pastry.

Her hair had grown and been shaved off many times in the correction centre and now it was a short bob, a dark lifeless tangle streaked with silver. Combs were non-existent in the correction centre. The smart clothes she'd worn on admission couldn't be found and they'd given her an ill-fitting black skirt, a white blouse and a navy-blue top coat of cheap, shoddy material.

She had nowhere to go except the convent. She showed her letter of introduction, was given a bowl of soup, a hunk of bread and a cot for the night and was sent out early the next morning to find work.

Previously in Barcelona she'd earned well and spent lavishly. But now she saw the seamy side of Barcelona. It was unnerving. There was severe unemployment and although Rosemarie searched diligently the only jobs available paid so little that they were only acceptable to girls living with their parents.

She'd known this before she began her search and did not waste too much time futilely. She went to an address she knew and when the door was opened by a white-aproned maid she asked for La Señora.

La Señora was a plump, middle-aged woman who listened sympathetically but shook her head as soon as she'd looked Rosemarie up and down.

'You've been in a correction centre, dear?'

Rosemarie made a face.

'We're full up,' sighed La Señora. She eyed Rosemarie critically. 'I don't want to be hurtful, my dear, but you won't get far as you are. You need flesh on your bones. There's not enough of you for a man to get his teeth into. Hair like rat tails and your hands ... a man wouldn't want you to touch him with hands like those!'

Rosemarie flushed. 'As soon as I earn a little money I'll look nice again.'

'Why don't you go home to your parents and rest.'

'I ... I'm an orphan.'

'Haven't you a boy friend who ...' La Señora broke off. She saw Rosemarie's pinched face, hollow cheeks, haunted eyes and shrunken chest. 'No. I suppose not.'

'All I need is a start and then I'll be all right. I used to earn big ...'

'Yes,' sighed the Señora. 'We all used to earn big. There's a time for it, but you never know until it's over. It doesn't ever come back. Our profession is unique. We start at the top and there's only one way we can go ... down!'

'Can't you do anything for me?' pleaded Rosemarie.

'I'll be honest, girl. Even if I had a vacancy I *couldn't* have you. My house has to maintain standards.'

Rosemarie got to her feet sadly. 'Can you recommend anywhere?'

La Señora opened a drawer, took from it a visiting card and scribbled an address on its back. 'Try Lola's. You might think it's below you, but the way things are you'll be lucky to get in.'

'How about going on the streets?'

'Very risky. You don't want to go back to a correction centre, do you?'

Rosemarie shuddered.

'Perhaps this will help.' La Señora thrust a hundred peseta note into Rosemarie's hand.

'No. You mustn't. I couldn't,' whispered Rosemarie.

'Don't be silly, girl. We're all up against it at some time. You look as if you could use a good meal. When things get better you can pay me back.'

'I will,' promised Rosemarie sincerely. Tears were in her eyes. 'I'll pay you back soon,' she promised.

Rosemarie called at other houses without success. Business was bad and there were more girls than clients. But faced with returning for the night to the convent, Rosemarie went to Lola's.

173

Lola's was in the grey back streets of the dock area. The Madam was a vixenish woman of sixty with skin the colour of a toadstool and black beady eyes. She looked Rosemarie up and down critically. 'You haven't much to offer a man.'

'I'll be all right when I get started.'

'We usually have twenty girls but one left yesterday.'

'Will I suit?' Rosemarie said quickly.

'We can give it a try,' said the Madam doubtfully.

'I'd like to,' said Rosemarie eagerly.

'Each girl has her own room,' said the Madam. 'There's a common room when you're not working where you eat. Don't bring a lot of baggage. There's not room for it.'

'I haven't any,' said Rosemarie quietly.

'We're a fixed price house. The price is painted on the door. There's a percentage deduction for taxes and living expenses. The balance is shared equally between the girl and the house.'

Rosemarie asked timidly: 'What's the fixed price?'

'Five pesetas,' said the Madam.

Rosemarie was shocked. 'So little!'

'Times are bad.'

'When I was working I earned fifty times as much.'

The Madam smiled venomously. 'You can make up for it with the number of clients.'

'But . . . it's throwing yourself away.'

The Madam shrugged her shoulders. 'I'm not short of girls, dearie. Think it over. But I can't hold it open for you if another girl comes along.'

Rosemarie thought quickly. It would be a stop-gap until she got a start. 'I'll stay,' she decided. Then seeing the glitter in the Madam's eyes she added humbly: 'If you will permit me, Señora.'

'Another thing.'

Rosemarie looked at her anxiously.

'Anything goes. The client pays and you give him what he wants. A girl who's fastidious about what she does or turns up her nose because she doesn't fancy a client gives us a bad name.'

Rosemarie nodded. It would only be for a short time, she reassured herself. 'I understand.'

Business started at seven in the evening when the twenty girls filed downstairs into a large, dimly lit hall with wooden benches placed round the walls. There were waist-high swing doors opening on to the street which never stopped flapping until closing time at five a.m. A red light burned above the entrance doors and a placard warned: 'Minors below the age of eighteen not admitted'. The fixed price was painted on each

174

door flap.

In theory the girls sat on the benches while clients strolled round inspecting them. But as soon as the doors were opened, the hall was thronged with men and the girls mingled with them. The smell of cigar smoke blended with the odour of cheap perfume and body sweat. It was the port area and the house catered for lowly paid Spaniards, dock labourers, seamen and lascars.

Rosemarie's first customer was a dark-skinned man with thick lips and cropped black hair. He wore a striped sailor's jersey and grubby white pants. She led him through the turnstile, collected her red plastic disc from the Madam and ushered him upstairs.

The cot was stripped down with a cotton sheet over the mattress. In one corner was a cracked and brown-veined wash basin and her surprised client had to stand on a chair so that she could wash him.

It was her first physical contact with a man since entering the correction centre and his forceful impatience made her cry out. But when he growled: 'What's the matter, woman?' she feared he might complain about her. 'It's nothing. It's all right.'

It was a long night but she learned quickly that for their modest payments clients expected not lovemaking but physical relief and were content with simple climatic satisfaction. They didn't expect a diamond ring for a peseta or a Venus for five pesetas. They were resentful and even suspicious of her cleanliness. The other girls were slick, leading clients upstairs and bringing them down again with startling rapidity, doubling and trebling her own trade.

She learned that although the hall was always crowded with youths and men, only a few were potential customers. Most drifted from house to house inspecting the girls and stimulating their appetites, but without money to satisfy them. She learned she was not expected to wear underclothing. The men pressed round her, face after face stared into hers and it was impossible to know who was a possible client and who was amusing himself. So the girls held still for them all and smiled mechanically while exploring fingers stroked with an insulting casualness.

Despite the throng of men, few were customers and Rosemarie learned she must encourage men and brazenly arouse them. Once, that first night, she thought of Escoleras. The Man was a big drunken Swede who buried her in the mattress so that she couldn't move. He huffed stale wine and garlic fumes into her face and bruised her shoulders. He was a ship's engineer and his skin smelt of diesel oil. He sweated profusely and great beads of it dripped from his forehead on to her face.

And while she was ground beneath his weight, she reflected that nothing could be as bad as this. She thought of Escoleras and Josefina. She pictured Josefina, laughing, bright-eyed and big-breasted. She would have opened her eyes to Rosemarie. Perhaps she still would if she went to her. But Rosemarie blanked the thought out of her mind. Escoleras was a part of her life which was dead. Here she could suffer shocking indignities yet hold her head high because she felt no shame. But in Escoleras she'd not be able to face anyone.

Her last client that night was a Lascar with tattooed arms and a shaven head. One leg had been crushed and he dragged it when he walked. He watched her undress. 'You're not much to look at!'

'I've been ill.'

'You're all bone.'

'I'm sorry.'

'Look at those ribs. Like a scrub board. I can play a tune on them.' He ran his knuckles down them and she flinched.

'Do you want me to wash you?' she asked.

'I'm sweet enough as I am.' He roared with laughter and slapped her hard. 'Call that an ass? No flesh.'

She glowered and rubbed her haunch.

'Come on, girl,' he snorted. He threw himself down and bunched up the pillow beneath his head. When she stooped over him he grasped the shrunken pouches of her breasts. 'What d'you call these?'

'I've been ill,' she said. She moved closer to him but he placed his hands on her shoulders and pressed down.

'Kiss me, girl,' he ordered. 'Kiss me!'

After they closed, Madam settled accounts. Rosemarie had only eleven plastic discs and the other girls smiled their contempt. She'd earned only a few pesetas. Madam explained the accounts. There were many hidden expenses, the rent of the premises, the wages of the cleaners, the door-keeper, tips to the night guards who were always on hand to quell disturbances, gifts to government inspectors who turned a blind eye upon minor infringements of the law, medical fees and so on. A percentage of all these costs was deducted from each girl's earnings and she took fifty per cent of what was left.

'You'll earn more when you get into the way of it, dearie,' encouraged Madam. 'All the other girls do. Otherwise you won't be much good to yourself or to us!'

Wearily Rosemarie made her way upstairs to her tiny room

and lay down tiredly on her cot with its soiled sheet steeped in the smell of man. She'd stick it a while longer, she resolved. And when she'd saved enough to pretty herself she'd get her own flat.

The doctor came the next day for his weekly check-up. The girls sat in the common room reading, talking, listening to the radio or playing cards while awaiting their turn to be examined. The door was left open and Rosemarie saw what was expected of her. The Madam gave her a test tube with her name written on it and the doctor didn't even look at her when she entered. She waited until he glanced up. 'Ah. You're new.' He shredded cotton wool from a roll and wound it round two fingers. 'Brace yourself against the table. That's the way.'

He was a middle-aged man with a bony face. He looked tired and hadn't any interest in her as a woman which made her feel less embarrassed while she held her skirt up round her waist and braced herself.

'Feet astride,' he said briskly, and his fingers sank deep and then withdrew with a sweeping pressure like a hungry man wiping his plate clean with a piece of bread. Pain hissed out between her teeth.

He looked at her sharply. 'Don't move.' He thrust the cotton wool smear into her test tube, corked it and placed it in his bag.

'Sit on the table.' He shone a torch on her, probing gently with his sensitive fingers.

'How long have you been here?'

'I started yesterday.'

'Not used to it?'

'I've been in a correction centre for a long time.'

'Is this sore?'

Again she hissed.

'All right,' he said.

She stood up and shook down her skirt.

'You'd better rest for a few days,' he said. 'I'll tell the Madam.'

'Please don't,' she said quickly. 'I need the money.'

He looked at her unhappily then as his hand moved towards his pocket, she said quickly: 'It's not only the money. I need the job.'

He sighed. 'I suppose so.' He searched his bag and produced a small glass bottle. 'Use this,' he said. 'It's a soothing lubricant.'

His kindness was almost calamitous. Her first client was a German sailor who raged furiously because he couldn't feel anything. She had to wash quickly to appease him.

Rosemarie despised the girls she worked with. They sensed her contempt, kept apart from her and called her a snooty Catalan whore! Most of them were from isolated villages in Andalucia where living conditions had scarcely changed in the last hundred years. They'd been turned out of home for waywardness and had their babies adopted. Their manners were coarse. They would spit on the floor or unconcernedly break wind at the dining table. Some could only sign their names with a cross and those who could read bought only paperbacked romance novels or comics. Their conversation was filthy and their language vile. Their passions were easily aroused and they would scream, tear and claw at one another and sometimes snatch up knives and throw them.

The first days were hard for Rosemarie, but as time passed she adapted. The food in the house was sustaining and she put on flesh until her hip bones didn't stand out so starkly and her breasts, although sagging lifelessly, became pear-shaped. It was hard to save. She needed a new dress and shoes. They were essential. So were her visits to the hairdresser to get her hair looking right again. She adapted to her nightly stint. Her calf muscles, strained taut by high-heeled shoes, grew accustomed to the long hours of standing. She had a false smile ever ready. She learned to recognise hundreds of the faces which laughed into hers and even began to remember those who tested the fruit for ripeness but never purchased.

The weeks drifted into months but her savings increased only very slowly. There was always something she had to buy, another dress, cough medicine, headache pills or cosmetics. The lighting in the hall was dim and the girls needed garish make-up to attract attention, crimson lipstick, thick rouge, heavily pencilled eyebrows and darkly purpled eyelids.

The months passed and one day she realised with surprise that she had been in the house a year. It wouldn't be long now before she got away, she promised herself. Every day she scanned the classified advertisements for furnished flats, mentally selecting the districts and accommodation which would suit her. A flat was too much money to manage at the moment but she was saving hard.

Her small, drab room with its iron cot and soiled sheets had become an integral part of her life. The grunts and gasps and the sweat of men who laboured with her was the same monotonous way of life as the scrubbing at the correction centre. It went on into eternity.

She would break free soon, she vowed. She'd cut away from the foul-mouthed women she was obliged to live with and become her true self.

CHAPTER NINE

THE speedboat was a crimson splash against the blue of the sea and trailing wings of white spray were thrown up on either side. The youth who weaved across its wake on one ski was like a bronzed god flying across the water. Great plumes of spray sometimes enveloped him like puffs of white smoke.

The speedboat made a curving approach to the sand in front of the hotel and tourists watched the bronzed youth with admiration and envy as he swooped in towards the beach, his speed increasing as the speedboat curved out to sea and he released the tow-cord. He hissed on across the water, balanced beautifully, a superb statuette, poised and steering the ski across the shallows with such precision that he glided up the sloping beach and ground gently to a standstill. Leon stepped from it, wetting no more than the soles of his feet.

Instantly he was surrounded by a laughing throng of young people of his own age. Roguish-eyed girls in scanty bikinis asked questions about skiing techniques and youths waded out to meet the speed launch as it returned for its next skiier.

He joined the young people sitting on the hot sand, watching the skiing while they sang. One of them strummed a guitar. There were about twenty of them of mixed nationalities and Leon was their natural leader. The speedboat was a present from Teresa and he was an expert on skis and taught the others. He switched easily from French to Italian, to German and into English and welded together the different nationalities. He was handsome, his hair was silvery-blonde and he was physically beautiful. His long legs were well shaped, his hips were narrow and his shoulders wide. He was strong but without the bulging muscles of a muscle-man. The girls clustered round him eagerly, daring to singe their wings, while youths envied him because he had everything, health, good looks and wealth. He handled his red sports car expertly and it was always full of pretty girls who perched on the back seat with their long hair streaming behind them.

From spring until autumn Leon lived in the hotel like a privileged guest. He was helpful and solicitous to the holiday-makers and the mainspring of their social life. He introduced them to other guests, broke down formal restraints, organised outings, arranged beach sports, encouraged elderly couples to dance and was never without attractive girls at his elbow.

That morning the group sang a German folk song with a German boy playing the guitar accompaniment with professional sensitivity. Leon lay back on the sand with his eyes closed and the English girl beside him happily watched the rhythmic rise and fall of his chest.

Abruptly Leon sat up and saw Silvana who had stared hard at him as she walked past. She looked away from him quickly.

He got to his feet. 'Excuse me, darling,' he said to the English girl with his musical foreign accent which she found so enchanting.

He followed Silvana along the beach. He knew she had walked past him deliberately and he wanted her to look back. But she walked on, confident that he was following her.

He caught up with her and paced at her side. The gentle surf washed in and lapped round their ankles. 'You were looking for me, Silvana?'

'You flatter yourself.'

'Then ... you don't mind me being here with you?'

There was a pause. 'You know that's not true, Leon.'

'Why are you angry?' he asked.

'I suppose I have no right to be angry? Is that it?'

'I know of no reason,' he said quietly.

'You never have time for me, Leon. I never see you. Always you are with other ... friends!'

'I want you as my friend too, Silvana.' He sighed. 'We live in different worlds. I can enter your world but you'll never enter mine.'

'I do not blame you, Leon,' she said slowly, picking her words carefully. 'It is your business to be pleasant to your guests. But you are *always* with them!'

'Then join us,' he encouraged. 'Come now and sit with us. My friends will be your friends.'

She shook her head. 'It cannot be, Leon.' Her cotton swim suit was the only one she possessed. It was a year old and she'd outgrown it. It cut so revealingly into her crotch that she was continually tugging down its brief skirt. She'd seen how those shameless foreign girls behaved, stretched out on the sand with legs shamelessly flung apart, displaying themselves and not caring that their wet bikinis exposed them as though they were naked. Silvana would *never* join such a group.

They had walked a long way along the beach. Leon pointed inland. 'Let's walk over there, Silvana.'

They would be lost to sight among the sand dunes almost at once. Silvana said: 'Let's turn back.'

'You see,' he sighed. 'We are of different worlds. You dare not walk with me among the sand dunes, out of sight of your mother and the gossips, for fear of scandal.'

'I did not make the laws, Leon. They were made by our parents. A girl may not go alone with a boy and retain her good reputation.'

'It's not my fault either, Silvana. I am young. I have a love of life and enjoy it to the full. I want you as my friend, Silvana, but to be your friend I must sit at your side only. We may not picnic without your parents. Your mother's always too tired to come and your father always too busy. And even if they did come they would be a hindrance. How can we talk when every word we utter is overheard?'

'It is not as bad as that, Leon. You can sit with my own group and swim with us in the mornings. Then in the evenings you can call at home and sit with me. I would love it, Leon, and I would not expect you to come every night.'

He tossed his head, flicking his long, fair hair away from his forehead. 'Silvana. I could call upon you for one night, perhaps even two nights. But I could endure no more. I am young and want to live. I can't bear being cramped into a mould of convention.'

'If you liked me, Leon, you would do it.'

He looked at her steadily. 'I'm sorry, Silvana,' he said honestly. 'It must be that I do not like you enough!'

Silvana was silent.

They paced along side by side while he sensed the hurt which chilled her. When she spoke her voice was toneless with her effort to be unemotional.

'I understand you, Leon. You have everything you want. A good life and . . . good friends.'

'Yes,' he agreed. 'I am very lucky.'

'But some day you will want to marry?'

He hesitated. 'Yes . . . some day . . . perhaps.'

'Will it be a Spanish girl?'

He shrugged his shoulders. 'How can I know? They say Spanish girls make good wives, but it is not always so.'

Silvana feared he was thinking of her mother.

'I might marry an English girl, or perhaps a Swiss girl, but marriage is something of which I will not think for many years. Marriage offers me nothing. I have everything to lose!'

'You are selfish, Leon.'

He was surprised. 'Selfish? Why? How? Is it wrong to seek happiness?'

They had walked too far along the beach. She turned back and the jealousy simmering inside her could not be restrained.

'What do these foreign girls mean to you, Leon? Are they truly your friends?'

'Yes,' he said quietly. 'While they are here they are my friends.'

'They ... you kiss them?'

He chuckled. 'How different are our two worlds, Silvana. You may not kiss until you are engaged. But in my world a kiss is a greeting, not a promise of marriage.'

'Is a kiss not something more, Leon?'

'It can be,' he agreed. 'It can be an encouragement to deeper understanding.'

'And do you have a deeper understanding with ... your friends, Leon?'

He said flatly: 'Never be surprised that a man has the desires of a man.'

Although she had been driving him to make this admission, the knowledge was a pain. She thought of the shameless girls displaying their oiled limbs to catch his eye and who, for the brief weeks of their holidays, could see Leon every day and defiance swelled up in her. She said breathlessly: 'I will see you too, Leon. I will enter your world.'

He looked at her curiously. 'This is what I have always wanted, Silvana. Come, I will introduce you to my friends.'

She shrank back. 'No. Not *now*!'

'When, then?'

'It must be at night.'

'At night it is impossible for you.'

'It isn't. I can slip out when everybody is in bed.'

He said slowly: 'It would be wrong, Silvana. I won't encourage you to do it.'

'It's nothing to do with you, Leon. If I decide to escape from my prison, it is *my* decision.'

'We will talk about it,' he said, shelving the slightly alarming suggestion.

'Tonight,' she insisted. 'I will see you tonight.'

He hesitated. 'I've fixed something for tonight.'

'And I'm not welcome?'

'There are five of us. Two German boys and a couple of French girls they've just met. We're going out along the coast in the speedboat for a midnight picnic in a little cove which can only be reached by sea.'

Her voice was dead. 'I understand. You don't want me along.'

'It's not that, Silvana. It's ... not suitable for a Spanish girl.'

'I *do* understand,' she said bitterly. 'You want to take

another girl. I hope you enjoy yourself.'

He'd intended to invite the English girl, but he said quickly:
'I have invited nobody else so if you want to come you can.'

'I do.'

He took a deep breath. 'It's a big risk for you.'

'If you don't want me to come, say so. Don't keep raising obstacles.'

'All right. I've said you can come.'

'Where shall I meet you?'

'On the beach. We're setting off at eleven.'

2

The two German boys spoke a little French, but neither they nor the French girls spoke Spanish, so when Silvana joined them on the beach she learned only their names. Leon introduced her and then she sat quietly while the others chatted excitedly.

Leon drove with his arm firm against her shoulder as they roared out across the sea. The other four in the rear of the boat were accustomed to speeding but Silvana was thrilled by the breathless beauty of the boat's power. It didn't seem to touch the still water as it skimmed across it effortlessly. She looked back at the wake. It was churned up like milk and when the spray was thrown high it flashed with luminous colours like a handful of scattered diamonds. When it splashed down it turned the sea alive with phosphorous radiance.

'Was it difficult to get away?' asked Leon.

She shouted to be heard above the roar of the engine. 'I locked the door of my bedroom and climbed out through the window.'

'It's not good. It's underhand.'

'It's the *only* way.'

'You should have told your father you were coming and insisted upon your right to do so.'

'I haven't any rights,' she said quietly. 'I'm not yet twenty-five.'

'It was risky. You can easily be found out.'

'I don't care,' she said. Defiance was so bracing that she shouted it again. 'I don't care!'

They sped on, paralleling the towering cliffs of the Costa Brava until, far from Escoleras, Leon throttled down and eased the boat into a narrow channel in the cliff face. Presently the channel widened out into a cove and at the end of it was a tiny beach where they drew the boat up out of the water.

The German boys gathered drift wood and lit a fire while

183

Leon and the others unloaded the boat. There were plastic covered cushions, a transistor radio, a picnic basket containing cold chicken, ham, wine, champagne and hot coffee in a thermos flask. It was late, the sea air gave an edge to their appetites and they ate with relish, laughing and joking and drinking a great deal of wine and champagne. Silvana felt apart from the others who enjoyed themselves without restraint. The French girls had met the boys that morning but behaved as though they had known them for years. One girl shared a chicken leg with a boy, teasing him, pulling it away before he could get his teeth into it, shredding flesh from it with her own white teeth and then offering him her mouth so he could take it directly from her, a lip-to-lip tug-of-war and finally lip-to-lip giggling and passing food from mouth to mouth.

Leon was strangely quiet as though her presence subdued his high spirits. He ate sparingly and Silvana wondered if she dared offer him a chicken bone to bite.

The coffee was rich and black and the brandy was heady. It loosened her restraint. The French girls had changed partners and embraced abandonedly. They liked interminable kisses.

Leon sat beside Silvana with his shoulder touching hers and presently he slipped his arm round her shoulder. She snuggled up to him, but when he lowered his lips to her cheek she turned her face away.

They danced. The champagne had made them all gay and as they danced they sang and the German boys banged spoons against aluminium picnic plates.

Just when Silvana was thinking it was time to leave for home, there was a wild clamour for a midnight swim. Silvana couldn't believe it when the German boys and the girls stripped off their clothes and stood stark naked in the moonlight in full view of each other. If the beach had permitted she would have walked away, but it was so small that she couldn't avoid seeing them.

Leon asked quietly: 'Are you swimming, Silvana?'

To her acute embarrassment he unbuckled his belt and pulled his shirt over his head.

She looked away quickly.

They waded, swam and splash-fought. The night was warm and so was the sea. Silvana was the only one who was embarrassed. The others behaved so naturally that presently she could master her impulse to look away from their nudity.

They frolicked in the water until they were cold. Then a French girl ran from the water shivering, picked up a towel and dried herself. She stood watching the others romp, her firm flesh silvered and the tips of her breasts stood hard, the triangle of her pelvis a black smudge. The others ran out of the water, laughing and shivering. Without bothering to dry themselves, the German boys lay down upon boat cushions with blankets pulled over them. The girls snuggled under the blankets with them, squealing with cold and giggling at the contact.

Leon walked over to Silvana and stood drying himself, making no attempt to conceal his nudity.

She kept her head turned from him.

'This is my world,' he said.

'You're welcome to it!'

He picked up a blanket and spread it over himself as he lay out on the cushions.

'It was wrong of me to come,' she said.

'I think so, Silvana,' he agreed.

She was furious with him for agreeing. She looked slyly at the other couples. Both girls' silvered shoulders showed over the tops of the blankets as they browsed over their companions' lips, tasting them as though they had exquisite savour.

'If I hadn't come you'd have had some other girl here, kissing her?'

'Yes,' he said quietly.

She was acutely aware of his nakedness under the blanket. He wanted to emphasise how she had deprived him of pleasure.

'You think *that's* the way a decent girl should behave?' She asked scornfully.

'Every generation has a new attitude to life, Silvana. But Spain rarely moves with the times.'

'It's . . . cheap to behave like that.'

'No it isn't, Silvana,' he said gently. 'Not if you're sincere.'

'How can you be sincere with somebody you've only just met?'

'It's easy to feel sincerity quickly. But often it isn't a lasting sincerity.'

'I've spoilt your night, haven't I?'

'I'm unhappy for you,' he said.

'Why for me?'

'Because . . . you're so repressed you couldn't let yourself go even if you wanted to.'

She was angered by his criticism. She moved over to him, pulled back the blanket and slipped in under it. Her skirt rode up but she quickly pulled it down. She lay with her back towards him, sensing the heat of him but not actually touching him. 'I can do anything those other girls can do,' she said. 'It's not a matter of being repressed. It's a matter of what is *decent*!'

'Don't measure them with *your* yardstick, Silvana.'

'I hate them,' she said.

'They've done nothing to hurt you.'

'Don't you think I want to be kissed as they are?'

'Then do not set a price on kisses,' he said, and although his voice was gentle it was accusing.

She turned to face him. 'It is not as you think, Leon. I have learned not to give myself cheaply.'

'We are in different worlds, Silvana. You talk with the tongue of the elders who make what is exciting and sweet into something shameful and nasty.'

'Would you have all girls behave like prostitutes?'

'You do not understand. Petting is one of the greatest joys of youth. To lie together, to embrace, to caress and arouse emotions!'

'You have a glib tongue, Leon. But once these things start . . .'

'What do *you* know of these things and what happens when they start?' he asked, and when she remained silent he chuckled.

'I am a woman,' she said. 'A woman knows things by instinct.'

'Yet you have never kissed.'

'Do you think I do not know how to kiss?'

'I doubt it.'

'I'll show you!'

He raised his hand quickly and his fingers covered her mouth. 'No, Silvana. We are friends and it must remain thus. I am young and free and will make no promise to marry. Perhaps . . . perhaps I will never marry!'

'I shall still kiss you. Not to make you my fiancé but to prove I know how to kiss.' She propped herself on her elbow like the French girls and stared down into his face.

He smiled and the moonlight gave the whites of his eyes a silvery glitter. She pressed her mouth against his for long seconds, then browsed across his cheek, drawing a line of little kisses from the point of his chin to his ear.

Leon lay quite still, strangely unmoved, and she too was surprised that she felt so little emotion. She wondered why the French girls were so passionately absorbed in kissing.

'You see, Leon,' she said. 'I too know how to kiss.'

He shook his head, laughing at her silently.

'Shall I show you again?'

'You forget that a kiss is a symbol of deeper understanding.'

'I am happy to be with you, Leon. Does my kissing not show that?'

'Shall I teach you how to kiss?'

'I shall show you again that I know how to kiss.'

She pressed her lips on his and thrilled at his closeness and the intimacy of their mouths touching. But the kiss lacked delight and she thought again of the French girl's passion and wondered if it came only after prolonged kissing.

Then Leon's lips swelled up warmly and moistly, parted hers until startlingly she was overwhelmed by a shaft of surging emotion. Nothing so dreamily wonderful had ever happened before. Her mouth shared the intimacy of his and their tongues clung lovingly until she trembled. She abandoned herself to the pleasure of his mouth and lips, her tongue caressed the beloved contours of his face, the tip of it explored his ear, moistened the line of his eyebrows, brushed gently down across his cheek, neck and throat and then upwards again, searching his hot, moist mouth for the sweetness of its hidden recesses. Her long hair hung down curtaining his cheek and she was breathless as his hands stole under her blouse and ran up and down her spine, sending such shivers of delight running through her that she hugged him. 'Leon. Leon. I love you, Leon!'

His caresses were heavenly and she made no protest when he unhooked her brassiere so that his fingers could stroke the full length of her spine from neck to waistline. She knew a moment of alarm and tried to stop him, but desisted because it was already too late when he cupped her breasts in his hands.

She was champagne dreamy and drugged by the pleasure of his caresses and every moment her body became more alive and more aware until his hot nakedness became essential and as her pleasure mounted she ground against him and moaned. And then a passion-hungry urge swelled up within her and she whimpered while he fought off her searching hands.

'Oh, yes, yes, yes, Leon, darling,' she gasped, her body and hands insistent. 'Yes, Leon. Oh, yes, darling. I don't care at all. I *don't* care!' She was angry with him for denying her and fought with him but he held her in a strong embrace and caressed her in such a way that the ecstasy of it turned her tense. She was rigid, deliciously tense and being borne ever higher on a cloud which exploded into a million shooting stars all spurting higher and higher and then slowly floating down in the peace of aftermath.

After a time she said tonelessly: 'You're disgusted with me now?'

He laughed. 'Of course not.'

'I ... I ... what happened?'

'It is the first time you've ever kissed?'

'Yes,' she admitted softly.

'And the first time you've had ... these feelings?'

She nodded. There were tears on her cheeks.

'It is natural to cry,' he told her.

'It was wonderful. But it was terrible too. I didn't know what was happening. I was weak ... I hadn't the strength to move.'

'But for a time you were very strong.'

She flushed, recalling hazily how she had fought to get at the root of him and had risen up on him in the grip of an emotional compulsion until he sensed her hunger and appeased it.

'I must love you deeply, Leon, to give myself to you thus.'

'Do not speak this way, Silvana. A girl does not give herself. Lovemaking is a mutual pleasure.'

'Am I still a virgin, Leon?'

'Have no fear. I only caressed you.'

She gulped. 'Even to be touched there by a man ... is a shameful thing.'

He sighed.

'Moreover,' she said bitterly. 'I have disgusted you. I cheapened myself, brazenly threw myself at you and you did not want me.'

'Listen, Silvana,' he said gently. 'This talk of not wanting you is nonsense. You are attractive and I love to have you with me. But when you are overwhelmed by emotion and do not know what you are doing it would be wrong to take advantage of you.'

'You didn't want me!'

'I wanted you,' he said quietly. 'A man always wants a woman. But the thoughtlessness of a man for a few moments can change a woman's entire life. I did not want you to do anything you would regret later.'

'You talk of *me*, Leon,' she said. 'But what of *you*?'

'It is pleasant to make love,' he said quietly. 'But it is a pleasure I can forgo when there is need.'

One of the boys called to Leon and he replied in German.

'It is time to go, Silvana.' He helped her to rearrange her clothing and she was surprised at how natural it all seemed. Earlier that day she would have died at the thought of him touching her. Now when the French girls stood up and dressed leisurely, the shock of it was no longer great because she felt she could almost do it herself if only Leon were present.

They set off back to Escoleras and the sea was smooth and

silvery. The engine roared powerfully, white wash creamed back behind them into an ever-widening highway and they sped away from the towering cliffs, out to sea, heading in a straight line to their destination instead of following the coastal contours.

Silvana sat beside Leon and his forearm touched her in the warm contact of companionship. His calm confidence when the trouble started was very reassuring.

They were hissing smoothly across the silver surface of the sea when there was a loud jarring clang. The speed launch leaped high for some yards and then splashed down. The engine roared frenziedly, vibrating and threatening to shake the boat apart.

Leon righted the boat after it bucked and quickly cut the engine. In the sudden silence the lapping of the disturbed water was loud and mocking.

'What's happened?' she choked.

'We hit something,' said Leon grimly.

'We're not holed? We're not sinking?'

'No. But we've stripped the prop.' Leon climbed over the driving seat. His face was grim.

'How bad is it?' she asked anxiously.

'We hit a chunk of drift wood. No propellor.'

'What do we do?'

'The current's in the right direction. We'll drift with it.'

'It'll take hours to reach land.'

He nodded. 'That's the trouble. I'm worried about you. You'll have to explain at home about . . . tonight!'

She nodded. Her face was composed, but there was cold anxiety within her.

The couples behind them were warm under their blankets and they began to sing softly. Drifting wasn't any hardship for them. One of the boys threw a blanket over the driving seat.

'Are you cold?' asked Leon.

'A little.'

He spread the blanket over them, put his arm round her and she snuggled up to him. The simple act of concealment aroused sweet memories and she whispered: 'Kiss me, Leon. Kiss me.' She turned her mouth to him, lips moist and parted. 'Darling, caress me again. Ah, Leon. Yes! YES!'

A fisherman in a small boat came upon them just after dawn and took them in tow. When they saw the fisherman approaching Leon folded the blanket but as they were being towed to Escoleras she held his hand. The fisherman glanced back over his shoulder and saw it. Leon detached his hand from hers, but she grasped it again firmly. 'Don't you like holding my hand?'

'It's you I'm thinking of. It's bad enough as it is. You know the way people talk.'

'I don't care, Leon,' she said recklessly. 'I don't care.' Her eyes shone and she held her head high.

'I was thinking about you.'

'I don't care what they say!' she said. 'I don't care. Something's happened to me, Leon. I ... I've become free! I've learned and now I see it all quite differently!'

When the speed launch was beached in front of the Marvista the other couples hurried away to breakfast.

'They'll know by now what you've done,' said Leon.

Silvana nodded.

'I'll take you home so they'll know who you've been with.'

'It's better not.'

'I'll accompany you,' he insisted.

But when they reached the drive she said firmly: 'Don't come any further, Leon.'

'I'll explain where you've been.'

'Later, if you must. But not now. Please. It's better this way, Leon.'

'If you're sure.'

'I'm sure.' Her eyes caressed his face. 'Thank you for everything.' There was a break in her voice and she turned quickly and hurried up the gravel drive.

Her father was waiting on the terrace. He had seen her arrive with Leon from an upper window and as she climbed the steps he asked coldly: 'Was the boy afraid to face me?'

'No, Father. I begged him to go away.'

'Why?'

'Because I'm tired and don't want a scene.'

Her mother choked: '*You're* tired! And we were worried out of our minds!'

'Where have you been?' asked Anselmo in a dead voice.

'We went out along the coast. It was a beautiful night.'

'Without my permission?'

'I wanted to go, Father. It would have been useless to ask you.'

'How many were you?'

'Six.'

'Three couples?'

She met his eyes steadily. 'Yes.'

'What happened?'

'We lost the propellor.'

'What happened to *you*? Out there alone with that boy!'

'Leon is well-mannered and a gentleman.'

Anselmo's eyes glittered. 'I want to know what *happened*!'

190

Silvana tossed her head and flared: 'I'm tired. Leave me alone!'

Her mother intervened. 'I'll handle this, Anselmo. I'll find out. I'm her mother.' She glared. 'We'll talk in your room, my girl!'

Silvana held her head high and her mother panted and puffed as she waddled along behind her. But once inside the bedroom her mother locked the door. 'Now,' she said. Her black eyes glittered balefully. 'Let's have a look at you.' Her piggy eyes in their pouches of fat examined her daughter sharply. 'How did your blouse get creased in this way? And your skirt?'

'Sitting in the boat.'

'Creased like *that*! How were you sitting then? With your skirt up round your waist?'

'Really, Mother. Clothes crease so easily.'

'Get undressed.'

'Why should I?'

'You're my daughter and I'm telling you. That's why. You'll do what I say or get my hand across your face.'

Pale-faced, Silvana took off her blouse and skirt. Her mother snatched them and threw them across the room. 'That's a fine way to go out,' she said disgustedly. 'Practically nothing on underneath. Take *that* off.' She examined the brassiere carefully. 'What about this hook?' she demanded. 'Half pulled off!'

'I've been meaning to sew it for days.'

'And this broken shoulder strap!'

'It snapped without my noticing it.'

'Without you noticing!' sneered her mother. She scrutinised her daughter intently, handling her breasts to see them better. 'What's this mark here? This red mark?'

'I can't see any mark, Mother.'

'And this mark here. You can't deny that that's a bruise, can you?'

'Perhaps ... perhaps I banged myself.'

'Perhaps you held yourself too tightly. Those are finger marks as plain as plain, aren't they?'

'Mother ... I don't know what you think ...'

'Take that off,' grated her mother and panted wheezily as her daughter stepped out of her last garment. She looked at it closely and turned it inside out. Suddenly she lashed out. The flat of her hand slapped the girl's cheek and hurled her back on the bed. She stood over the girl, her fat face working with rage, her eyes furious. 'You dirty little slut,' she panted. 'A daughter of mine behaving like an alley-cat!'

'Mother ... please!' choked Silvana. She was crying.

'You think you can hide it from your own mother! I know what you've been up to, you dirty little bitch. Don't deny it. I can smell it on you! You think I've had all my children without knowing what it's all about? Something'll be done about this, my girl!'

'Please, Mother. You don't understand ...!'

Her mother waddled to the door, unlocked it and flung it open. 'Anselmo!' she screamed along the wide empty corridor and when he came hurrying anxiously she screamed: 'It's that Coruna boy. He's had her!'

3

Teresa received Anselmo in her office. They had seen little of each other these past few years, only occasionally meeting each other in the street. Anselmo was astonished at the size of the hotel. He'd never visited it until now and was impressed by the sumptuousness of the reception hall and Teresa's private office.

Teresa ordered the Buttons who had shown him in: 'Tell the desk I'm in conference and I'm not to be disturbed unless it's urgent.'

As soon as the door closed she came round from behind her desk and walked to Anselmo, smiling with such warmth that he was embarrassed. 'It's good to see you, Anselmo. You never call on us. It's a pity because we'd be delighted to see more of you.'

He said uncomfortably: 'It's Narcisus I want to see.'

'You mean you *don't* want to see *me*?' she chuckled.

Despite himself he smiled. 'You know that isn't true, Teresa.'

'Make yourself comfortable, Anselmo. What would you like to drink?'

'Er ... nothing, thanks. It will soon be lunch time.'

'That's why. An aperitif. What do you fancy?'

'Aah ... nothing. Thank you, Teresa. I'd rather not.'

'Nonsense.' She dismissed his protest. 'What was it you used to like? Yes. Now I remember. Black Cinzano, a little gin and a few drops of Picon.'

It was years since Anselmo had drunk an aperitif and he was a little awed by Teresa's self-assurance as she prepared the drinks. He was pleasantly surprised to see how young she looked, as though the years had not touched her. Almost, it seemed, she had improved as she'd grown older. She used to be thin and angular but now she was firm-fleshed and wirily slim.

192

She wore a tight dress which emphasised the thrust of her breasts and her slim waist, and from behind she could have been taken for a girl in her twenties.

How old was she, he wondered, and reckoned back, startled to realise she must be forty-five or forty-six.

Teresa turned round from the portable bar and came over to him, carrying two tall glasses. She sat on her desk, swinging one leg. In these days of short skirts the soft skin of her knees was excusably exposed.

'It's been a long time, Anselmo,' she sighed. 'Time passes so quickly. Have you found it the same? The children grow up and there's no time for anything. How is Silvana and the rest of the family?'

'Well,' he said. 'Quite well.' He gulped, remembering the purpose of his visit. 'That is . . .'

'I'm sorry about your financial troubles, Anselmo.'

'Ah, yes!' he said, nodding sadly. He'd been dogged by bad luck. He'd sold a farm at a giveaway price to buy a tractor and the first week it was in use, before he'd insured it, an inexpert driver had overturned it into a ditch. The driver's cigarette had ignited spilt fuel and the tractor had burned until the fuel tank exploded. He'd had a rich crop of wheat with heavily ripening heads, but the north wind blew with hurricane force for three days and stripped the wheat clean so that only the stalks could be reaped. A herd of cattle had died off down to the last calf before he'd found the poisonous plant they were feeding on. One of his farm horses fell, broke its leg, overturned the cart upon the driver and Anselmo had had to compensate him for the loss of an arm.

Teresa talked with Anselmo about his misfortunes and he was surprised that she knew as much about them as he did himself. He discussed his other problems with her and was delighted to be able to confide in someone who was understanding.

'I was unlucky,' he sighed. 'I sold off all the land I had near the sea and was paid a pittance. It's changed hands a dozen times since and now they're building on it. If I'd held on a few years I'd have been wealthy today.'

'Have you thought of leaving farming and doing something else?'

He sighed. 'Many times. But I'm trapped. Antonia and Pilar still need help. They're not married and can't make enough to live on teaching. Then there's Manolo. He's not doing well in Barcelona and I send him something. And I have my own family. All these expenses have to be paid by the farm and when there's bad luck or bad crops I can't make ends meet. I've sold almost all the land that's saleable, but unless things get better soon...' Anselmo shrugged his shoulders dismally.

'How about the farm?' she asked. 'Have you thought of selling it?'

'Farming's not good business these days. Too many government restrictions. If I found a buyer he'd pay me next to nothing.'

'And Rafael?' she asked. 'Any news of him?'

He shook his head. 'After mother's death we had a property settlement. Since then ... we've heard nothing.'

'You look tired, Anselmo,' she said, and he saw she was looking at him tenderly.

'I do a lot of work on the farm. Labour is a big problem. Everybody has gone into building. It pays much better wages than I can afford.'

'You've lost weight.'

'Being active keeps my weight down.' He laughed, showing his strong white teeth and the firm line of his jaw. The corners of his eyes crinkled and she had a glimpse of the happy, carefree youth she had known before the war.

'It is not good to be too fat,' she agreed solemnly. 'But ... are you sure you're not working too hard?' She'd wanted to ask if he was eating enough, but it was a question too critical of Silvana.

'Work rarely kills,' said Anselmo. He took out his handkerchief and wiped his forehead. He'd put on his best jacket for this formal visit and it was tight under the armpits. Teresa noticed his discomfort and encouraged him: 'Take your coat off, Anselmo.'

'I'm just going now and ...'

'Take your coat off even if it's just for a few minutes. Be comfortable while you're here.' She helped him off with his jacket, draped it over a hangar and hung it in the wardrobe. Then, brushing aside his protests, she freshened his glass. He watched her deft movements and when she handed him his drink there was something in her poise that took him back over the years. He remembered her standing with her feet astride, leaning her weight against the tug of the net, her dress floating in the water, blackly wet to the hips, her brown arms straining and her face alight with eagerness. Above her, seagulls cawed angrily and Paco Barras urged rhythmically: 'Heave ... heave ... heave.' There was the gentle swish of the surf lapping at the beach, the smell of mussels and seaweed and faintly too the warm, milky, body scent of a young girl. Then there was ...

'Would you like more ice?' Teresa asked, and abruptly he

was back in the present, a little hazy because it was a long while since he had drunk an aperitif and he was sad with the loss of something that had eluded him.

'No, thanks,' he said. When a man makes his bed he must lie on it. He said abruptly: 'It is Narcisus I wish to see.'

'He's away today. But you can talk to me, Anselmo. Anything which concerns Narcisus concerns me.'

She was looking at his arm and he glanced down and saw the long, white scar. He moved his arm slightly. 'A constant reminder, Teresa. I was ... ungrateful to you. I hope you forgive me.'

'When we are young we do many things for which we need forgiveness.'

The conversation was escaping again, turning into byways which he dared not enter. 'I called to see Narcisus about a serious matter,' he said.

'Yes?' Her eyes widened.

'Leon, your son. Do you know where he was last night?'

'He said something about a midnight picnic. The engine broke down and he didn't get back until this morning.'

'Do you know who was with him?'

She shrugged her shoulders disinterestedly. 'He usually makes up a party of guests from the hotel.'

'Silvana was with him,' Anselmo said quietly. He took out his handkerchief and mopped his forehead. 'All night!' he added.

Teresa's eyes narrowed. She studied him thoughtfully but said nothing.

'That's why I want to talk to you and Narcisus.'

'Yes?' said Teresa. Her voice was quiet.

Anselmo spread his hands. 'You understand. Something must be done. Soon the whole village will know.'

'No. I don't understand, Anselmo. What are you telling me?'

He was surprised. 'My daughter's reputation is at stake. Your son is responsible.'

Teresa picked up a packet of cigarettes, selected one and placed it between her lips. She offered the packet to Anselmo. He waved it away.

Teresa snapped a lighter, held the flame to the tip of the cigarette and puffed it to life. She inhaled and slowly blew out a thin plume of smoke. Only when she was quite sure she was under control did she say: 'My son is responsible? For what?'

He was puzzled by her attitude. 'For my daughter's reputation.'

'Tell me, Anselmo,' she said gently. 'Did Leon carry her off by force?'

'Of course not. I'm not suggesting . . .'

'She went with him willingly?'

'But without our knowledge and against our wishes.'

'But she went with him voluntarily?'

'She should never have done it. But it happened. And . . . they were together all night!'

'Engine trouble was the cause. These accidents happen.'

'Teresa. You and Narcisus must talk to your boy and arrange something.'

'Arrange what, Anselmo?' Teresa's voice was ominously quiet.

'They must marry,' he said flatly.

Teresa arched one eyebrow. 'Is Silvana pregnant?'

He flushed. 'If she is we won't know for some time.'

'What does Silvana want?'

'She's difficult. She won't talk about it. Her mother can't get sense out of her.'

'Perhaps . . . nothing happened?'

'That's too much to expect.'

'They're young. Perhaps it went no further than kissing and cuddling.'

'What they did doesn't affect the issue, Teresa. Silvana's reputation is in jeopardy.'

Teresa turned and paced to the window. She stood staring out and said over her shoulder: 'What do you expect me to do?'

'Talk to Leon. He can call and ask for Silvana's hand. I will agree, of course. The sooner they are married the better . . . just in case!'

'Does Silvana want to marry Leon?'

'She'll do what I say.'

Teresa turned round and said carefully: 'I'll talk to Leon. If he wants to marry Silvana I will raise no objections.'

Anselmo gaped: '*If!*' he said. 'On an important issue like this the parents make the decision.'

'No,' she said quietly. 'Leon makes his *own* decisions.'

Anselmo couldn't believe his ears. 'Have you no influence over him?'

'A great deal. Probably too much. That's one reason for not using it.'

'You've got to be firm, Teresa. The younger generation has got out of hand. Too much money and not enough self-control. Your Leon's had my daughter and, as parents, you and Narcisus have a duty to see he does the right thing.'

'I'm sorry, Anselmo,' she said firmly. 'I won't influence

Leon. He must make his own decisions.'

Anselmo got to his feet. He breathed hard. 'I'm shocked, Teresa,' he said bitterly. 'I was confident that as a lifelong friend of the family you would do the right thing.'

'Don't you see, Anselmo? I'm *trying* to do the right thing.'

'Then oblige your son to marry my daughter.'

'Leon must decide.'

'Teresa, do you want to destroy our friendship?'

Teresa studied him for a very long time. Then she said clearly: 'Long ago I gave way to a natural impulse and became what you called "soiled". I became unworthy of you and we never married. Now, when you demand that my son marries your daughter I can only ask this. If I was not fit to marry because I was "soiled", why should your own "soiled" daughter be good enough to marry my son?'

Anselmo turned pale. Without a word he got to his feet and put on his jacket. Without another glance at Teresa he strode to the door and went out.

When the door closed behind him Teresa sighed sadly, crossed to the bar and poured herself another drink.

CHAPTER TEN

1

IT was the worst winter the old people could remember. The rains were heavy, the wind fierce and the cold intense. One morning the Serras rose before dawn, hitched up their skin and bone horse to their old cart and set off into the mountains. Some months earlier at an auction Vicente Serra had snapped up a few acres of agricultural land, unwanted because it was too far from the village. Now he and Maria set off to gather its potato crop.

It was a long, uphill journey along rough, rutted paths and boulder-strewn slopes. Their aged mare's bones stood out from its mangy hide as she wearily hauled the cart. On the steeper slopes Vicente Serra walked in front and pulled the lead rein while Maria pushed behind the cart.

The rarified air on the higher mountain slopes was much colder than at sea level and as they hobbled the mare and took up their tools, the north wind began to blow. They stooped over the furrows and chipped at the frosty, iron hard earth while the wind cut cruelly through their clothing. But work kept them warm, although their hands were blue and each gust drove grit at them like invisible needles. At midday, when they stopped to chew a hunk of bread and drink a little wine, the cold was so intense that they were eager to start work again. By late afternoon the cart was piled high with potatoes and could carry no more.

The aged mare had been standing in the shafts all day and they had to rub warmth into her legs before she could walk without stumbling and they'd covered only a few hundred yards of their return journey when one wheel skidded off the side of a large boulder and sprang free from its axle. The cart gave a wild lurch and dropped, the hub scored a groove in the earth and the mare was dragged to a standstill. The potatoes avalanched and Serra swore violently to the heavens as the wheel rolled on for several yards before it toppled on its side.

The fury of the Tramontana eased a little, as it always did before sunset, '*showing reverence to the setting sun*', as the villagers said, and Serra shouted fiercely: 'Hurry, woman. Help me before it is dark.'

Half the load of potatoes had spilled out and they gathered large stones and built them up under the axle. They levered, using a pickaxe handle as a crowbar and pushed more stones under the axle. It was slow, laborious work and it was dusk before the cart was propped up level. Maria trundled the wheel to Vicente who was working under the cart. They had only to fit the wheel on to the axle, improvise a pin to hold it and they could be on their way. But the axle had to be raised another inch and while Vicente levered with his crowbar, the aged mare, mistaking his grunts of effort for a command, gathered her strength and lurched forward. The cart toppled slowly forward off the small mountain of stones and, seeing his danger, Serra tried frantically to escape. The full weight of the cart crunched down upon his leg. The cracking of the bone was startlingly loud.

'Holy Mother of Jesus!' gasped Serra.

'Your leg. Your leg!' screamed Maria.

'Don't be hysterical, woman,' shouted Serra. 'Get busy. Do something.'

The mare's ears pricked and she made another half start, tugging on the shafts and increasing the pressure on Serra's leg. 'Do something!' he choked.

'What must I do, Vicente?' whimpered Maria.

'That whore of a horse is tearing my leg apart.'

She loosened the traces and slapped the mare until she stepped free from the shafts.

'Daughter of a whore!' Serra shouted and the mare trotted away apprehensively, ears pricking as she lowered her long, tired neck to graze.

'Have you much pain, Vicente?' asked Maria, white faced.

'Not yet,' he said. 'Hurry. Before the pain begins.'

'What must I do?'

'Get two big boulders. One to slide under the axle as you raise it and the other to brace the pickaxe handle on.'

Maria was thin but wiry and concern for her husband gave her a strength she might not have otherwise possessed. When everything was prepared as he directed, she strained her weight upon the crowbar and raised the cart high enough for him to pull his leg free. It was by now quite dark.

'Are you in much pain, Vicente?'

'Help me mount the mare,' he growled.

But the mare was nervous and distrusted the woman's increasingly angry efforts to catch her. Maria stalked her a long time, never able to get close enough to seize her and finally lost her in the darkness. She returned to her husband.

'Help me,' he said. 'I'll try to walk.'

He leaned heavily upon her and used a pick handle as a walking stick. They made tortuously slow progress. The

Tramontana blew again with full fury and its icy fingers cut through their clothing like knives. Its force often threatened to hurl them forward on their faces and they had to lean their weight against it. There was no moon, the rock-strewn slopes were treacherous and they stumbled often. The temperature went down and down, numbing their limbs until they ached and presently snow flakes drove against them, coating them and spreading a white carpet on the ground. Half blinded by whirling snow they didn't see where the earth had broken away and fell in a tangle of limbs. Serra screamed.

'I am sorry, Vicente. I lost my footing.' Maria had to shout to make herself heard above the wind.

He groaned.

'Come, Vicente. I will help you.'

He held back. 'It cannot be. The pain will kill me.'

She took him in her arms and rocked gently, her back turned to the fury of the wind to protect him. Snow gathered on them and numbness crept through her.

'Listen, Vicente. I will go for help.'

He held her tightly. 'Don't leave me.'

She warmed him with her own thin body and when he began to whimper she crooned to him. The cold penetrated and drained away consciousness until she slept. She was awakened by the slash of an uprooted thorn bush flung against her by the wind. 'Vicente,' she choked. 'Vicente!'

He did not answer. He was breathing quickly, his hands were icy and she knew he would die if she did not go for help. She tucked his hands into his jacket, covered him with her shawl and got to her feet. The joints of her limbs were stiff and she stumbled along on feet so numbed that she lost one rope-soled sandal without knowing it. She fought on grimly through the driving snow, teeth chattering and often floundering knee-deep in snow drifts. Presently she became light-headed and hazy about direction. She saw distant pin points of light and staggered on amidst the icy wind for an eternity before she reached the stream that flowed through Escoleras. There had been torrential rain the previous day and the stream was waist deep. But its surface was frozen and covered with snow and when Maria blundered on to it the ice broke under her and she sank to her armpits.

When she reached Escoleras her clothes were frozen hard, her hair was white with frost and her flesh was blue.

Rescue volunteers prepared warm clothing and a stretcher while others tried to warm Maria. They stripped off her clothing, rubbed her chilled flesh with alcohol and placed her before a roaring fire enveloped in blankets. Her teeth chattered so violently that she could tell where she had left Vicente only with the greatest difficulty.

After a time Maria slept. But even in sleep she shivered violently, her teeth chattered and her flesh remained as hard as frozen beef. Presently she began to cough. It was a body cough which came from the depths of her being and shook her body convulsively. The rescue volunteers with Doctor Aldo and four Civil Guards set off into the cold night.

It was the worst winter anyone could remember. Eucalyptus trees, more than two hundred years old, perished. Few olive trees survived and the cactus bushes which marked the boundaries between properties turned black and withered.

Escoleras was cut off from the outside world for seven days until snow ploughs were brought down from the mountain passes to open the roads, leaving banks of snow eight feet high on either side.

The rescue party searched all night and most of the next day but Vicente was not found until the snows melted three weeks later. Maria died of exposure, slipping away swiftly, never once having committed the sin of extravagance ... nor known the joy of it!

Asuncion bore the loss of her parents stoically, went on living in the same tumble-down cottage, was grateful for the sympathy of her neighbours and worked every day in the grocery store.

The Barcelona solicitor who handled Serra's affairs presently informed Asuncion that as Serra's only daughter she inherited everything!

2

Asuncion Serra called to see Doctor Aldo. She was mature now and womanly-wise, slim, dark-eyed and attractive although, to the doctor, her face had never quite lost its pinched and hungry expression.

'I trust you, Doctor Aldo. I know nobody else I can ask for advice.'

'I'll help if I can, Asuncion. What's your problem?'

'I want to marry.'

Doctor Aldo was not surprised. Long before her parents' death, Asuncion had shown her liking for Diego Munez. He was a cheerful, dark-eyed, curly-haired gipsy youth who would strum a guitar for hours but who loathed work. Vicente and Maria Serra had kept Diego away from their daughter, but since their death the doctor had often seen Asuncion with him.

'It is Diego Munez you want to marry?' asked the doctor, and tried to stop his voice sounding like a sigh.

Asuncion nodded. 'I hope I can make him happy and I know he will make me happy.'

'You should be able to make him happy,' said the doctor dryly, thinking of her inheritance.

And then the girl surprised him.

'Diego will want my money, Doctor Aldo. I don't think it's *only* my money he's after, but in his happy-go-lucky way he'll expect to handle my money as though it's his own.'

He was delighted that she could see so clearly. 'You could come to a financial arrangement,' he suggested delicately.

'I've discussed it with my solicitor, Doctor. I won't deny Diego anything that's reasonable. But I don't want *everything* squandered. My solicitor has listed ways to invest the money so it can't be touched while it yields a reasonable income.' Asuncion pushed a thick manilla envelope across the desk. 'I don't understand these things much and I'd like you to advise me which you think are best.'

Doctor Aldo took the sheaf of documents from the envelope and his eyebrows raised. It was hard to believe that Serra and his wife could have made such a fortune. Every peseta the frugal couple had earned must have been invested again and again. Serra had bought land in Barcelona during the depression and had sold it later for a fortune. He owned stocks and shares, houses, flats and factories. The amount of property he'd bought in and around Escoleras was startling. He'd ferreted out the owners of land long disused and bought it cheaply. The solicitor had prepared a number of sound schemes and Doctor Aldo told Asuncion which he thought suited her best.

'Thank you for your help, Doctor.'

'I've done very little. But I'm curious, Asuncion. What will you do with the rest of the property?'

Her eyes glowed. 'I'll sell it and put the money in the bank for Diego to squander.'

'You think you'll be happy, Asuncion?'

'Diego hasn't anything except his sunny nature, Doctor. But I don't mind him having my money if he'll give me a little of his sun.'

Doctor Aldo gave Asuncion away at the wedding. The honeymoon was to have lasted a month but within a few days the couple were back in Escoleras. Diego was bored with travelling. The newly-weds rented a luxury flat on the front with a dominating view of the sea and the rest of the Munez family moved into the two flats above it. The many Munez children had new clothes and bright new toys and Diego's parents blossomed out like lottery winners, swaggering along the promenade wearing expensive, eye-catching clothes, the man wreathed in the blue smoke of Havana cigars and the woman in a cloud of expensive perfume. Diego bought a speedboat for himself and another for his parents. He chose a red sports car for his own use and a gleaming six-seater limousine with a chauffeur for his parents. Every night the entire family, including Diego and Asuncion, dined out at expensive restaurants. They were like children with money, having no sense of its value. In the bars they paid for everybody's drinks and in restaurants sent champagne to other tables. They tipped so extravagantly that worried waiters sometimes begged them to take some back.

One day Doctor Aldo and Paco Barras were strolling along the promenade and came upon Diego in leather jeans and jacket, strumming his guitar and singing softly. Asuncion sat beside him, listening with dreamy eyes. Diego courteously exchanged greetings and resumed playing when they had passed.

Paco Barras shook his head wryly. 'Serra would go mad if he could see what's happening to his money. He and Maria pinched and scraped and starved and finally died to hoard a few pesetas. And for what? So the laziest people in Escoleras can spend their money like water.'

'It may be for the best,' said Doctor Aldo.

'You could be right,' chuckled Paco Barras. 'Sometimes a cat chokes itself with cream.'

'I'm thinking of the girl,' said Doctor Aldo. 'Did you see the look in her eyes? She's a sensible girl. And that's probably why she's one of the happiest girls we've known.'

3

Rosemarie's determination to get her own flat was a forgotten dream. She tried to save but she earned so little and there were always little expenses which nibbled away her reserves. The years passed quickly and she lost the will to escape from her environment until finally it became a natural part of her background.

One night as the men milled round her, Rosemarie found herself among a group of students. It was a stifling evening, the hot air reeked of sweat and scented bodies and she had to shout to make herself heard. The students hemmed her in, joked with her tipsily and laughed uproariously. She knew you could never tell with students. They might mean business or merely be slumming. But the chance wasn't to be lost because if a girl could take a number of students up to her room for tricks, it was easy money.

She laughed with them, touched them with quick fingers, smiled with big, crimson lips and widened her eyes so that the whites would gleam. 'Why not all of you together?' she wheedled. 'We'll all have fun.'

'How's that for a geometrical problem?' said one student.

They laughed uproariously. They were drunk.

'An accumulator?' hooted another.

Again the laughter.

She gripped the nearest student's arm strongly. 'Come with me, darling. You've never known anything like it!'

'Why? What are you? Male, female or hermaphrodite?'

She arched her loins at him and slitted her eyes invitingly. 'Find out,' she said huskily.

She held still for him. 'Aaaah!' She hissed her pleasure, slitted her eyes and tensed as though in ecstasy. She revolved her hips round his touch. 'I want you, darling,' she panted. 'I want you!'

He moved his hand, then abruptly tugged hard, uprooting so fiercely that she cried out with the stinging pain.

'Another for the collection,' he chortled, flourishing his wispy trophy.

'I knew they wouldn't be blonde,' said another student.

Rosemarie smarted intolerably. As the student flourished his trophy, anger overwhelmed her and using her knowledge mercilessly she drove her knee hard up into his groin. The boy doubled up and gasped in agony.

Her anger gushed out in words. A part of her seemed to stand on one side and listen to the torrent of filth and abuse which poured from her lips and watch her obscene actions and gestures. The students helped their companion to stand as she stormed shockingly. A space cleared round them and she became the focus of all eyes. But she couldn't stop herself. It was as though all her resentment at life had at last to pour out in this great flood of obscenity. Her fury finally ebbed and she finished. 'I shit upon all of you and your whoring mothers!' Then she spat.

The students supported their companion whose face was grey and strained. One said bitterly: 'It was only a joke.'

'A fine joke! I'm bleeding!'

'I'm sorry about that,' said the student sincerely and she was suddenly deeply ashamed of herself.

'I'm sorry too,' she gulped. 'I ... I couldn't help myself. He hurt me. He really *hurt* me.'

'I'll pay you,' he said.

'All of you?' she asked quickly.

'No. Just me.'

'All right. Come upstairs and I'll show you what he did to me.'

The student drew back. 'I'll . . . I'll give you the money.'

She saw in his eyes his reluctance to go with her and perversely she determined that he should. 'Come on. You have to have what you pay for.'

'No,' he said. 'I'll give you the money.' He fumbled in his pocket. His companions were moving away and he wanted to go with them.

She held on to his arm. 'I don't want you to *give* me the money. Come upstairs.'

He tried to pull away. 'No.'

'What's the matter? Are you a maricon?' She touched him.

'Leave me alone,' he said desperately. 'I'll give you the money. What more do you want?'

'*You*, darling.' She thrust against him. 'Come along.'

He struggled, his boyish face was flushed and his eyes alarmed. 'Let me go!'

But she clung to him. 'I won't let you go. Come upstairs.'

'No,' he choked. 'I won't!'

'You will,' she said and tried to kiss him.

He recoiled. She saw the revulsion in his eyes and the hurt of it was upon her before he shouted: 'I couldn't touch an old hag like you. I'd . . . vomit!'

She was only vaguely aware that he'd broken away and was shouldering through the crowd. As though dazed she made her way to the turnstile, nodded at the Madam and climbed the stairs to her room. She bolted the door behind her, crossed to the cracked mirror and stared at her reflection.

Old hag!

The awful realisation that it was true shocked her.

She saw herself through the eyes of the young student. Make-up was caked on her face and mascara mingled with perspiration and ran into the crow's feet at the corners of her eyes. The pupils were shiny, the whites yellowy and below them the flesh was dark and baggy. Under the crimson lipstick her mouth was a mean, pinched line and the deep creases in her neck ran down to the raddled flesh of the vee between her breasts.

I *can't* be old, she thought wildly. I can't be! But she was, she realised. Not only in age but with the long years of staring up at the ceiling over the Man's shoulder, her mind detached from the activity, nerves, muscle and skin wearing away, senses blunted, existence a perpetual false smile and mindless submission.

She looked at her cracked mirror with horror. I'm *old,* she thought frantically. *Old!* I'm on the road to fifty!

Then she thought panic-strickenly: *What will happen to me?*

In the next instant she knew. She remembered the old crones garbed in black who crouched over trays of matches on the pavements outside the brothels.

4

The meeting was called for eleven. The mayor and the town council secretary were present, the authorised architect and the surveyor. The four businessmen from Barcelona sat on one side of the long table facing Teresa, Narcisus and the bank manager.

After a whispered conference with the secretary, the mayor rose to his feet. 'As you know, gentlemen . . .' he began. Then he remembered Teresa. 'Pardon me. *Ladies* and gentlemen. An official permit has been granted for your urbanisation plan. Work can begin at once. Some modifications have been suggested, however. I understand they are probably acceptable to the syndicate but we must legalise it.' He glanced at the businessmen from Barcelona who looked bored so he finished quickly: 'I'll ask Señor Narcisus Coruna to carry on.'

Narcisus smiled feebly, his plump white hands fluttered nervously and his voice was thin and reedy. 'My wife knows this matter inside out so perhaps she'll discuss it instead of me.'

Teresa smiled, rose gracefully and pressed her chair away with the back of her legs. The businessmen came to life and eyed her with interest. Teresa said crisply: 'I'm not proposing any change in our plans but I'm suggesting an additional development.'

As she talked the official architect studied her with concealed admiration. Teresa was a remarkable woman and he knew it better than anyone. The entire project was her idea and had reached fruition because of her determination and drive. Teresa was a modern counterpart of the American pioneers who had driven out westwards, overcoming all obstacles with courage and determination and laying the foundations upon which great cities were later built.

He'd worked for months with Teresa, producing plans, and was amazed at the breadth of her vision. When she'd taken out

206

an option on the land many years ago, it was worthless, half mud half swamp. But the land flanked the beach and Teresa was turning waste land into a garden city. She'd formed the syndicate by going after hard-headed businessmen and convincing them that her plans were sound. Now they were about to be put into practice. Retaining walls would be built along the beach and tipping trucks would fill in the swamp with grit and rubble until it was above sea-level. Then roads would be run through, electric light installed, water and sewage pipes laid and housing sites marked out for a garden city. There was even an area allocated for light industry factories. It was a ten-year plan and at the end of it, Escoleras would be a thriving tourist resort with a population of thirty thousand and an industrial centre to provide employment during the winter months. The Government in Madrid had approved the plan, the Admiralty had undertaken to build a splendid promenade lined with palm trees, the governor of the Province had promised every assistance and three of the big banks would make extensive loans.

Today's meeting was called because Teresa needed approval for a new suggestion. She had a map spread put on the table and everyone gathered round it as she talked.

'The front-rank promenade bordering the beach is of primary importance,' she said, indicating the esplanade. 'Behind it we must leave a wide strip of land for public gardens where people can stroll in the cool of the evening. Next, we've got our building area. Bungalows in the first rank, two-storey villas in the second rank and so on, back to eight-storey apartment blocks. A view of the sea for everyone. Here, the hotels and recreation grounds. Then, right back, we've got the factory area plan which I'd like modified. I don't think we've allocated enough space to it. We should go deeper inland. I've made pencil lines showing how this section should be expanded.'

The Barcelona men studied the plan. One asked: 'The syndicate land ends here?'

Teresa nodded.

'This other land can be bought cheaply?'

Teresa eyed him steadily. 'I haven't enquired.'

'Any land so far from the sea front is valueless,' he said. 'Even when we build up to its boundary it is still valueless without the right to use our roads.'

'I feel it's important that the syndicate buys this land. We can afford to pay a good price,' said Teresa.

'How much do you think of paying?'

'Five million pesetas.'

207

They took out their slide rules, calculated the price per square metre and looked at Teresa in surprise. 'It's ... it's as much as we pay for your land, Señora Coruna!'

'But my land has to be filled in!'

'But it has direct frontage to the beach.'

Teresa smiled. 'Our project is costing hundreds of millions. Need we quibble about the price of a small piece of land, gentlemen?'

'Señora. It's our duty to our shareholders to buy at a keen price.'

Teresa chose her words carefully so that they would not sound like a threat. 'My contract with the syndicate gives me the option to retain twenty per cent of my land. Our plans have gone ahead swiftly and I shan't exercise this option because it will disrupt our development. But I say this, gentlemen. If I am co-operative, it makes me unhappy if the syndicate is reluctant to co-operate when I ask for a fair deal for a small land-owner.'

The men from Barcelona smiled at Teresa. 'Buy the land, Señora Coruna. We're sure your judgment is sound.'

Before she left the town hall, Teresa took the architect by his arm and led him to one side. 'You will call on Señor Ledesma with the documents and complete the purchase?'

'This afternoon if you wish, Señora.'

'The sooner the better.'

He sensed that she was searching for words. 'Anything else, Señora?' he asked.

'Yes. Don't mention that I am connected with the transaction.'

'As you wish, Señora.'

'One other thing,' she said slowly. 'Anselmo ... Señor Ledesma ... You can be useful to Señor Ledesma. When he sells the farm he'll have money to invest. Why don't you suggest he pulls down his residence and builds a block of flats. His home and its ground are large enough for a six-storey block. You could design elegant apartments for him.'

The architect's quick mind snapped up her idea. Most of his designs had to cramp living conditions into a minimum of space. His clients had to pay top prices for every square yard of ground and wanted it to yield the maximum. But Señor Ledesma would be an ideal client. He'd want a building of grace and dignity. The architect could be extravagant with space because although it would earn less in rent, Señor Ledesma would want a cultured landmark.

'Thank you for the suggestion, Señora.' His eyes were shining. Already he was visualising the tall, proud apartment block he would build where the Ledesma house now stood.

Narcisus was waiting for Teresa outside the town hall and when they arrived back at the Marvista she sensed that he wanted to talk to her. She took him into her office. 'I know it's early but pour me a cocktail, darling.'

Narcisus mixed a cocktail and poured from the shaker into cut glass tumblers.

'To health and money,' Teresa toasted.

'To *your* happiness,' he said, looking at her intently.

She savoured her drink. He was good at mixing cocktails. 'What are you thinking?'

'I congratulate you.'

She raised one eyebrow. 'On what, darling?'

'On finding a way to help Anselmo.'

She said slowly: 'Let's hope this stops the decline. His farm was always a headache and perhaps now he'll be able to invest shrewdly.'

'You've always worried about him, haven't you?'

'Was it so evident?'

'To me it was. But that's because I'm your husband, I suppose.'

'Do you mind very much?'

'I face facts, Teresa. It was Anselmo you wanted to marry.'

'That was a long, long time ago, Narcisus.'

'He would have been much happier with you.'

She said quietly: 'I think so. But I've discovered something, Narcisus. If I had my time again and could marry Anselmo, I wouldn't do it. I would marry ... you!'

Narcisus smiled weakly. 'A sweet white lie. I've always taken second place to Anselmo.'

She smiled softly. 'You're wrong, foolish one. Quite wrong. Young girls have their romantic dreams. But few wives get the faith, tenderness and respect you've always given me.'

He looked away from her, blinking quickly.

'Anselmo won't ever speak to either of us again because of that business with Leon.' She shrugged her shoulders. 'It doesn't worry me at all, darling. Not at all!'

5

Teresa was walking across the vestibule towards the dining room when something strangely familiar about the man standing at the reception desk caught her attention. Her step faltered and as though he could feel her eyes upon him, he turned slowly. Her heart leaped and for a moment her breathing seemed to cease. He was tall and dark and his lean, handsome face and brooding eyes recalled instantly the infinitely sweet pleasure of caressing hands.

He came to her, but the recognition in his eyes was veiled. When he drew close he said in a low-toned, excited voice: 'Chiquita. Chiquita!'

'Capitan!' Her eyes searched his face and she saw that her memory had tricked her. He was not dark. His hair was streaked with silver and his sideboards were quite white. His darkly handsome face was fleshy and red-veined and the whites of his eyes were yellowy. '*Mother of God*,' she thought. '*He's old, terribly old!*' And reckoning back she realised he must be sixty. The absurdity of a lover of sixty made her want to laugh.

'Come,' she said. 'Let us sit and talk.'

He looked guiltily at the ladies' room. 'Can't I see you later? Privately?'

'If you wish, Capitan. But is it necessary?'

He flashed a furtive glance round him. 'Have you forgotten? I'm a political refugee.'

'But if they allowed you into the country . . .'

'I've a French name and passport.'

'If you'd like to come up to my private room?'

'Later,' he said quickly. 'Later.' Again he looked at the ladies' room. 'My wife's with me and she's very inquisitive. I'd rather she . . .'

His nervousness irritated her and she said coldly: 'It's up to you, Capitan.'

'Where can I meet you?'

'Room sixty-five.'

'When?'

'This afternoon.'

'What time?'

'Between three and four. Is that all right?'

'She always sleeps in the afternoons. I'll tell her I'm going for a walk.' Again his sly manner irritated her. 'I'll leave you now, Chiquita. I don't want her to see us talking.'

'As you wish,' she said coldly and hurried away.

But from within the dining room she watched him join the plump little woman who came out of the ladies' room. She was his own age, Teresa judged. Dyed auburn hair set as hard as bronze and as lifeless. A pronounced double chin, a costume skirt and jacket which betrayed that she was tightly corseted and high-heeled shoes which were much too small. She walked to the lift as though her feet were tender. He followed attentively, ready to cope with all the minor problems she encountered.

All that morning her thoughts kept returning to him, but when she was in her room awaiting his visit she almost regretted inviting him. She lowered the shutters so that the room was in cool shadow, kicked off her shoes and put on comfortable sandals. When he knuckled the door she was relaxed on her lounging couch. She put down her magazine, straightened the cushions and called: 'Come in.'

As soon as the door was closed behind him he sighed with relief. 'She's asleep.'

'Please sit down,' she said formally.

He sat down and smiled at her.

'How about a drink?'

'Something long. A mineral water or a beer.'

She poured him San Miguel and mineral water for herself.

'Seeing you again makes it seem that I was only here yesterday. You haven't changed at all, Chiquita.'

'You haven't changed much either, Capitan.'

'I heard about ... your brother.'

'Miguel?'

He nodded. 'It must have been a terrible blow.'

She said quietly: 'He was lost to us long before he died.'

'Everything has changed so much, Chiquita. There's nothing here that I recognise.'

She nodded. 'Everything's changing. *Everything!*'

'Everything except ... except the system, the repression and the corruption.'

She was surprised. 'I don't understand, Capitan.'

'There's no freedom. You can't speak your mind. It's a fascist country.'

'It's not as bad as that, Capitan.'

'The things I read about Spain in the newspapers make me ashamed.'

'The French newspapers, Capitan?'

'Naturally,' he said. 'The Spanish press daren't print criticisms of the regime.'

'Why are you bitter, Capitan?' You weren't interested in politics. You were simply an officer doing his duty.'

'Spain is my country, Chiquita. I love Spain and her people. I did my duty as a soldier and an officer. But the corrupt men in power have deprived me of my nationality.'

'You can come back, Capitan. There's an amnesty. Many, many Spaniards have returned.'

'How many trusting fools walked into a trap? How many were beaten up, imprisoned and executed?'

'Those were criminals. Murderers who tried to return under the protection of political amnesty.'

'It's easy to accuse a political opponent of murder when he is denied a public trial and is found guilty by a secret court.'

'Nevertheless, many have returned to Spain and picked up the threads of their lives again, Capitan.'

He studied her carefully. 'I'm risking my life here. I've got French nationality, daughters at college and a sound family business. I'm afraid, Chiquita. What's to stop them arresting me and charging me with treason, an offence punishable by death?'

'They won't do that, Capitan.'

'But they did it, Chiquita. Officers who remained loyal to the Spanish Government and refused to revolt were shot by the Nationalists when they were taken prisoner.'

'But that was years ago!'

His eyes stared intently. 'Do you think things have changed?'

'I *know* they've changed.'

He shook his head. 'How many are in jail now without ever having had a trial? How many are still awaiting execution? How many are today arrested without charge and beaten up? What happened to you when they learned that Scarface was your brother?'

'All that was so long, long ago.'

'What did they do, Chiquita. Did they tie you down and beat your bare feet with canes? Did they keep you without food and water until you talked?'

'You exaggerate, Capitan. I won't deny that sometimes somebody vicious and unbalanced is in authority and thirty years ago political hatred was so intense that people killed because of it. But things have changed, Capitan. A new generation has grown up. Those who were leaders during the Civil War are nearly all dead or are very old men. Those who were young and fanatically idealistic are like you, Capitan, no longer young. The new generation hasn't any resentment or hatred. It lives in a different world that doesn't give rise to them. Spain is on the crest of a wave of prosperity and there's work for everyone. Spain lagged far behind other European countries but now we're catching up fast. Working people who once couldn't afford a radio are buying television sets and washing machines! There are still many things wrong in Spain, Capitan. But nine people out of ten will sign on for another ten years of prosperity, like these we've had under Franco.'

'You're biased, Chiquita. You've done well out of the regime.'

'We were a simply family of fishermen, Capitan. What we

212

did, anyone could have done.'

'But Spain is a fascist dictatorship, Chiquita. People can't choose their representatives and vote them into the Cortes.'

She smiled slowly. 'We Spanish are temperamental, Capitan. Perhaps we need firm rule. Left alone, we'd never reach agreement, all of us pulling a dozen different ways.'

'The British have learned how to govern themselves.'

'But . . . we're Spanish, Capitan!' she said and chuckled.

'Perhaps you are right,' he agreed reluctantly.

'How long are you staying?'

'I'm feeling my way. I'd like to go home. My parents died, but I have a sister.'

'How long will you stay in Escoleras?'

'I leave tomorrow.' He walked across to the window and stared out. 'The sea is the one thing which hasn't changed. After our retreat to France, while I was in a concentration camp, this view dominated my memory, the deep blue of the sea and the softer blue of the sky. You were a part of it all, Chiquita. Those months I spent here were the happiest of my life.'

She too thought back.

'You did not marry Anselmo?'

She shook her head slowly. 'I was not worthy of him.'

He came away from the window and stood looking down at the parting of her hair. 'Were you unhappy?'

'Terribly.'

'What went wrong?'

'It was . . .' she began. 'It was Anselmo's vanity and pride.'

'I'm sorry,' he said sincerely.

'You needn't be. I know now I couldn't have been truly happy with him. Anselmo is steeped in old Spanish traditions. I'd have been a respected hostess in my home, the mother of his children, and I would have had his affection, care and security. But he would never have permitted me to be other than his wife. I would have presided at the dining table but only the men would have retired to the lounge to smoke and discuss business. I would have accepted decisions . . . but never made them. I would never have known the thrill of achievement or the pleasure of accomplishment.'

'And your husband. Are you happy with him?'

'He is sweet and he is weak which is good because I am strong and otherwise we would clash.'

'And he makes you happy in . . . every way?'

'He's thoughtful, gentle, sensitive and tender.'

He moved behind her and too late she realised what he intended. His hand brushed across her shoulder, slipped swiftly

213

down inside her dress and cupped her breast as, many years
ago, he had touched her for the first time. And because of that
intimacy she could not be offended. She maintained her dignity
by being impervious to his touch. 'You'll get a crick in your
neck stooping over me that way, Capitan.'

'This is the way I first touched you, Chiquita. Do you
remember? All these years I've remembered it.'

'You have a tiresome memory, Capitan.' Her breast was cool
and slack and soon he would understand.

'I wanted you to be my wife.'

She remembered how dashing and gallant he had looked,
splashing through the river shallows and galloping up to the
gun emplacements to return the fire of the warship which
shelled the town. And his caressing aroused her despite herself.
Her breast tautened as his stimulation stiffened her nipple.
'Please don't do this,' she said.

'I'm not hurting you?'

'Things are different now. We're both married.'

'Nothing changes the way I feel about the touch of you, the
smoothness of your skin, the warmth of your response.'

'Doesn't your wife satisfy you?'

'You should see her! She's a good wife, helps with the
business and is a good mother, but ... she doesn't have much
energy.'

'So you want to work off your excess energy on me?'

There was hurt in his voice. 'You know how I feel about
you, Chiquita.'

'Please stop. You'll snap my bra strap.'

'There's a good way to avoid that danger.' He tried to pull
her dress down off her shoulder, but she grasped his wrists. 'I
asked you to stop. Do I have to become unpleasant?'

He desisted at once. He was hurt. 'I did not intend to offend.
If you knew how all these years I've relived again and again
the memories of the happy times we spent together ... you
would understand better.'

She *could* understand because her memories too were vivid,
the joy of innocence and of exploring each other with sweet
tenderness.. They were memories to be cherished and she
almost yielded to him.

'We cannot live with our memories, Capitan. We must live
in the real world.'

'A man likes to dream.' His black eyes were compelling. 'I
long to caress you, Chiquita. To kiss you and feel you respond
as once you did. The desire is an ache. Is it too much to
ask?'

For one fleeting moment the temptation was enormous. It

would have been easy to abandon herself to this elderly man while remembering his darkly handsome face smiling tenderly while his lingering caresses sent her floating away into ecstasy.

She all but surrendered to him. Then she heard herself say: 'You've developed into a dirty old man!'

The words wiped away the tender memories like chalk from a blackboard. He withdrew sharply, becoming icily polite to protect his inner sensitivity from the cruel rasp of her indifference.

'And how is your father?' he asked formally.

'He is well. He will be pleased to see you.'

He shook his head. 'Before I meet those who know me, I must feel my way. I have a good friend in Sevilla, a retired officer. I will seek his advice.'

'If I can help you I shall be happy, Capitan.'

'Thank you, Chiquita.' He glanced at his wrist watch. 'Yvonne will be awaking soon. I must go.'

'Next time you call perhaps Narcisus will be here. I'd like you to meet him.'

'I hope so too,' he said politely but she knew she would never see him again.

They shook hands.

'Adios, Chiquita.'

'Adios, Capitan.'

CHAPTER ELEVEN

PACO BARRAS came downstairs in his stockinged feet and grunted as he sat down and pulled on his rubber-soled boots. He sighed, rose to his feet, crossed to the kitchen and stood staring in at Elisa. Her white hair was in bobby pins. She was washing up and looked no different from behind than she had for almost all the years of their marriage.

'What's for lunch, woman?' he demanded.

'Something you like. Paella.'

'With gambas?'

'Plenty.' The crockery rattled. 'Did you put on the clean shirt I put out?'

'I did.' He chuckled. 'I must look my best when I go walking with the doctor!'

'You're a conceited old man,' she scolded.

He stole up behind her and slapped her buttock. 'And you're a nagging old woman.'

'On your way back try to remember to buy a few boxes of matches.'

'Ah! Woman! You want to set me on fire? To burn you up!'

'Away with you,' she scolded happily. 'Talking like that at your age.'

Paco opened the back door, stepped outside and scowled. Most of his life he had walked bare-footed upon the beach. He was still not used to the wide promenade which replaced the sand. He never would be. In summer the promenade was thronged with tourists. They strolled there with their children, sunbathed in deck chairs, talked, shouted and played games. They thronged round the door and windows of his cottage, peering inside with wide-eyed curiosity as though he and Elisa were museum exhibits. If he stepped outside barefoot, they stared at him as though he was a peculiar biological specimen.

Paco sighed, placed his feet astride, looked out to sea and drew fresh air into his lungs. Then he lit a black cheroot. All had changed so much, he thought sadly. The joy of living in Escoleras had dissolved away. All that remained of his happy way of life was this cottage. It was an anachronism now, overtowered in a newly built street by smart shops and blocks of flats.

It was one of those January days when the sun blazed down hotly, the blue sky tinted the sea and the distant Pyrenees seemed only a few miles away, standing out clearly with their peaks snow-capped.

Presently he saw Doctor Aldo and the two old friends slowly strolled the promenade.

'Don't walk so fast,' grumbled Doctor Aldo.

Paco Barras gave him a sly sideways glance. 'What's the matter, Doctor? Getting old?'

'A touch of lumbago.' Doctor Aldo frowned indignantly. 'What do you mean, old? You're older than me.'

'We all have to get old.'

Doctor Aldo looked at Paco's sunburned face, his clear blue eyes and his shock of blonde hair and realised with surprise that it was almost all silver. El Rubio had been so fair that its change in colour had been imperceptible. 'How old are you, Paco?' He asked, envious of his friend's effortless gait.

'Seventy-six next Thursday.'

'And you still go fishing!'

'That's when I'm happiest.' He chuckled. 'It gets me away from all this.'

They walked on slowly, past the hot-dog kiosk closed for the winter, the small pier where passengers queued for excursion boat trips and the town hall's information office built squarely in the centre of the promenade.

Presently they stopped and watched the Pradas sitting on the promenade wall and eating garrotas. They had a porron of wine, a long loaf and gaily-coloured napkins. They chopped open the sea urchins with kitchen knives to spoon out the rich, yellow meat. Isabel and Marcel Prada glanced up and saw the two men watching them.

'You are welcome,' invited Marcel.

'Thank you,' they said, shaking their heads. They walked on.

'What happened to Rosemarie?' asked Paco Barras.

Doctor Aldo took out his watch and glanced at it. He'd been retired a year and the alert young doctor who'd taken over his practice rarely called upon him for assistance. He sighed. 'Before he died, Serra told me he'd been with her in a Barcelona brothel. You know how mean-fisted he was, so you can imagine the cheap type of brothel he would go to.'

'She was a good girl. It's hard to believe,' said Paco.

'If it *was* Rosemarie, heaven knows what she's doing now they've cleaned out all those places.'

'She'll be getting past that kind of thing anyway.'

'She'll be getting on for fifty,' said Doctor Aldo.

'We were all to blame for what happened to her,' said Paco Barras, shaking his head sadly. 'One of us should have taken her in.' He shrugged his shoulders wryly. 'But with the Nationalists occupying the village and . . . everything!'

'Life deals us all a hand of cards,' philosophised Doctor Aldo. 'Lucky people get the trumps. But once you've got your cards, all you can do is play them the best way you can. Rosemarie was dealt a very poor hand.' He sighed and thought of Rafael Ledesma's hard, black eyes and sneering lips. And because Paco was a close friend he could trust and because he had grown garrulous, he asked: 'Did I tell you about Rafael?'

Paco shook his head.

'Anselmo Ledesma would not like it to get round . . . !'

'You can trust me.'

'Rafael's been put away. There was always something strange . . . even when he was a boy. Did you see him when his mother died? He had a tic . . . the corner of his mouth kept twitching. I thought it might be the strain of war service. It wasn't.'

'You mean he's . . . loco?'

'I don't know the details. Anselmo isn't even aware I know. A couple of years ago I received a letter from a specialist in Madrid. They were treating Rafael and referred to me for his medical history. He was detained as a result of a pretty nasty business. He and another man had a girl tied up in their flat for days, cut her about, cigar ends and things like that!'

'Some men do things which make other men ashamed of being men,' said Paco.

They came to a standstill at the concrete base of a towering flagstaff and looked up at the red and gold Spanish flag fluttering in the light breeze.

'Our flag, the symbol of Nationalism,' said Doctor Aldo tonelessly.

'Hernando was a great anarchist,' mused Paco. 'This would have been his final humiliation.'

The flagstaff was erected on the site of Hernando's stone hut.

The two men walked on towards the Marvista Hotel and their thoughts were with Hernando, remembering his smiling brown face, his neatly trimmed goatee beard and his bristling waxed moustache.

'Do you remember when Hernando caught that two hundred kilo tunny fish three miles off the coast in his small rowing boat? He fought it for sixteen hours and finally had to tow it rowing because it was too big to lift into his boat.'

'And that wild boar that blundered into the village, fleeing

218

from the hunters,' said Paco Barras. 'I was with Hernando, and when we saw it he snatched up his gun and went after it. I didn't see him again for three days. But he brought back the boar. He carried it across his shoulders for fifteen kilometres.'

'They don't make men like him these days,' said Doctor Aldo and shook his head sadly.

'He was the old Spain,' said Paco. He paused and then added slowly. 'Perhaps ... the *true* Spain!'

'The world is changing and Spain changes with it,' said the doctor. 'We've changed our way of life so much that there's no room left for folk like Hernando.'

'We live in a different world now,' agreed Paco. 'But I doubt if it's a better one. Before the war we lived leisurely. We didn't have much money but we didn't need it. Everyone lived. Nowadays, everybody works so hard to earn money and spend it. There's no leisure. The only truly happy man I've ever known was Hernando and I don't remember he ever had a peseta to spend.'

They'd reached the wide highway that swept past the rear of the Hotel Marvista. A streamlined, crimson sports car snarled past and sounded a fierce blast on its hooter. A brown arm waved and a shout of greeting was torn away on the wind and floated to them. Leon's hair shone in the sun as silvery as his grandfather's. The girl beside him fluttered a blue chiffon scarf in the slipstream.

'I'm told my grandson is now called El Rubio,' said Paco contentedly.

'He's called Young Rubio and you're called Old Rubio.'

'He's just off to Barcelona,' said Paco.

'And the girl?'

'She's Swiss. Wealthy family. Her father built that big villa with the swimming pool on the slope overlooking the church.'

'Leon's a lucky boy. He's got the world at his feet,' said Doctor Aldo.

'I hope he knows how to treat it.'

'Wasn't there some kind of childhood romance between him and Silvana Ledesma?'

Paco Barras shrugged his shoulders. 'There may have been. Teresa says he's thinking of marrying this Swiss girl. They're a fine couple and go everywhere together.'

They reached the Marvista Hotel and a smartly uniformed Buttons took them up in the lift to the top floor. They walked the last flight of stairs to the roof terrace and seated themselves under gaily coloured parasols on chairs placed ready for them. The weekly aperitifs with Teresa and Narcisus had become a regular and pleasant routine.

A white-jacketed waiter served them, setting out dishes of cockles, mussels, baby octopus and other savouries. 'El Señor y La Señora Coruna will join you almost at once,' said the waiter.

'Thank you,' said Paco Barras. He leaned forward, speared three baby octopus with a toothpick, popped them into his mouth and chewed with relish.

Doctor Aldo looked out at the expanse of blue sea flecked with the silver fish scales of sun-dappled water. Then he turned his gaze to the long sweep of beach stretching into the distance. A new wide highway was being made. Tractors, trucks and mechanical shovels were scattered over the area and great cranes reared up like monster skeletons.

'It's hard to realise our village has become a town in a few short years, Paco.'

'I want nothing of towns. I wish this tourist boom had never started!'

'Are you seriously thinking of leaving Escoleras, Paco?'

'Perhaps. It would not be difficult. Every year my neighbours compete for my cottage. Every year they offer me a million more.' He chuckled. 'With what they will pay me I can buy a large house inland with many acres of good land.' He shrugged his shoulders. 'But I will die if when I look out of my window I cannot see the sea.'

'If you intend to sell your cottage, Paco, perhaps this year is the year to sell. Next year may be too late.'

'Too late?'

'For many years Spain has ridden on the crest of a wave of prosperity. Every year we build like beavers and double the number of our hotels and apartments. Every year industry gears itself up to higher production. It's an enormous snowball which is growing frighteningly. It can't go on ... for ever! One year there will be only the same number of tourists as the year previously. Then will come disaster because we Spaniards are sublime optimists and will never believe we have over-produced until there are thousands of apartments with no buyers and hundreds of hotels only half full.'

'There are already signs of this,' said Paco quietly. 'I've been told of new apartments which cannot be sold and of builders who cannot pay their debts.'

'The snowball can easily break,' said Doctor Aldo. 'Everyone owes, confidently expecting to sell and pay. But when there are no sales there are no payments. And when there are no payments the banks themselves may collapse beneath the strain of unpaid loans.'

'Such problems are not now,' said Paco Barras. 'They have

220

all happened before.' He sounded strangely contented.

'Are you not worried for Teresa and Narcisus? If the hotel business fails they will lose everything.'

Paco chuckled delightedly. 'Let them fail. Let them crash. What does it matter as long as nobody is injured. They have lived as wealthy people for a time and it will be no hardship for them to become simple people again.'

Doctor Aldo strolled across the terrace and looked out in the other direction. 'I see Pepita's building another wing to *her* hotel.'

Paco joined him, leaning over the stone parapet. 'They've had some good years. Luis is a hard working boy and doesn't squander money. All he earns he ploughs back. I'm pleased, because if things go badly in future, Pepita is provided for.'

Doctor Aldo's gaze wandered on. 'They're getting on with Anselmo Ledesma's flats.' He sighed. 'All the old landmarks are disappearing, Paco. Another fifty years and the memories will be gone too. But perhaps that's just as well.'

Paco shook his head. 'We've some bitter memories, eh, Juan? The Communist Committee and that mad fanatic who ordered the executions.'

'It doesn't seem possible now that men were shot in cold blood for their opinions, does it, Paco?'

'Don Carlos too,' sighed Paco Barras. 'A fine old man murdered because he was a priest.'

'And that young priest ... what they did to him!' Doctor Aldo shuddered. 'And poor Morales. Shot because he was mayor when he didn't want to be mayor!'

'We Spaniards are a cruel people,' said Paco Barras.

'We are foolishly proud and ridiculously brave,' said Juan Aldo. His eyes twinkled. 'All we have in our favour is that foreigners inexplicably find us so charming and friendly that they flock to visit us.'

Behind them Narcisus and Teresa came out on to the terrace and the two old men went to join them.

'You're looking lovelier than ever, Teresa,' said Doctor Aldo.

'You old charmer,' she chuckled.

Paco Barras reached for his drink and stood with feet astride as though digging his brown toes into the hot sand. Raising his glass high he said with a twinkle in his eyes: 'A toast. A toast to Spain. The old Spain ... and the new!'

ALL QUIET ON THE WESTERN FRONT

ERICH MARIA REMARQUE

Erich Maria Remarque belongs to a family of French extraction that emigrated into Germany at the time of the French Revolution and settled in the Rhineland. In 1914 at the age of 18 he went straight from school into the army and was sent to the Western Front. During the course of the war his mother died and all his friends were killed. At the end of the war he found himself alone in the world.

He wrote his book, without taking previous thought, about his own and his friends' experiences in the war. It arose out of the consideration that so many men of his generation, who were yet still young, nevertheless lived a friendless, embittered, resigned life without knowing why.

ALL QUIET ON THE WESTERN FRONT sets out to describe three things: the war, the fate of a generation and true comradeship.

5/-

A MAYFLOWER PAPERBACK

THE CAMP
by Gordon M. Williams

THE SIZZLING EXPOSÉ
OF THE <u>OTHER</u> SIDE OF
SERVICES LIFE:

by the author of *The Man Who
Had Power Over Women.*

THE CAMP is RAF Zeedorf in post-war Germany. To it comes National Serviceman SAC Ritchie Brown. His patriotic illusions are soon shattered. Sex, booze, fighting, dangerous horseplay and an unvarying crudity of language are the order of the day. But Zeedorf is at least a 'cushy' camp—until (following a rape case) the arrival of martinet Group-Captain House. Then sadism and brutality take over . . . and, eventually, violent death.

THE CAMP is a frighteningly authentic novel about the side of RAF life *not* featured in the recruiting advertisements.

'The rawest and savagest study of RAF life ever to come my way.'
—*Sunday Citizen*

'Earns high honours.'
—*Sunday Times*

'Not a book to buy your maiden aunt.'
—*Sheffield Morning Telegraph*

A MAYFLOWER BOOK   5/-

BUDDWING

EVAN HUNTER

Evan Hunter's magnificent novel is the story
of a journey of discovery. Its nameless prota-
gonist wakes up in Central Park, faced with
a terrifying riddle: who am I? His quest takes
him into the myriad city: Chinatown and the
wild spree with a sailor; the Italian all-night
wedding feast; the scavenger hunt with the
glossy rich woman on an emotional bender;
Harlem . . . and at the last shift of the kaleido-
scope, the final revelation.

5/-

A MAYFLOWER PAPERBACK

THE BITTER SEEDS OF HATE
The fourth and final novel in THE SPANISH SAGA.

With the Civil War officially over, an uneasy peace comes to Spain. But the instinct for revenge has not died. On the one hand, summary trials, disciplinary and correction camps . . . on the other, sabotage, daring bank-raids to provide funds for a movement now gone underground. The Civil War has been Hitler's rehearsal for the war in Europe, and in France many defeated Republicans prepare for a second, more direct clash with the hated German leader.

Teresa has married the plain but honest Narcisus Coruna, although she still loves Anselmo whom she lost through her affair with another man. Rosemarie Prada, driven from her house, discovers that there can be profit as well as comfort in the pleasure she gives to men . . .

Then a new word bursts on Spain. Tourism. And Teresa finds herself at the centre of a different kind of revolution . . .

U.K. 5/-   AUSTRALIA 80c   NEW ZEALAND 75c   SOUTH AFRICA 60c